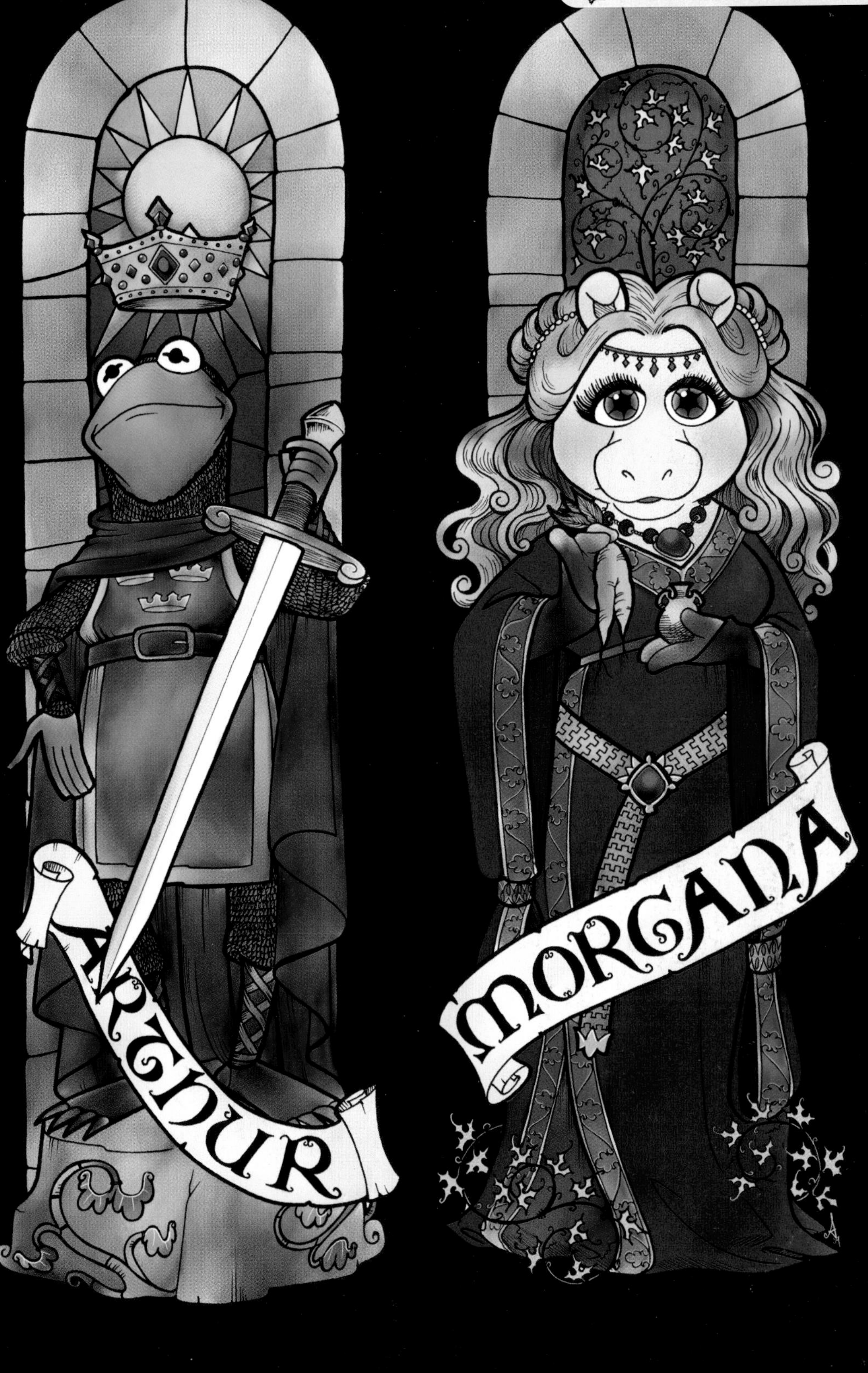
ARTHUR
MORGANA

MUPPET KING ARTHUR

BOOM KIDS!

ROSS RICHIE
chief executive officer

MARK WAID
editor-in-chief

ADAM FORTIER
vice president,
publishing

CHIP MOSHER
marketing director

MATT GAGNON
managing editor

JENNY CHRISTOPHER
sales director

FIRST EDITION: APRIL 2010

10 9 8 7 6 5 4 3 2 1

FOR INFORMATION REGARDING THE CPSIA ON THIS PRINTED MATERIAL CALL: 203-595-3636 AND PROVIDE REFERENCE # EAST – 66358

Office of publication: 6310 San Vicente Blvd Ste 404, Los Angeles, CA 90048-5457.

A catalog record for this book is available from OCLC and on our website www.boom-kids.com on the Librarians page.

Writers:
Paul Benjamin and
Patrick Storck

Artists:
Dave Alvarez
Issue 1
James Silvani
Issues 2-4

Colors:
Digikore Studios
Issue 1
Eric Cobain
Issues 2-4

Letterer:
Deron Bennett

Assistant Editor:
Jason Long

Editor:
Aaron Sparrow

Designer:
Erika Terriquez

Cover:
David Petersen

Special Thanks:
Jesse Post and Lauren Kressel of
Disney Publishing and our friends
at The Muppets Studio

Additional Visual Design by Sonny Strait

chapter one

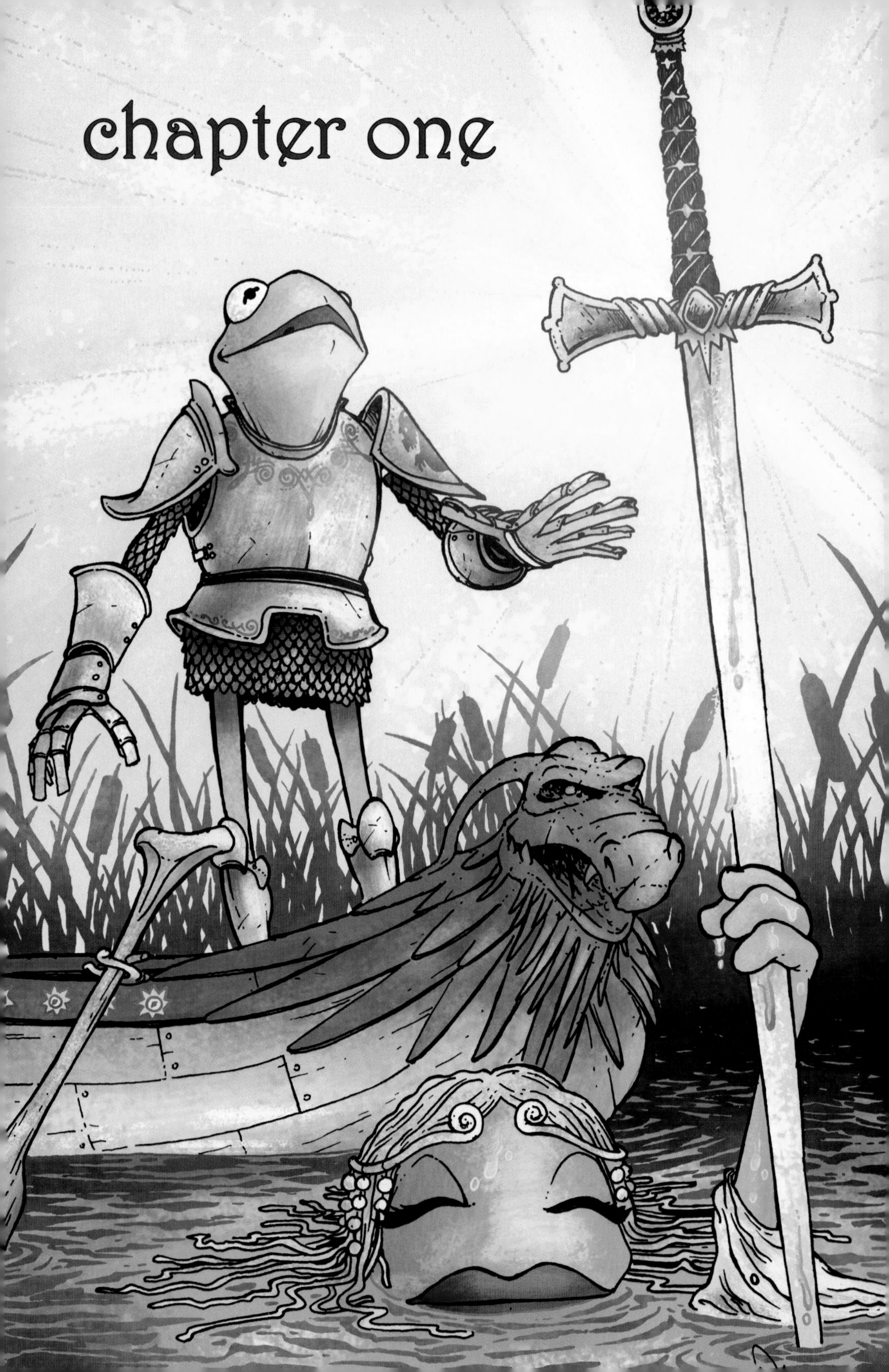

Britain without a king.
A dark, foreboding place.*

*EDITOR'S NOTE: SERIOUSLY? THE DARK AGES WEREN'T *THIS* DARK. GIVE THE ARTIST SOMETHING TO DRAW OR WE'RE ALL OUT OF A JOB!

A contest to remove the fabled sword Excalibur from its hold / begins our story of this tale oft told.

THAT'S RIGHT, KNIGHTS AND NOBLES, I HAVE HERE THE MAGIC SWORD, EXCALIBUR!

IT'S A ONE OF A KIND; CAN'T LIVE WITHOUT IT, *SUPER-RARE* COLLECTABLE!

STORED IN THIS FINE, QUARRY-THEMED, WEATHER-RESISTANT CASING FOR YEARS! AND WITH THE BLADE'S NON-STICK SURFACE, EVEN THE MOST TROUBLESOME DRAGON'S BLOOD COMES *CLEAN OFF!*

LOOK AT THAT EDGE! IT SLICES, IT DICES, IT PUTS ALL OF BRITAIN UNDER YOUR COMMAND IN JUST ONE EASY TUG! *

*BY AGREEING TO PARTICIPATE IN THE "EXCALIBUR: KING FOR LIFETIME CONTEST," ENTRANT FOREGOES LIKENESS RIGHTS IN BECOMING A PUBLIC (UP TO AND INCLUDING LEGENDARY) FIGURE. POSITION OF KING NON-TRANSFERABLE.

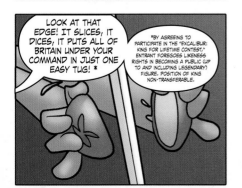

Knights from all over the kingdom of Camelot prepare for their chance / through wit and strength with sword and lance.

But the lonely page Arthur is not considered worthy to try. / He simply watches the action and lets out a

÷SIGH÷

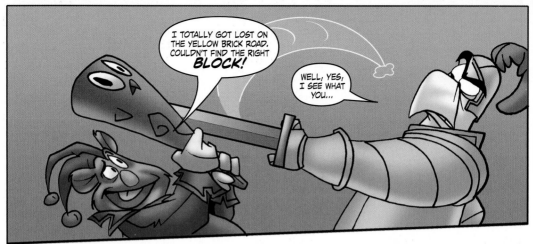

I TOTALLY GOT LOST ON THE YELLOW BRICK ROAD. COULDN'T FIND THE RIGHT *BLOCK!*

WELL, YES, I SEE WHAT YOU...

WHY DID THE PLAYGROUND RETIRE? IT HAD LOST ITS *SWING!*

YOU'LL NEVER WIN A DUEL IF YOU KEEP TELEGRAPHING YOUR MOVES, SIR PERCIVAL!

HOLD THAT THOUGHT.

HOW MANY DOTS AND DASHES IN P-A-R-R-Y?

DEE DEET DEE DEE DEET!

I'VE COMPLETELY BLUNTED MY EDGE BLOCKING THAT JESTER KNIGHT'S RIDICULOUS WEAPON. GO AND GET ME A FRESH SWORD, PAGE.

WOULDN'T IT MAKE MORE SENSE TO JUST GET IT SHARPENED?

WE NEED TO STIMULATE OUR ECONOMY, ARTHUR! THERE'S NO POINT IN FIXING SOMETHING YOU ALREADY HAVE WHEN YOU CAN THROW IT AWAY AND BUY SOMETHING NEW INSTEAD!

EDITOR'S NOTE: WANT TO STIMULATE THE ECONOMY SAM'S WAY? BE SURE TO GIVE YOUR FRIENDS YOUR SINGLE ISSUES OF MUPPET KING ARTHUR AND BUY THE TRADE PAPERBACK VERSION FOR YOURSELF!

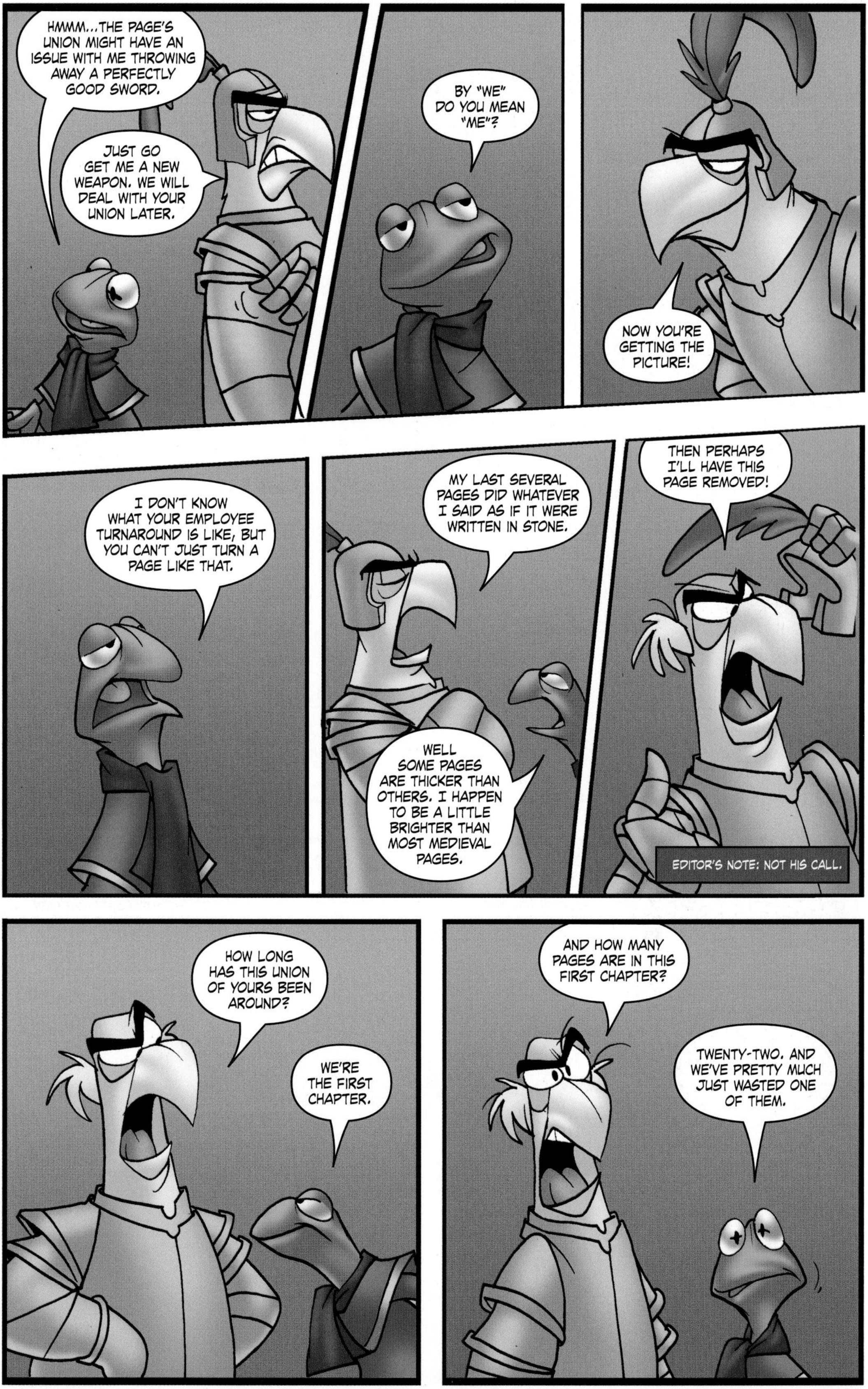
HMMM...THE PAGE'S UNION MIGHT HAVE AN ISSUE WITH ME THROWING AWAY A PERFECTLY GOOD SWORD.
JUST GO GET ME A NEW WEAPON. WE WILL DEAL WITH YOUR UNION LATER.
BY "WE" DO YOU MEAN "ME"?
NOW YOU'RE GETTING THE PICTURE!
I DON'T KNOW WHAT YOUR EMPLOYEE TURNAROUND IS LIKE, BUT YOU CAN'T JUST TURN A PAGE LIKE THAT.
MY LAST SEVERAL PAGES DID WHATEVER I SAID AS IF IT WERE WRITTEN IN STONE.
WELL SOME PAGES ARE THICKER THAN OTHERS. I HAPPEN TO BE A LITTLE BRIGHTER THAN MOST MEDIEVAL PAGES.
THEN PERHAPS I'LL HAVE THIS PAGE REMOVED!
EDITOR'S NOTE: NOT HIS CALL.
HOW LONG HAS THIS UNION OF YOURS BEEN AROUND?
WE'RE THE FIRST CHAPTER.
AND HOW MANY PAGES ARE IN THIS FIRST CHAPTER?
TWENTY-TWO. AND WE'VE PRETTY MUCH JUST WASTED ONE OF THEM.

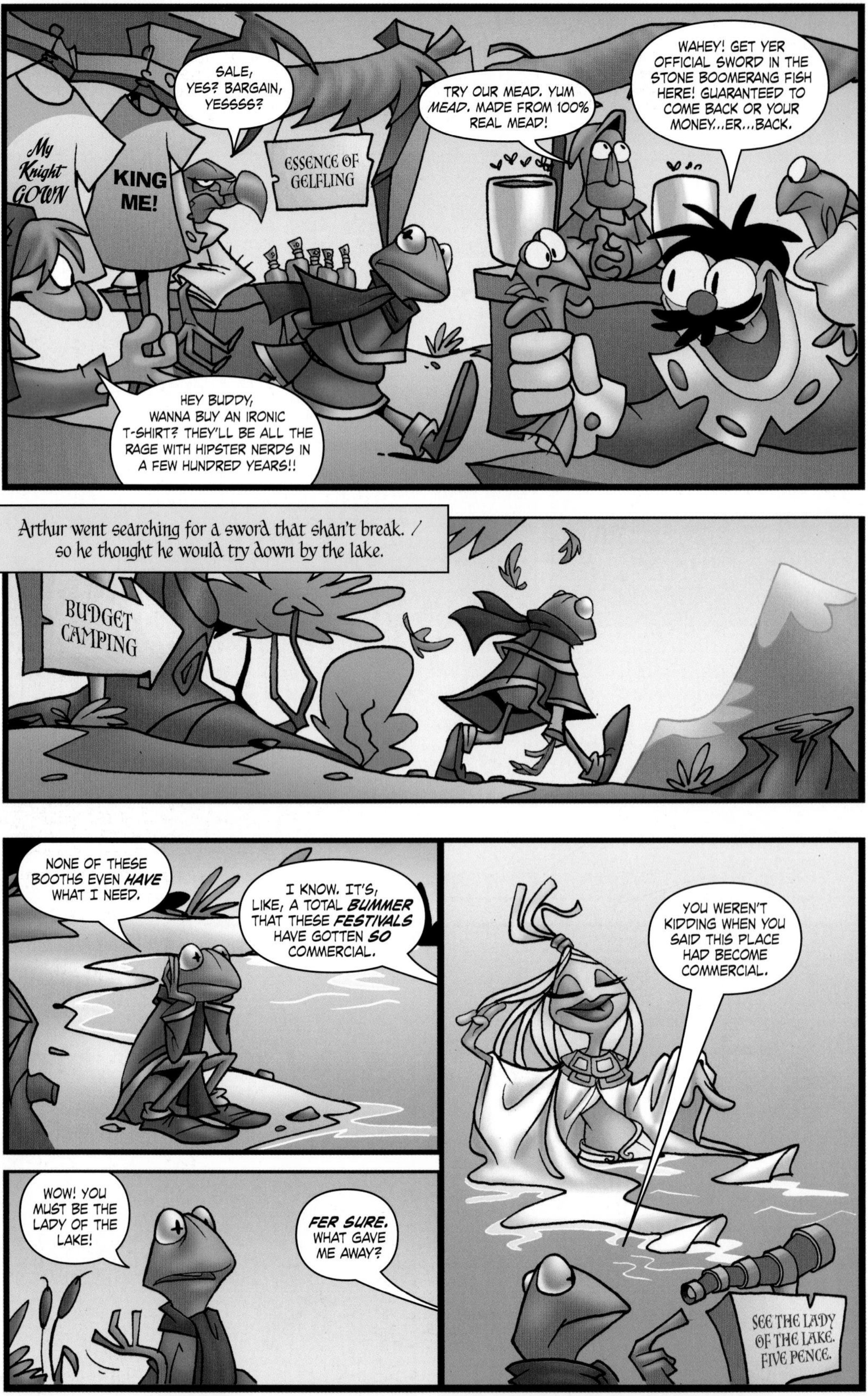
My Knight GOWN
KING ME!
SALE, YES? BARGAIN, YESSSS?
ESSENCE OF GELFLING
TRY OUR MEAD. YUM MEAD. MADE FROM 100% REAL MEAD!
WAHEY! GET YER OFFICIAL SWORD IN THE STONE BOOMERANG FISH HERE! GUARANTEED TO COME BACK OR YOUR MONEY...ER...BACK.
HEY BUDDY, WANNA BUY AN IRONIC T-SHIRT? THEY'LL BE ALL THE RAGE WITH HIPSTER NERDS IN A FEW HUNDRED YEARS!!
Arthur went searching for a sword that shan't break. / so he thought he would try down by the lake.
BUDGET CAMPING
NONE OF THESE BOOTHS EVEN HAVE WHAT I NEED.
I KNOW. IT'S, LIKE, A TOTAL BUMMER THAT THESE FESTIVALS HAVE GOTTEN SO COMMERCIAL.
WOW! YOU MUST BE THE LADY OF THE LAKE!
FER SURE. WHAT GAVE ME AWAY?
YOU WEREN'T KIDDING WHEN YOU SAID THIS PLACE HAD BECOME COMMERCIAL.
SEE THE LADY OF THE LAKE. FIVE PENCE.

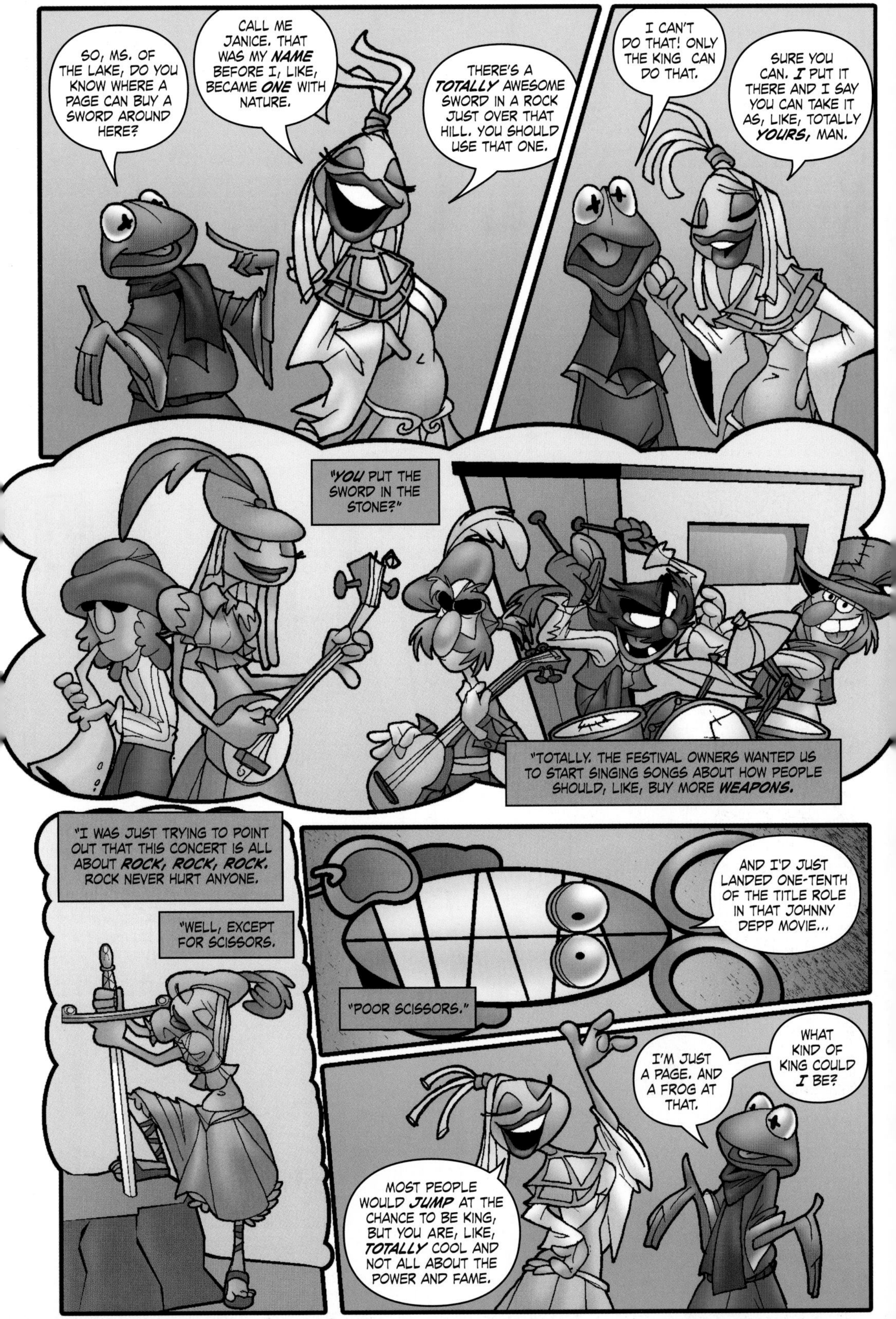

SO, MS. OF THE LAKE, DO YOU KNOW WHERE A PAGE CAN BUY A SWORD AROUND HERE?
CALL ME JANICE. THAT WAS MY NAME BEFORE I, LIKE, BECAME ONE WITH NATURE.
THERE'S A TOTALLY AWESOME SWORD IN A ROCK JUST OVER THAT HILL. YOU SHOULD USE THAT ONE.
I CAN'T DO THAT! ONLY THE KING CAN DO THAT.
SURE YOU CAN. I PUT IT THERE AND I SAY YOU CAN TAKE IT AS, LIKE, TOTALLY YOURS, MAN.
"YOU PUT THE SWORD IN THE STONE?"
"TOTALLY. THE FESTIVAL OWNERS WANTED US TO START SINGING SONGS ABOUT HOW PEOPLE SHOULD, LIKE, BUY MORE WEAPONS.
"I WAS JUST TRYING TO POINT OUT THAT THIS CONCERT IS ALL ABOUT ROCK, ROCK, ROCK. ROCK NEVER HURT ANYONE.
"WELL, EXCEPT FOR SCISSORS.
AND I'D JUST LANDED ONE-TENTH OF THE TITLE ROLE IN THAT JOHNNY DEPP MOVIE...
"POOR SCISSORS."
I'M JUST A PAGE. AND A FROG AT THAT.
WHAT KIND OF KING COULD I BE?
MOST PEOPLE WOULD JUMP AT THE CHANCE TO BE KING, BUT YOU ARE, LIKE, TOTALLY COOL AND NOT ALL ABOUT THE POWER AND FAME.

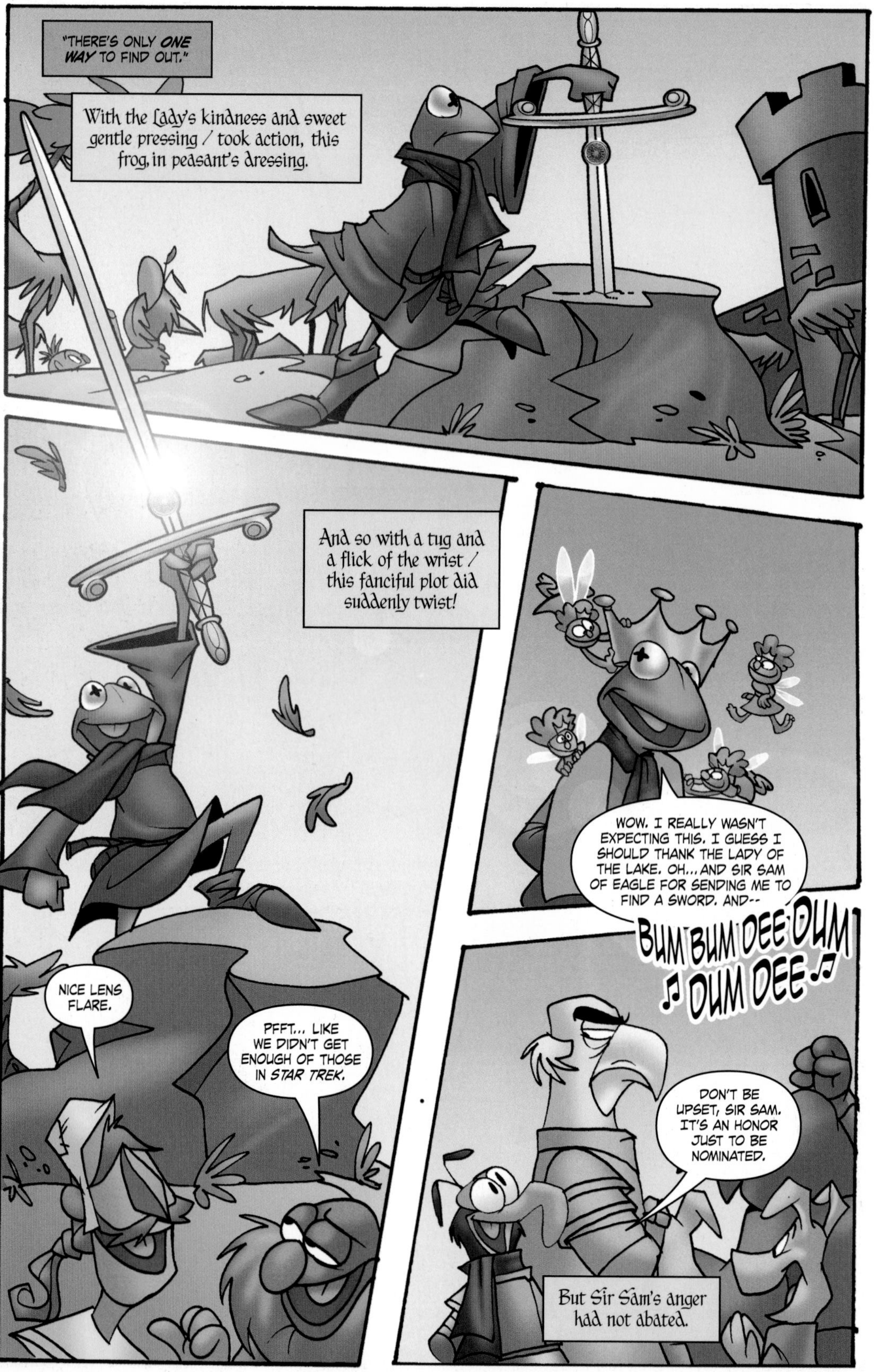
"THERE'S ONLY ONE WAY TO FIND OUT."
With the Lady's kindness and sweet gentle pressing / took action, this frog, in peasant's dressing.
And so with a tug and a flick of the wrist / this fanciful plot did suddenly twist!
WOW. I REALLY WASN'T EXPECTING THIS. I GUESS I SHOULD THANK THE LADY OF THE LAKE. OH... AND SIR SAM OF EAGLE FOR SENDING ME TO FIND A SWORD. AND--
NICE LENS FLARE.
PFFT... LIKE WE DIDN'T GET ENOUGH OF THOSE IN STAR TREK.
BUM BUM DEE DUM
DUM DEE
DON'T BE UPSET, SIR SAM. IT'S AN HONOR JUST TO BE NOMINATED.
But Sir Sam's anger had not abated.

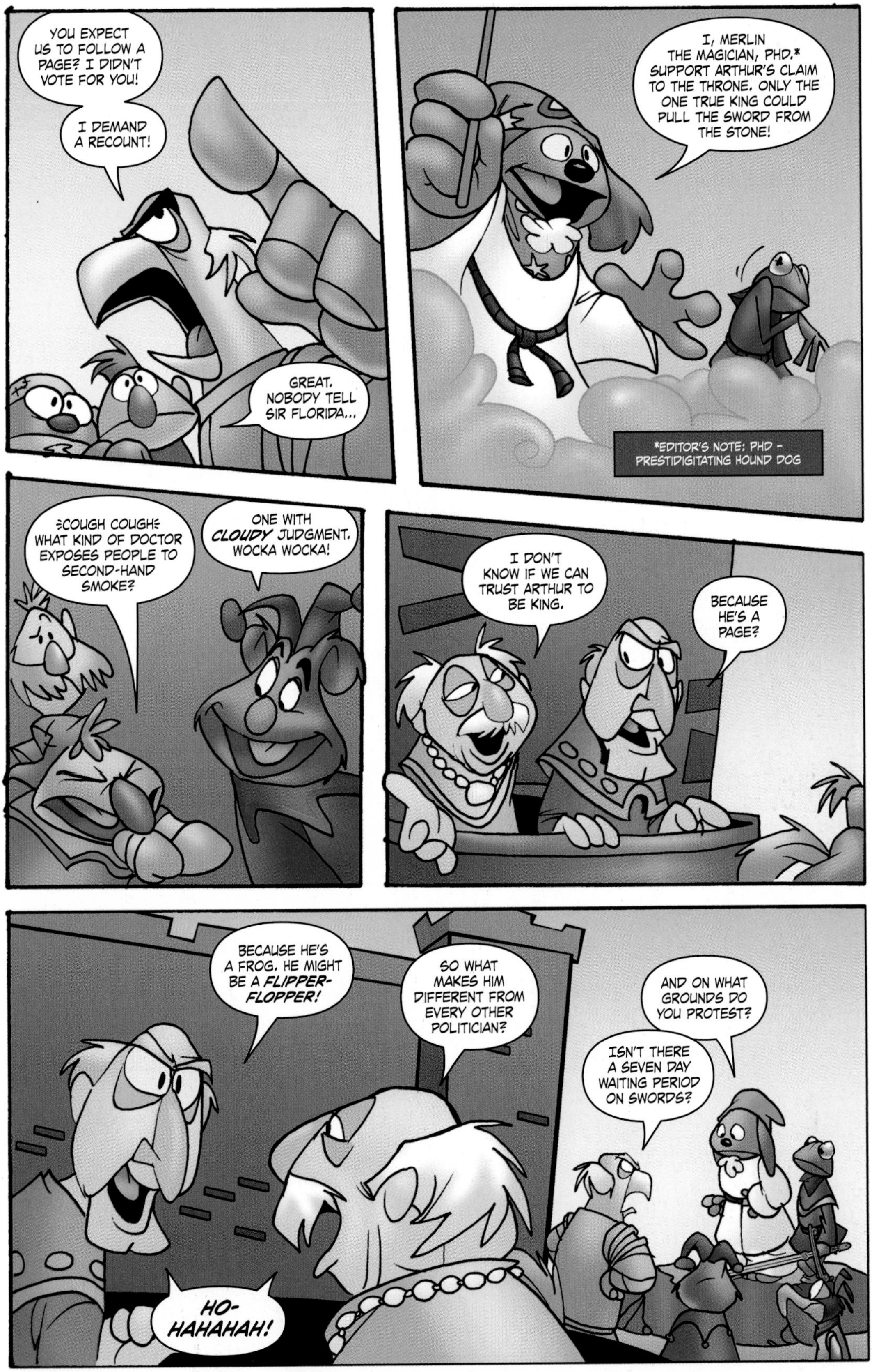
YOU EXPECT US TO FOLLOW A PAGE? I DIDN'T VOTE FOR YOU!
I DEMAND A RECOUNT!
GREAT. NOBODY TELL SIR FLORIDA...
I, MERLIN THE MAGICIAN, PHD.* SUPPORT ARTHUR'S CLAIM TO THE THRONE. ONLY THE ONE TRUE KING COULD PULL THE SWORD FROM THE STONE!
*EDITOR'S NOTE: PHD - PRESTIDIGITATING HOUND DOG
COUGH COUGH WHAT KIND OF DOCTOR EXPOSES PEOPLE TO SECOND-HAND SMOKE?
ONE WITH CLOUDY JUDGMENT. WOCKA WOCKA!
I DON'T KNOW IF WE CAN TRUST ARTHUR TO BE KING.
BECAUSE HE'S A PAGE?
BECAUSE HE'S A FROG. HE MIGHT BE A FLIPPER-FLOPPER!
SO WHAT MAKES HIM DIFFERENT FROM EVERY OTHER POLITICIAN?
AND ON WHAT GROUNDS DO YOU PROTEST?
ISN'T THERE A SEVEN DAY WAITING PERIOD ON SWORDS?
HO-HAHAHAH!

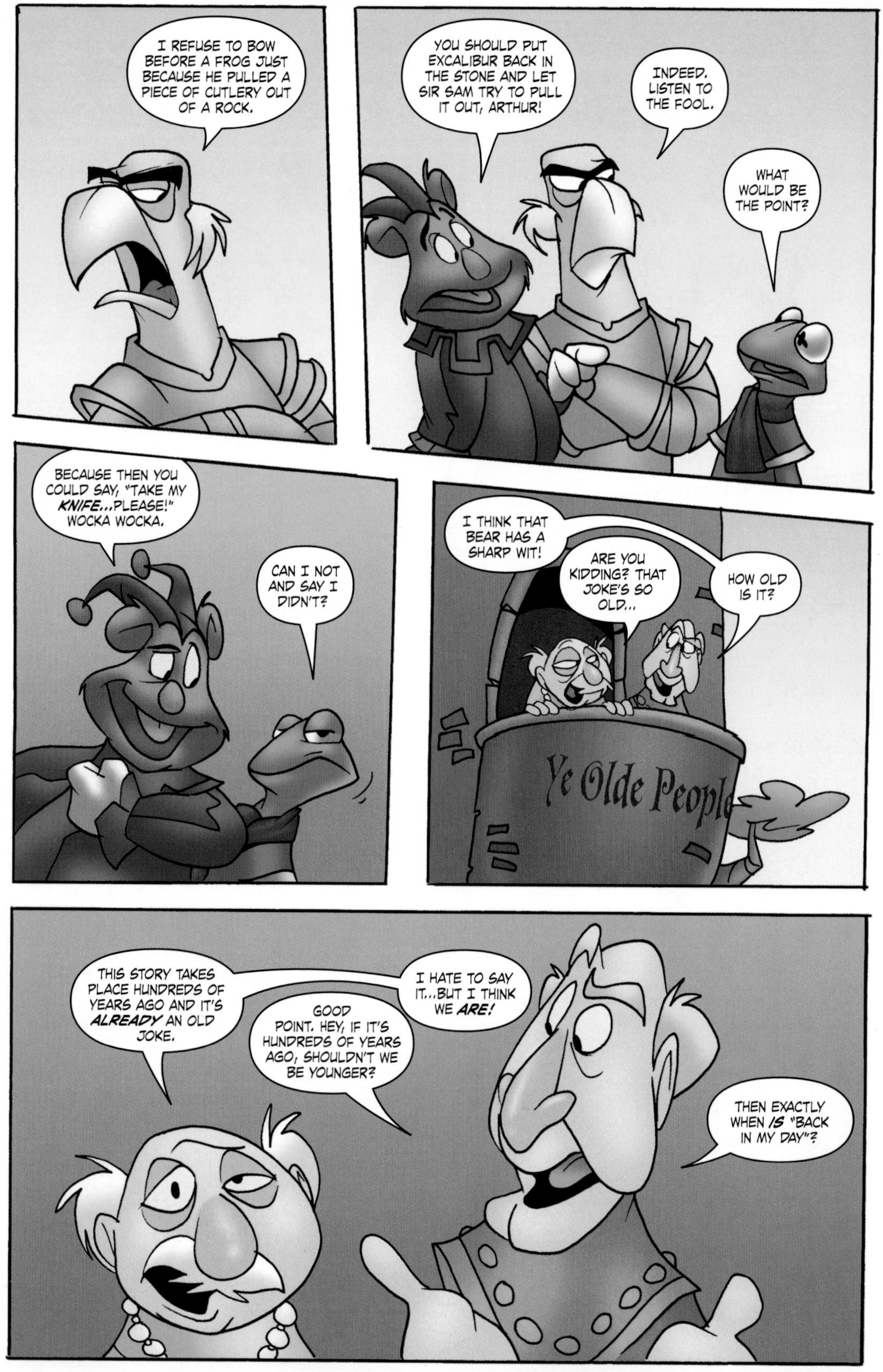
I REFUSE TO BOW BEFORE A FROG JUST BECAUSE HE PULLED A PIECE OF CUTLERY OUT OF A ROCK.
YOU SHOULD PUT EXCALIBUR BACK IN THE STONE AND LET SIR SAM TRY TO PULL IT OUT, ARTHUR!
INDEED. LISTEN TO THE FOOL.
WHAT WOULD BE THE POINT?
BECAUSE THEN YOU COULD SAY, "TAKE MY *KNIFE*...PLEASE!" WOCKA WOCKA.
CAN I NOT AND SAY I DIDN'T?
I THINK THAT BEAR HAS A SHARP WIT!
ARE YOU KIDDING? THAT JOKE'S SO OLD...
HOW OLD IS IT?
Ye Olde People
THIS STORY TAKES PLACE HUNDREDS OF YEARS AGO AND IT'S *ALREADY* AN OLD JOKE.
I HATE TO SAY IT...BUT I THINK WE *ARE!*
GOOD POINT. HEY, IF IT'S HUNDREDS OF YEARS AGO, SHOULDN'T WE BE YOUNGER?
THEN EXACTLY WHEN *IS* "BACK IN MY DAY"?

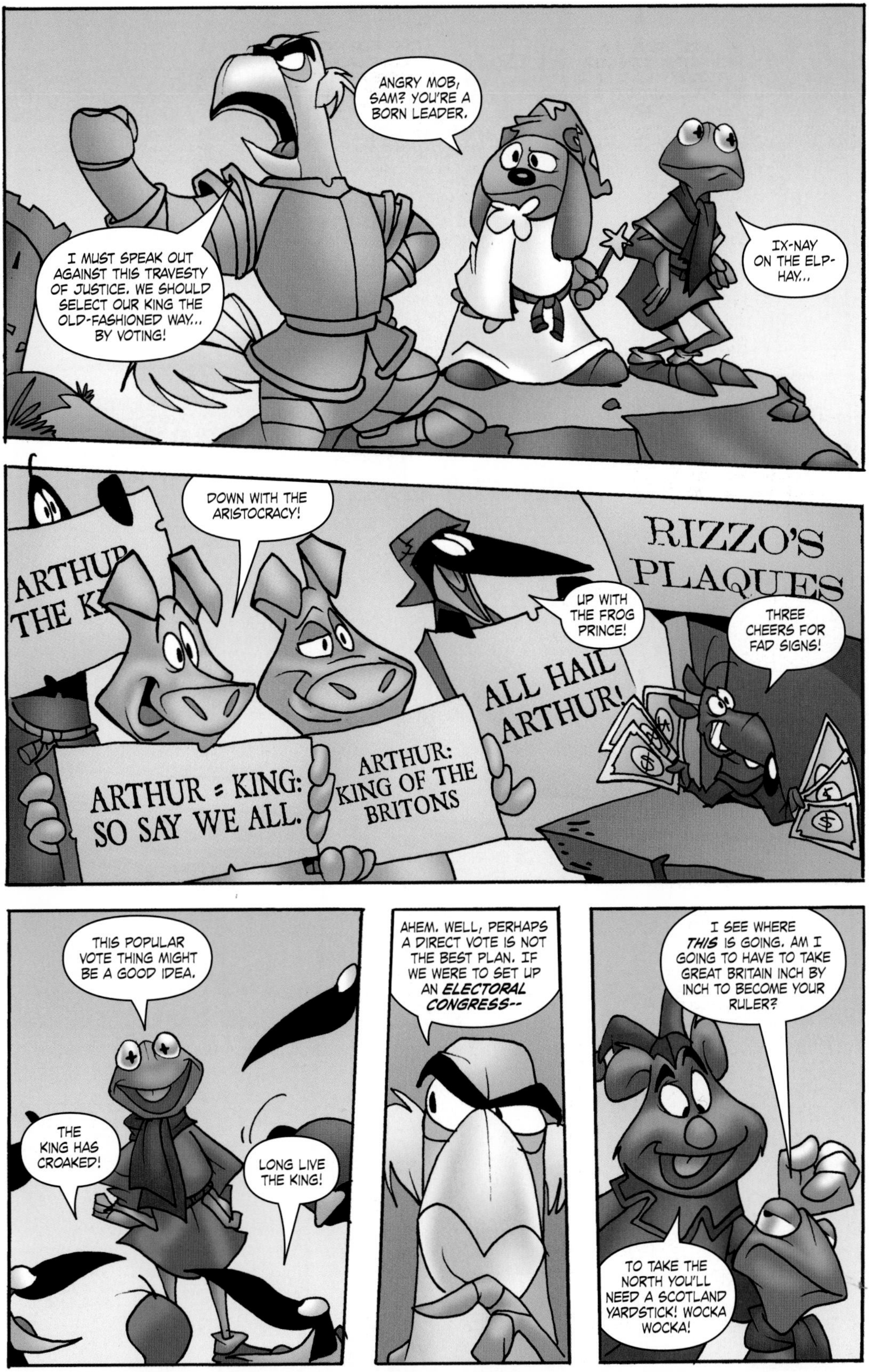
ANGRY MOB, SAM? YOU'RE A BORN LEADER.
I MUST SPEAK OUT AGAINST THIS TRAVESTY OF JUSTICE. WE SHOULD SELECT OUR KING THE OLD-FASHIONED WAY... BY VOTING!
IX-NAY ON THE ELP-HAY...
DOWN WITH THE ARISTOCRACY!
ARTHUR THE K
ARTHUR = KING: SO SAY WE ALL.
ARTHUR: KING OF THE BRITONS
ALL HAIL ARTHUR!
UP WITH THE FROG PRINCE!
RIZZO'S PLAQUES
THREE CHEERS FOR FAD SIGNS!
THIS POPULAR VOTE THING MIGHT BE A GOOD IDEA.
THE KING HAS CROAKED!
LONG LIVE THE KING!
AHEM. WELL, PERHAPS A DIRECT VOTE IS NOT THE BEST PLAN. IF WE WERE TO SET UP AN *ELECTORAL CONGRESS--*
I SEE WHERE *THIS* IS GOING. AM I GOING TO HAVE TO TAKE GREAT BRITAIN INCH BY INCH TO BECOME YOUR RULER?
TO TAKE THE NORTH YOU'LL NEED A SCOTLAND YARDSTICK! WOCKA WOCKA!

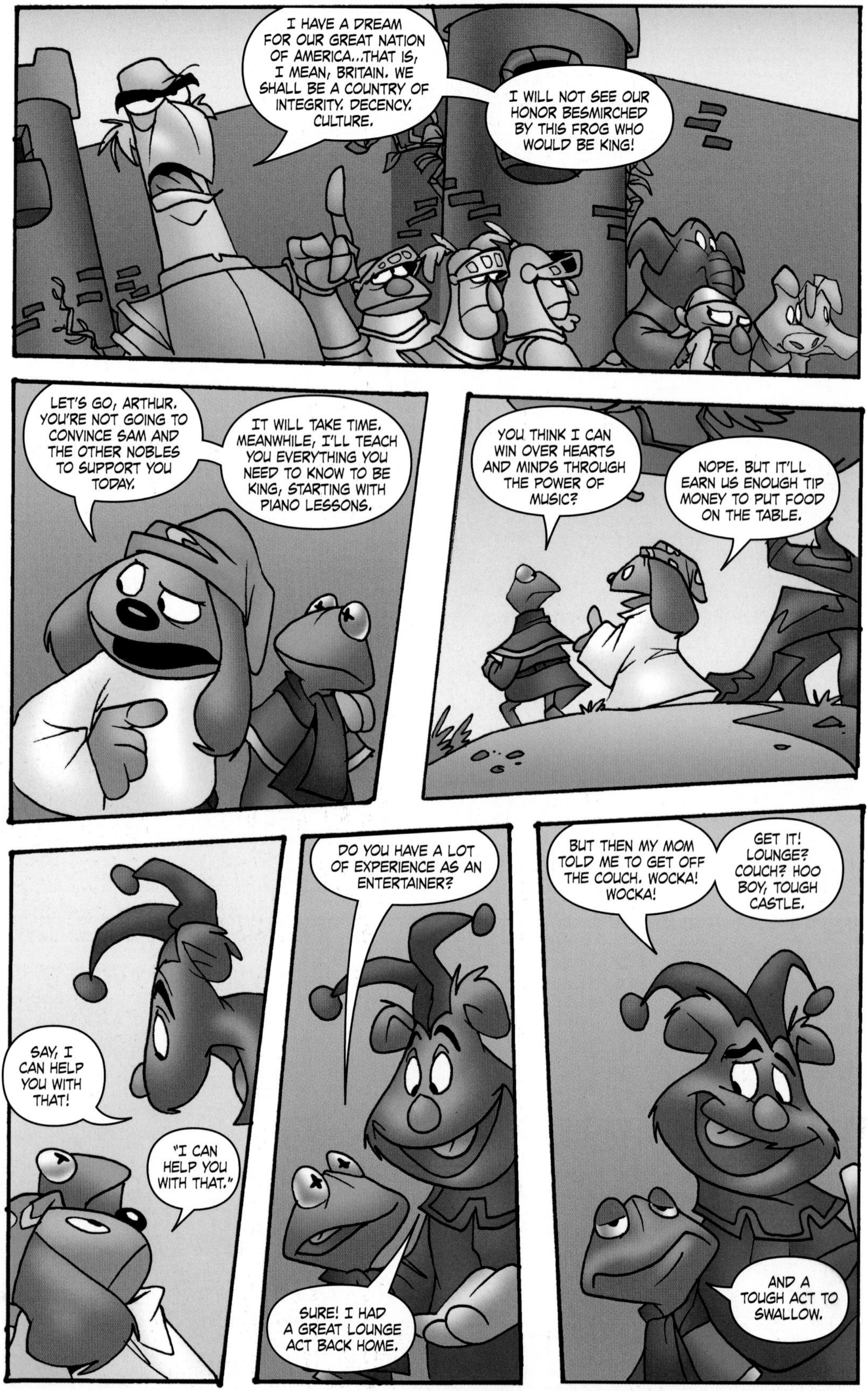
I HAVE A DREAM FOR OUR GREAT NATION OF AMERICA...THAT IS, I MEAN, BRITAIN. WE SHALL BE A COUNTRY OF INTEGRITY. DECENCY. CULTURE.
I WILL NOT SEE OUR HONOR BESMIRCHED BY THIS FROG WHO WOULD BE KING!
LET'S GO, ARTHUR. YOU'RE NOT GOING TO CONVINCE SAM AND THE OTHER NOBLES TO SUPPORT YOU TODAY.
IT WILL TAKE TIME. MEANWHILE, I'LL TEACH YOU EVERYTHING YOU NEED TO KNOW TO BE KING, STARTING WITH PIANO LESSONS.
YOU THINK I CAN WIN OVER HEARTS AND MINDS THROUGH THE POWER OF MUSIC?
NOPE. BUT IT'LL EARN US ENOUGH TIP MONEY TO PUT FOOD ON THE TABLE.
SAY, I CAN HELP YOU WITH THAT!
"I CAN HELP YOU WITH THAT."
DO YOU HAVE A LOT OF EXPERIENCE AS AN ENTERTAINER?
SURE! I HAD A GREAT LOUNGE ACT BACK HOME.
BUT THEN MY MOM TOLD ME TO GET OFF THE COUCH. WOCKA! WOCKA!
GET IT! LOUNGE? COUCH? HOO BOY, TOUGH CASTLE.
AND A TOUGH ACT TO SWALLOW.

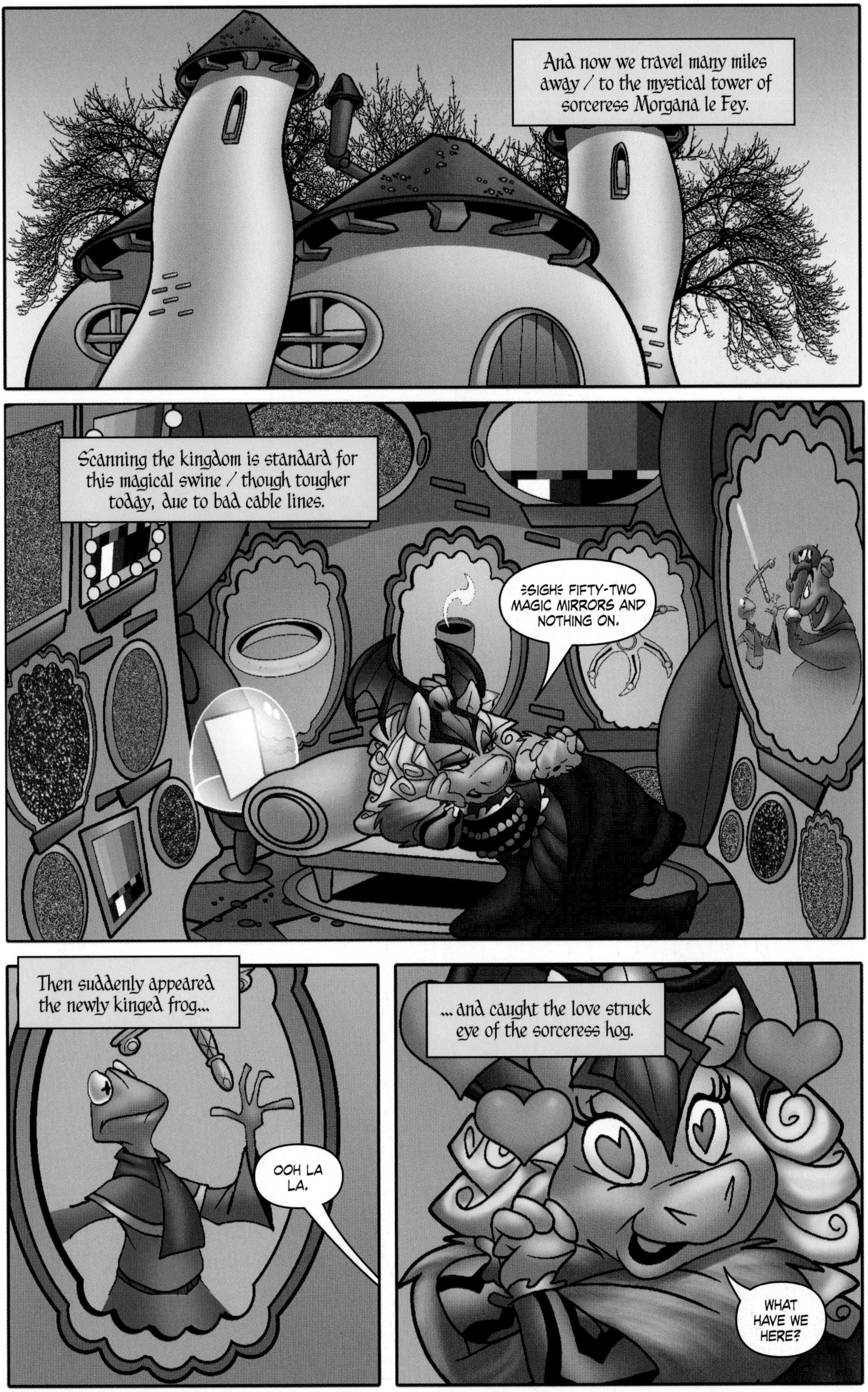
And now we travel many miles away / to the mystical tower of sorceress Morgana le Fey.
Scanning the kingdom is standard for this magical swine / though tougher today, due to bad cable lines.
=SIGH= FIFTY-TWO MAGIC MIRRORS AND NOTHING ON.
Then suddenly appeared the newly kinged frog...
OOH LA LA.
... and caught the love struck eye of the sorceress hog.
WHAT HAVE WE HERE?

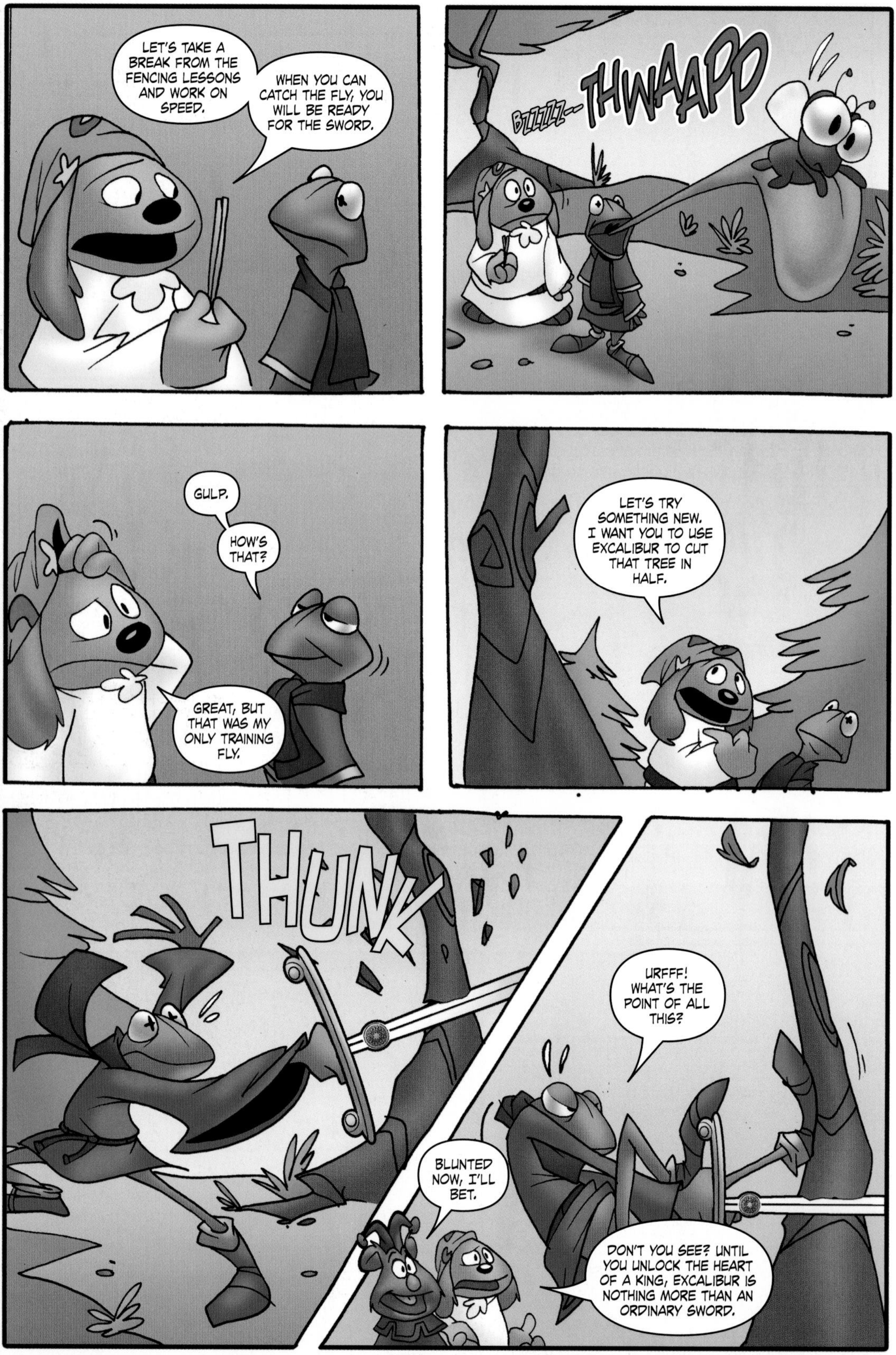
LET'S TAKE A BREAK FROM THE FENCING LESSONS AND WORK ON SPEED.
WHEN YOU CAN CATCH THE FLY, YOU WILL BE READY FOR THE SWORD.
BZZZZZ--THWAAPP
GULP.
HOW'S THAT?
GREAT, BUT THAT WAS MY ONLY TRAINING FLY.
LET'S TRY SOMETHING NEW. I WANT YOU TO USE EXCALIBUR TO CUT THAT TREE IN HALF.
THUNK
URFFF! WHAT'S THE POINT OF ALL THIS?
BLUNTED NOW, I'LL BET.
DON'T YOU SEE? UNTIL YOU UNLOCK THE HEART OF A KING, EXCALIBUR IS NOTHING MORE THAN AN ORDINARY SWORD.

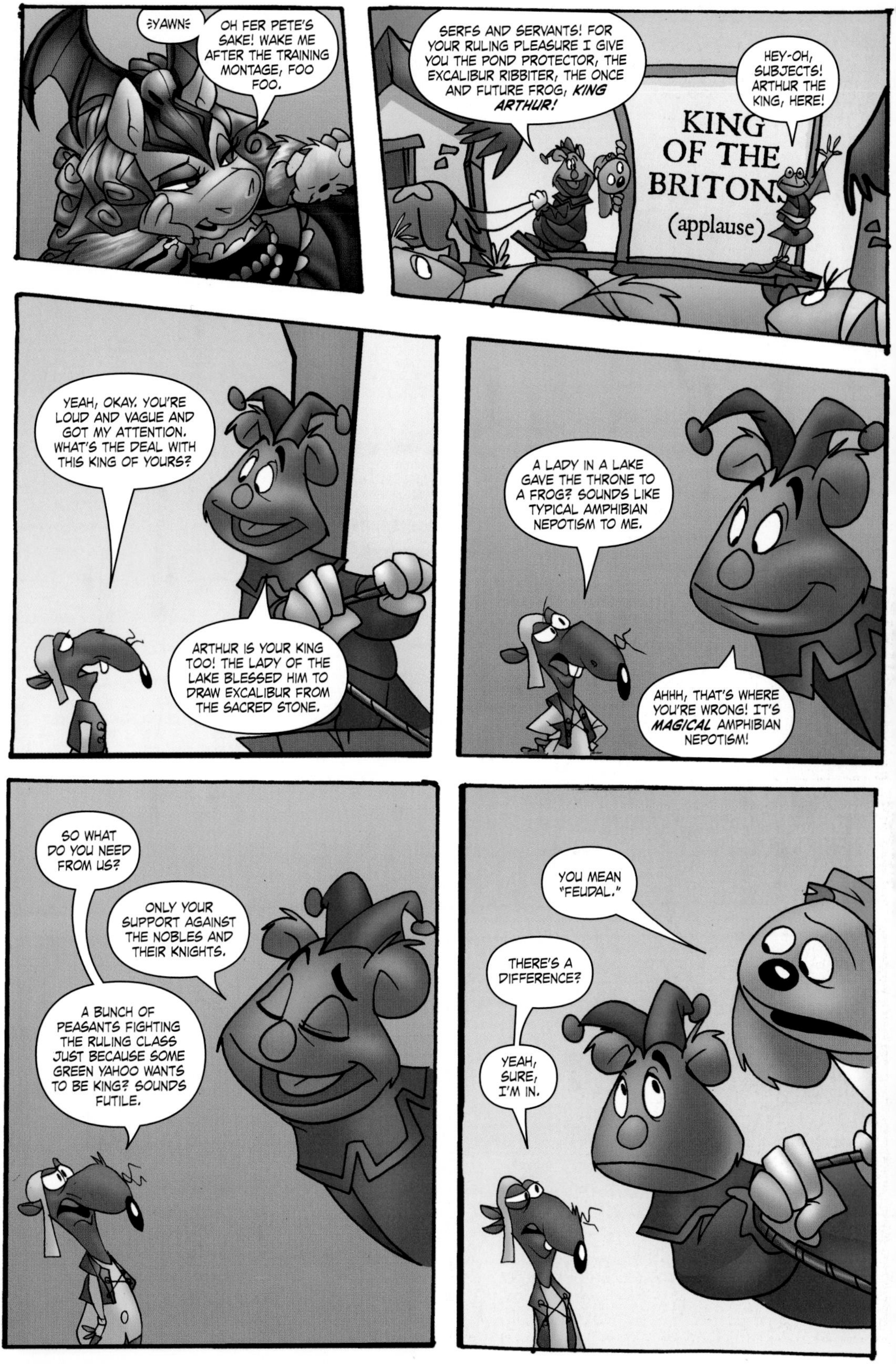

ƸYAWNƷ
OH FER PETE'S SAKE! WAKE ME AFTER THE TRAINING MONTAGE, FOO FOO.
SERFS AND SERVANTS! FOR YOUR RULING PLEASURE I GIVE YOU THE POND PROTECTOR, THE EXCALIBUR RIBBITER, THE ONCE AND FUTURE FROG, KING ARTHUR!
HEY-OH, SUBJECTS! ARTHUR THE KING, HERE!
KING OF THE BRITONS
(applause)
YEAH, OKAY. YOU'RE LOUD AND VAGUE AND GOT MY ATTENTION. WHAT'S THE DEAL WITH THIS KING OF YOURS?
ARTHUR IS YOUR KING TOO! THE LADY OF THE LAKE BLESSED HIM TO DRAW EXCALIBUR FROM THE SACRED STONE.
A LADY IN A LAKE GAVE THE THRONE TO A FROG? SOUNDS LIKE TYPICAL AMPHIBIAN NEPOTISM TO ME.
AHHH, THAT'S WHERE YOU'RE WRONG! IT'S MAGICAL AMPHIBIAN NEPOTISM!
SO WHAT DO YOU NEED FROM US?
ONLY YOUR SUPPORT AGAINST THE NOBLES AND THEIR KNIGHTS.
A BUNCH OF PEASANTS FIGHTING THE RULING CLASS JUST BECAUSE SOME GREEN YAHOO WANTS TO BE KING? SOUNDS FUTILE.
YOU MEAN "FEUDAL."
THERE'S A DIFFERENCE?
YEAH, SURE, I'M IN.

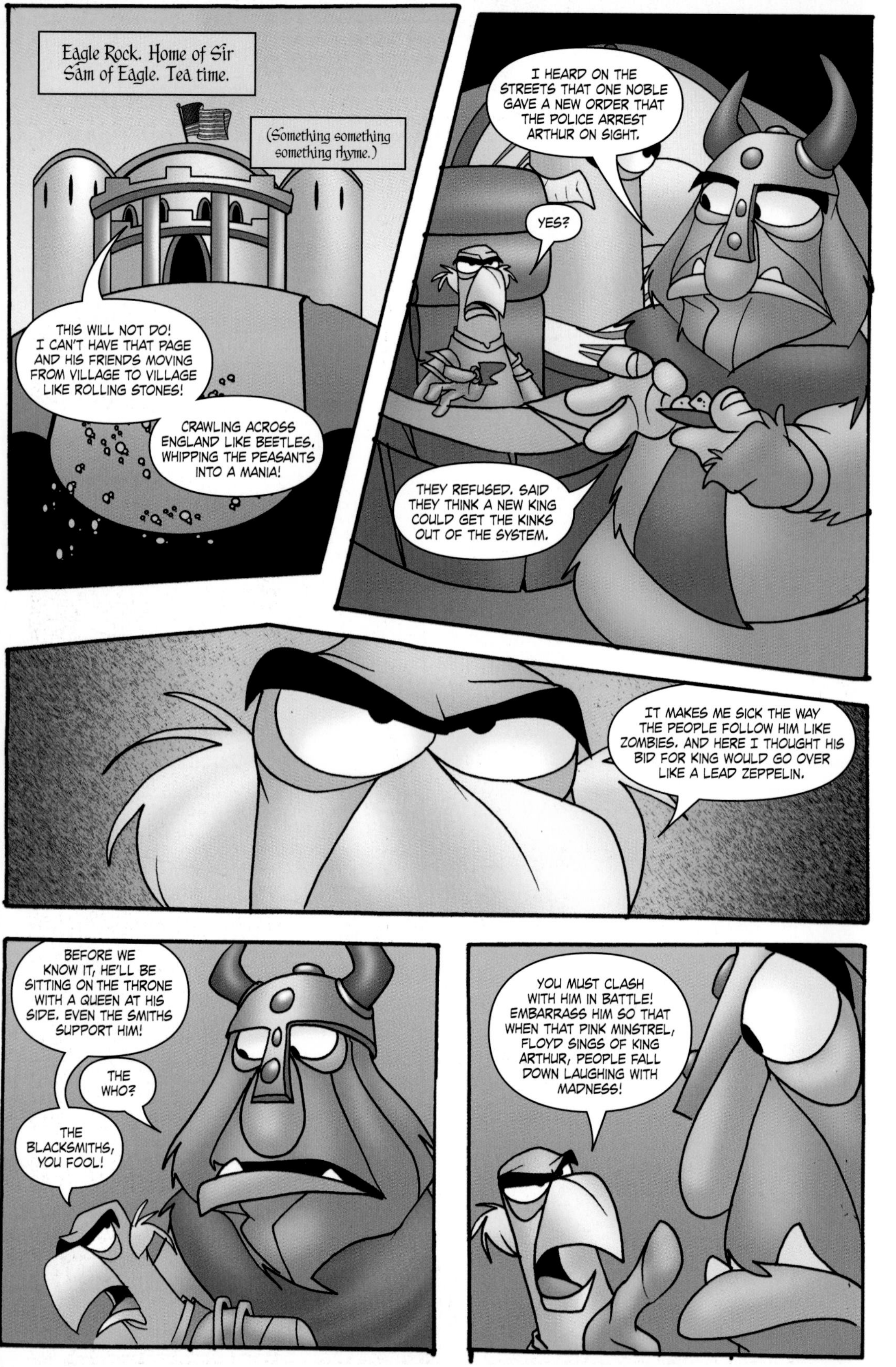

Eagle Rock. Home of Sir Sam of Eagle. Tea time.
(Something something something rhyme.)
THIS WILL NOT DO! I CAN'T HAVE THAT PAGE AND HIS FRIENDS MOVING FROM VILLAGE TO VILLAGE LIKE ROLLING STONES!
CRAWLING ACROSS ENGLAND LIKE BEETLES. WHIPPING THE PEASANTS INTO A MANIA!
I HEARD ON THE STREETS THAT ONE NOBLE GAVE A NEW ORDER THAT THE POLICE ARREST ARTHUR ON SIGHT.
YES?
THEY REFUSED. SAID THEY THINK A NEW KING COULD GET THE KINKS OUT OF THE SYSTEM.
IT MAKES ME SICK THE WAY THE PEOPLE FOLLOW HIM LIKE ZOMBIES. AND HERE I THOUGHT HIS BID FOR KING WOULD GO OVER LIKE A LEAD ZEPPELIN.
BEFORE WE KNOW IT, HE'LL BE SITTING ON THE THRONE WITH A QUEEN AT HIS SIDE. EVEN THE SMITHS SUPPORT HIM!
THE WHO?
THE BLACKSMITHS, YOU FOOL!
YOU MUST CLASH WITH HIM IN BATTLE! EMBARRASS HIM SO THAT WHEN THAT PINK MINSTREL, FLOYD SINGS OF KING ARTHUR, PEOPLE FALL DOWN LAUGHING WITH MADNESS!

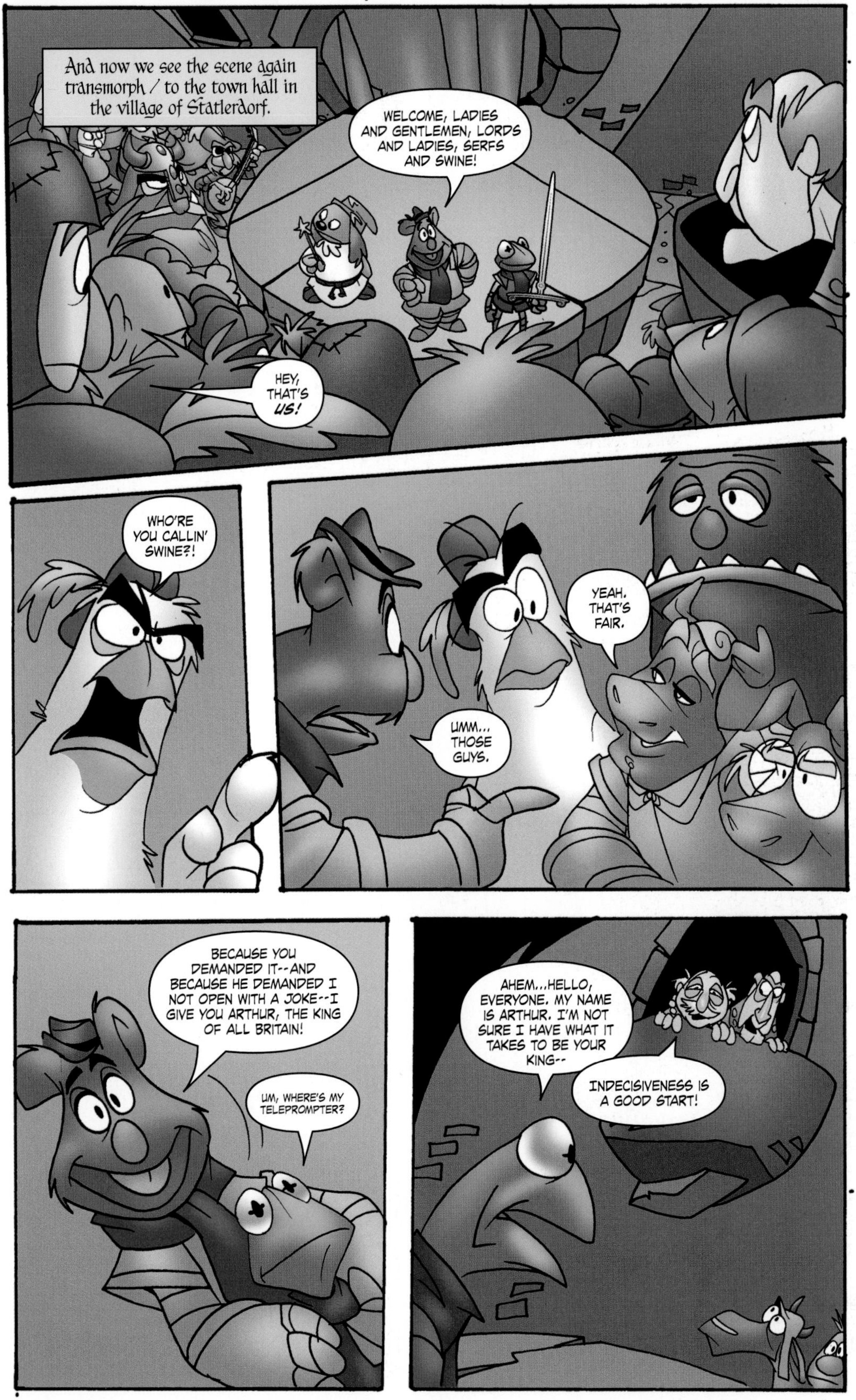
And now we see the scene again transmorph / to the town hall in the village of Statlerdorf.
WELCOME, LADIES AND GENTLEMEN, LORDS AND LADIES, SERFS AND SWINE!
HEY, THAT'S US!
WHO'RE YOU CALLIN' SWINE?!
YEAH. THAT'S FAIR.
UMM... THOSE GUYS.
BECAUSE YOU DEMANDED IT--AND BECAUSE HE DEMANDED I NOT OPEN WITH A JOKE--I GIVE YOU ARTHUR, THE KING OF ALL BRITAIN!
UM, WHERE'S MY TELEPROMPTER?
AHEM...HELLO, EVERYONE. MY NAME IS ARTHUR. I'M NOT SURE I HAVE WHAT IT TAKES TO BE YOUR KING--
INDECISIVENESS IS A GOOD START!

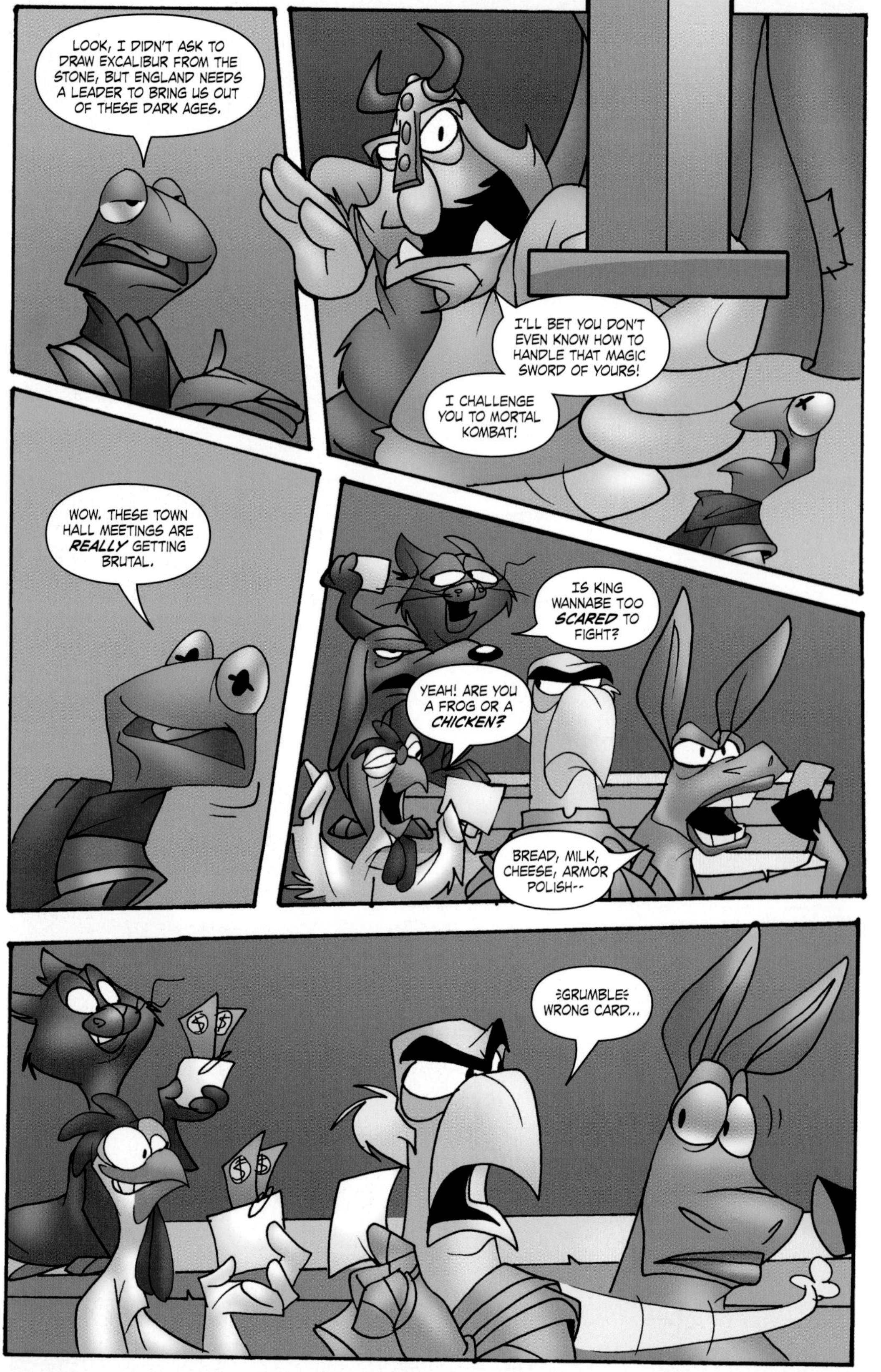
LOOK, I DIDN'T ASK TO DRAW EXCALIBUR FROM THE STONE, BUT ENGLAND NEEDS A LEADER TO BRING US OUT OF THESE DARK AGES.
I'LL BET YOU DON'T EVEN KNOW HOW TO HANDLE THAT MAGIC SWORD OF YOURS!
I CHALLENGE YOU TO MORTAL KOMBAT!
WOW. THESE TOWN HALL MEETINGS ARE REALLY GETTING BRUTAL.
IS KING WANNABE TOO SCARED TO FIGHT?
YEAH! ARE YOU A FROG OR A CHICKEN?
BREAD, MILK, CHEESE, ARMOR POLISH--
=GRUMBLE= WRONG CARD...

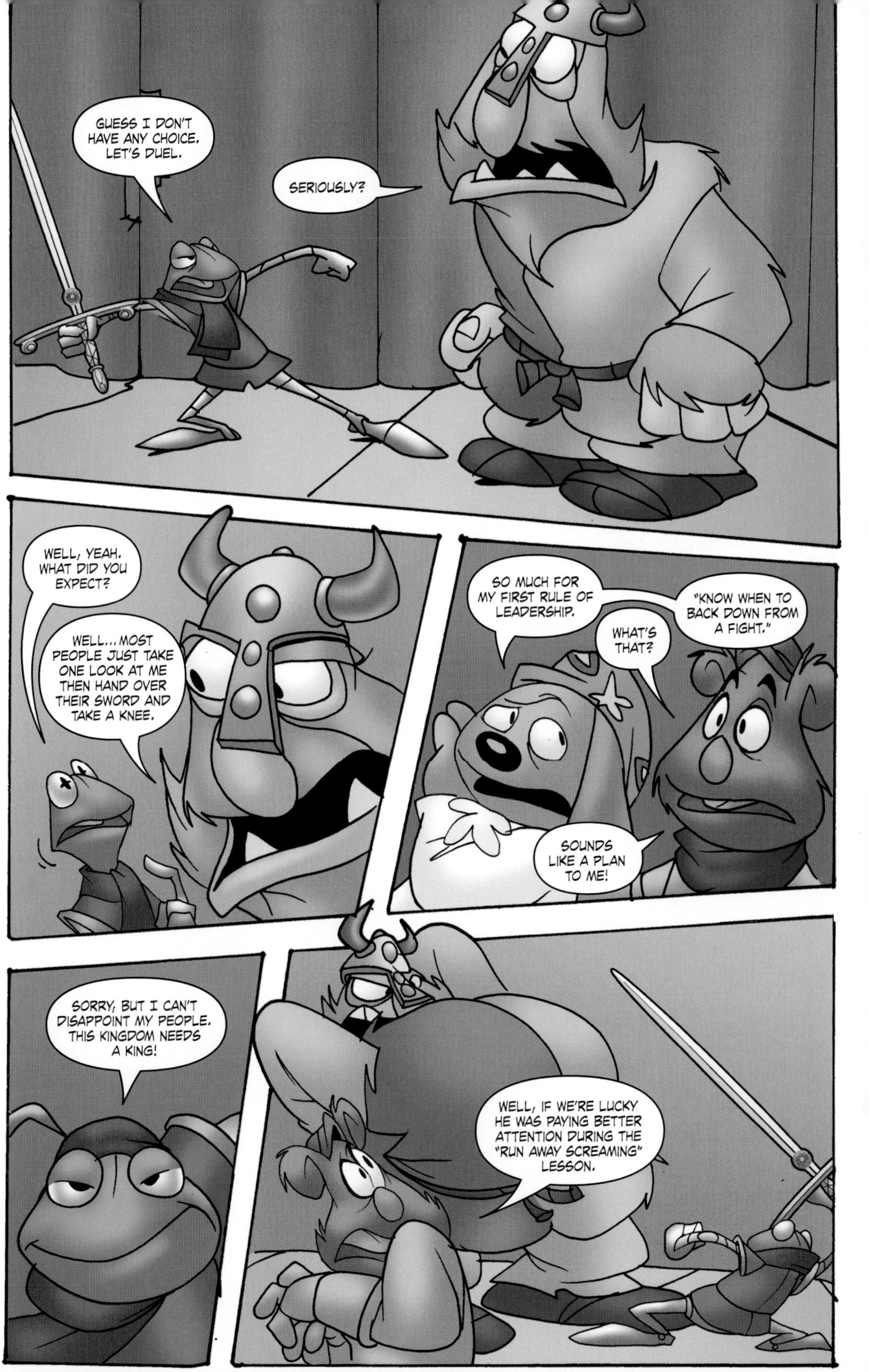
GUESS I DON'T HAVE ANY CHOICE. LET'S DUEL.
SERIOUSLY?
WELL, YEAH. WHAT DID YOU EXPECT?
WELL... MOST PEOPLE JUST TAKE ONE LOOK AT ME THEN HAND OVER THEIR SWORD AND TAKE A KNEE.
SO MUCH FOR MY FIRST RULE OF LEADERSHIP.
WHAT'S THAT?
"KNOW WHEN TO BACK DOWN FROM A FIGHT."
SOUNDS LIKE A PLAN TO ME!
SORRY, BUT I CAN'T DISAPPOINT MY PEOPLE. THIS KINGDOM NEEDS A KING!
WELL, IF WE'RE LUCKY HE WAS PAYING BETTER ATTENTION DURING THE "RUN AWAY SCREAMING" LESSON.

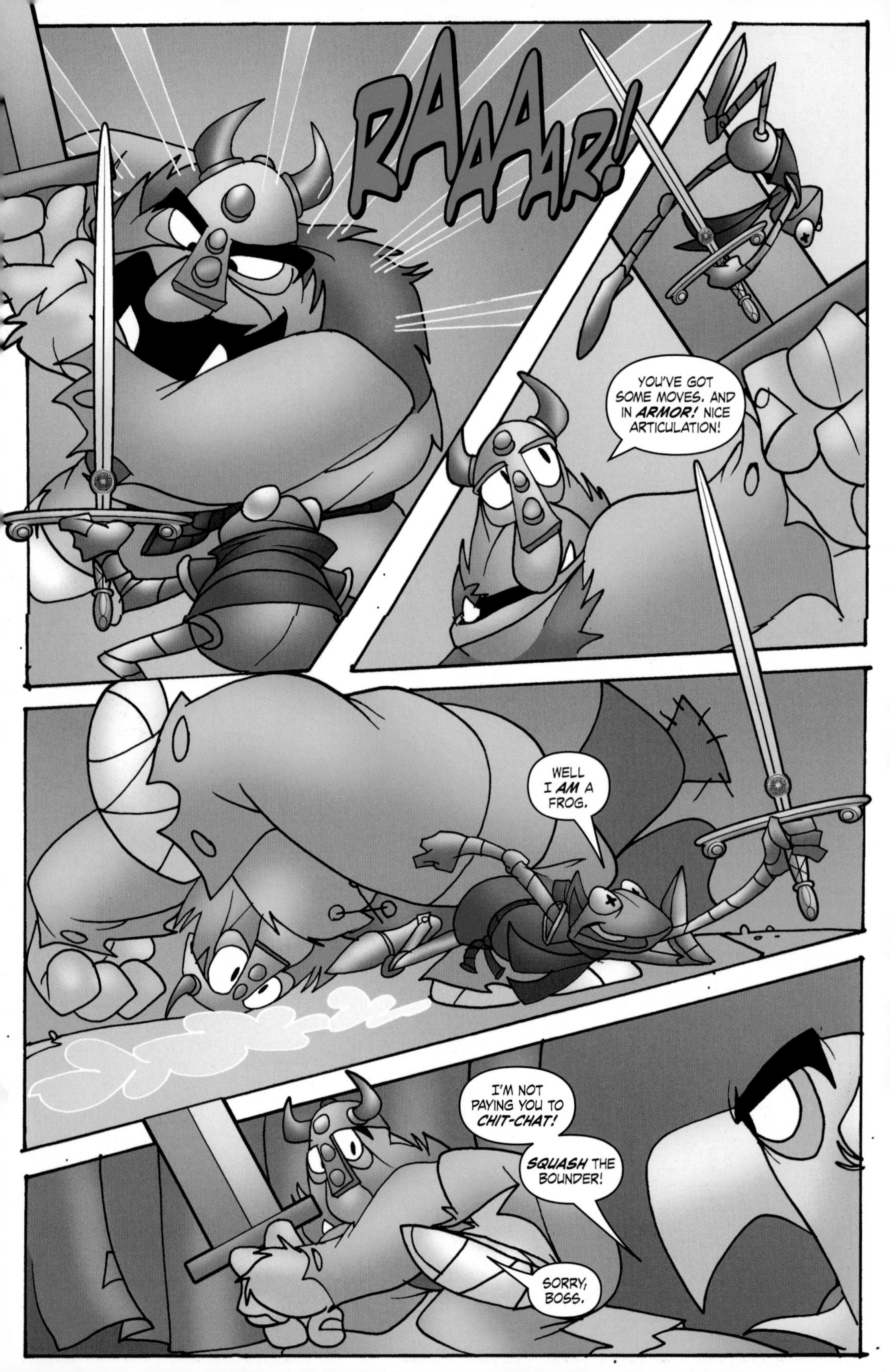
RAAAAR!
YOU'VE GOT SOME MOVES. AND IN ARMOR! NICE ARTICULATION!
WELL I AM A FROG.
I'M NOT PAYING YOU TO CHIT-CHAT!
SQUASH THE BOUNDER!
SORRY, BOSS.

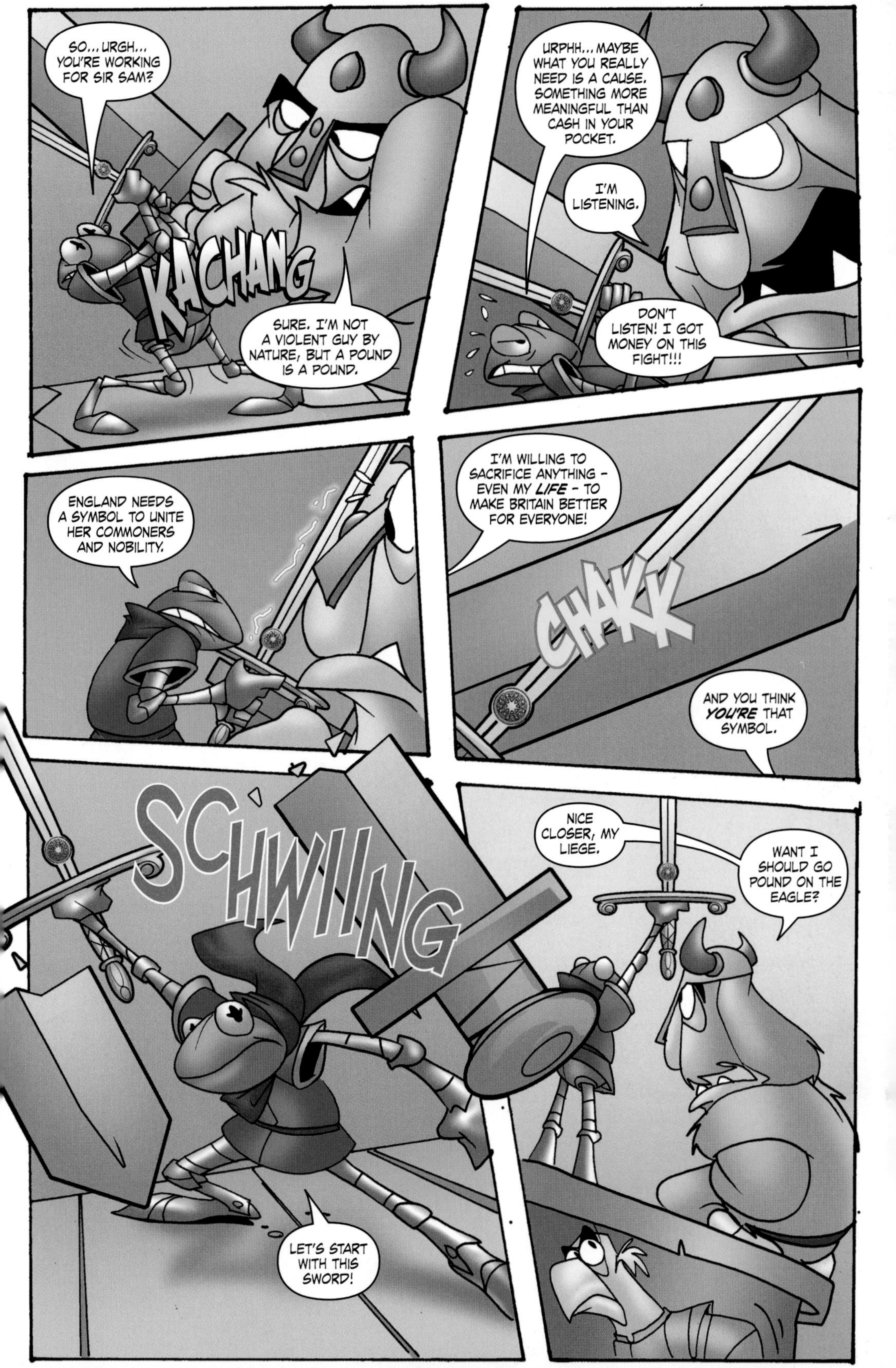
SO... URGH... YOU'RE WORKING FOR SIR SAM?
KACHANG
SURE. I'M NOT A VIOLENT GUY BY NATURE, BUT A POUND IS A POUND.
URPHH... MAYBE WHAT YOU REALLY NEED IS A CAUSE. SOMETHING MORE MEANINGFUL THAN CASH IN YOUR POCKET.
I'M LISTENING.
DON'T LISTEN! I GOT MONEY ON THIS FIGHT!!!
ENGLAND NEEDS A SYMBOL TO UNITE HER COMMONERS AND NOBILITY.
I'M WILLING TO SACRIFICE ANYTHING - EVEN MY *LIFE* - TO MAKE BRITAIN BETTER FOR EVERYONE!
CHAKK
AND YOU THINK *YOU'RE* THAT SYMBOL.
SCHWIING
LET'S START WITH THIS SWORD!
NICE CLOSER, MY LIEGE.
WANT I SHOULD GO POUND ON THE EAGLE?

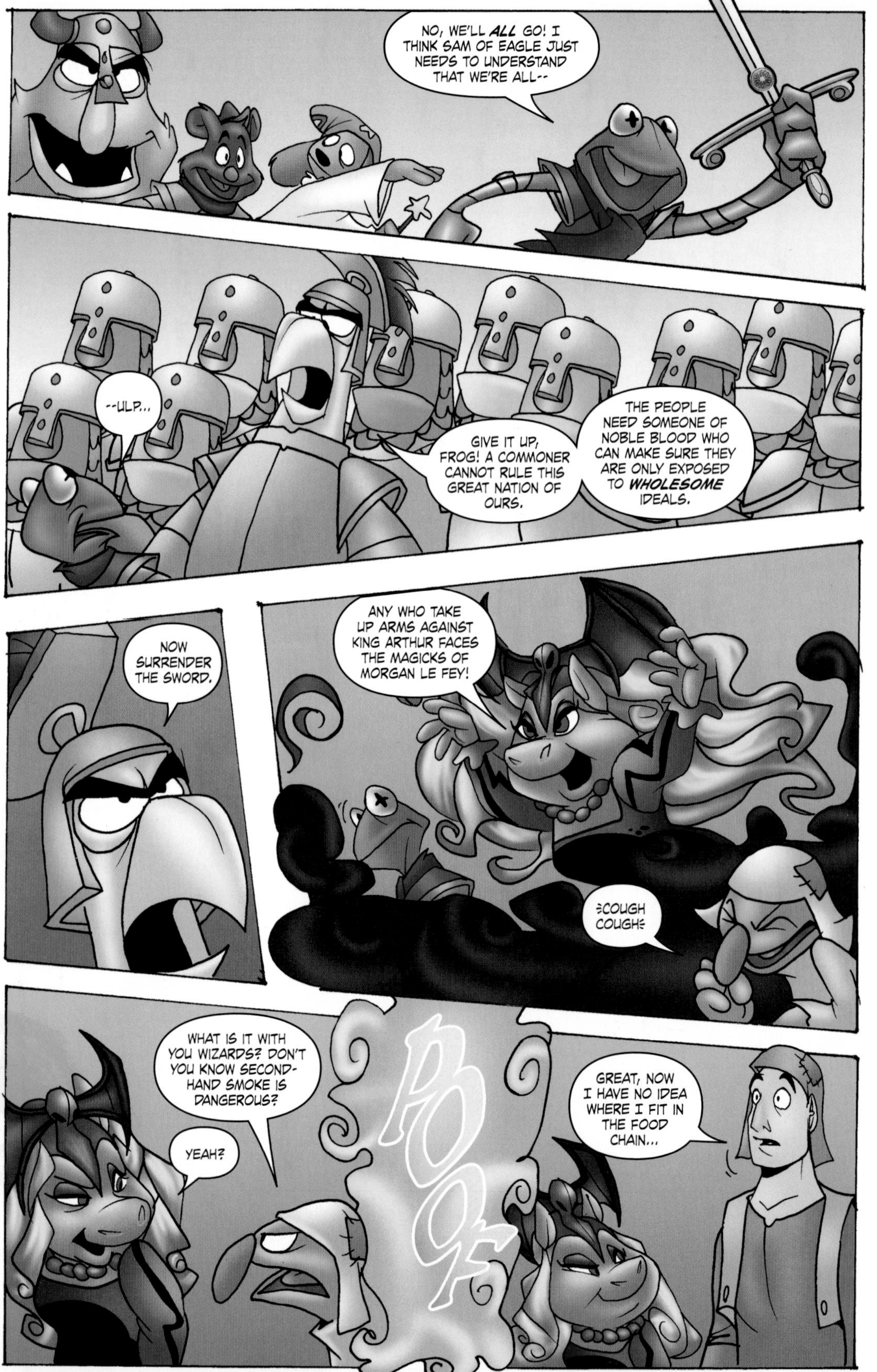
NO, WE'LL ALL GO! I THINK SAM OF EAGLE JUST NEEDS TO UNDERSTAND THAT WE'RE ALL--
--ULP...
GIVE IT UP, FROG! A COMMONER CANNOT RULE THIS GREAT NATION OF OURS.
THE PEOPLE NEED SOMEONE OF NOBLE BLOOD WHO CAN MAKE SURE THEY ARE ONLY EXPOSED TO WHOLESOME IDEALS.
NOW SURRENDER THE SWORD.
ANY WHO TAKE UP ARMS AGAINST KING ARTHUR FACES THE MAGICKS OF MORGAN LE FEY!
COUGH COUGH
WHAT IS IT WITH YOU WIZARDS? DON'T YOU KNOW SECOND-HAND SMOKE IS DANGEROUS?
YEAH?
POOF
GREAT, NOW I HAVE NO IDEA WHERE I FIT IN THE FOOD CHAIN...

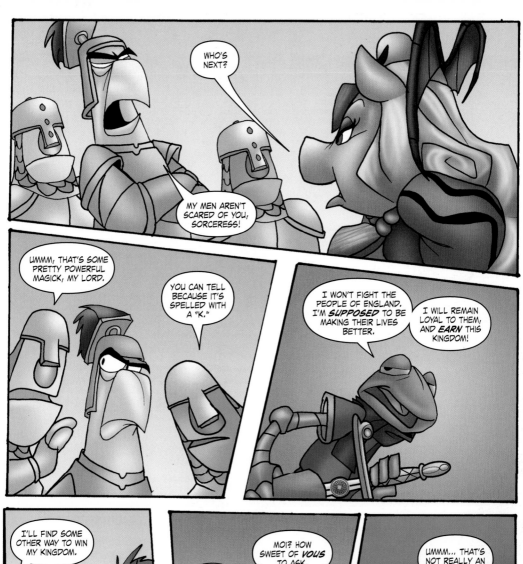

WHO'S NEXT?

MY MEN AREN'T SCARED OF YOU, SORCERESS!

UMMM, THAT'S SOME PRETTY POWERFUL MAGICK, MY LORD.

YOU CAN TELL BECAUSE IT'S SPELLED WITH A "K."

I WON'T FIGHT THE PEOPLE OF ENGLAND. I'M *SUPPOSED* TO BE MAKING THEIR LIVES BETTER.

I WILL REMAIN LOYAL TO THEM, AND *EARN* THIS KINGDOM!

I'LL FIND SOME OTHER WAY TO WIN MY KINGDOM.

THAT'S RIGHT! HOP AWAY, LITTLE FROG!

"LE FEY," ARE YOU FRENCH?

MOI? HOW SWEET OF *VOUS* TO ASK.

UMMM..., THAT'S NOT REALLY AN ANSWER.

IT'S FOR MOI TO KNOW AND VOUS TO FIND OUT.

IF YOU SAY SO.

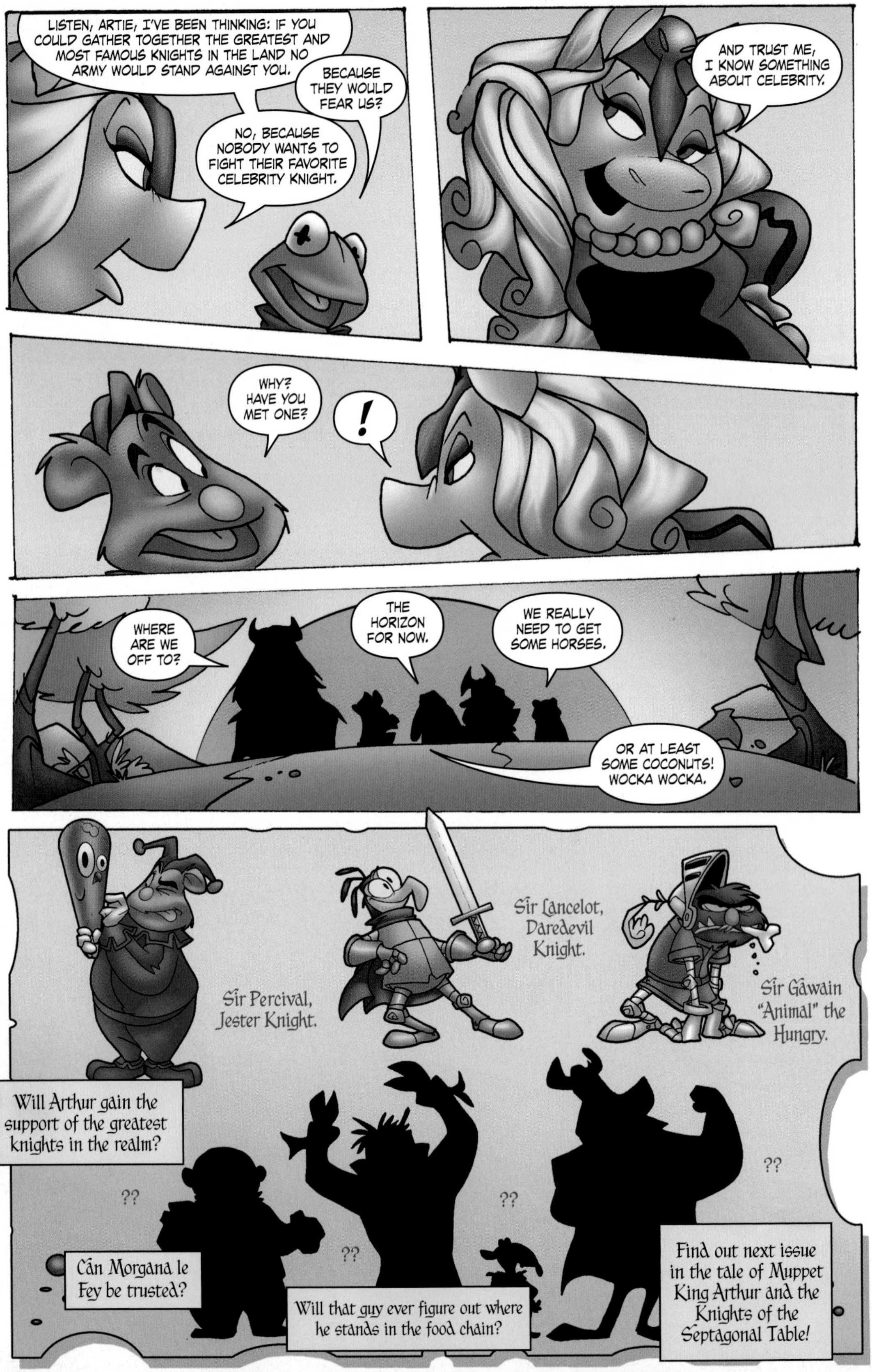
LISTEN, ARTIE, I'VE BEEN THINKING: IF YOU COULD GATHER TOGETHER THE GREATEST AND MOST FAMOUS KNIGHTS IN THE LAND NO ARMY WOULD STAND AGAINST YOU.
BECAUSE THEY WOULD FEAR US?
NO, BECAUSE NOBODY WANTS TO FIGHT THEIR FAVORITE CELEBRITY KNIGHT.
AND TRUST ME, I KNOW SOMETHING ABOUT CELEBRITY.
WHY? HAVE YOU MET ONE?
!
WHERE ARE WE OFF TO?
THE HORIZON FOR NOW.
WE REALLY NEED TO GET SOME HORSES.
OR AT LEAST SOME COCONUTS! WOCKA WOCKA.
Sir Percival, Jester Knight.
Sir Lancelot, Daredevil Knight.
Sir Gâwain "Animal" the Hungry.
Will Arthur gain the support of the greatest knights in the realm?
??
??
??
??
Cân Morgana le Fey be trusted?
Will that guy ever figure out where he stands in the food chain?
Find out next issue in the tale of Muppet King Arthur and the Knights of the Septâgonal Table!

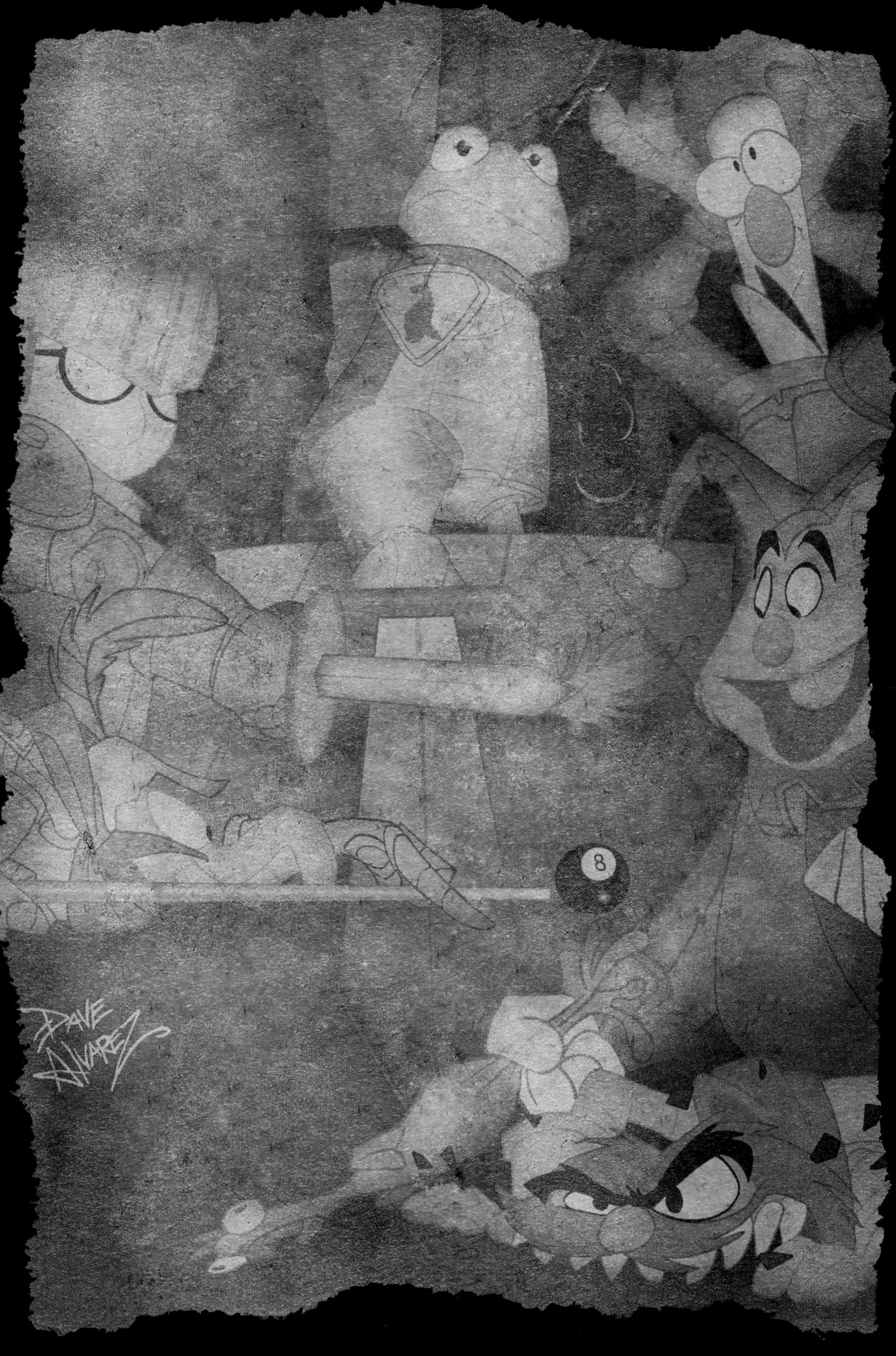
DAVE ALVAREZ
8

chapter two

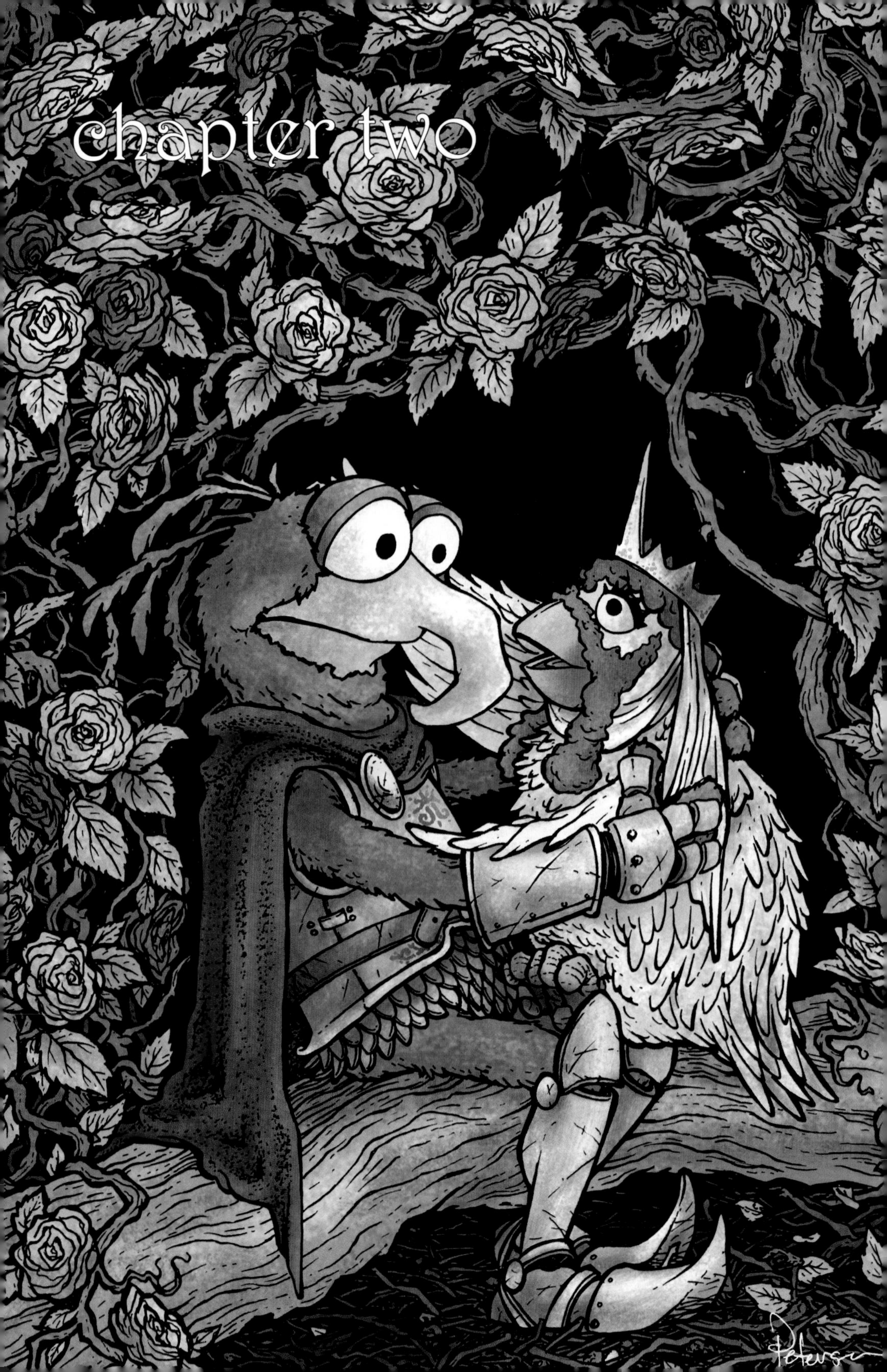

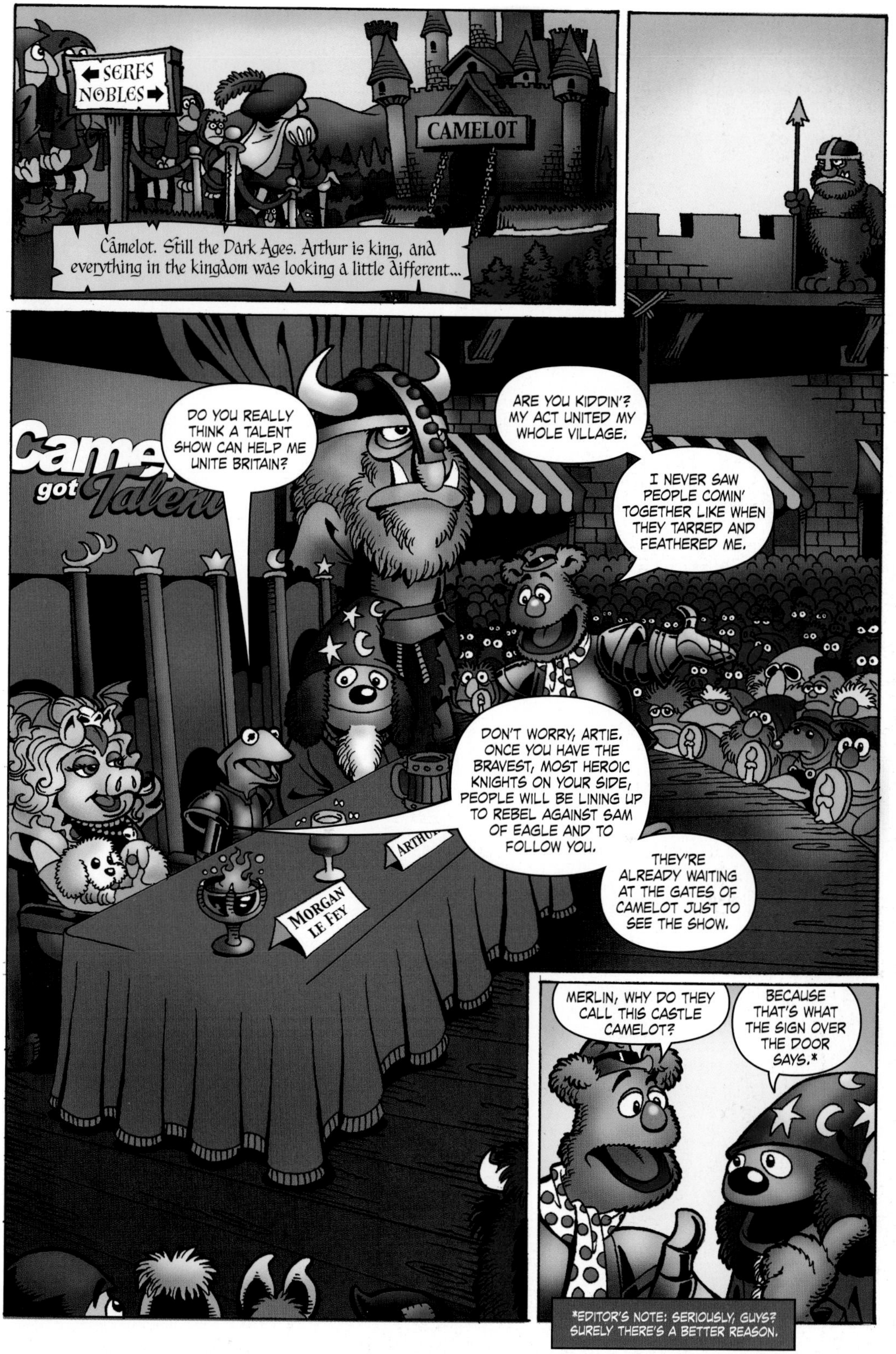

SERFS
NOBLES
CAMELOT
Câmelot. Still the Dark Ages. Arthur is king, and everything in the kingdom was looking a little different...
DO YOU REALLY THINK A TALENT SHOW CAN HELP ME UNITE BRITAIN?
ARE YOU KIDDIN'? MY ACT UNITED MY WHOLE VILLAGE.
I NEVER SAW PEOPLE COMIN' TOGETHER LIKE WHEN THEY TARRED AND FEATHERED ME.
DON'T WORRY, ARTIE. ONCE YOU HAVE THE BRAVEST, MOST HEROIC KNIGHTS ON YOUR SIDE, PEOPLE WILL BE LINING UP TO REBEL AGAINST SAM OF EAGLE AND TO FOLLOW YOU.
THEY'RE ALREADY WAITING AT THE GATES OF CAMELOT JUST TO SEE THE SHOW.
MORGAN LE FEY
MERLIN, WHY DO THEY CALL THIS CASTLE CAMELOT?
BECAUSE THAT'S WHAT THE SIGN OVER THE DOOR SAYS.*
*EDITOR'S NOTE: SERIOUSLY, GUYS? SURELY THERE'S A BETTER REASON.

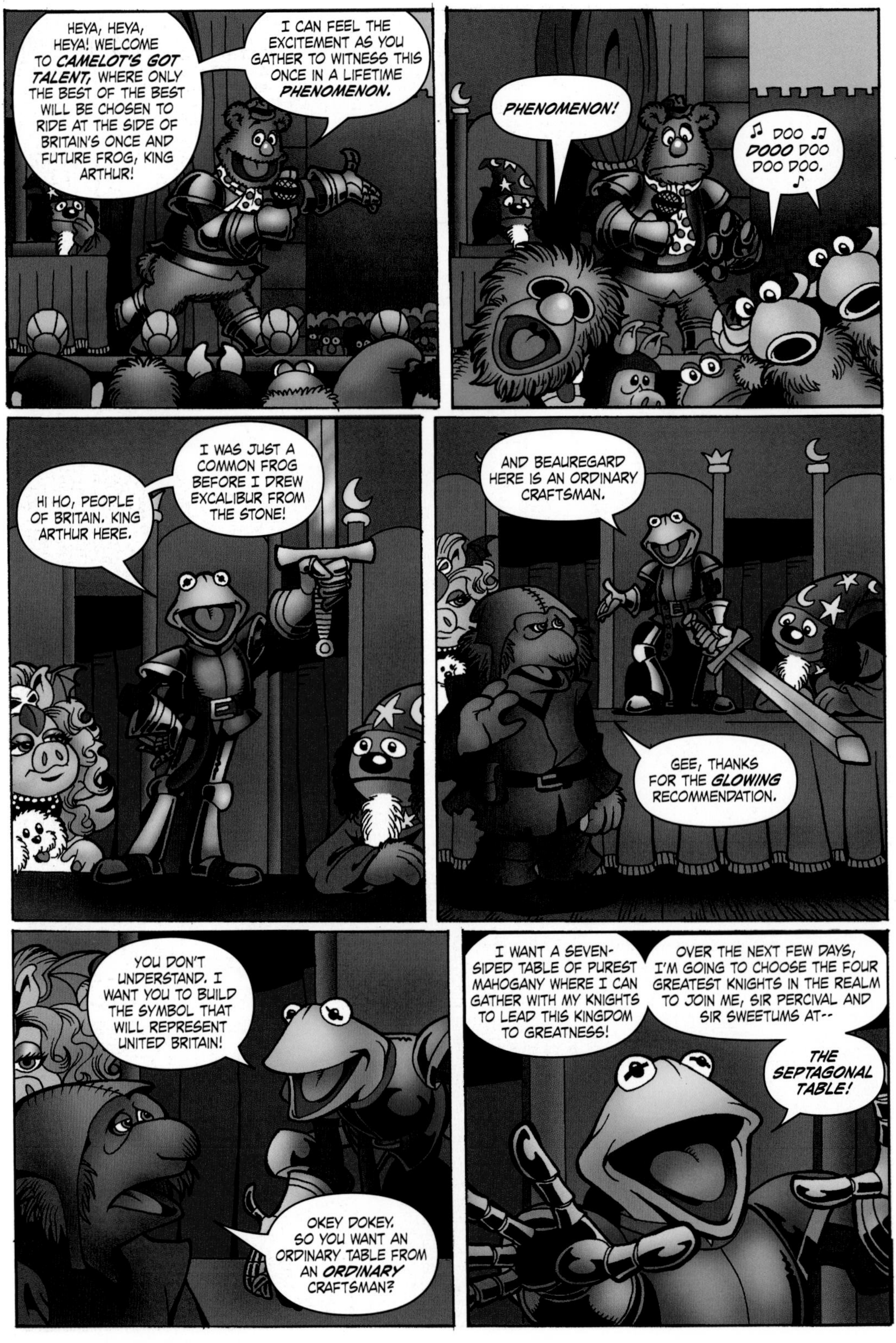
HEYA, HEYA, HEYA! WELCOME TO CAMELOT'S GOT TALENT, WHERE ONLY THE BEST OF THE BEST WILL BE CHOSEN TO RIDE AT THE SIDE OF BRITAIN'S ONCE AND FUTURE FROG, KING ARTHUR!
I CAN FEEL THE EXCITEMENT AS YOU GATHER TO WITNESS THIS ONCE IN A LIFETIME PHENOMENON.
PHENOMENON!
♫ DOO ♫ DOOO DOO DOO DOO. ♪
HI HO, PEOPLE OF BRITAIN. KING ARTHUR HERE.
I WAS JUST A COMMON FROG BEFORE I DREW EXCALIBUR FROM THE STONE!
AND BEAUREGARD HERE IS AN ORDINARY CRAFTSMAN.
GEE, THANKS FOR THE GLOWING RECOMMENDATION.
YOU DON'T UNDERSTAND. I WANT YOU TO BUILD THE SYMBOL THAT WILL REPRESENT UNITED BRITAIN!
OKEY DOKEY. SO YOU WANT AN ORDINARY TABLE FROM AN ORDINARY CRAFTSMAN?
I WANT A SEVEN-SIDED TABLE OF PUREST MAHOGANY WHERE I CAN GATHER WITH MY KNIGHTS TO LEAD THIS KINGDOM TO GREATNESS!
OVER THE NEXT FEW DAYS, I'M GOING TO CHOOSE THE FOUR GREATEST KNIGHTS IN THE REALM TO JOIN ME, SIR PERCIVAL AND SIR SWEETUMS AT--
THE SEPTAGONAL TABLE!

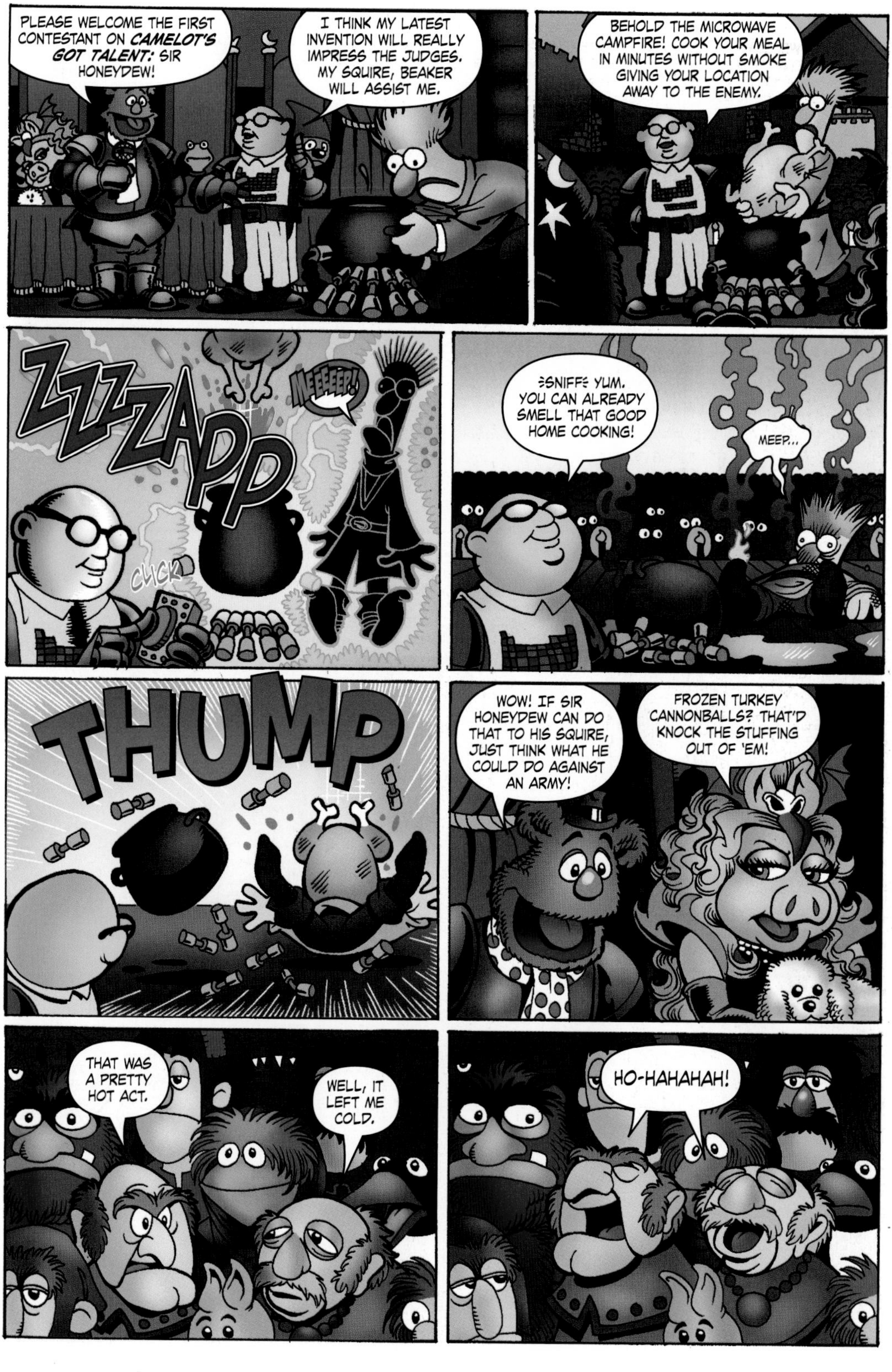
PLEASE WELCOME THE FIRST CONTESTANT ON CAMELOT'S GOT TALENT: SIR HONEYDEW!
I THINK MY LATEST INVENTION WILL REALLY IMPRESS THE JUDGES. MY SQUIRE, BEAKER WILL ASSIST ME.
BEHOLD THE MICROWAVE CAMPFIRE! COOK YOUR MEAL IN MINUTES WITHOUT SMOKE GIVING YOUR LOCATION AWAY TO THE ENEMY.
ZZZZAPP
MEEEEEP!
CLICK
SNIFF YUM. YOU CAN ALREADY SMELL THAT GOOD HOME COOKING!
MEEP...
THUMP
WOW! IF SIR HONEYDEW CAN DO THAT TO HIS SQUIRE, JUST THINK WHAT HE COULD DO AGAINST AN ARMY!
FROZEN TURKEY CANNONBALLS? THAT'D KNOCK THE STUFFING OUT OF 'EM!
THAT WAS A PRETTY HOT ACT.
WELL, IT LEFT ME COLD.
HO-HAHAHAH!

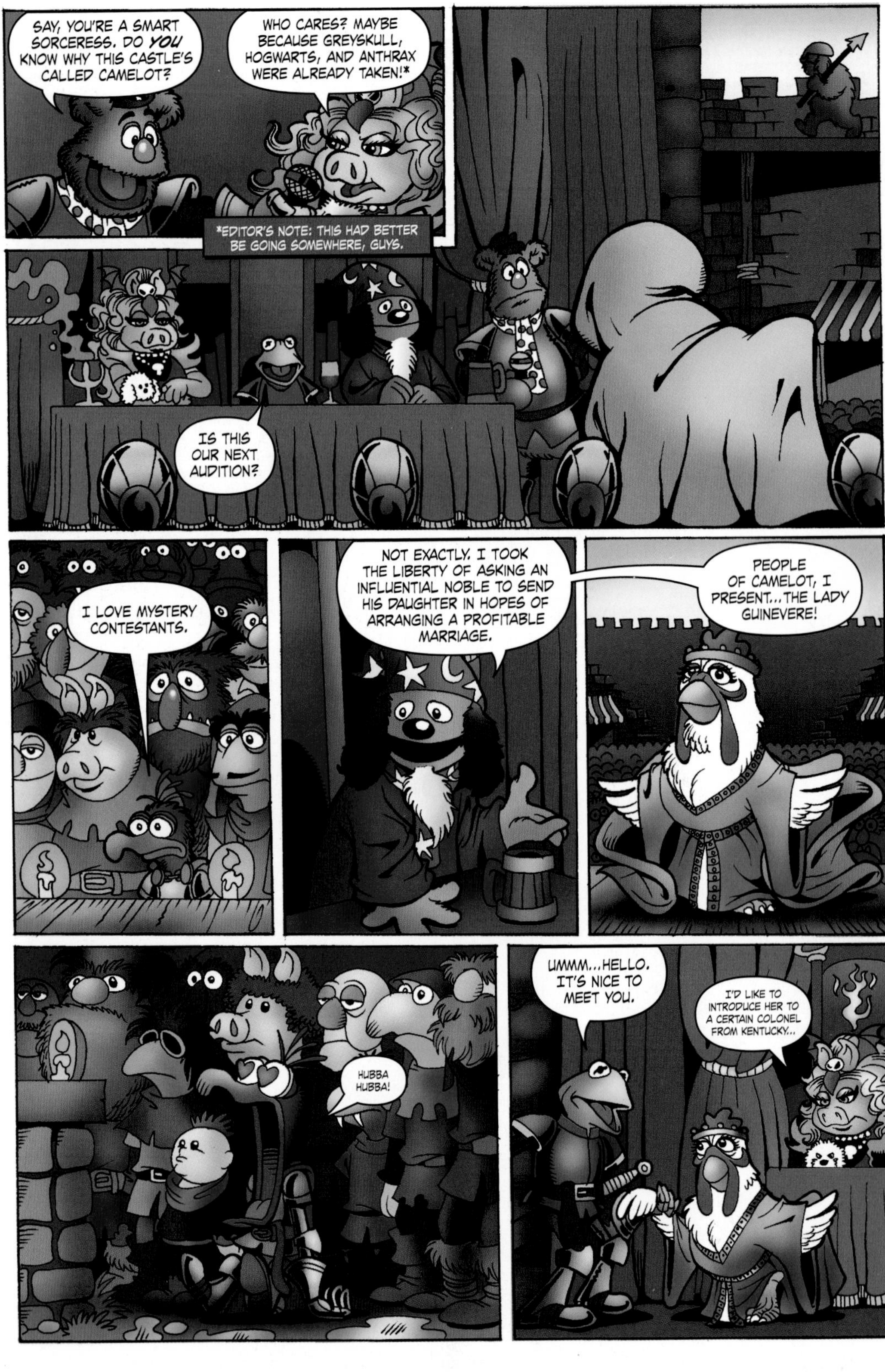
SAY, YOU'RE A SMART SORCERESS. DO YOU KNOW WHY THIS CASTLE'S CALLED CAMELOT?
WHO CARES? MAYBE BECAUSE GREYSKULL, HOGWARTS, AND ANTHRAX WERE ALREADY TAKEN!*
*EDITOR'S NOTE: THIS HAD BETTER BE GOING SOMEWHERE, GUYS.
IS THIS OUR NEXT AUDITION?
I LOVE MYSTERY CONTESTANTS.
NOT EXACTLY. I TOOK THE LIBERTY OF ASKING AN INFLUENTIAL NOBLE TO SEND HIS DAUGHTER IN HOPES OF ARRANGING A PROFITABLE MARRIAGE.
PEOPLE OF CAMELOT, I PRESENT...THE LADY GUINEVERE!
HUBBA HUBBA!
UMMM...HELLO. IT'S NICE TO MEET YOU.
I'D LIKE TO INTRODUCE HER TO A CERTAIN COLONEL FROM KENTUCKY...

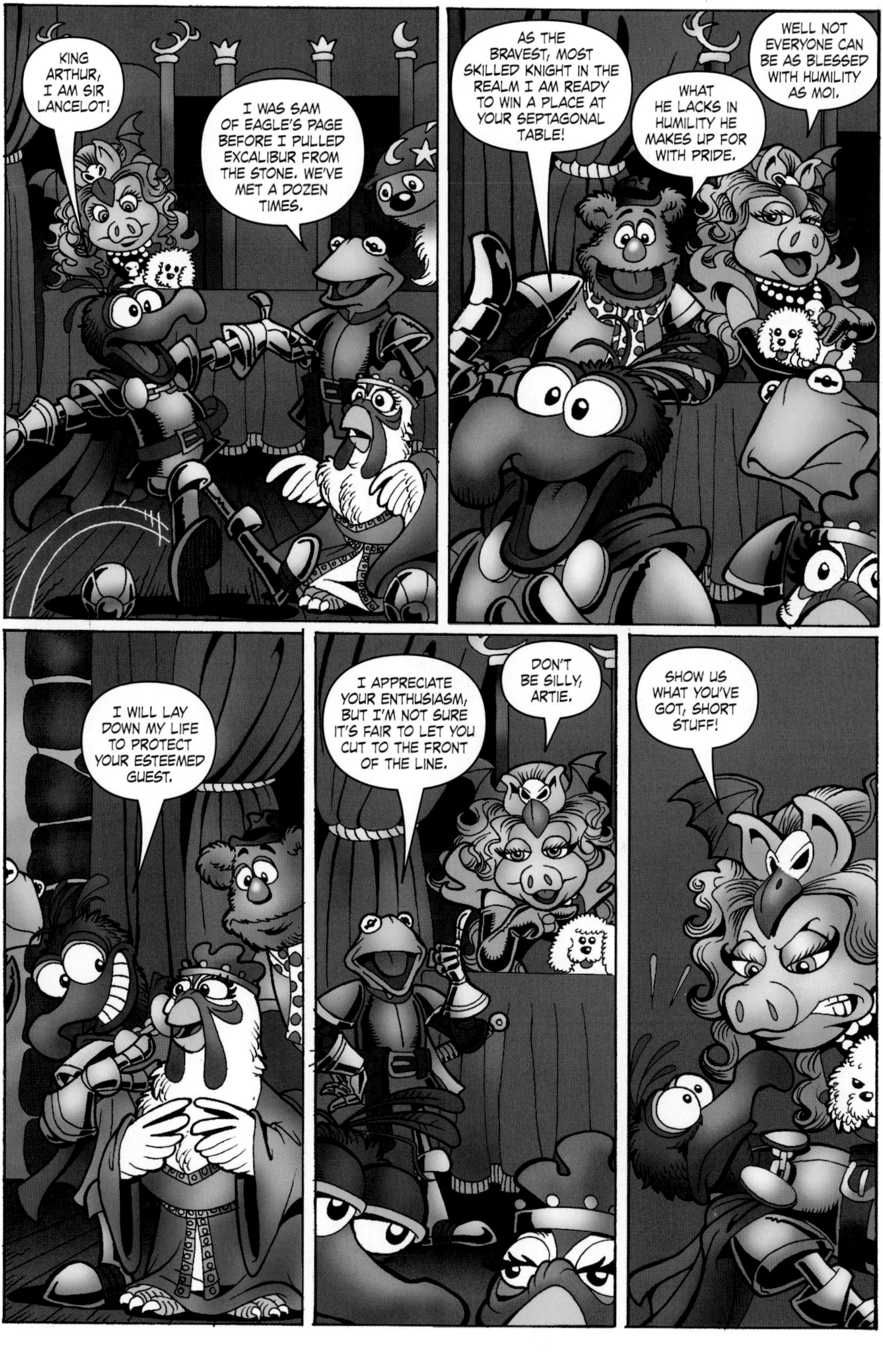
KING ARTHUR, I AM SIR LANCELOT!
I WAS SAM OF EAGLE'S PAGE BEFORE I PULLED EXCALIBUR FROM THE STONE. WE'VE MET A DOZEN TIMES.
AS THE BRAVEST, MOST SKILLED KNIGHT IN THE REALM I AM READY TO WIN A PLACE AT YOUR SEPTAGONAL TABLE!
WHAT HE LACKS IN HUMILITY HE MAKES UP FOR WITH PRIDE.
WELL NOT EVERYONE CAN BE AS BLESSED WITH HUMILITY AS MOI.
I WILL LAY DOWN MY LIFE TO PROTECT YOUR ESTEEMED GUEST.
I APPRECIATE YOUR ENTHUSIASM, BUT I'M NOT SURE IT'S FAIR TO LET YOU CUT TO THE FRONT OF THE LINE.
DON'T BE SILLY, ARTIE.
SHOW US WHAT YOU'VE GOT, SHORT STUFF!

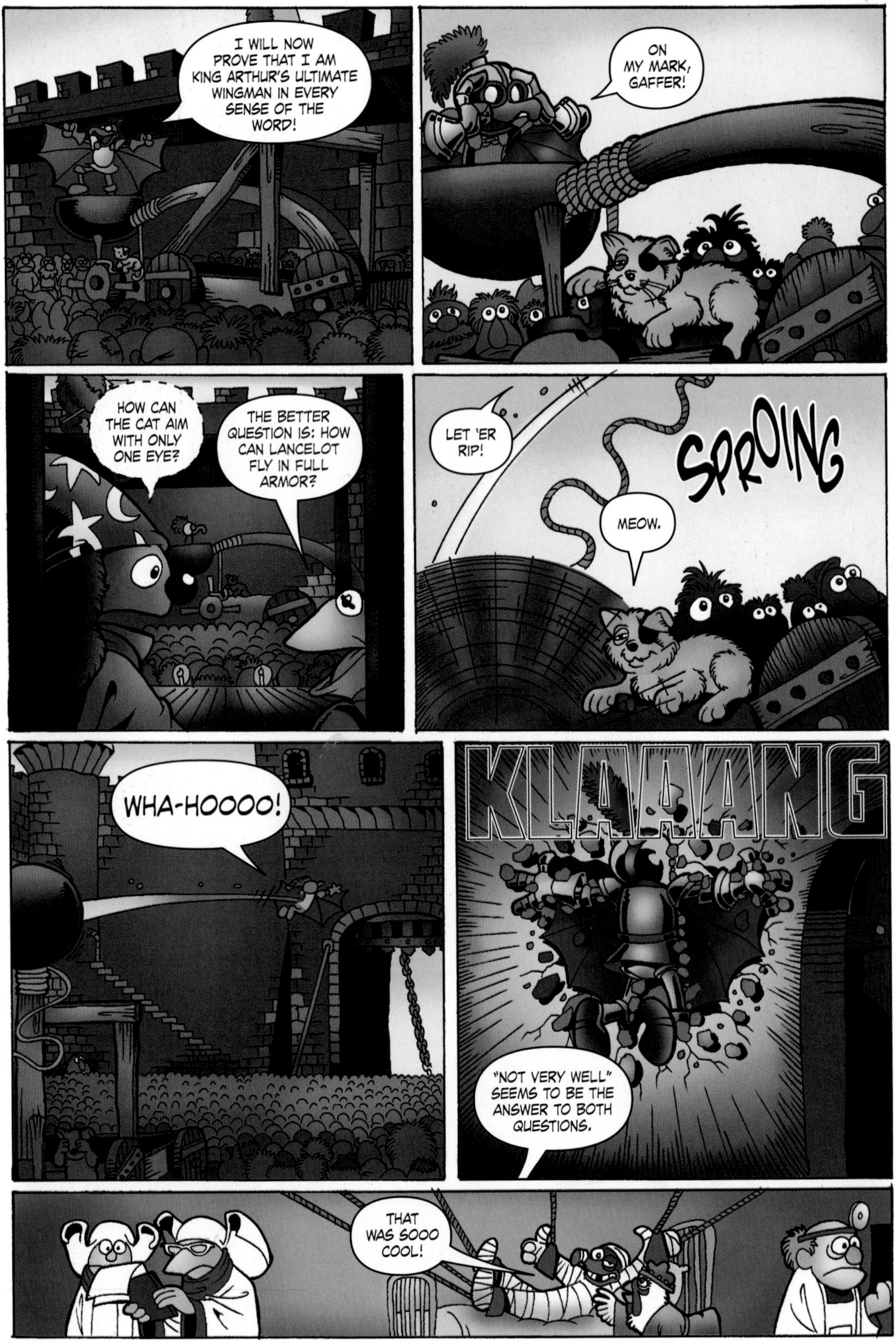
I WILL NOW PROVE THAT I AM KING ARTHUR'S ULTIMATE WINGMAN IN EVERY SENSE OF THE WORD!
ON MY MARK, GAFFER!
HOW CAN THE CAT AIM WITH ONLY ONE EYE?
THE BETTER QUESTION IS: HOW CAN LANCELOT FLY IN FULL ARMOR?
LET 'ER RIP!
SPROING
MEOW.
WHA-HOOOO!
KLAAANG
"NOT VERY WELL" SEEMS TO BE THE ANSWER TO BOTH QUESTIONS.
THAT WAS SOOO COOL!

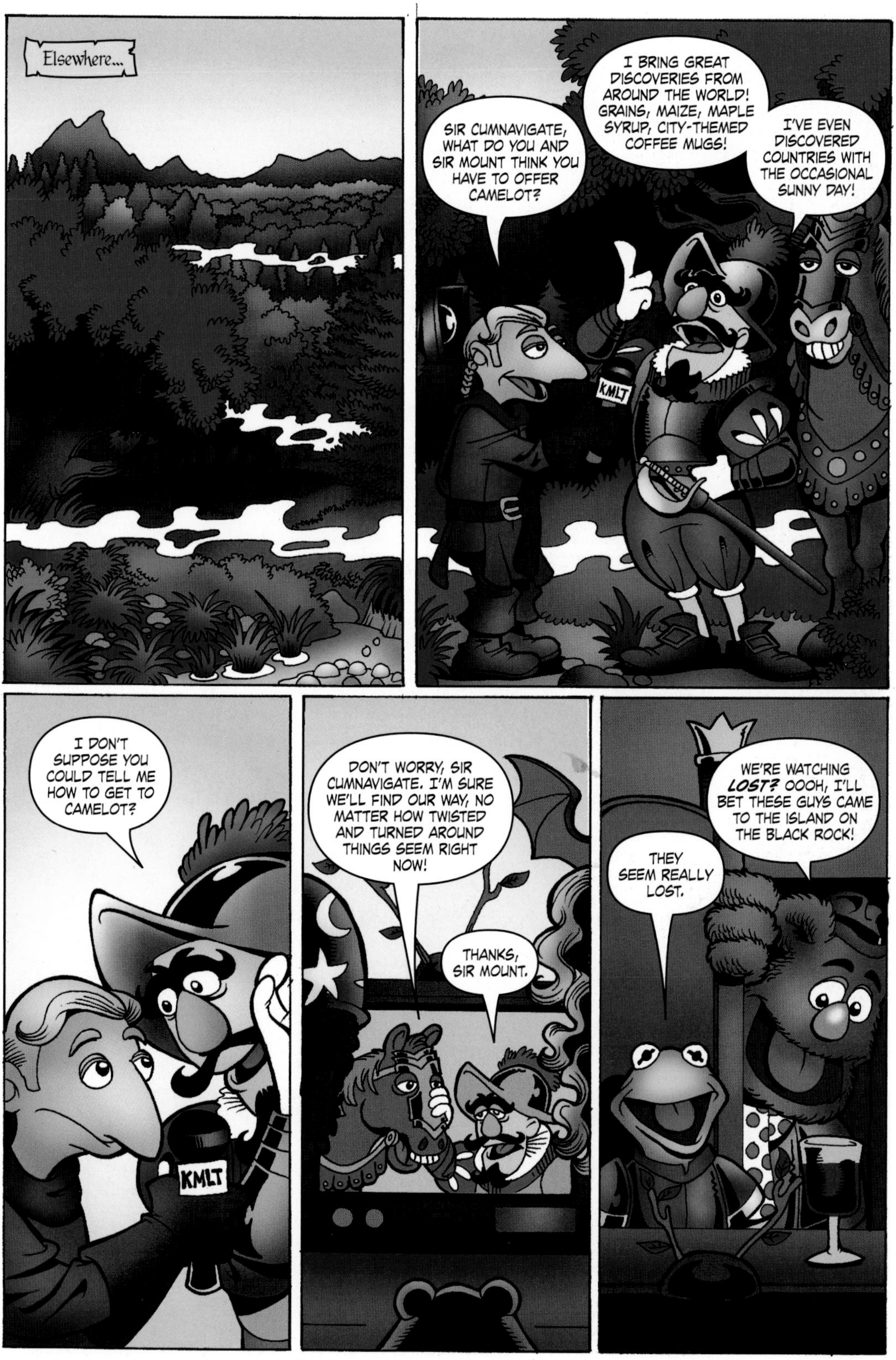
Elsewhere...
SIR CUMNAVIGATE, WHAT DO YOU AND SIR MOUNT THINK YOU HAVE TO OFFER CAMELOT?
I BRING GREAT DISCOVERIES FROM AROUND THE WORLD! GRAINS, MAIZE, MAPLE SYRUP, CITY-THEMED COFFEE MUGS!
I'VE EVEN DISCOVERED COUNTRIES WITH THE OCCASIONAL SUNNY DAY!
KMLT
I DON'T SUPPOSE YOU COULD TELL ME HOW TO GET TO CAMELOT?
KMLT
DON'T WORRY, SIR CUMNAVIGATE. I'M SURE WE'LL FIND OUR WAY, NO MATTER HOW TWISTED AND TURNED AROUND THINGS SEEM RIGHT NOW!
THANKS, SIR MOUNT.
WE'RE WATCHING LOST? OOOH, I'LL BET THESE GUYS CAME TO THE ISLAND ON THE BLACK ROCK!
THEY SEEM REALLY LOST.

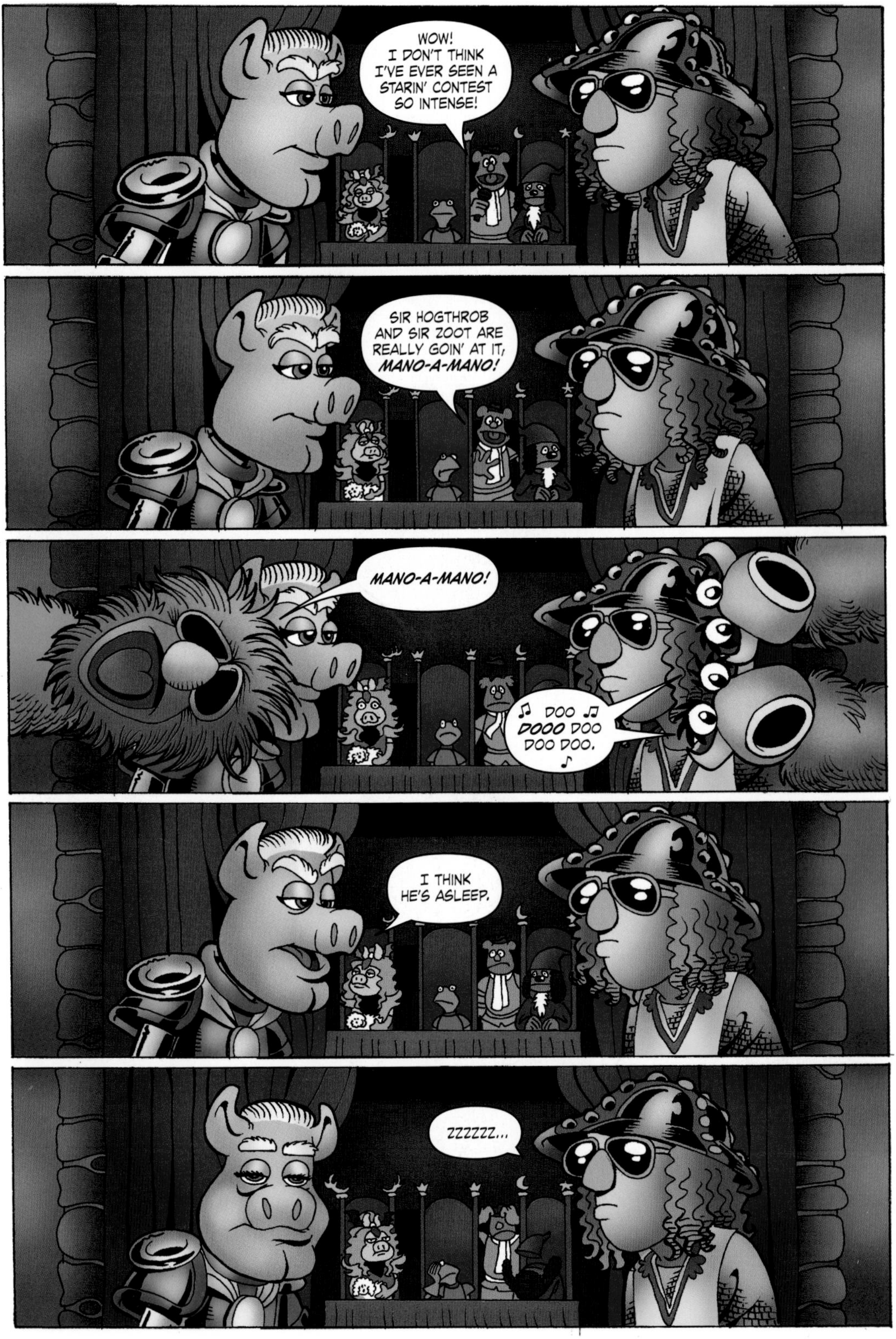
WOW! I DON'T THINK I'VE EVER SEEN A STARIN' CONTEST SO INTENSE!
SIR HOGTHROB AND SIR ZOOT ARE REALLY GOIN' AT IT, MANO-A-MANO!
MANO-A-MANO!
♫ DOO ♫ DOOO DOO DOO DOO. ♪
I THINK HE'S ASLEEP.
ZZZZZZ...

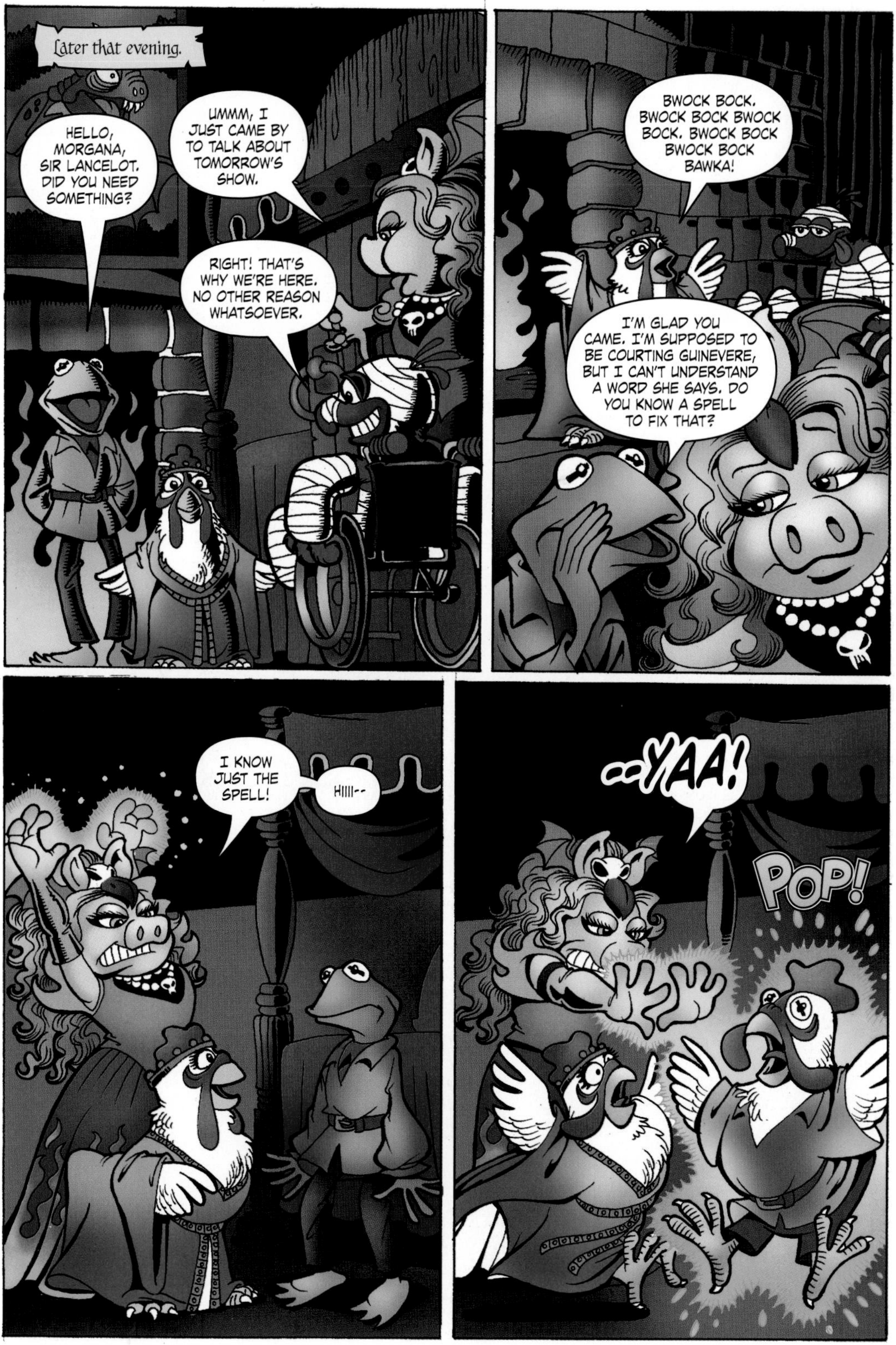

Later that evening.
HELLO, MORGANA, SIR LANCELOT. DID YOU NEED SOMETHING?
UMMM, I JUST CAME BY TO TALK ABOUT TOMORROW'S SHOW.
RIGHT! THAT'S WHY WE'RE HERE. NO OTHER REASON WHATSOEVER.
BWOCK BOCK. BWOCK BOCK BWOCK BOCK. BWOCK BOCK BWOCK BOCK BAWKA!
I'M GLAD YOU CAME. I'M SUPPOSED TO BE COURTING GUINEVERE, BUT I CAN'T UNDERSTAND A WORD SHE SAYS. DO YOU KNOW A SPELL TO FIX THAT?
I KNOW JUST THE SPELL!
HIIII--
--YAA!
POP!

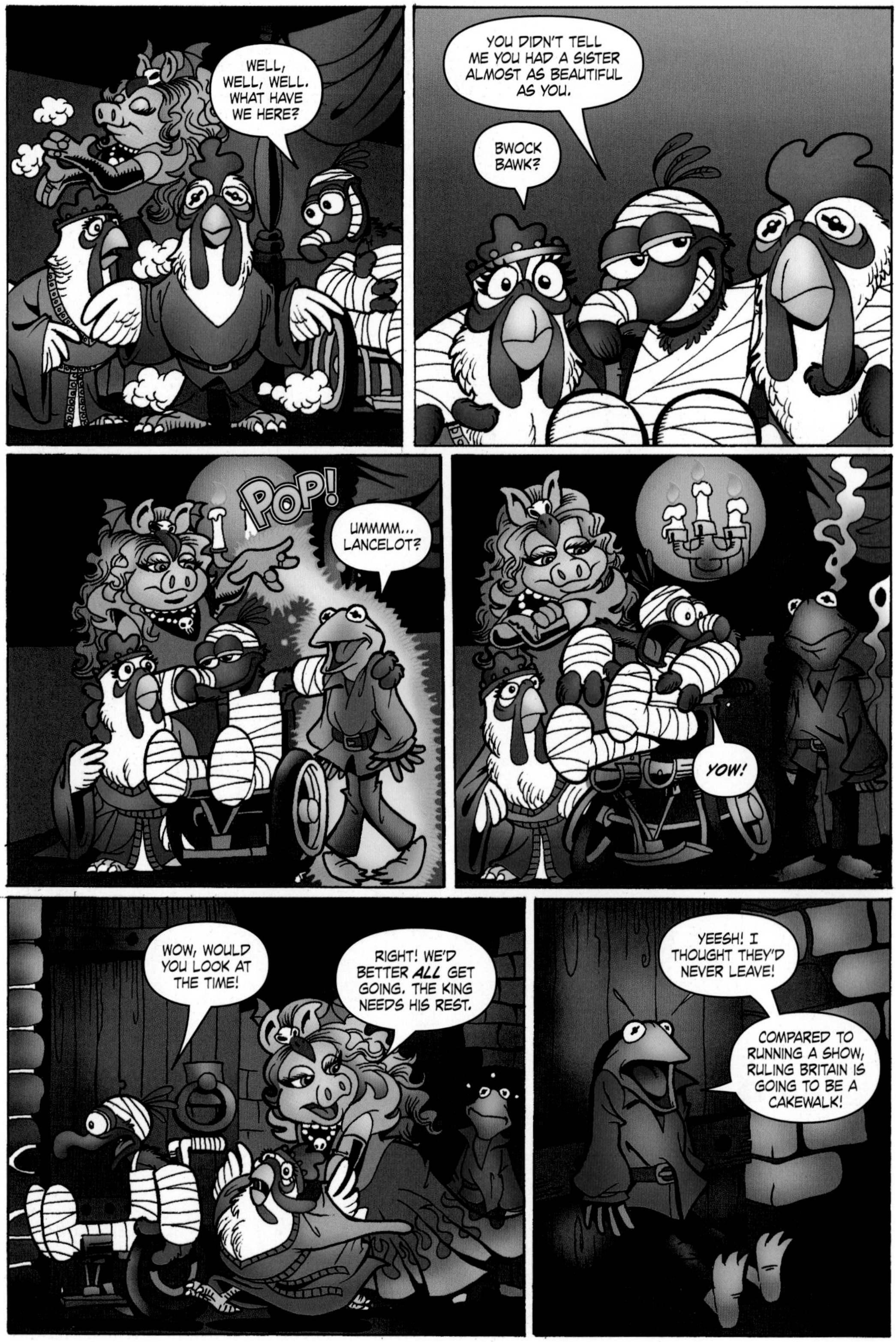
WELL, WELL, WELL. WHAT HAVE WE HERE?
YOU DIDN'T TELL ME YOU HAD A SISTER ALMOST AS BEAUTIFUL AS YOU.
BWOCK BAWK?
POP!
UMMMM... LANCELOT?
YOW!
WOW, WOULD YOU LOOK AT THE TIME!
RIGHT! WE'D BETTER ALL GET GOING. THE KING NEEDS HIS REST.
YEESH! I THOUGHT THEY'D NEVER LEAVE!
COMPARED TO RUNNING A SHOW, RULING BRITAIN IS GOING TO BE A CAKEWALK!

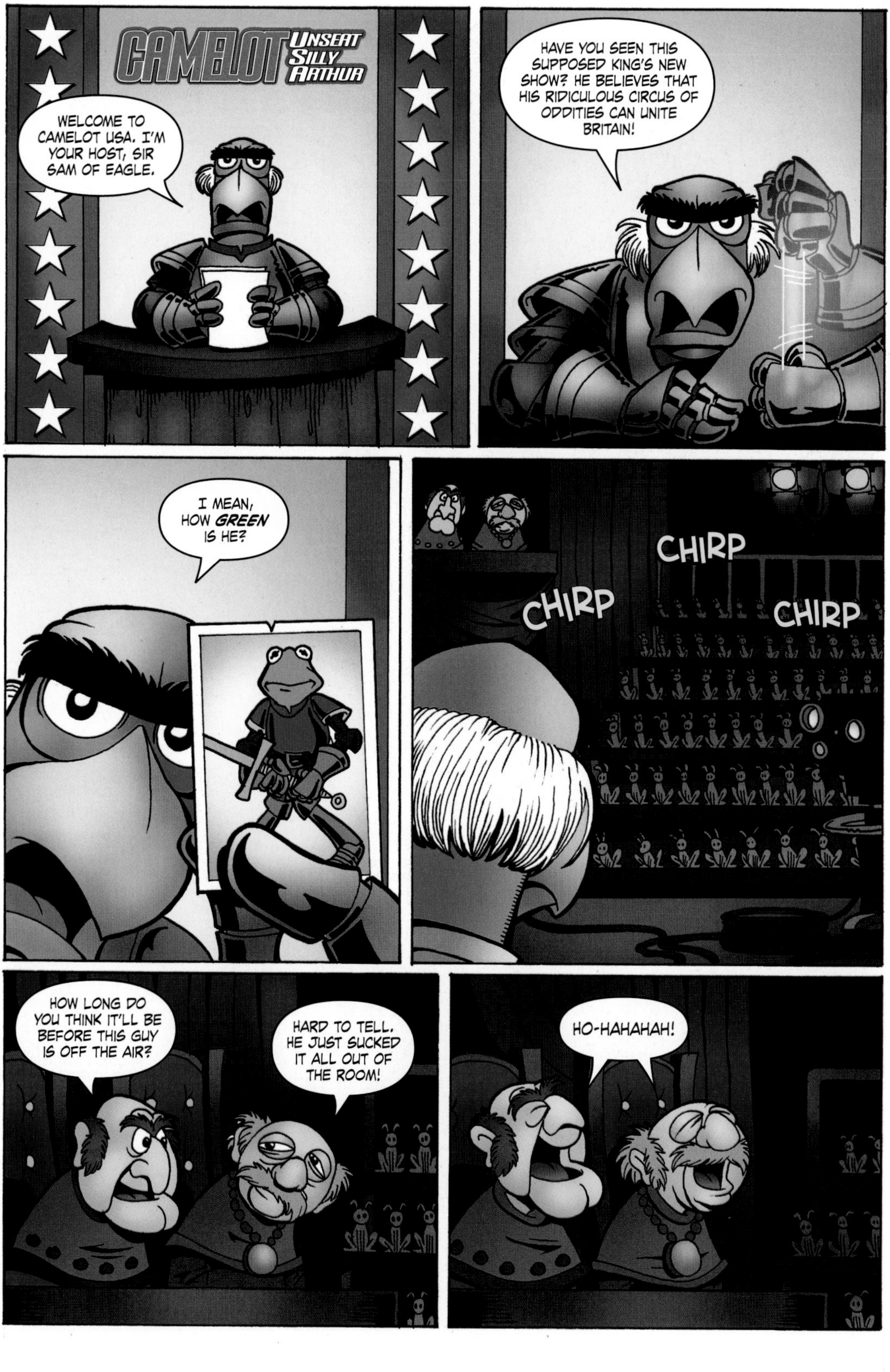
CAMELOT UNSEAT SILLY ARTHUR
WELCOME TO CAMELOT USA. I'M YOUR HOST, SIR SAM OF EAGLE.
HAVE YOU SEEN THIS SUPPOSED KING'S NEW SHOW? HE BELIEVES THAT HIS RIDICULOUS CIRCUS OF ODDITIES CAN UNITE BRITAIN!
I MEAN, HOW *GREEN* IS HE?
CHIRP
CHIRP
CHIRP
HOW LONG DO YOU THINK IT'LL BE BEFORE THIS GUY IS OFF THE AIR?
HARD TO TELL. HE JUST SUCKED IT ALL OUT OF THE ROOM!
HO-HAHAHAH!

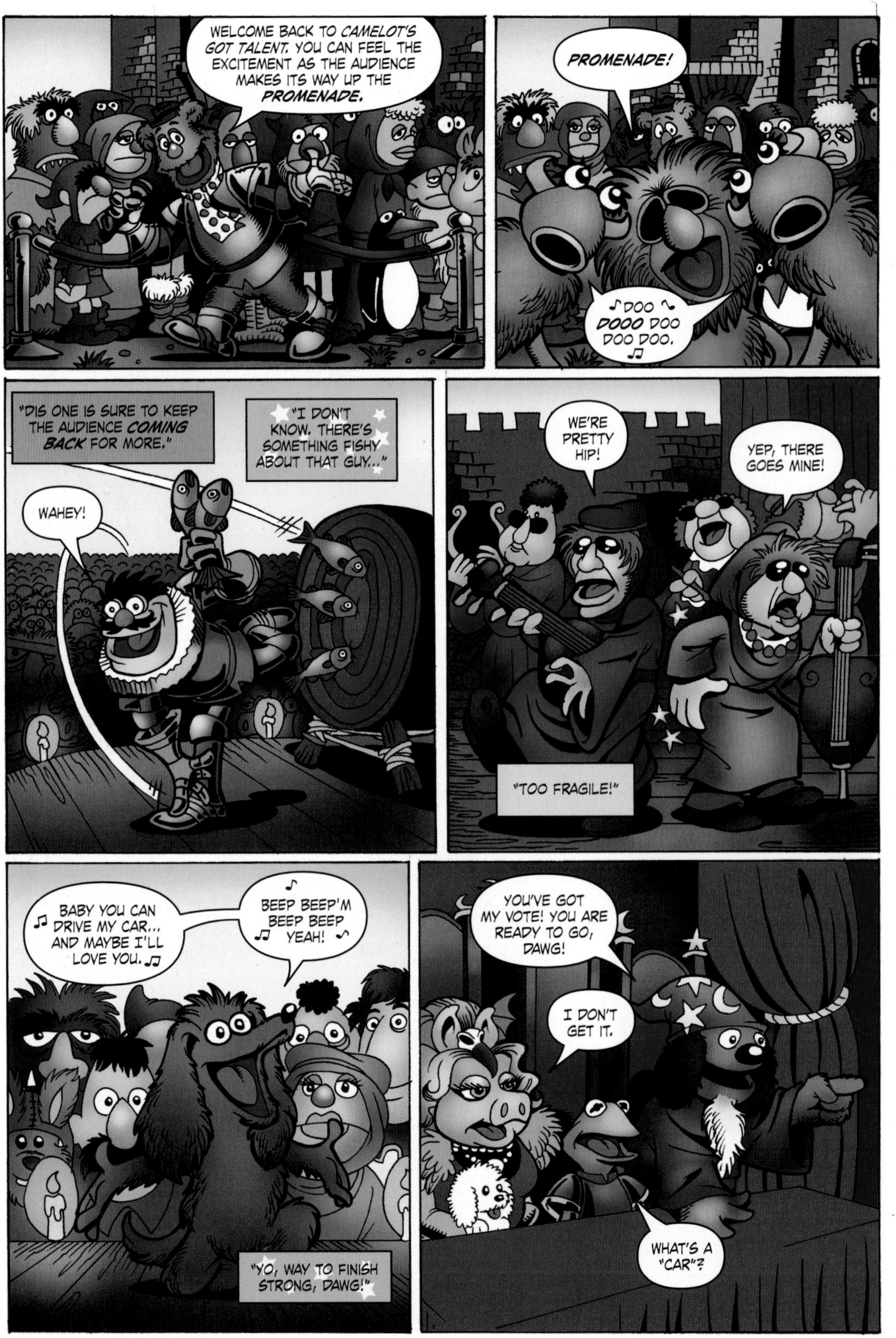
WELCOME BACK TO CAMELOT'S GOT TALENT. YOU CAN FEEL THE EXCITEMENT AS THE AUDIENCE MAKES ITS WAY UP THE PROMENADE.
PROMENADE!
♪DOO ♪ DOOO DOO DOO DOO. ♫
"DIS ONE IS SURE TO KEEP THE AUDIENCE COMING BACK FOR MORE."
"I DON'T KNOW. THERE'S SOMETHING FISHY ABOUT THAT GUY..."
WAHEY!
WE'RE PRETTY HIP!
YEP, THERE GOES MINE!
"TOO FRAGILE!"
♫ BABY YOU CAN DRIVE MY CAR... AND MAYBE I'LL LOVE YOU. ♫
♪ BEEP BEEP'M BEEP BEEP ♫ YEAH! ♪
"YO, WAY TO FINISH STRONG, DAWG!"
YOU'VE GOT MY VOTE! YOU ARE READY TO GO, DAWG!
I DON'T GET IT.
WHAT'S A "CAR"?

BRING OUT SIR VIVOR!

OH...ERRR...NEVER MIND. APPARENTLY HE'S STUCK ON AN ISLAND SOMEWHERE IN THE PACIFIC.

WHO'S NEXT, BEAR?

DEY CALL HIM "SIR RENDER."

"RENDER." DO THEY CALL HIM THAT BECAUSE HE TEARS HIS FOES APART IN BATTLE?

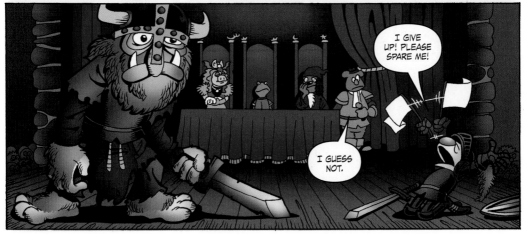

I GIVE UP! PLEASE SPARE ME!

I GUESS NOT.

WELL, THIS IS A SURPRISE.

WHAT, THAT HE'S SO SMALL?

NO, THAT'S HIS NAME: SIR PRIZE.

DON'T LET MY HEIGHT FOOL YOU. I'VE BEEN IN TONS OF GREAT BATTLES.

BATTLE OF THE PLANETS; BATTLE OF THE NETWORK STARS; NIGHT AT THE MUSEUM: BATTLE OF THE SMITHSONIAN; ALTAMONT...

YOUR VOICE SOUNDS AWFULLY FAMILIAR.

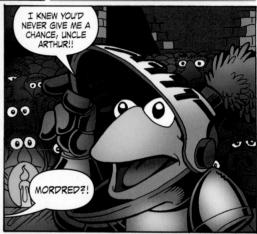

I KNEW YOU'D NEVER GIVE ME A CHANCE, UNCLE ARTHUR!!

MORDRED?!

WHAT ARE YOU DOING HERE?

I WANT TO BE A KNIGHT OF THE SEPTAGONAL TABLE.

YOU KNOW YOU'RE TOO YOUNG TO BE A KNIGHT, MORDRED.

BUT MY YOUTH IS AN ADVANTAGE. I COULD SERVE BRITAIN FOR MANY MOONS!

MANY MOONS!

♫ DOO ♫ DOOO DOO DOO DOO.

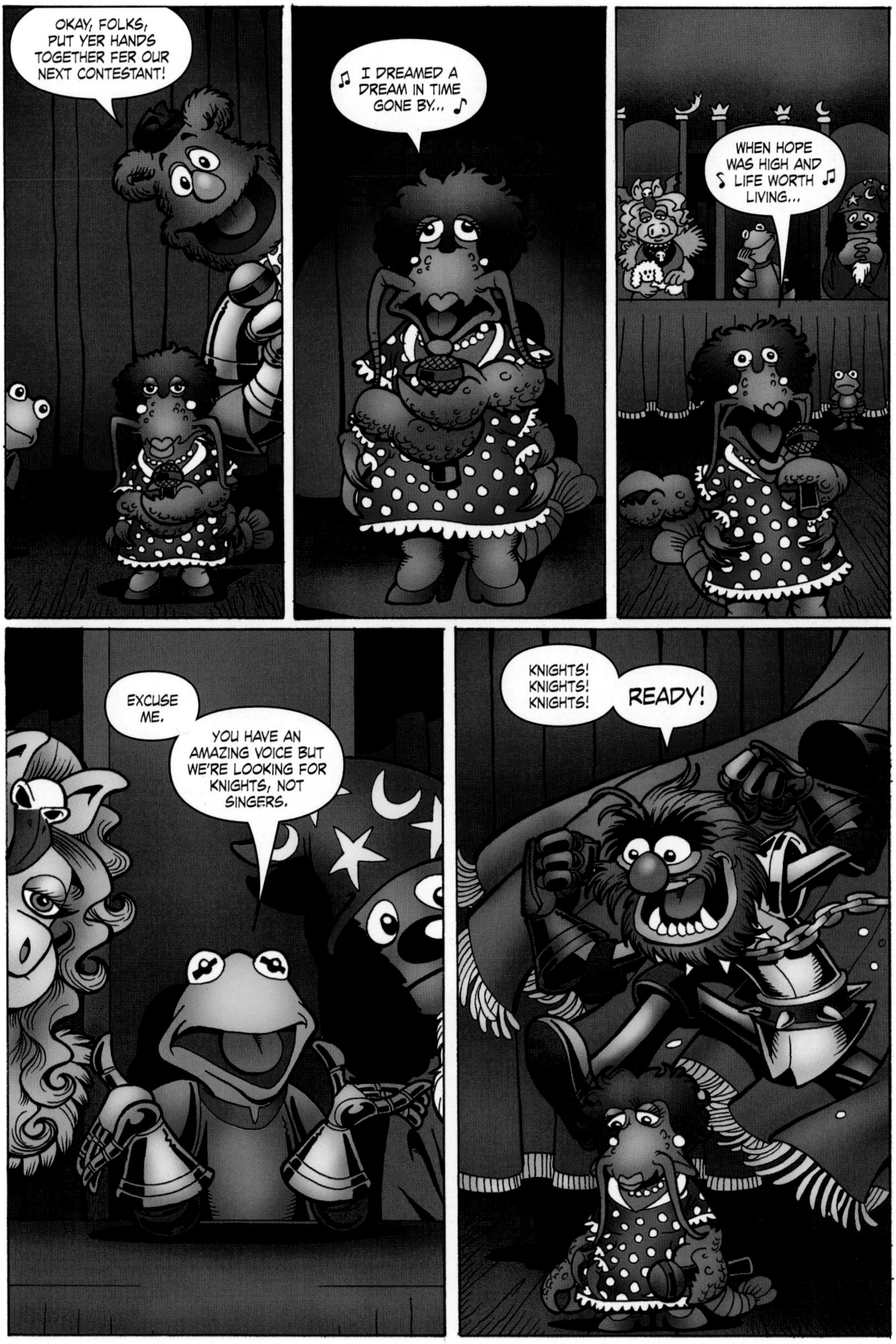
OKAY, FOLKS, PUT YER HANDS TOGETHER FER OUR NEXT CONTESTANT!
♫ I DREAMED A DREAM IN TIME GONE BY... ♪
WHEN HOPE WAS HIGH AND ♪ LIFE WORTH ♫ LIVING...
EXCUSE ME.
YOU HAVE AN AMAZING VOICE BUT WE'RE LOOKING FOR KNIGHTS, NOT SINGERS.
KNIGHTS! KNIGHTS! KNIGHTS!
READY!

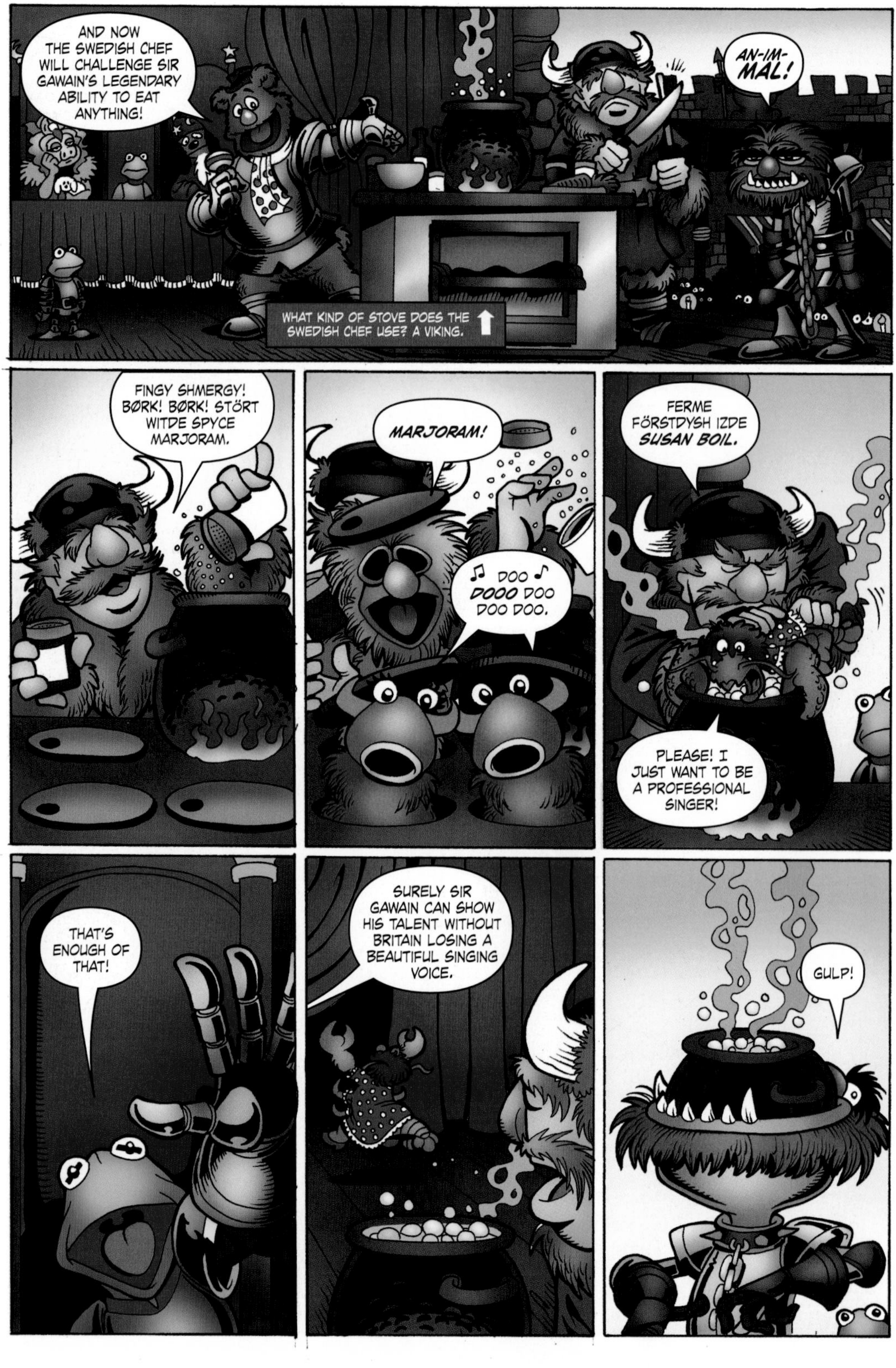
AND NOW THE SWEDISH CHEF WILL CHALLENGE SIR GAWAIN'S LEGENDARY ABILITY TO EAT ANYTHING!
AN-IM-MAL!
WHAT KIND OF STOVE DOES THE SWEDISH CHEF USE? A VIKING.
FINGY SHMERGY! BØRK! BØRK! STÖRT WITDE SPYCE MARJORAM.
MARJORAM!
♫ DOO ♪ DOOO DOO DOO DOO.
FERME FÖRSTDYSH IZDE SUSAN BOIL.
PLEASE! I JUST WANT TO BE A PROFESSIONAL SINGER!
THAT'S ENOUGH OF THAT!
SURELY SIR GAWAIN CAN SHOW HIS TALENT WITHOUT BRITAIN LOSING A BEAUTIFUL SINGING VOICE.
GULP!

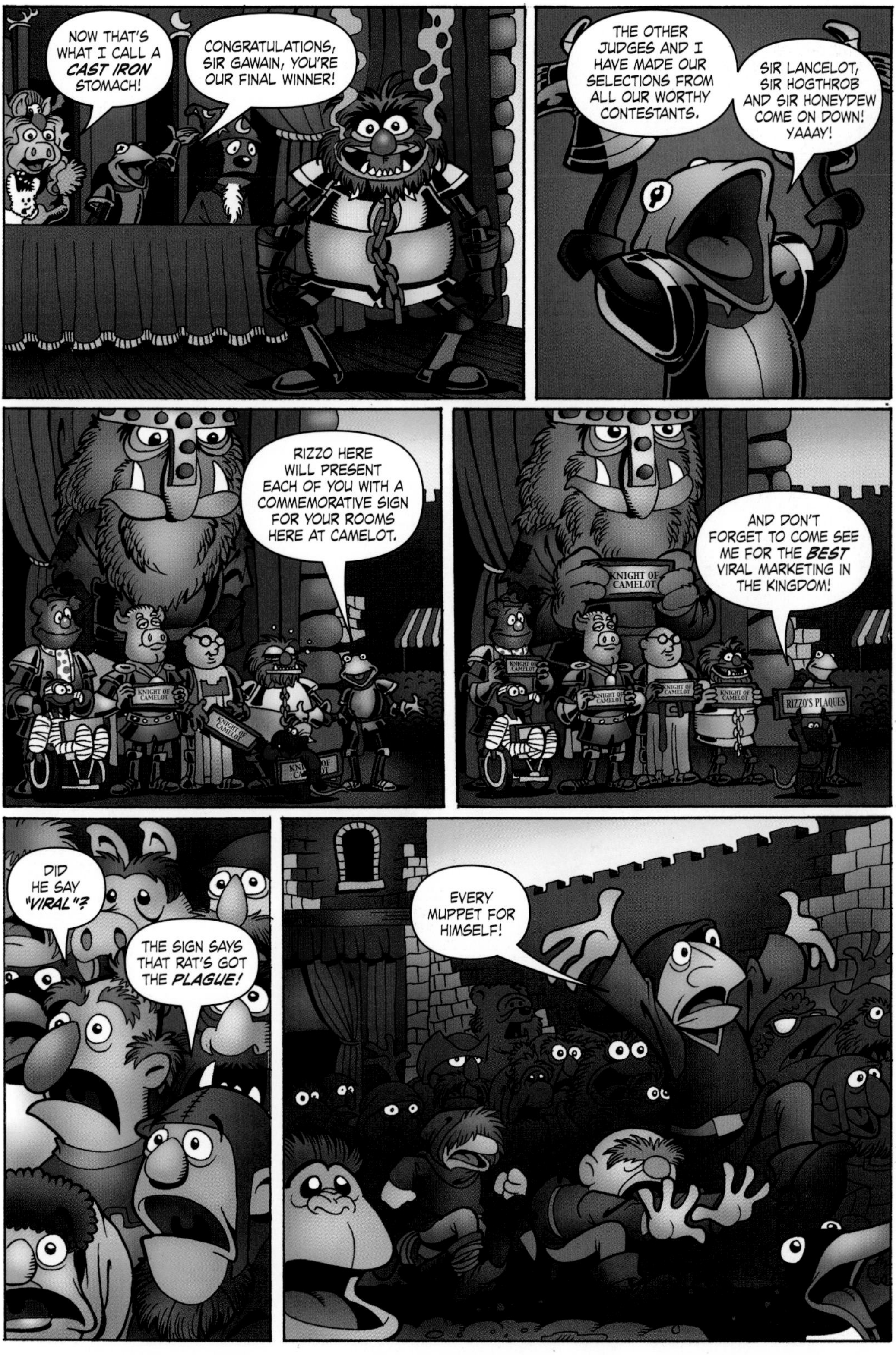
NOW THAT'S WHAT I CALL A *CAST IRON* STOMACH!
CONGRATULATIONS, SIR GAWAIN, YOU'RE OUR FINAL WINNER!
THE OTHER JUDGES AND I HAVE MADE OUR SELECTIONS FROM ALL OUR WORTHY CONTESTANTS.
SIR LANCELOT, SIR HOGTHROB AND SIR HONEYDEW COME ON DOWN! YAAAY!
RIZZO HERE WILL PRESENT EACH OF YOU WITH A COMMEMORATIVE SIGN FOR YOUR ROOMS HERE AT CAMELOT.
KNIGHT OF CAMELOT
KNIGHT OF CAMELOT
AND DON'T FORGET TO COME SEE ME FOR THE *BEST* VIRAL MARKETING IN THE KINGDOM!
RIZZO'S PLAQUES
DID HE SAY *"VIRAL"*?
THE SIGN SAYS THAT RAT'S GOT THE *PLAGUE!*
EVERY MUPPET FOR HIMSELF!

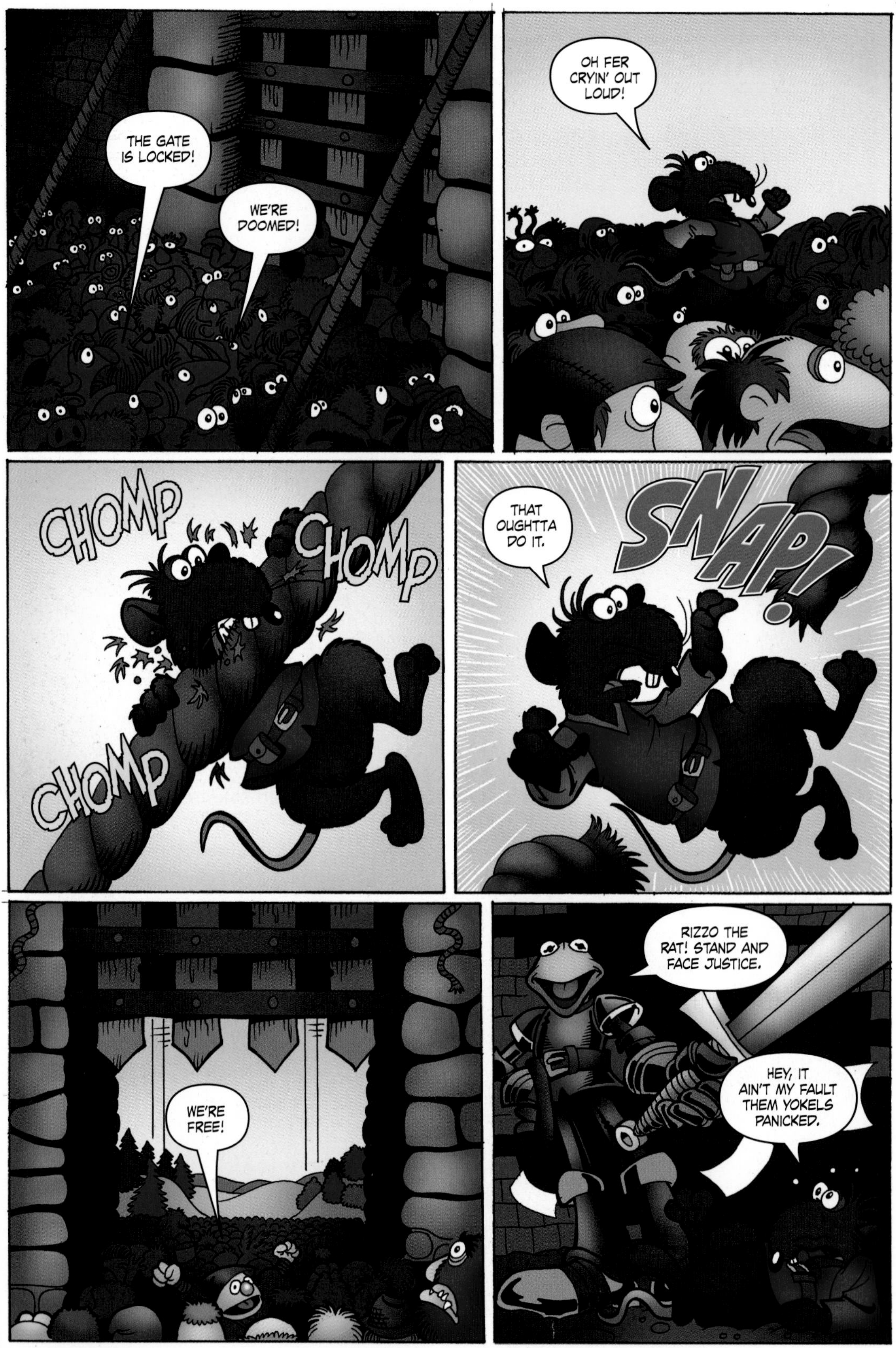
THE GATE IS LOCKED!
WE'RE DOOMED!
OH FER CRYIN' OUT LOUD!
CHOMP
CHOMP
CHOMP
THAT OUGHTTA DO IT.
SNAP!
WE'RE FREE!
RIZZO THE RAT! STAND AND FACE JUSTICE.
HEY, IT AIN'T MY FAULT THEM YOKELS PANICKED.

YET YOU NOBLY RISKED YOUR OWN SKIN TO OPEN THE GATE. THAT WAS A HEROIC GESTURE.

OH, RIGHT...IT *WAS* PRETTY HEROIC, WASN'T IT?

BY THE POWER OF THE GREAT SWORD EXCALIBUR, I DUB THEE *SIR* RIZZO!

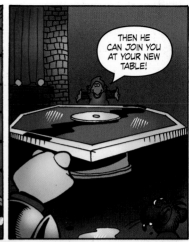

THEN HE CAN JOIN YOU AT YOUR NEW TABLE!

UMMM... WHAT'S THAT ON THE TOP?

A LAZY SUSAN. IN CASE YOU ORDER CHINESE...

UH OH. THE TABLE ONLY HAS SEVEN SIDES. WITH SIR RIZZO THERE ARE NOW *EIGHT* KNIGHTS!

BUT WHAT'S MORE IMPORTANT IS THAT *ALL* SIDES OF IT ARE *EQUAL* IN LENGTH. THERE IS NO HEAD OF THE TABLE.

MY KNIGHTS AND I WILL BE EQUALS AS WE BRING ORDER AND UNITY TO BRITAIN!

YEESH, WHAT'S WITH ALL THE DRAMA? IT AIN'T LIKE I CAN'T *SHARE* A SIDE WITH SOMEONE.

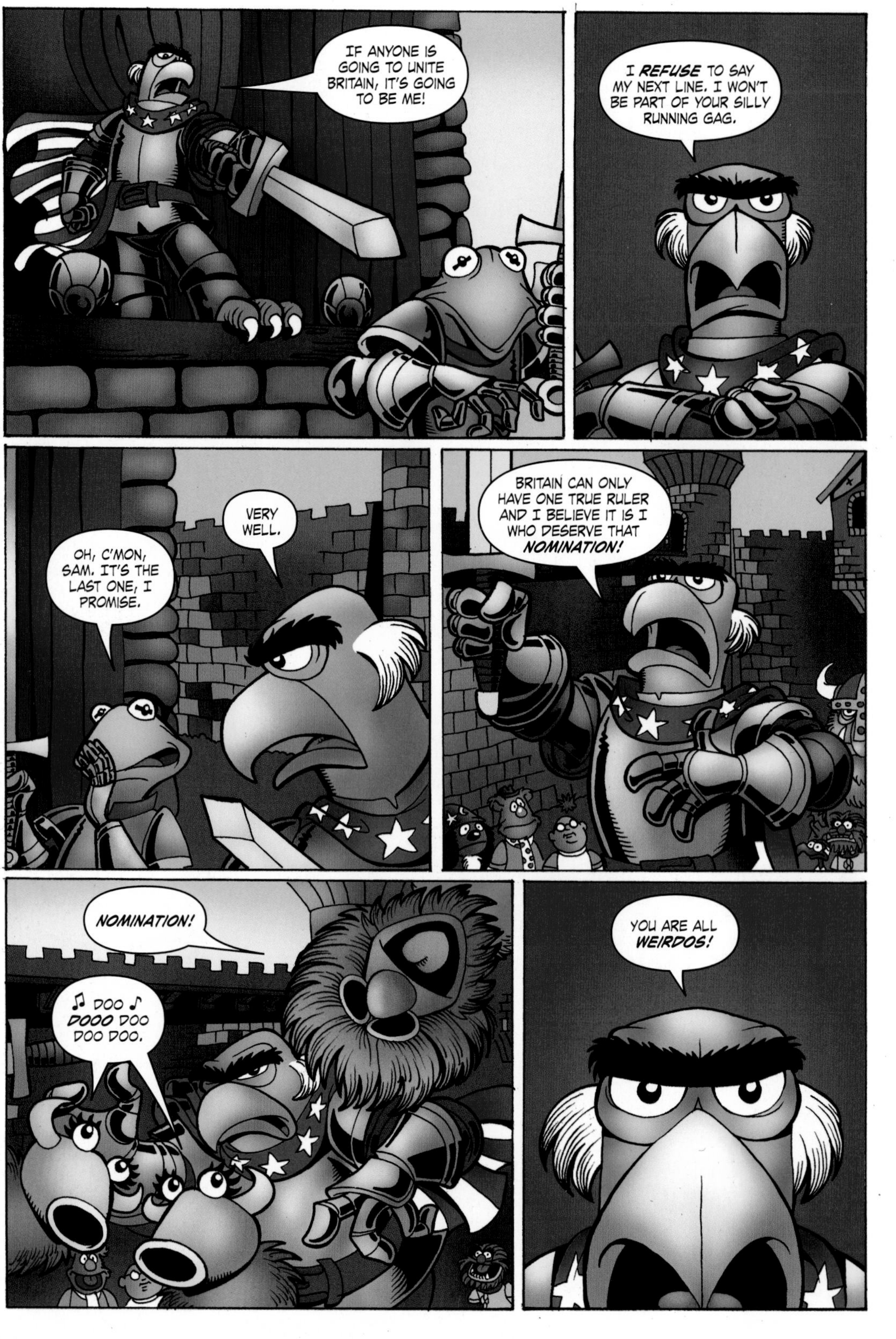
IF ANYONE IS GOING TO UNITE BRITAIN, IT'S GOING TO BE ME!
I **REFUSE** TO SAY MY NEXT LINE. I WON'T BE PART OF YOUR SILLY RUNNING GAG.
OH, C'MON, SAM. IT'S THE LAST ONE, I PROMISE.
VERY WELL.
BRITAIN CAN ONLY HAVE ONE TRUE RULER AND I BELIEVE IT IS I WHO DESERVE THAT **NOMINATION!**
NOMINATION!
♫ DOO ♪ **DOOO** DOO DOO DOO.
YOU ARE ALL **WEIRDOS!**

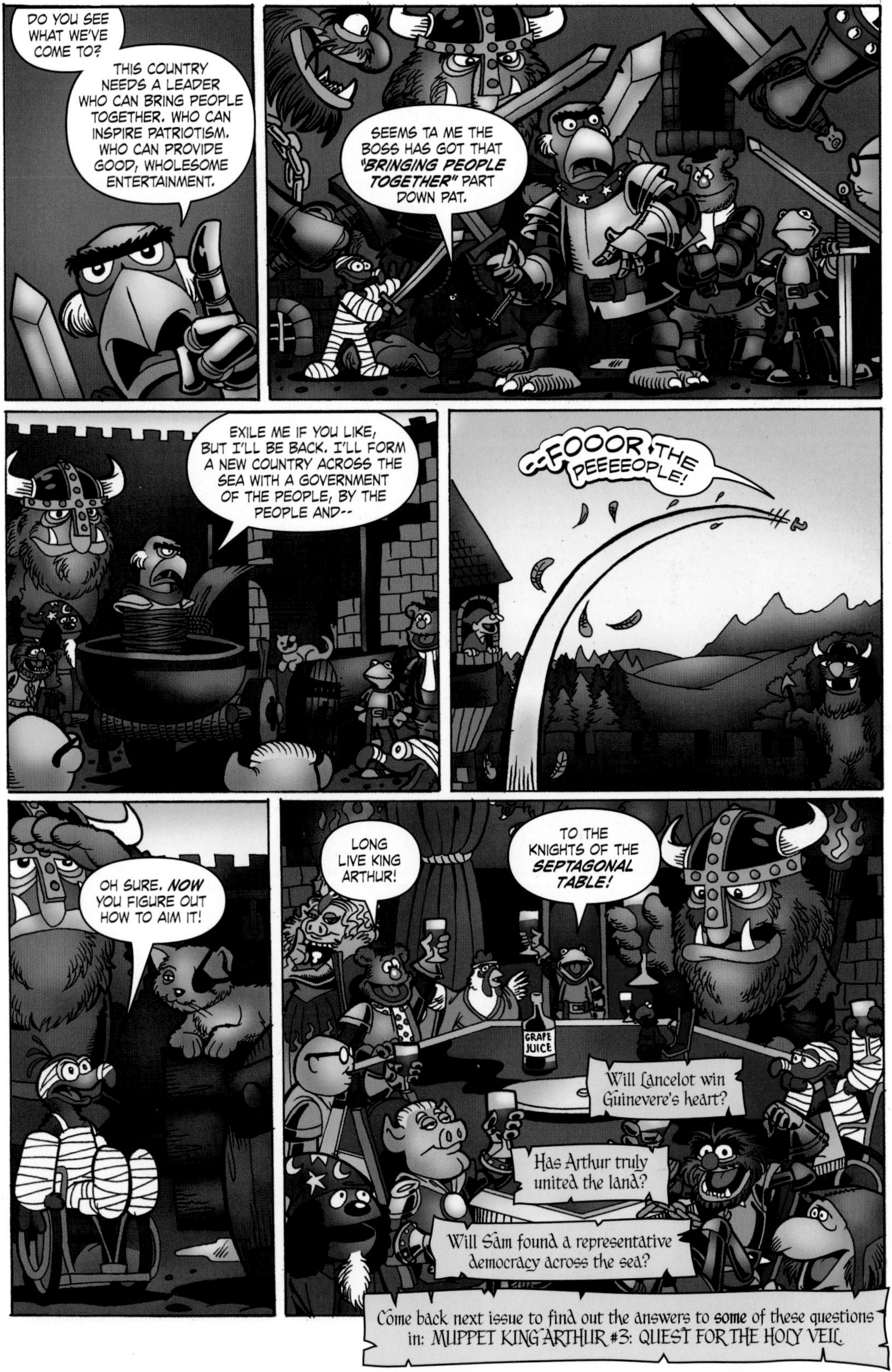
DO YOU SEE WHAT WE'VE COME TO?
THIS COUNTRY NEEDS A LEADER WHO CAN BRING PEOPLE TOGETHER. WHO CAN INSPIRE PATRIOTISM. WHO CAN PROVIDE GOOD, WHOLESOME ENTERTAINMENT.
SEEMS TA ME THE BOSS HAS GOT THAT "BRINGING PEOPLE TOGETHER" PART DOWN PAT.
EXILE ME IF YOU LIKE, BUT I'LL BE BACK. I'LL FORM A NEW COUNTRY ACROSS THE SEA WITH A GOVERNMENT OF THE PEOPLE, BY THE PEOPLE AND--
--FOOOR THE PEEEEOPLE!
OH SURE. NOW YOU FIGURE OUT HOW TO AIM IT!
LONG LIVE KING ARTHUR!
TO THE KNIGHTS OF THE SEPTAGONAL TABLE!
GRAPE JUICE
Will Lancelot win Guinevere's heart?
Has Arthur truly united the land?
Will Sam found a representative democracy across the sea?
Come back next issue to find out the answers to some of these questions in: MUPPET KING ARTHUR #3: QUEST FOR THE HOLY VEIL

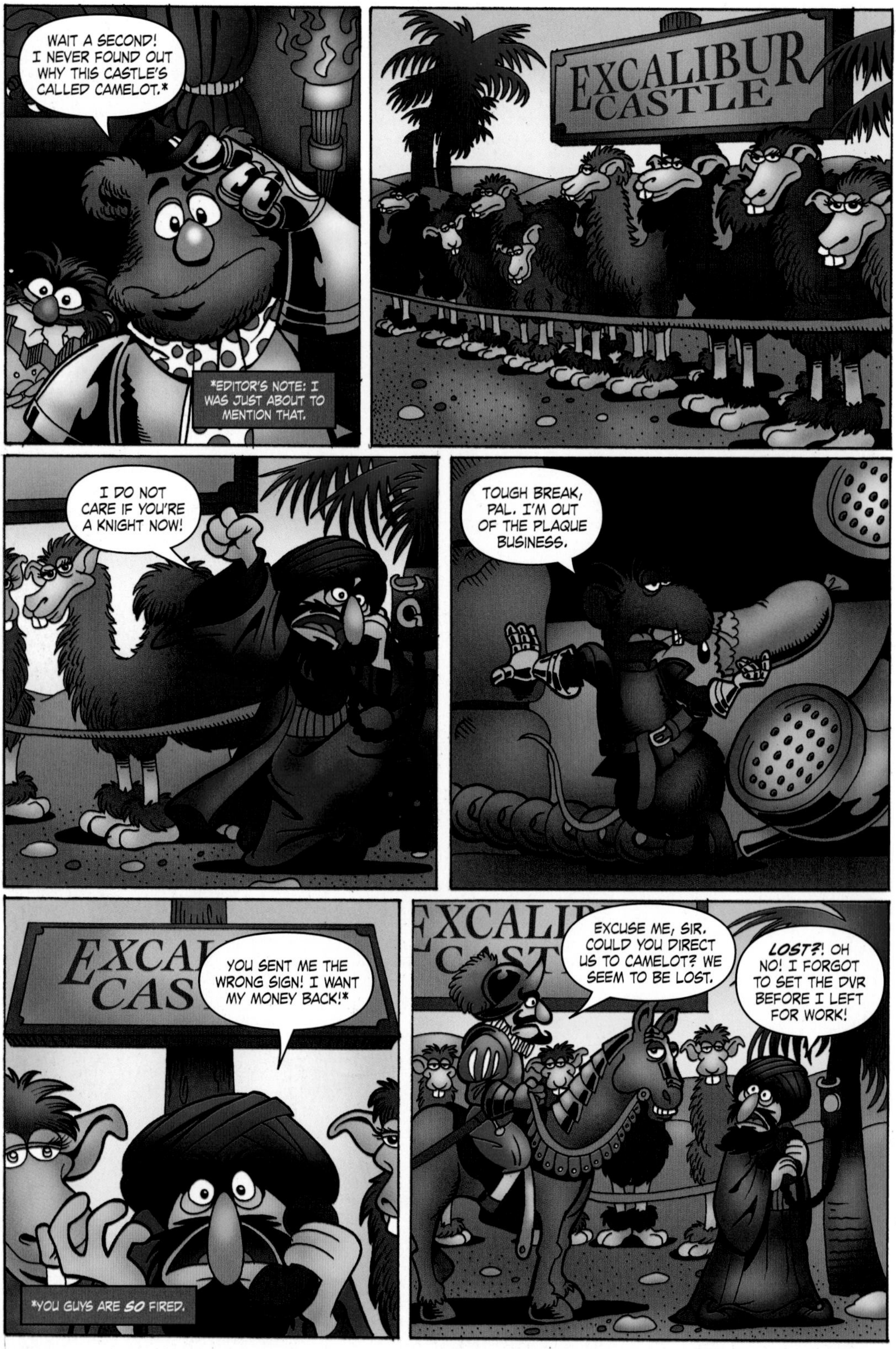
WAIT A SECOND! I NEVER FOUND OUT WHY THIS CASTLE'S CALLED CAMELOT.*
*EDITOR'S NOTE: I WAS JUST ABOUT TO MENTION THAT.
EXCALIBUR CASTLE
I DO NOT CARE IF YOU'RE A KNIGHT NOW!
TOUGH BREAK, PAL. I'M OUT OF THE PLAQUE BUSINESS.
EXCAL CAS
YOU SENT ME THE WRONG SIGN! I WANT MY MONEY BACK!*
*YOU GUYS ARE *SO* FIRED.
EXCALIB CAST
EXCUSE ME, SIR. COULD YOU DIRECT US TO CAMELOT? WE SEEM TO BE LOST.
LOST?! OH NO! I FORGOT TO SET THE DVR BEFORE I LEFT FOR WORK!

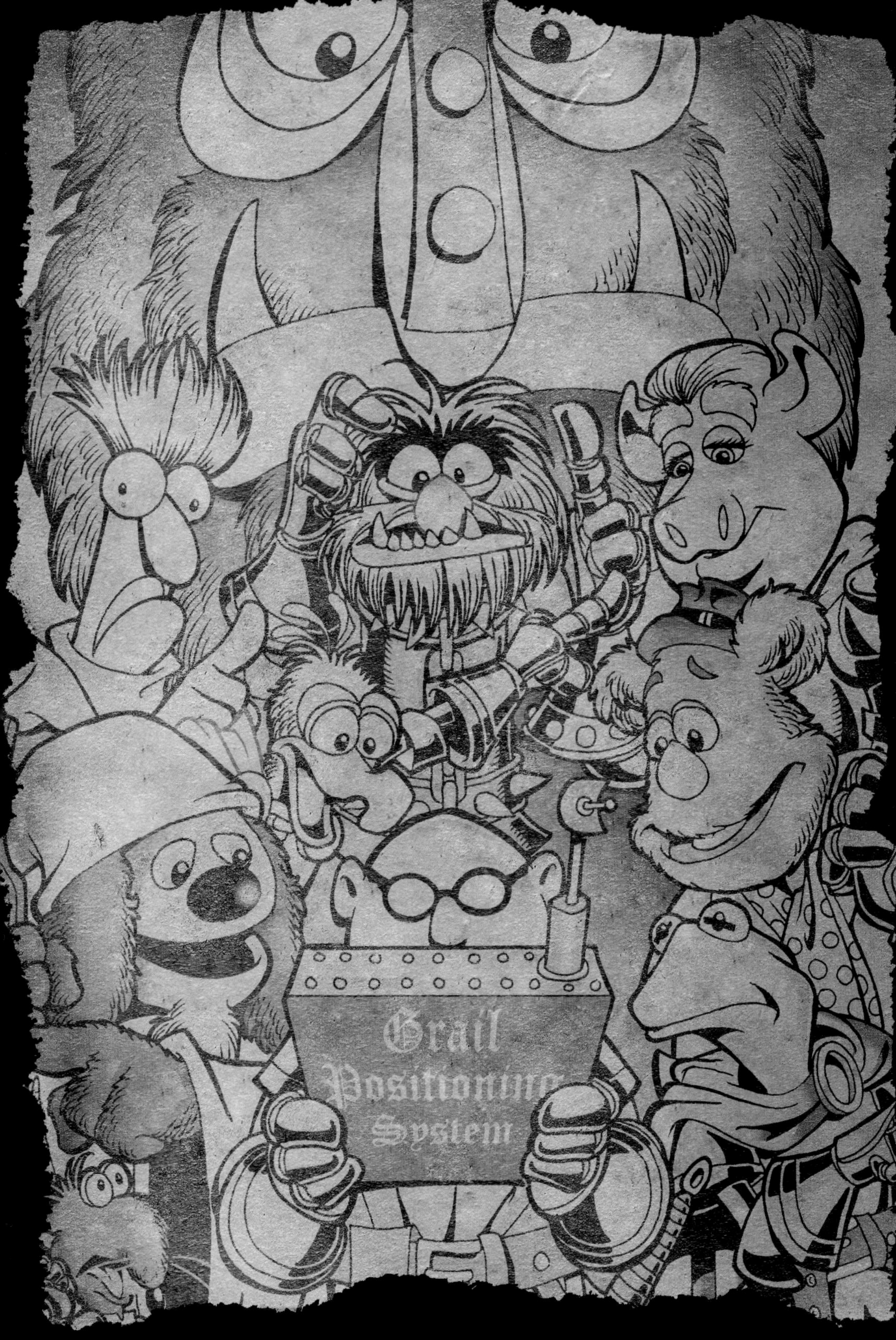
Grail
Positioning
System

chapter three

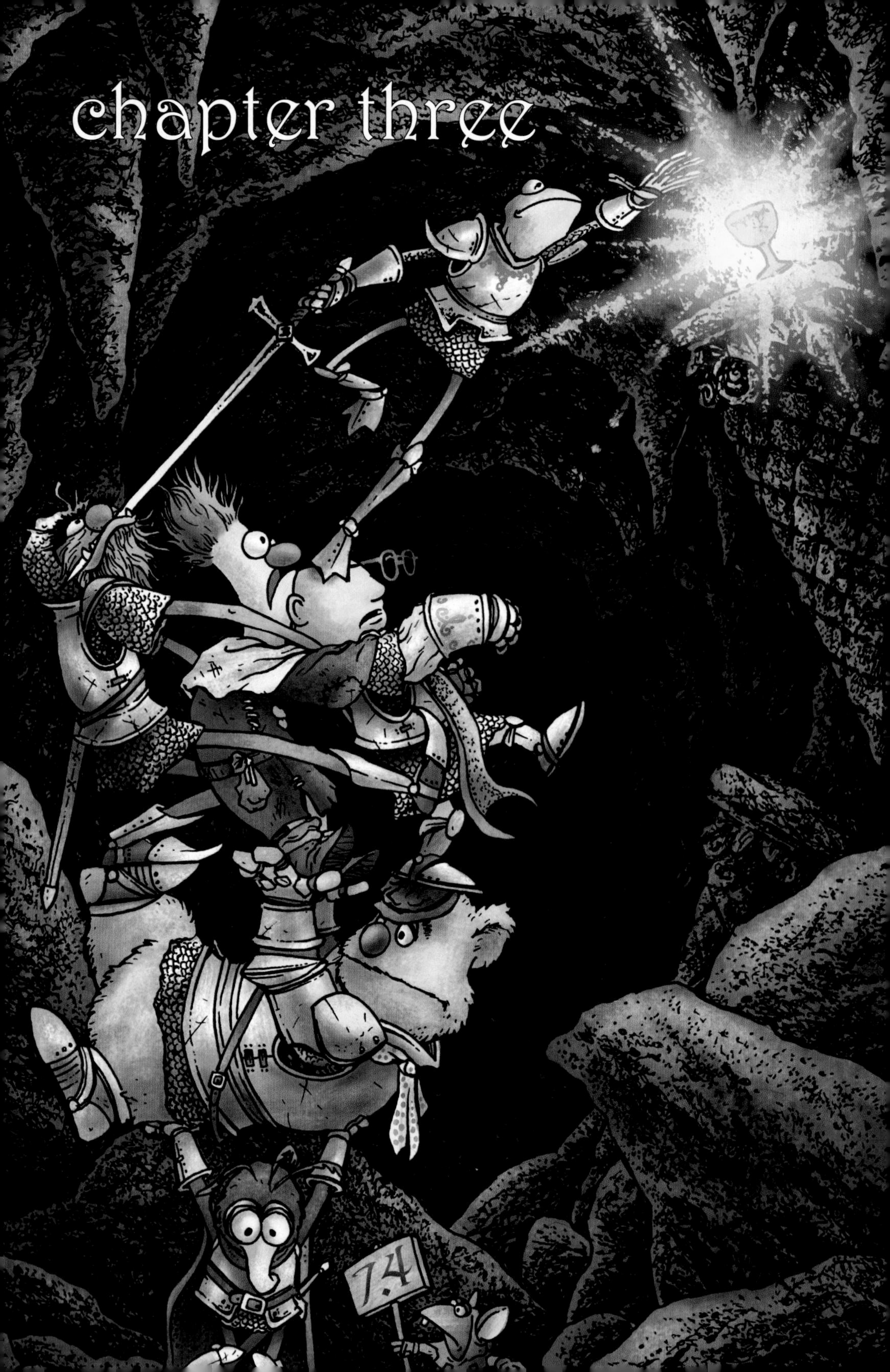
7.4

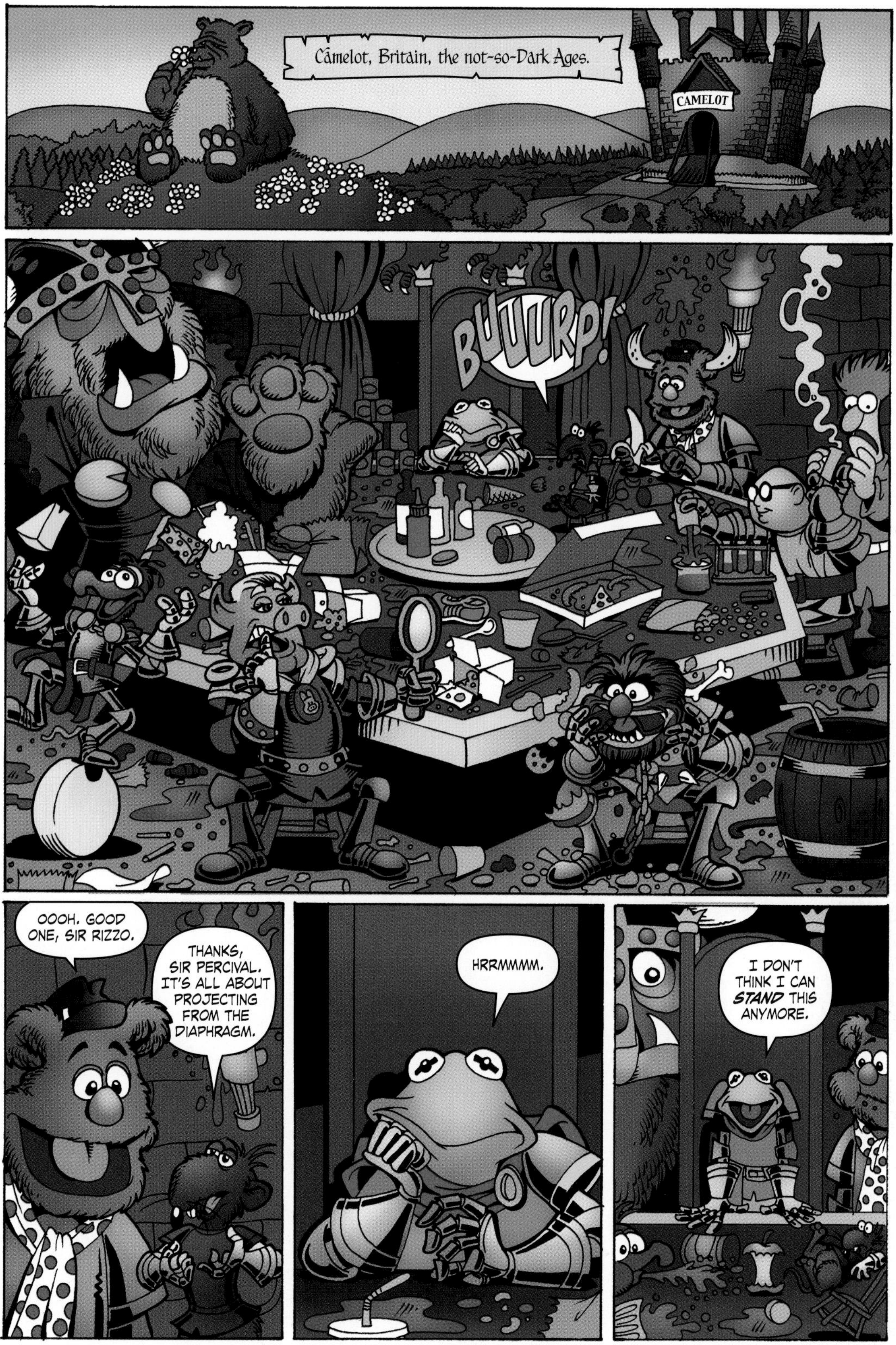
Câmelot, Britain, the not-so-Dark Ages.
CAMELOT
BUUURP!
OOOH. GOOD ONE, SIR RIZZO.
THANKS, SIR PERCIVAL. IT'S ALL ABOUT PROJECTING FROM THE DIAPHRAGM.
HRRMMMM.
I DON'T THINK I CAN *STAND* THIS ANYMORE.

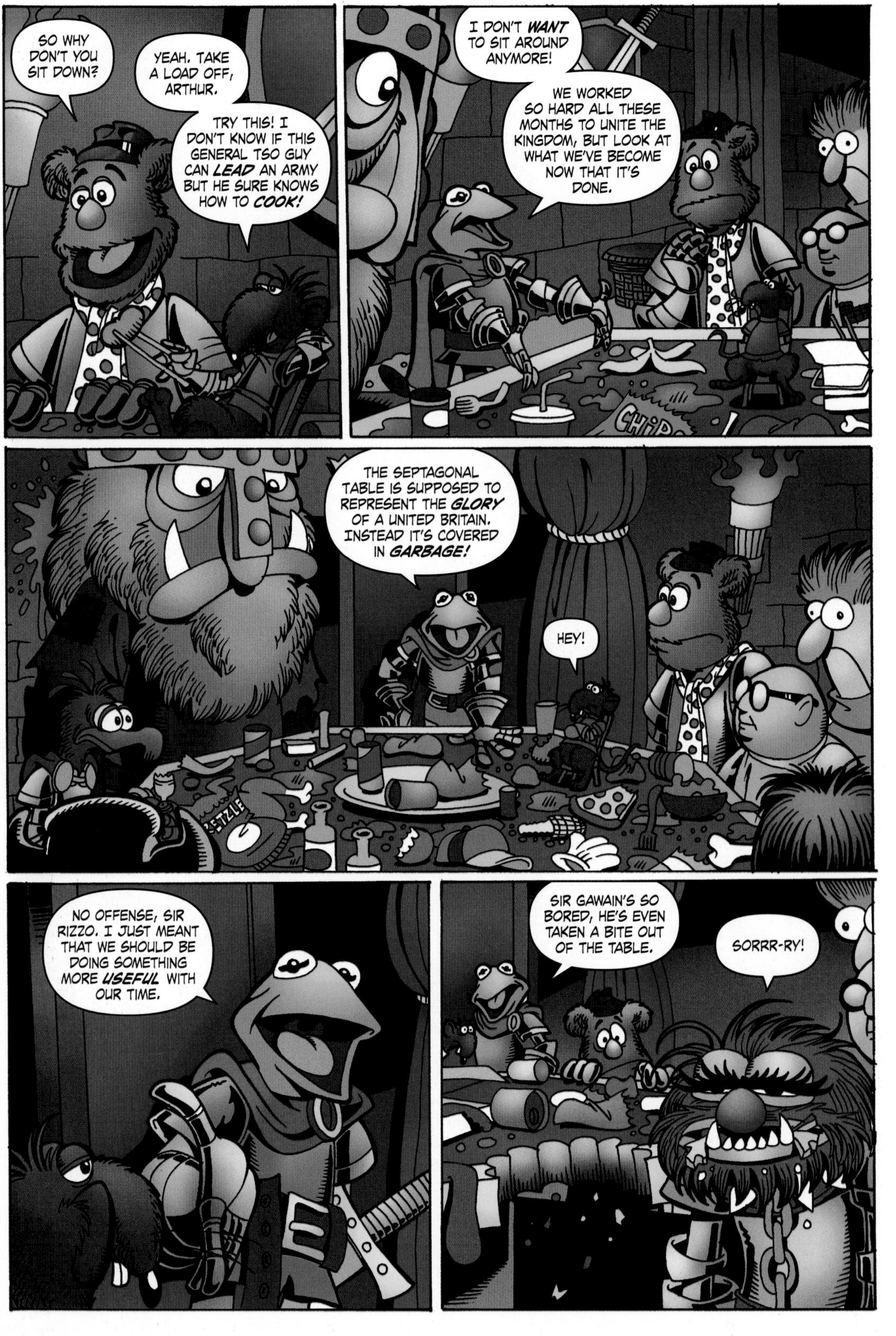
SO WHY DON'T YOU SIT DOWN?
YEAH. TAKE A LOAD OFF, ARTHUR.
TRY THIS! I DON'T KNOW IF THIS GENERAL TSO GUY CAN LEAD AN ARMY BUT HE SURE KNOWS HOW TO COOK!
I DON'T WANT TO SIT AROUND ANYMORE!
WE WORKED SO HARD ALL THESE MONTHS TO UNITE THE KINGDOM, BUT LOOK AT WHAT WE'VE BECOME NOW THAT IT'S DONE.
CHIPS
THE SEPTAGONAL TABLE IS SUPPOSED TO REPRESENT THE GLORY OF A UNITED BRITAIN. INSTEAD IT'S COVERED IN GARBAGE!
HEY!
NO OFFENSE, SIR RIZZO. I JUST MEANT THAT WE SHOULD BE DOING SOMETHING MORE USEFUL WITH OUR TIME.
SIR GAWAIN'S SO BORED, HE'S EVEN TAKEN A BITE OUT OF THE TABLE.
SORRR-RY!

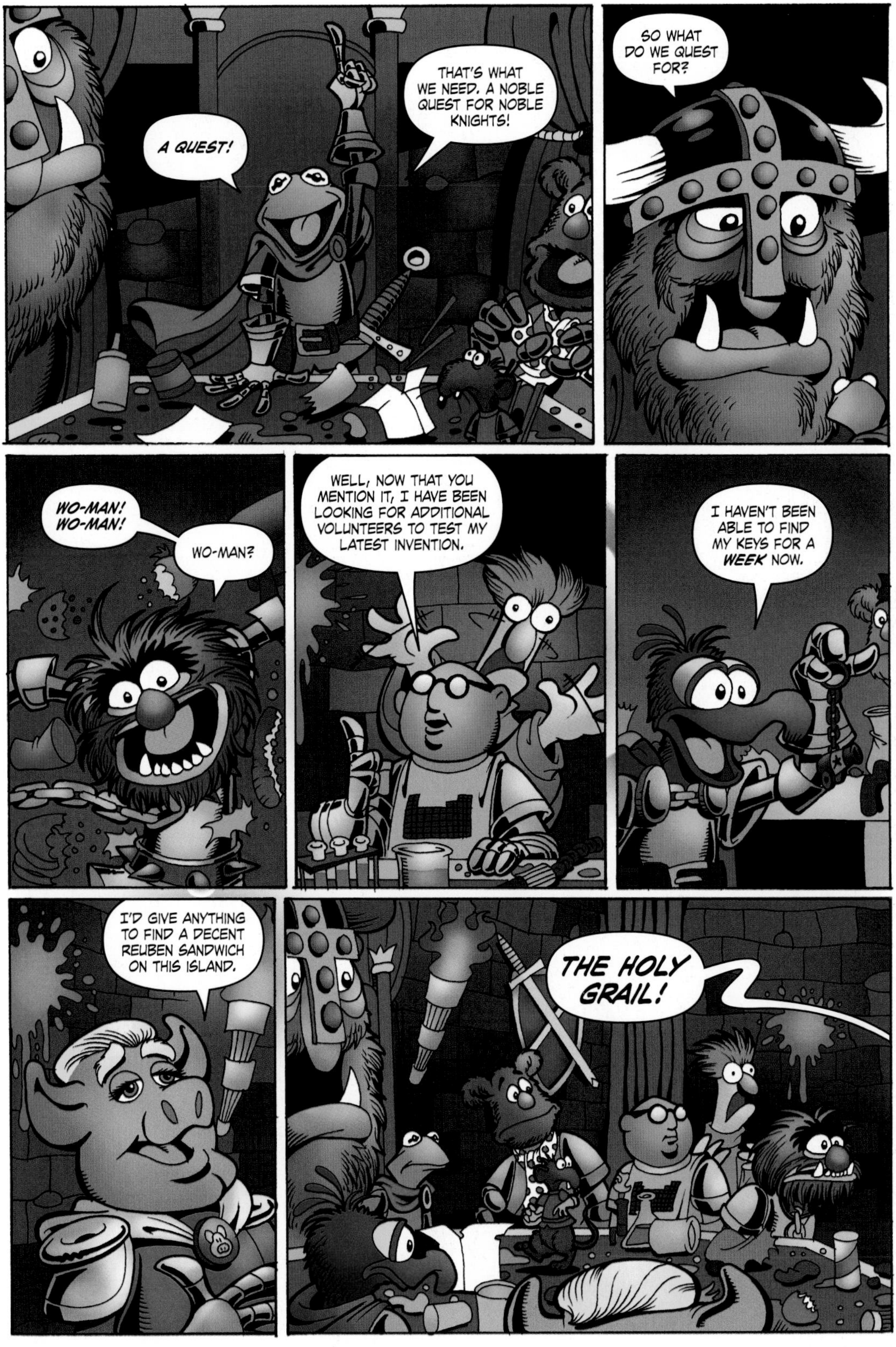

A QUEST!
THAT'S WHAT WE NEED. A NOBLE QUEST FOR NOBLE KNIGHTS!
SO WHAT DO WE QUEST FOR?
WO-MAN! WO-MAN!
WO-MAN?
WELL, NOW THAT YOU MENTION IT, I HAVE BEEN LOOKING FOR ADDITIONAL VOLUNTEERS TO TEST MY LATEST INVENTION.
I HAVEN'T BEEN ABLE TO FIND MY KEYS FOR A WEEK NOW.
I'D GIVE ANYTHING TO FIND A DECENT REUBEN SANDWICH ON THIS ISLAND.
THE HOLY GRAIL!

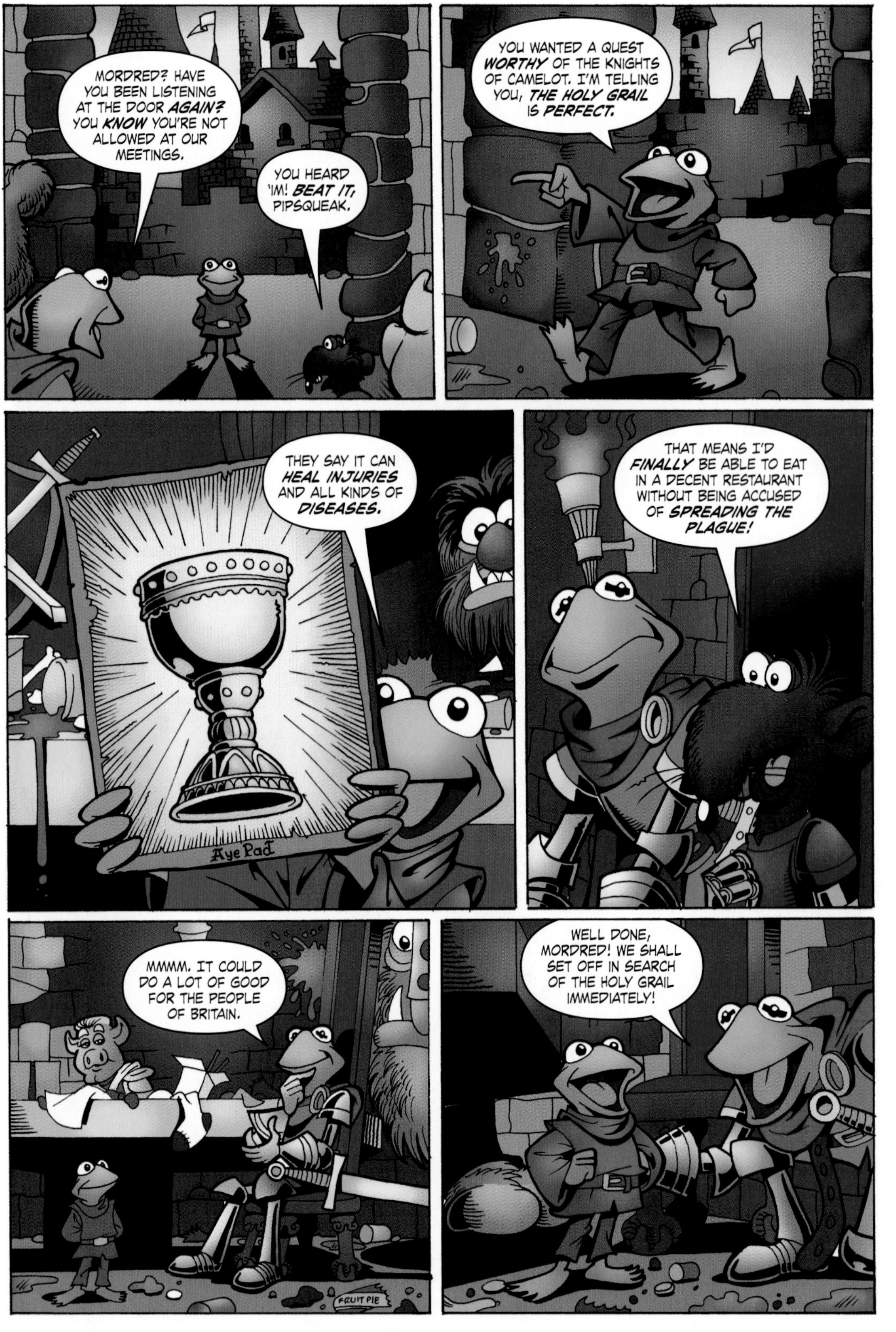
MORDRED? HAVE YOU BEEN LISTENING AT THE DOOR AGAIN? YOU KNOW YOU'RE NOT ALLOWED AT OUR MEETINGS.
YOU HEARD 'IM! BEAT IT, PIPSQUEAK.
YOU WANTED A QUEST WORTHY OF THE KNIGHTS OF CAMELOT. I'M TELLING YOU, THE HOLY GRAIL IS PERFECT.
THEY SAY IT CAN HEAL INJURIES AND ALL KINDS OF DISEASES.
Aye Pad
THAT MEANS I'D FINALLY BE ABLE TO EAT IN A DECENT RESTAURANT WITHOUT BEING ACCUSED OF SPREADING THE PLAGUE!
MMMM. IT COULD DO A LOT OF GOOD FOR THE PEOPLE OF BRITAIN.
FRUIT PIE
WELL DONE, MORDRED! WE SHALL SET OFF IN SEARCH OF THE HOLY GRAIL IMMEDIATELY!

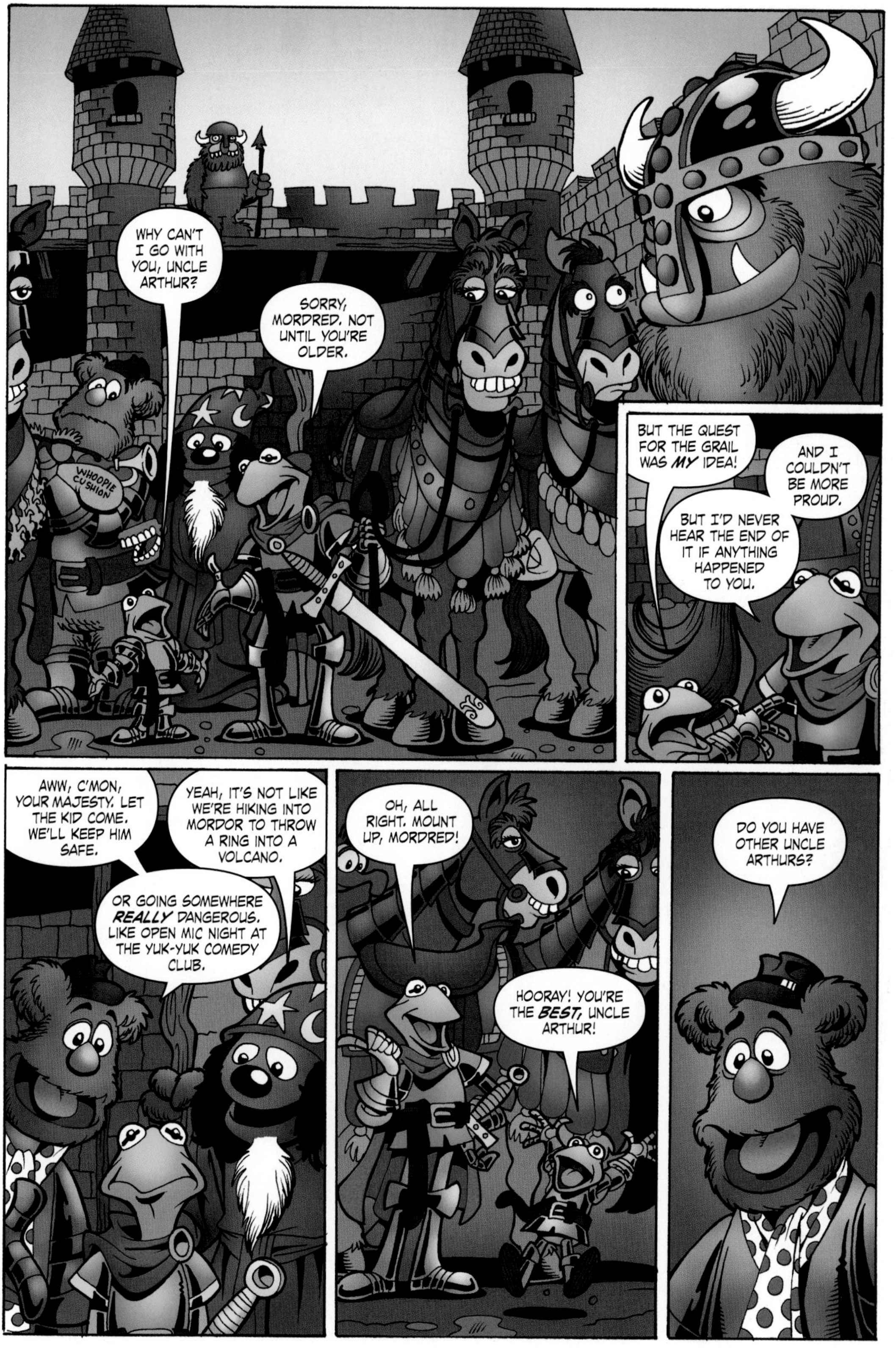
WHY CAN'T I GO WITH YOU, UNCLE ARTHUR?
SORRY, MORDRED. NOT UNTIL YOU'RE OLDER.
WHOOPIE CUSHION
BUT THE QUEST FOR THE GRAIL WAS MY IDEA!
AND I COULDN'T BE MORE PROUD.
BUT I'D NEVER HEAR THE END OF IT IF ANYTHING HAPPENED TO YOU.
AWW, C'MON, YOUR MAJESTY. LET THE KID COME. WE'LL KEEP HIM SAFE.
YEAH, IT'S NOT LIKE WE'RE HIKING INTO MORDOR TO THROW A RING INTO A VOLCANO.
OR GOING SOMEWHERE REALLY DANGEROUS. LIKE OPEN MIC NIGHT AT THE YUK-YUK COMEDY CLUB.
OH, ALL RIGHT. MOUNT UP, MORDRED!
HOORAY! YOU'RE THE BEST, UNCLE ARTHUR!
DO YOU HAVE OTHER UNCLE ARTHURS?

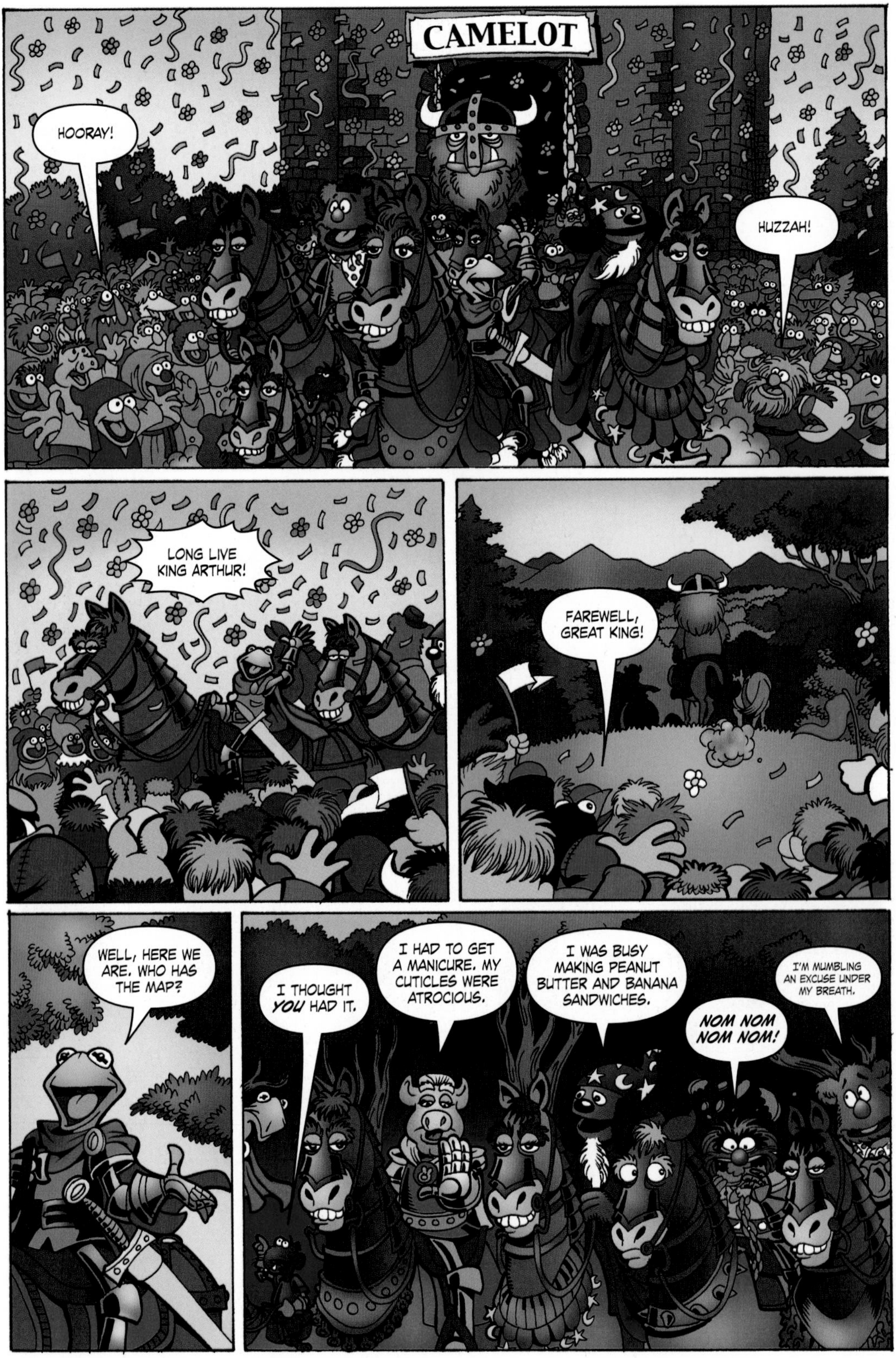
CAMELOT
HOORAY!
HUZZAH!
LONG LIVE KING ARTHUR!
FAREWELL, GREAT KING!
WELL, HERE WE ARE. WHO HAS THE MAP?
I THOUGHT *YOU* HAD IT.
I HAD TO GET A MANICURE. MY CUTICLES WERE ATROCIOUS.
I WAS BUSY MAKING PEANUT BUTTER AND BANANA SANDWICHES.
NOM NOM NOM NOM!
I'M MUMBLING AN EXCUSE UNDER MY BREATH.

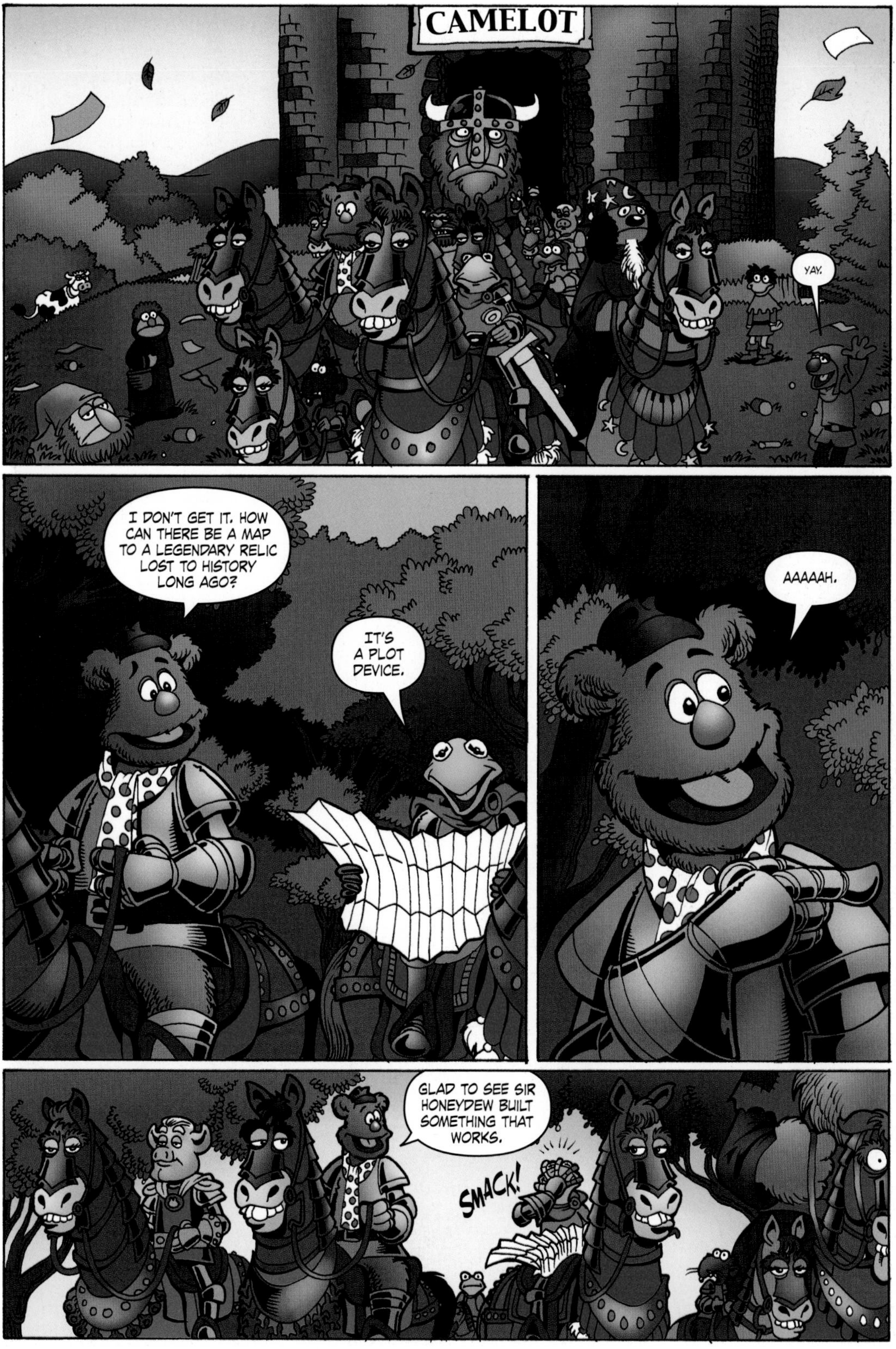
CAMELOT
YAY.
I DON'T GET IT. HOW CAN THERE BE A MAP TO A LEGENDARY RELIC LOST TO HISTORY LONG AGO?
IT'S A PLOT DEVICE.
AAAAAH.
GLAD TO SEE SIR HONEYDEW BUILT SOMETHING THAT WORKS.
SMACK!

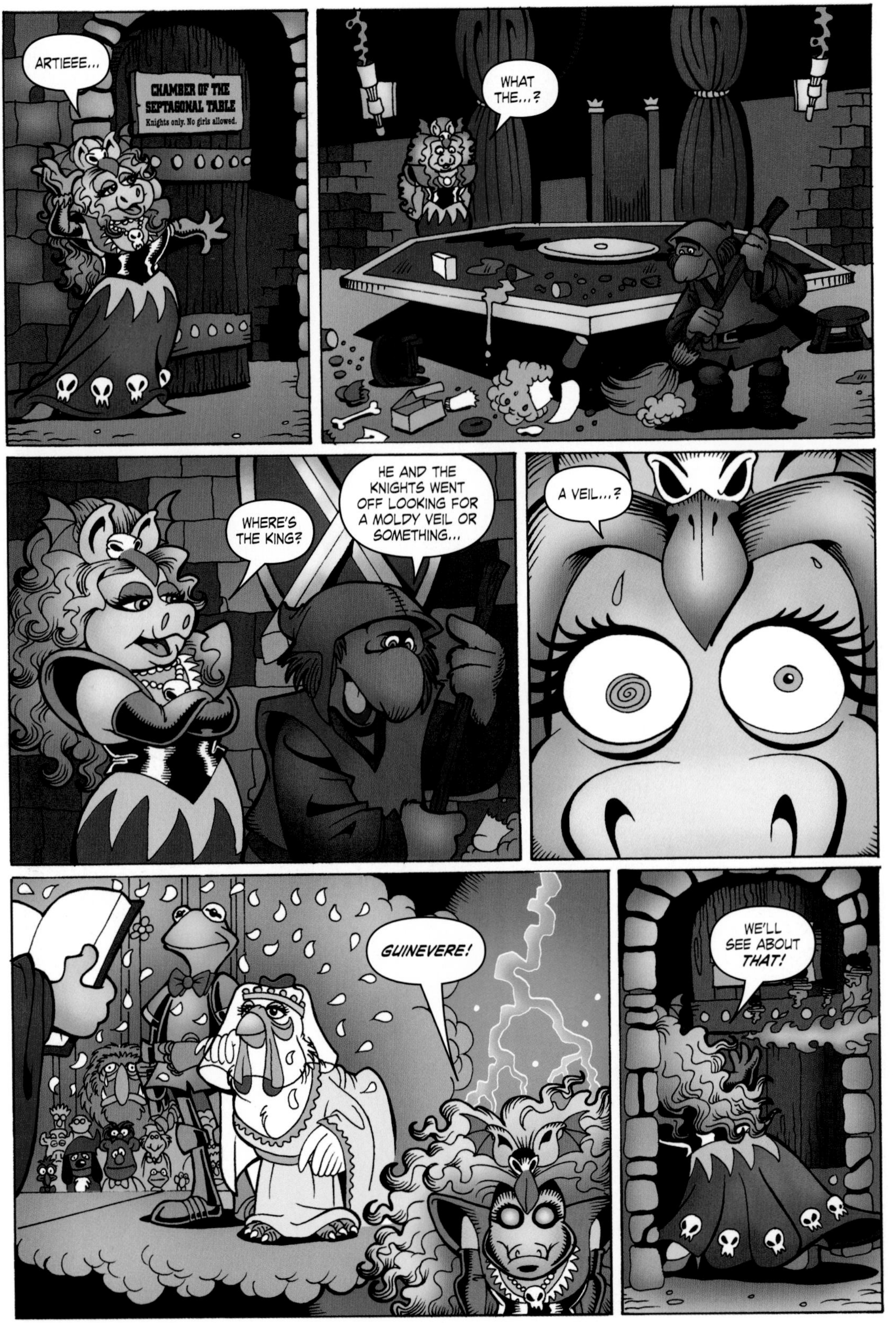
ARTIEEE...
CHAMBER OF THE SEPTAGONAL TABLE
Knights only. No girls allowed.
WHAT THE...?
WHERE'S THE KING?
HE AND THE KNIGHTS WENT OFF LOOKING FOR A MOLDY VEIL OR SOMETHING...
A VEIL...?
GUINEVERE!
WE'LL SEE ABOUT THAT!

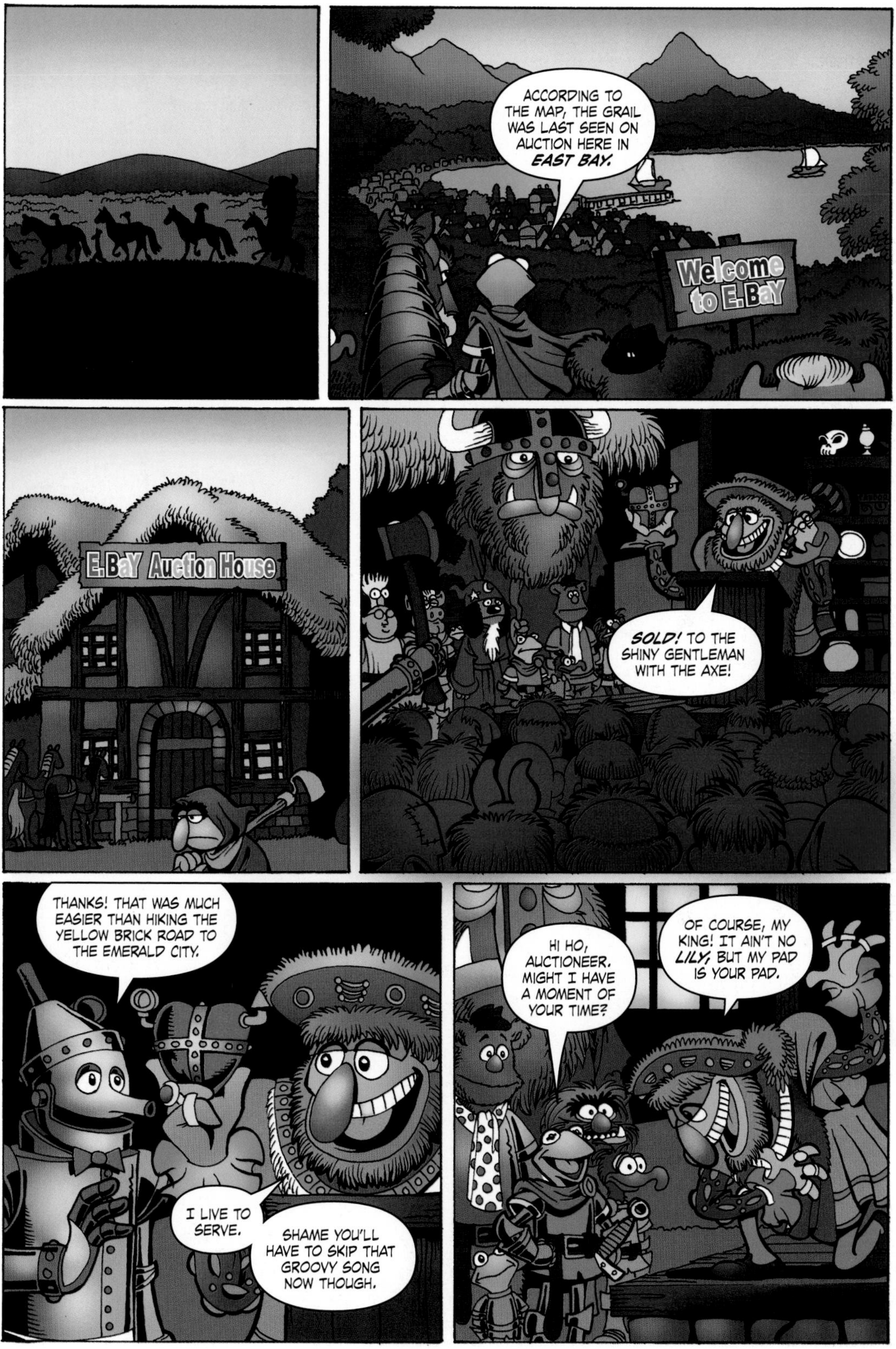
ACCORDING TO THE MAP, THE GRAIL WAS LAST SEEN ON AUCTION HERE IN *EAST BAY.*
Welcome to E. BaY
E. BaY Auction House
SOLD! TO THE SHINY GENTLEMAN WITH THE AXE!
THANKS! THAT WAS MUCH EASIER THAN HIKING THE YELLOW BRICK ROAD TO THE EMERALD CITY.
I LIVE TO SERVE.
SHAME YOU'LL HAVE TO SKIP THAT GROOVY SONG NOW THOUGH.
HI HO, AUCTIONEER. MIGHT I HAVE A MOMENT OF YOUR TIME?
OF COURSE, MY KING! IT AIN'T NO *LILY,* BUT MY PAD IS YOUR PAD.

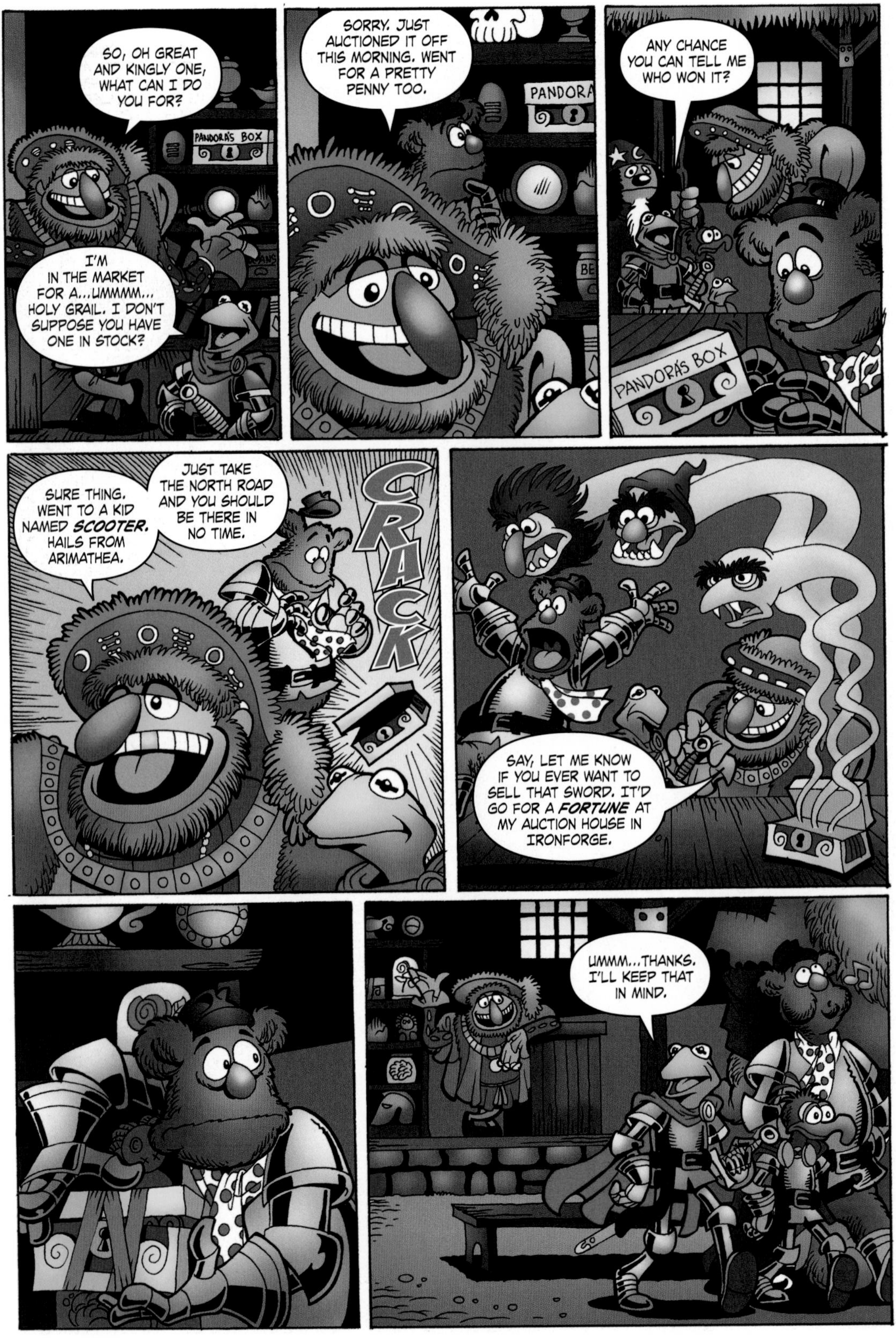
SO, OH GREAT AND KINGLY ONE, WHAT CAN I DO YOU FOR?
PANDORA'S BOX
I'M IN THE MARKET FOR A...UMMMM... HOLY GRAIL. I DON'T SUPPOSE YOU HAVE ONE IN STOCK?
SORRY. JUST AUCTIONED IT OFF THIS MORNING. WENT FOR A PRETTY PENNY TOO.
PANDORA
ANY CHANCE YOU CAN TELL ME WHO WON IT?
PANDORA'S BOX
SURE THING. WENT TO A KID NAMED *SCOOTER.* HAILS FROM ARIMATHEA.
JUST TAKE THE NORTH ROAD AND YOU SHOULD BE THERE IN NO TIME.
CRACK
SAY, LET ME KNOW IF YOU EVER WANT TO SELL THAT SWORD. IT'D GO FOR A *FORTUNE* AT MY AUCTION HOUSE IN IRONFORGE.
UMMM...THANKS. I'LL KEEP THAT IN MIND.

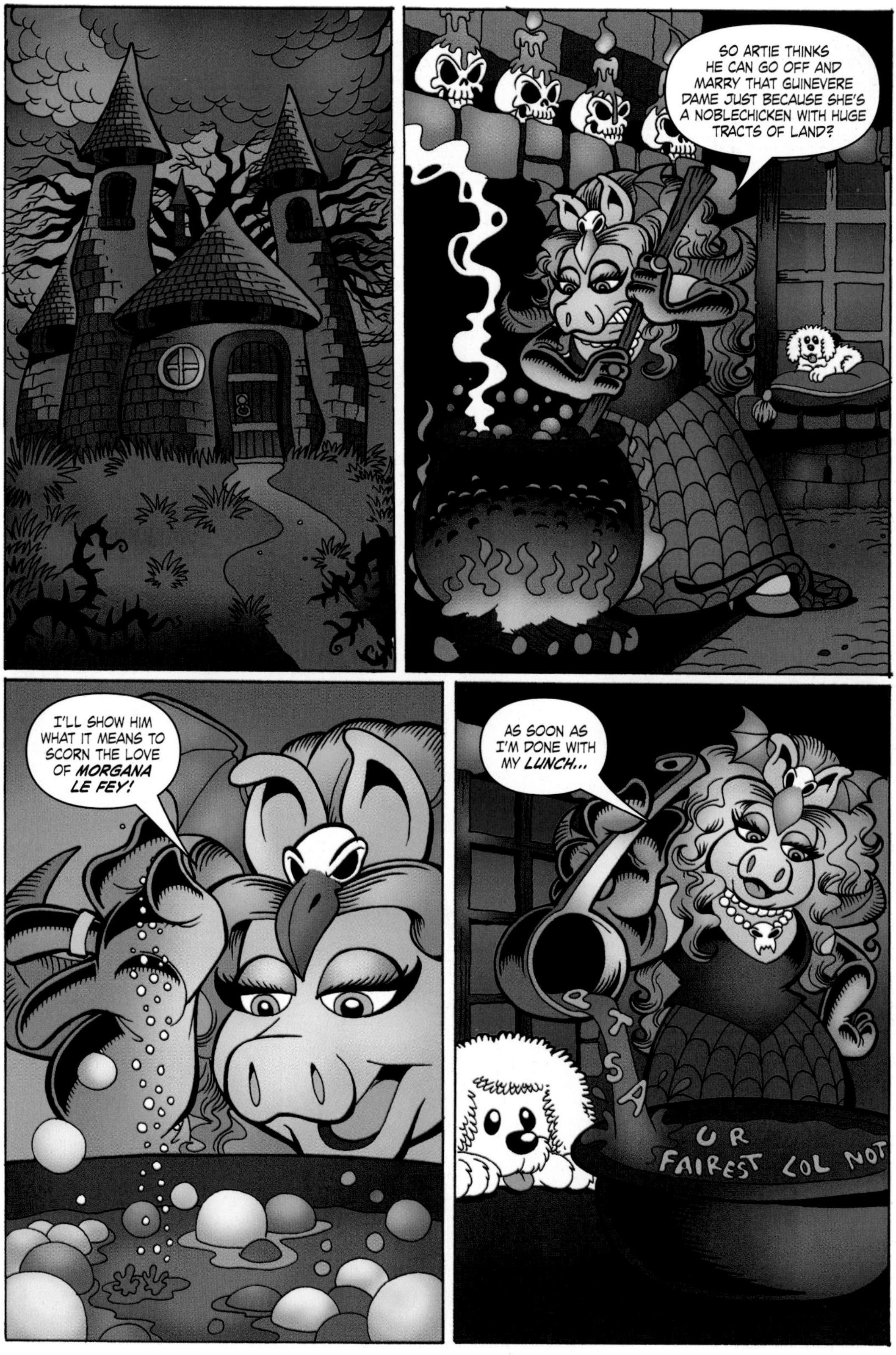
SO ARTIE THINKS HE CAN GO OFF AND MARRY THAT GUINEVERE DAME JUST BECAUSE SHE'S A NOBLECHICKEN WITH HUGE TRACTS OF LAND?
I'LL SHOW HIM WHAT IT MEANS TO SCORN THE LOVE OF ***MORGANA LE FEY!***
AS SOON AS I'M DONE WITH MY ***LUNCH...***
U R
FAIREST LOL NOT

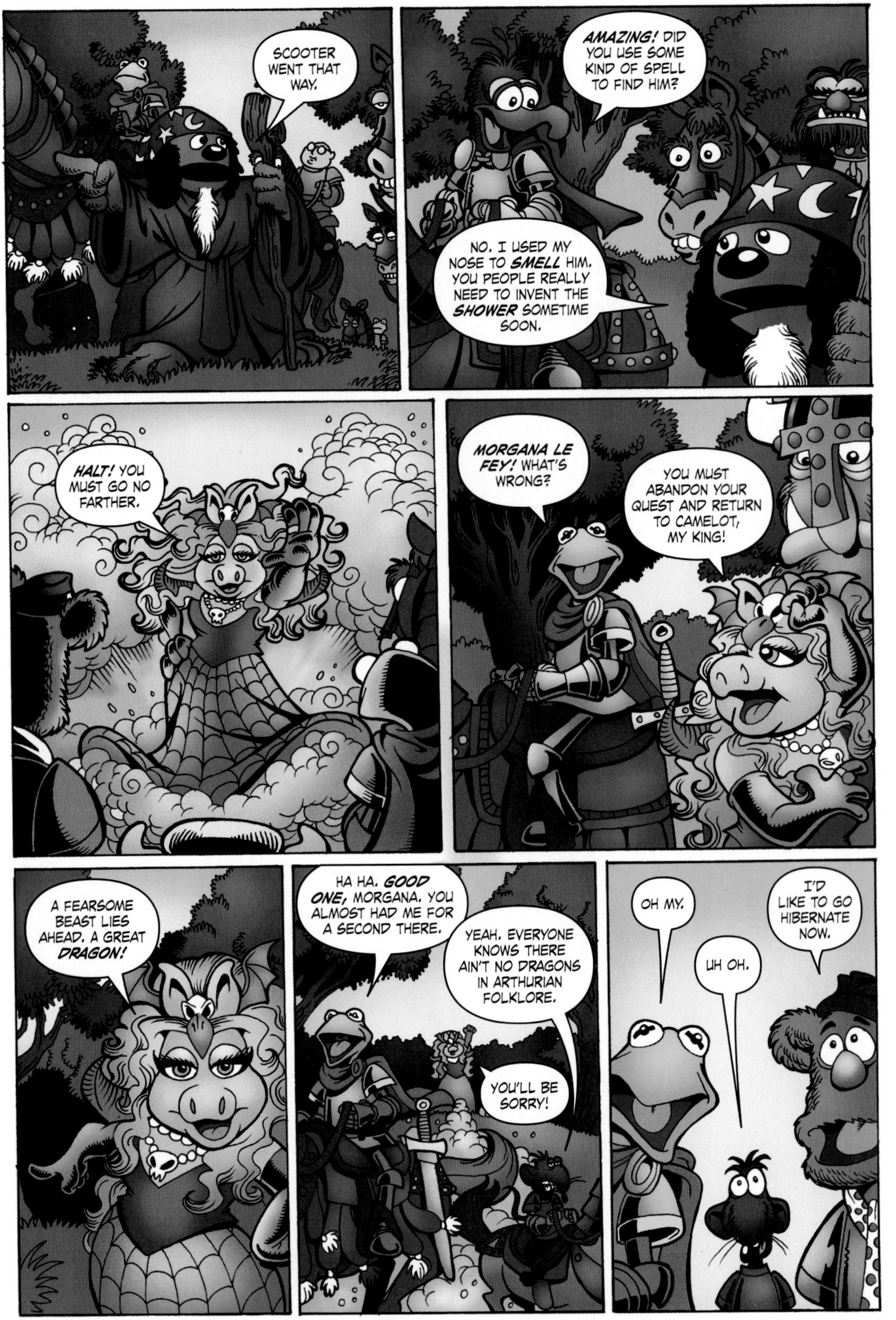
SCOOTER WENT THAT WAY.
AMAZING! DID YOU USE SOME KIND OF SPELL TO FIND HIM?
NO. I USED MY NOSE TO SMELL HIM. YOU PEOPLE REALLY NEED TO INVENT THE SHOWER SOMETIME SOON.
HALT! YOU MUST GO NO FARTHER.
MORGANA LE FEY! WHAT'S WRONG?
YOU MUST ABANDON YOUR QUEST AND RETURN TO CAMELOT, MY KING!
A FEARSOME BEAST LIES AHEAD. A GREAT DRAGON!
HA HA. GOOD ONE, MORGANA. YOU ALMOST HAD ME FOR A SECOND THERE.
YEAH. EVERYONE KNOWS THERE AIN'T NO DRAGONS IN ARTHURIAN FOLKLORE.
YOU'LL BE SORRY!
OH MY.
UH OH.
I'D LIKE TO GO HIBERNATE NOW.

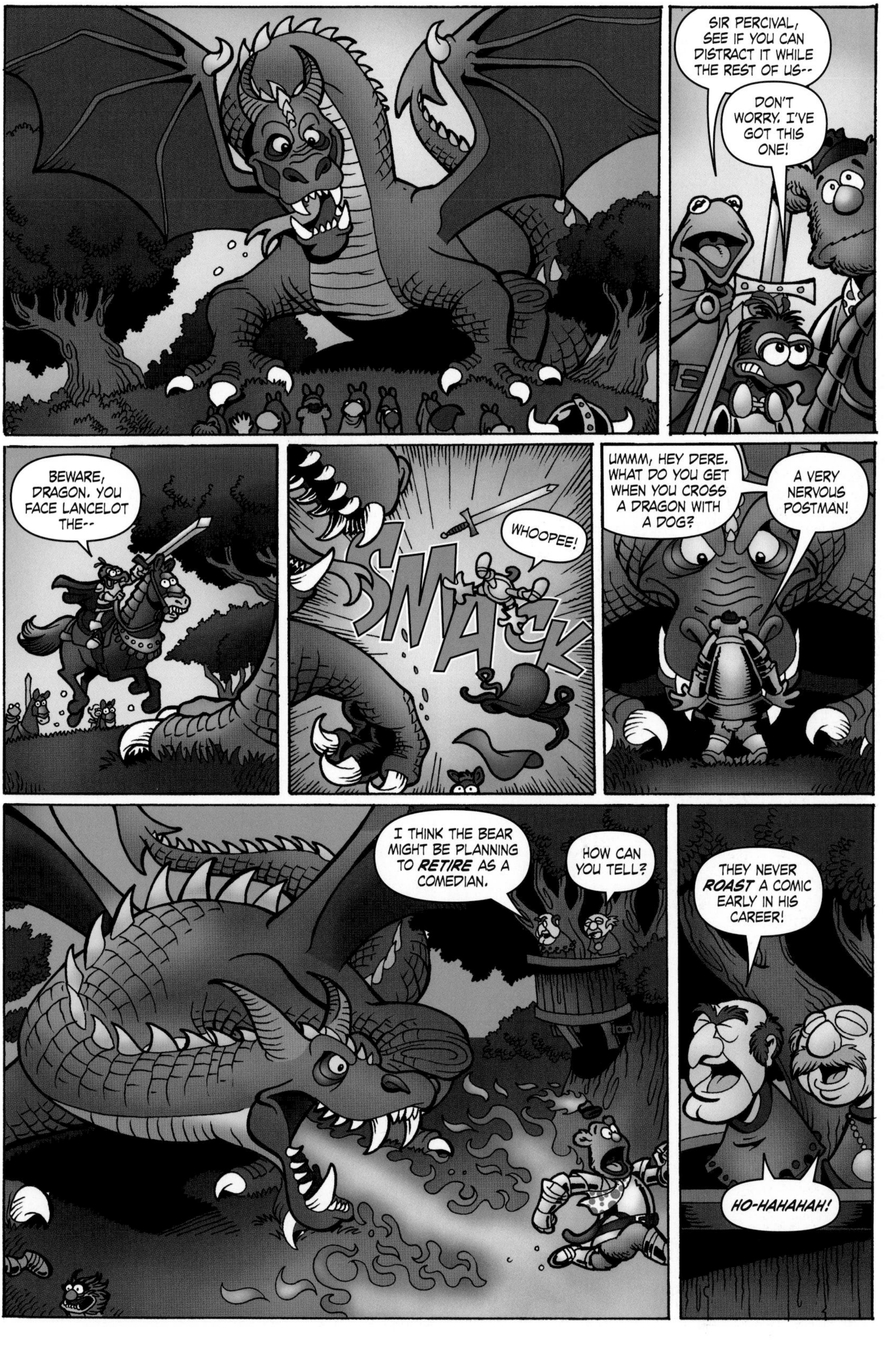
SIR PERCIVAL, SEE IF YOU CAN DISTRACT IT WHILE THE REST OF US--
DON'T WORRY. I'VE GOT THIS ONE!
BEWARE, DRAGON. YOU FACE LANCELOT THE--
SMACK
WHOOPEE!
UMMM, HEY DERE. WHAT DO YOU GET WHEN YOU CROSS A DRAGON WITH A DOG?
A VERY NERVOUS POSTMAN!
I THINK THE BEAR MIGHT BE PLANNING TO *RETIRE* AS A COMEDIAN.
HOW CAN YOU TELL?
THEY NEVER *ROAST* A COMIC EARLY IN HIS CAREER!
HO-HAHAHAH!

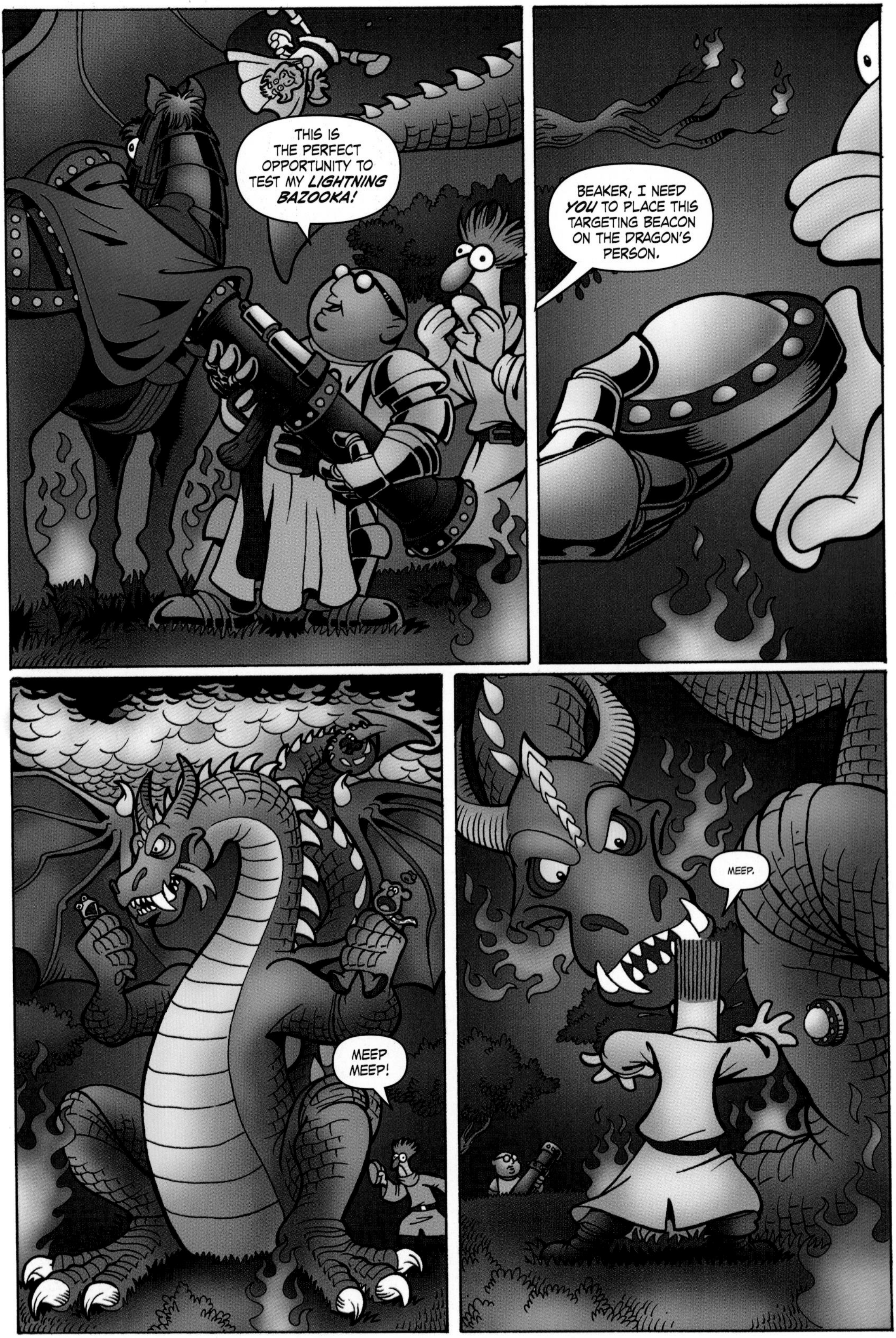
THIS IS THE PERFECT OPPORTUNITY TO TEST MY LIGHTNING BAZOOKA!
BEAKER, I NEED YOU TO PLACE THIS TARGETING BEACON ON THE DRAGON'S PERSON.
MEEP MEEP!
MEEP.

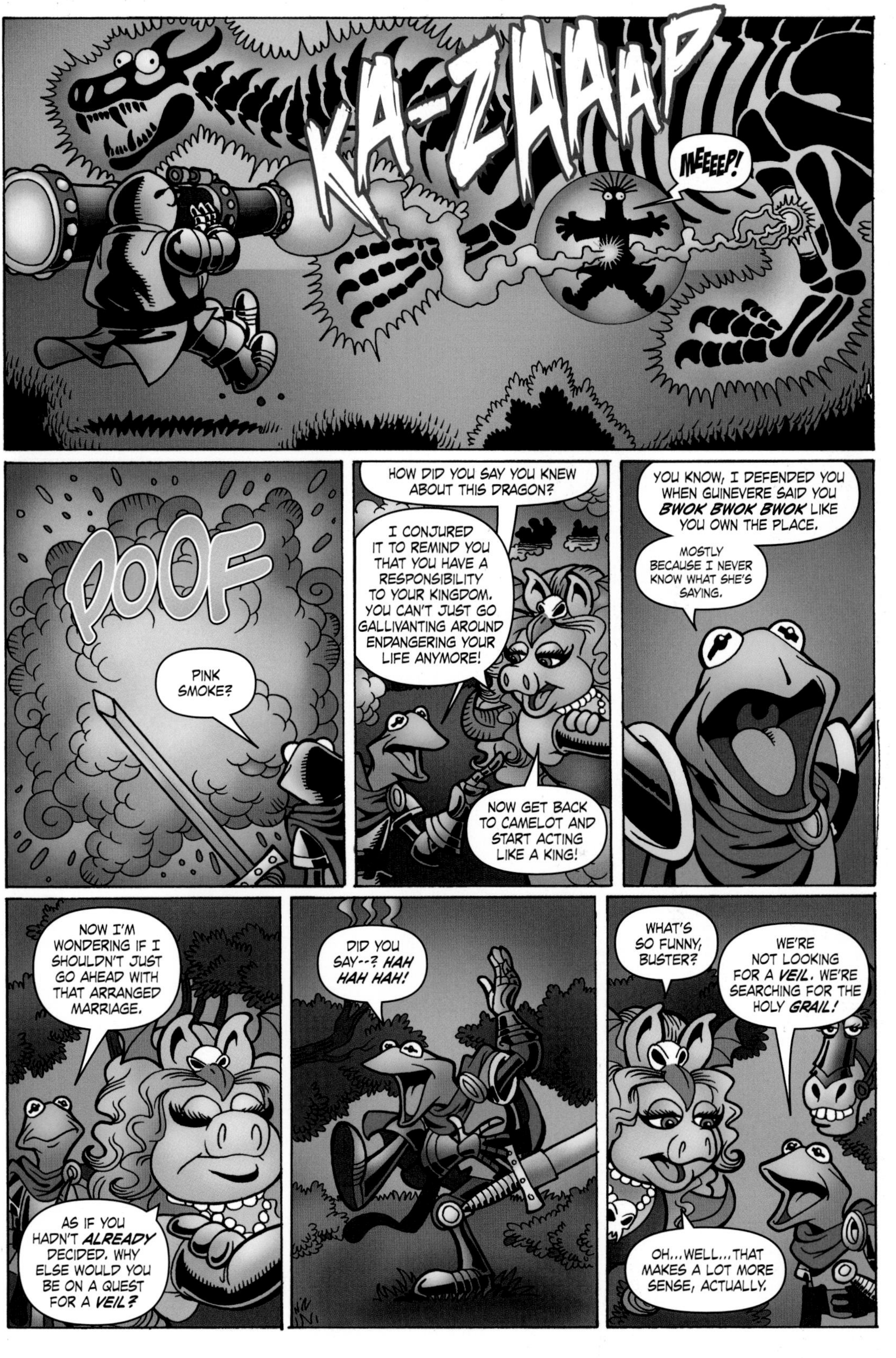
KA-ZAAAAP
MEEEEP!
POOF
PINK SMOKE?
HOW DID YOU SAY YOU KNEW ABOUT THIS DRAGON?
I CONJURED IT TO REMIND YOU THAT YOU HAVE A RESPONSIBILITY TO YOUR KINGDOM. YOU CAN'T JUST GO GALLIVANTING AROUND ENDANGERING YOUR LIFE ANYMORE!
NOW GET BACK TO CAMELOT AND START ACTING LIKE A KING!
YOU KNOW, I DEFENDED YOU WHEN GUINEVERE SAID YOU ***BWOK BWOK BWOK*** LIKE YOU OWN THE PLACE.
MOSTLY BECAUSE I NEVER KNOW WHAT SHE'S SAYING.
NOW I'M WONDERING IF I SHOULDN'T JUST GO AHEAD WITH THAT ARRANGED MARRIAGE.
AS IF YOU HADN'T ***ALREADY*** DECIDED. WHY ELSE WOULD YOU BE ON A QUEST FOR A ***VEIL?***
DID YOU SAY--? ***HAH HAH HAH!***
WHAT'S SO FUNNY, BUSTER?
WE'RE NOT LOOKING FOR A ***VEIL***. WE'RE SEARCHING FOR THE HOLY ***GRAIL!***
OH...WELL...THAT MAKES A LOT MORE SENSE, ACTUALLY.

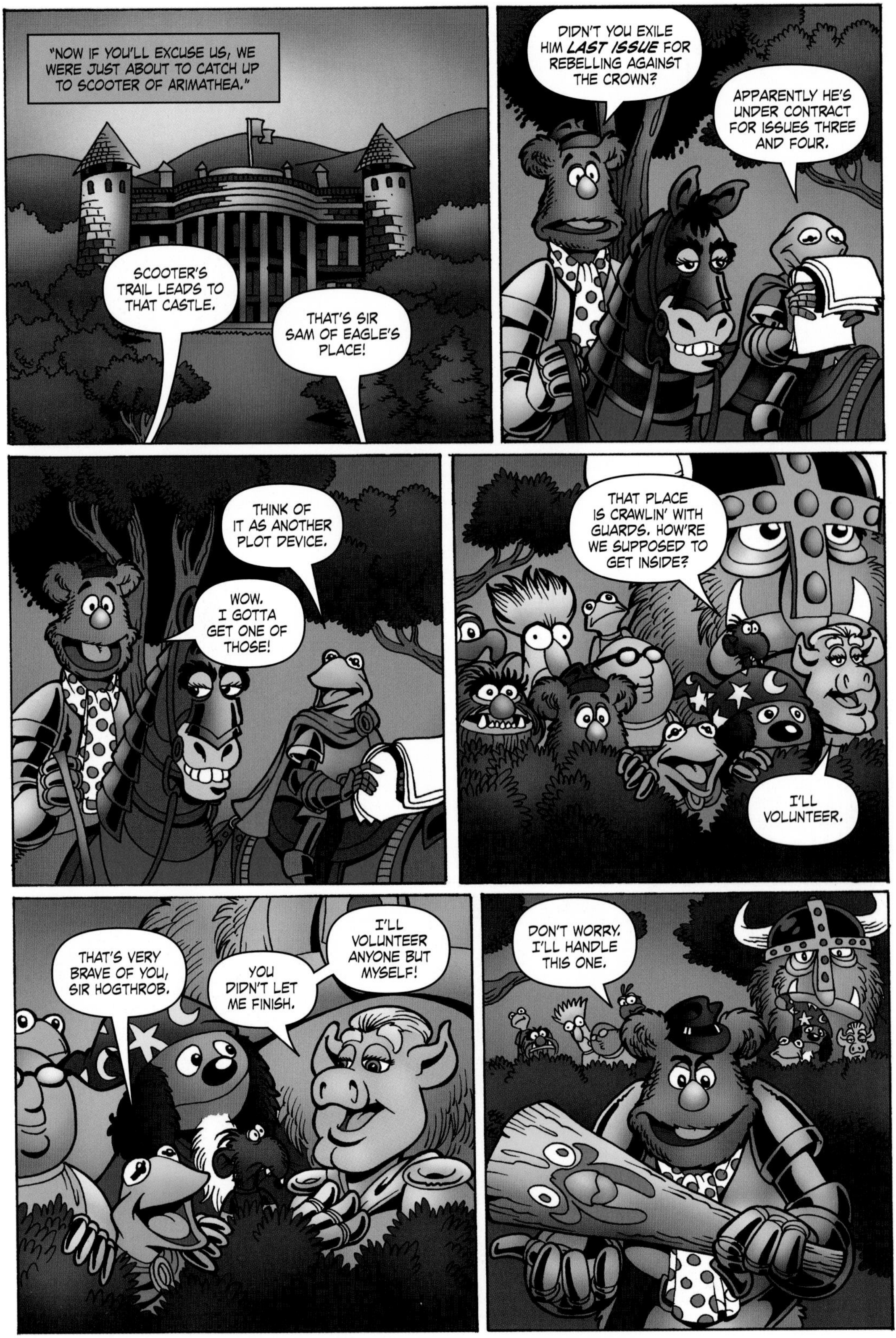
"NOW IF YOU'LL EXCUSE US, WE WERE JUST ABOUT TO CATCH UP TO SCOOTER OF ARIMATHEA."
SCOOTER'S TRAIL LEADS TO THAT CASTLE.
THAT'S SIR SAM OF EAGLE'S PLACE!
DIDN'T YOU EXILE HIM LAST ISSUE FOR REBELLING AGAINST THE CROWN?
APPARENTLY HE'S UNDER CONTRACT FOR ISSUES THREE AND FOUR.
THINK OF IT AS ANOTHER PLOT DEVICE.
WOW. I GOTTA GET ONE OF THOSE!
THAT PLACE IS CRAWLIN' WITH GUARDS. HOW'RE WE SUPPOSED TO GET INSIDE?
I'LL VOLUNTEER.
THAT'S VERY BRAVE OF YOU, SIR HOGTHROB.
YOU DIDN'T LET ME FINISH.
I'LL VOLUNTEER ANYONE BUT MYSELF!
DON'T WORRY. I'LL HANDLE THIS ONE.

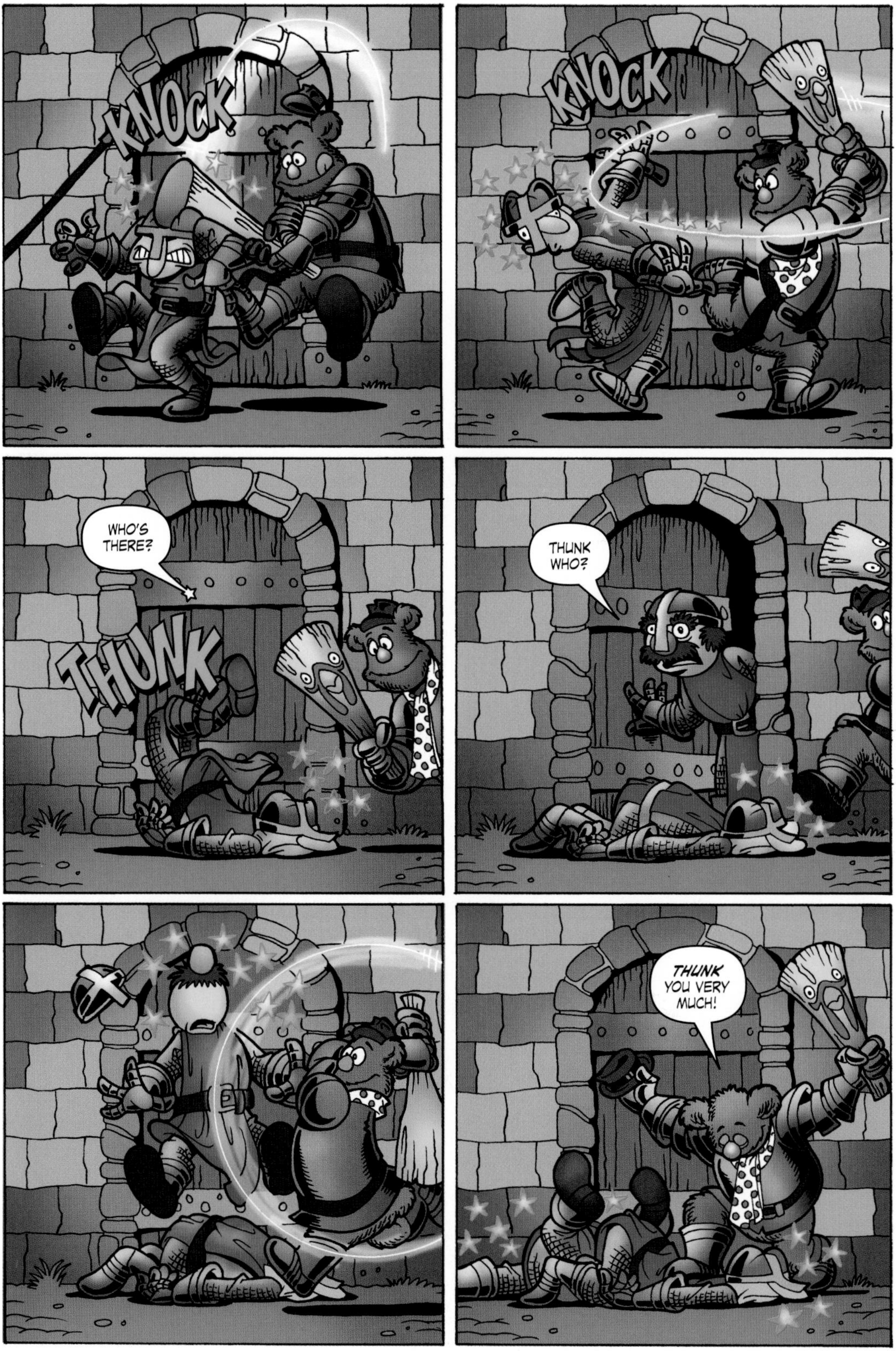
KNOCK
KNOCK
WHO'S THERE?
THUNK
THUNK WHO?
THUNK YOU VERY MUCH!

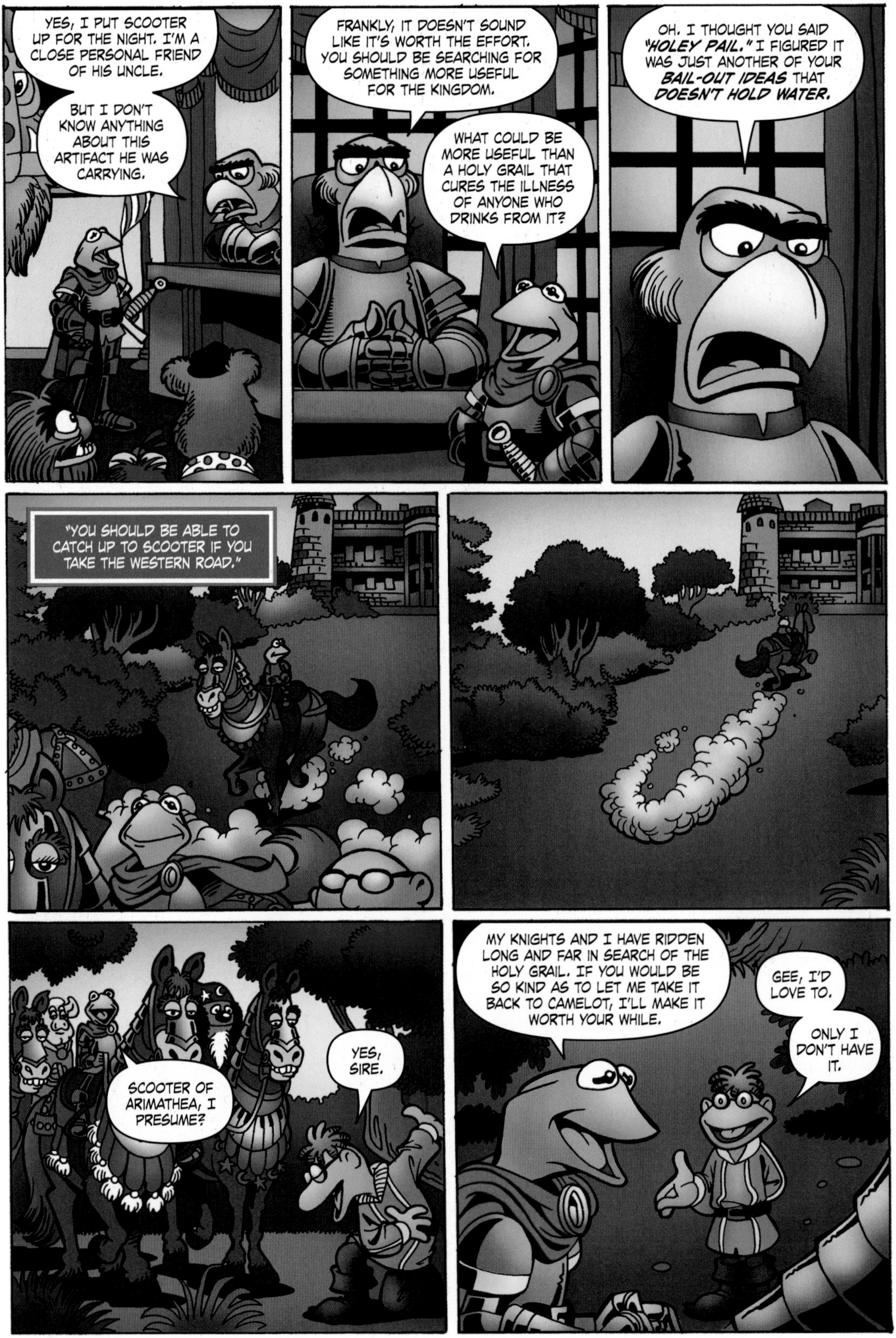
YES, I PUT SCOOTER UP FOR THE NIGHT. I'M A CLOSE PERSONAL FRIEND OF HIS UNCLE.
BUT I DON'T KNOW ANYTHING ABOUT THIS ARTIFACT HE WAS CARRYING.
FRANKLY, IT DOESN'T SOUND LIKE IT'S WORTH THE EFFORT. YOU SHOULD BE SEARCHING FOR SOMETHING MORE USEFUL FOR THE KINGDOM.
WHAT COULD BE MORE USEFUL THAN A HOLY GRAIL THAT CURES THE ILLNESS OF ANYONE WHO DRINKS FROM IT?
OH. I THOUGHT YOU SAID "HOLEY PAIL." I FIGURED IT WAS JUST ANOTHER OF YOUR BAIL-OUT IDEAS THAT DOESN'T HOLD WATER.
"YOU SHOULD BE ABLE TO CATCH UP TO SCOOTER IF YOU TAKE THE WESTERN ROAD."
SCOOTER OF ARIMATHEA, I PRESUME?
YES, SIRE.
MY KNIGHTS AND I HAVE RIDDEN LONG AND FAR IN SEARCH OF THE HOLY GRAIL. IF YOU WOULD BE SO KIND AS TO LET ME TAKE IT BACK TO CAMELOT, I'LL MAKE IT WORTH YOUR WHILE.
GEE, I'D LOVE TO.
ONLY I DON'T HAVE IT.

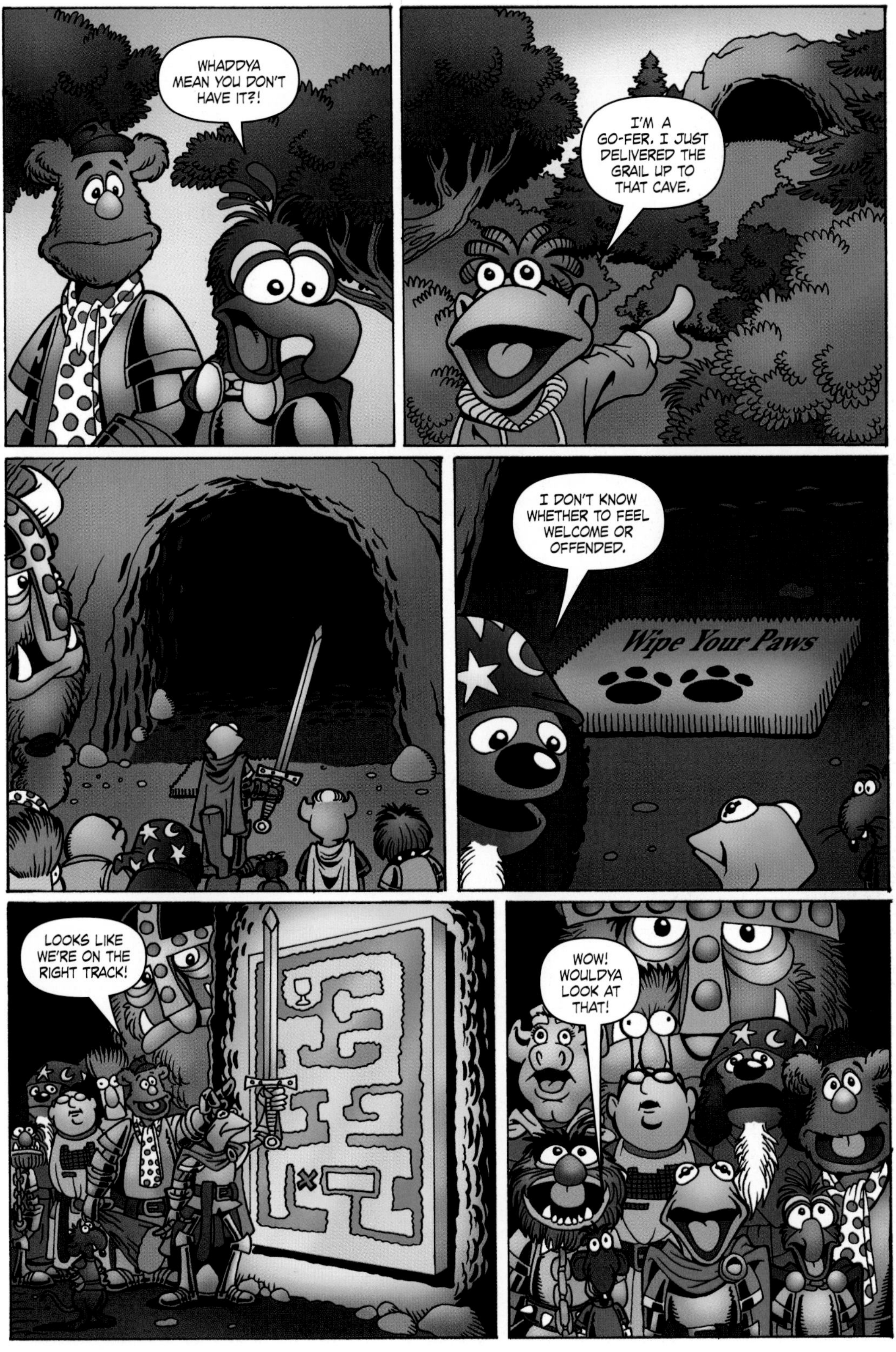
WHADDYA MEAN YOU DON'T HAVE IT?!
I'M A GO-FER. I JUST DELIVERED THE GRAIL UP TO THAT CAVE.
I DON'T KNOW WHETHER TO FEEL WELCOME OR OFFENDED.
Wipe Your Paws
LOOKS LIKE WE'RE ON THE RIGHT TRACK!
WOW! WOULDYA LOOK AT THAT!

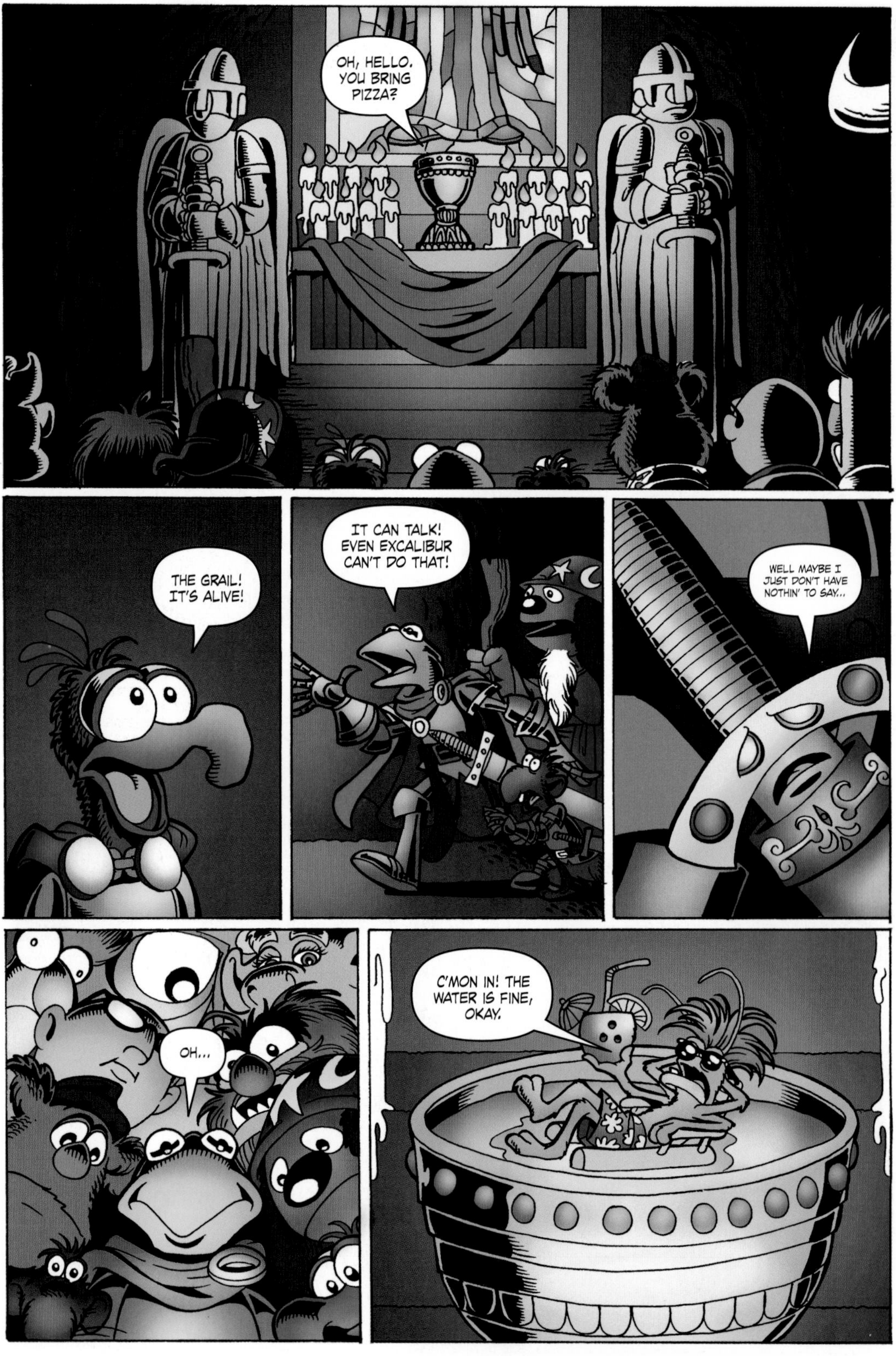
OH, HELLO. YOU BRING PIZZA?
THE GRAIL! IT'S ALIVE!
IT CAN TALK! EVEN EXCALIBUR CAN'T DO THAT!
WELL MAYBE I JUST DON'T HAVE NOTHIN' TO SAY...
OH...
C'MON IN! THE WATER IS FINE, OKAY.

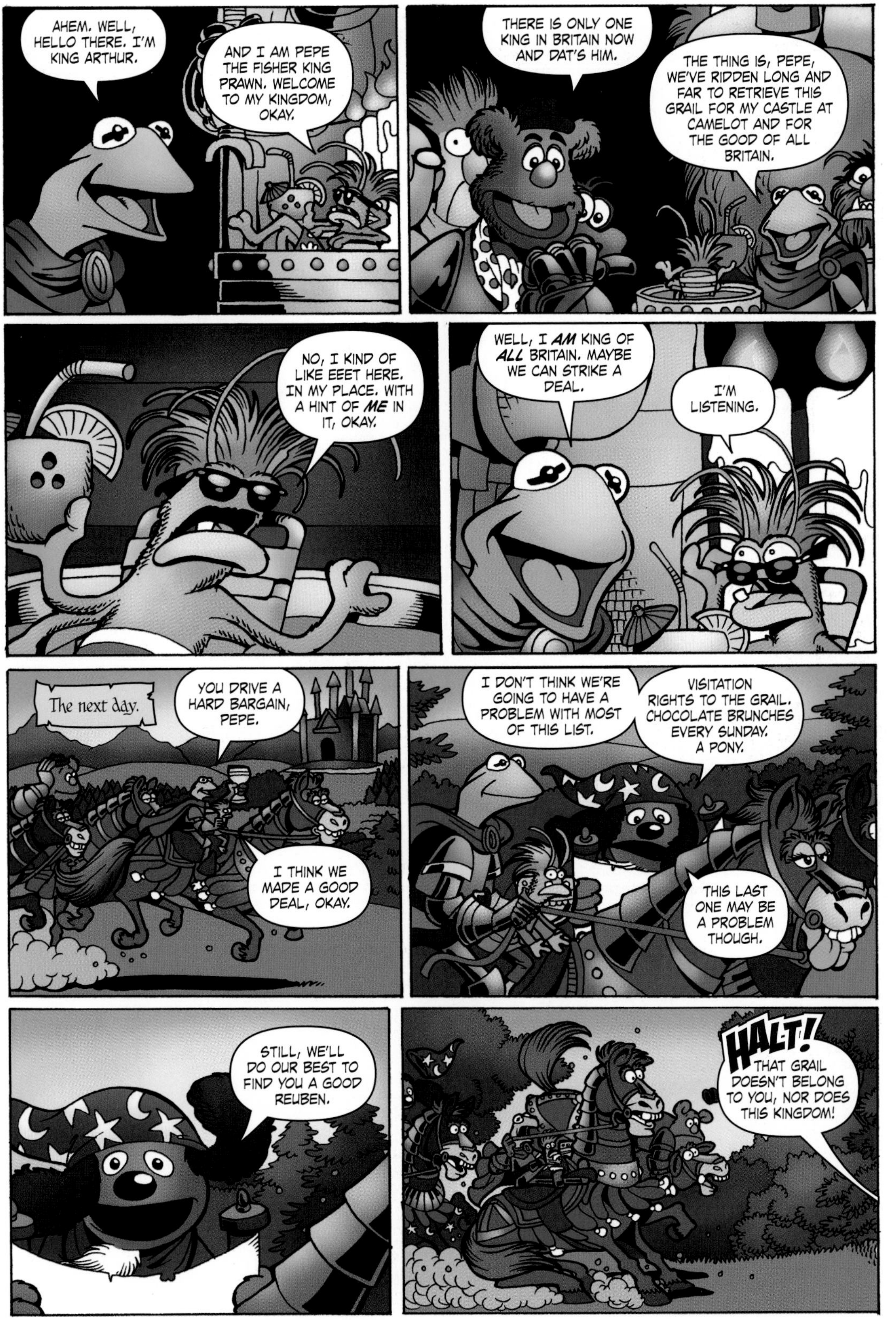
AHEM. WELL, HELLO THERE. I'M KING ARTHUR.
AND I AM PEPE THE FISHER KING PRAWN. WELCOME TO MY KINGDOM, OKAY.
THERE IS ONLY ONE KING IN BRITAIN NOW AND DAT'S HIM.
THE THING IS, PEPE, WE'VE RIDDEN LONG AND FAR TO RETRIEVE THIS GRAIL FOR MY CASTLE AT CAMELOT AND FOR THE GOOD OF ALL BRITAIN.
NO, I KIND OF LIKE EEET HERE. IN MY PLACE. WITH A HINT OF *ME* IN IT, OKAY.
WELL, I *AM* KING OF *ALL* BRITAIN. MAYBE WE CAN STRIKE A DEAL.
I'M LISTENING.
The next day.
YOU DRIVE A HARD BARGAIN, PEPE.
I THINK WE MADE A GOOD DEAL, OKAY.
I DON'T THINK WE'RE GOING TO HAVE A PROBLEM WITH MOST OF THIS LIST.
VISITATION RIGHTS TO THE GRAIL. CHOCOLATE BRUNCHES EVERY SUNDAY. A PONY.
THIS LAST ONE MAY BE A PROBLEM THOUGH.
STILL, WE'LL DO OUR BEST TO FIND YOU A GOOD REUBEN.
HALT!
THAT GRAIL DOESN'T BELONG TO YOU, NOR DOES THIS KINGDOM!

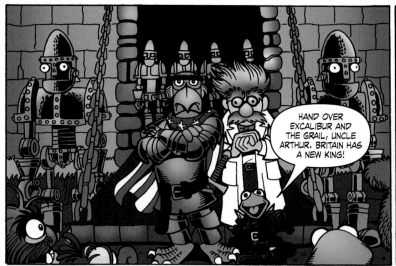

HAND OVER EXCALIBUR AND THE GRAIL, UNCLE ARTHUR. BRITAIN HAS A NEW KING!

MORDRED? WHY WOULD YOU TURN ON ME LIKE THIS?

I FINALLY FOUND SOMEONE WHO LISTENS TO ME. WHO TREATS ME LIKE A GROWN UP.

WHO DOESN'T KEEP ME IN THE BACKGROUND WITH TOKEN LINES AND THROWAWAY GAGS!

BUT WHERE DID YOU GET AN ARMY? ALL THE KNIGHTS IN BRITAIN ARE LOYAL TO ME NOW.

WHO NEEDS AN ARMY WHEN I'M FRIENDS WITH PROFESSOR PHINEAS A. PLOT?

THESE CLOCKWORK KNIGHTS ARE MY GREATEST PLOT DEVICES EVER!

Will Mordred overthrow King Arthur?

Can the Knights of the Round Table defeat an army of armored robots?

Is there a decent Reuben sandwich in all of Britain?

Find out next issue in: MUPPET KING ARTHUR #4: THE KING ARTHUR SHOW!

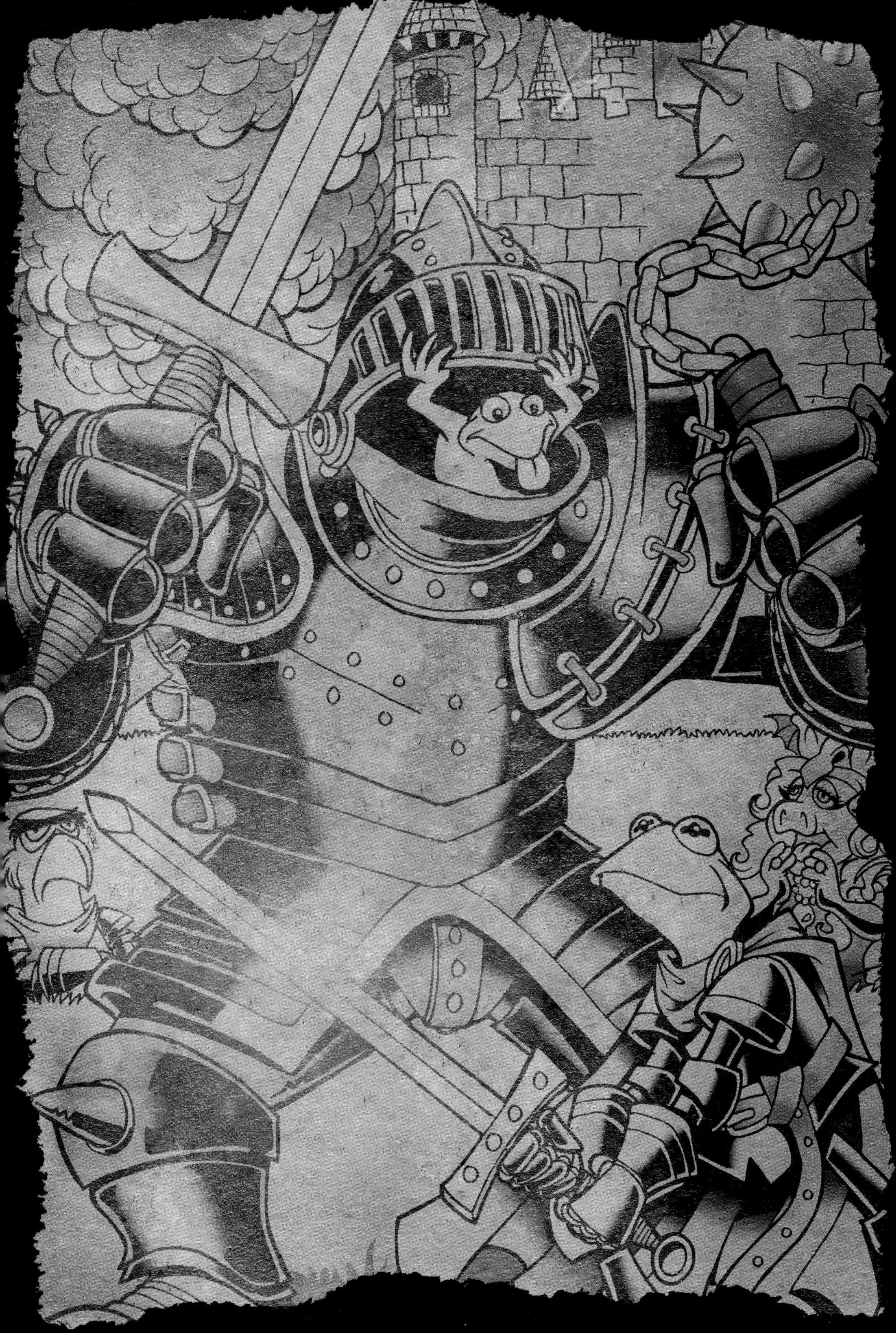

chapter four

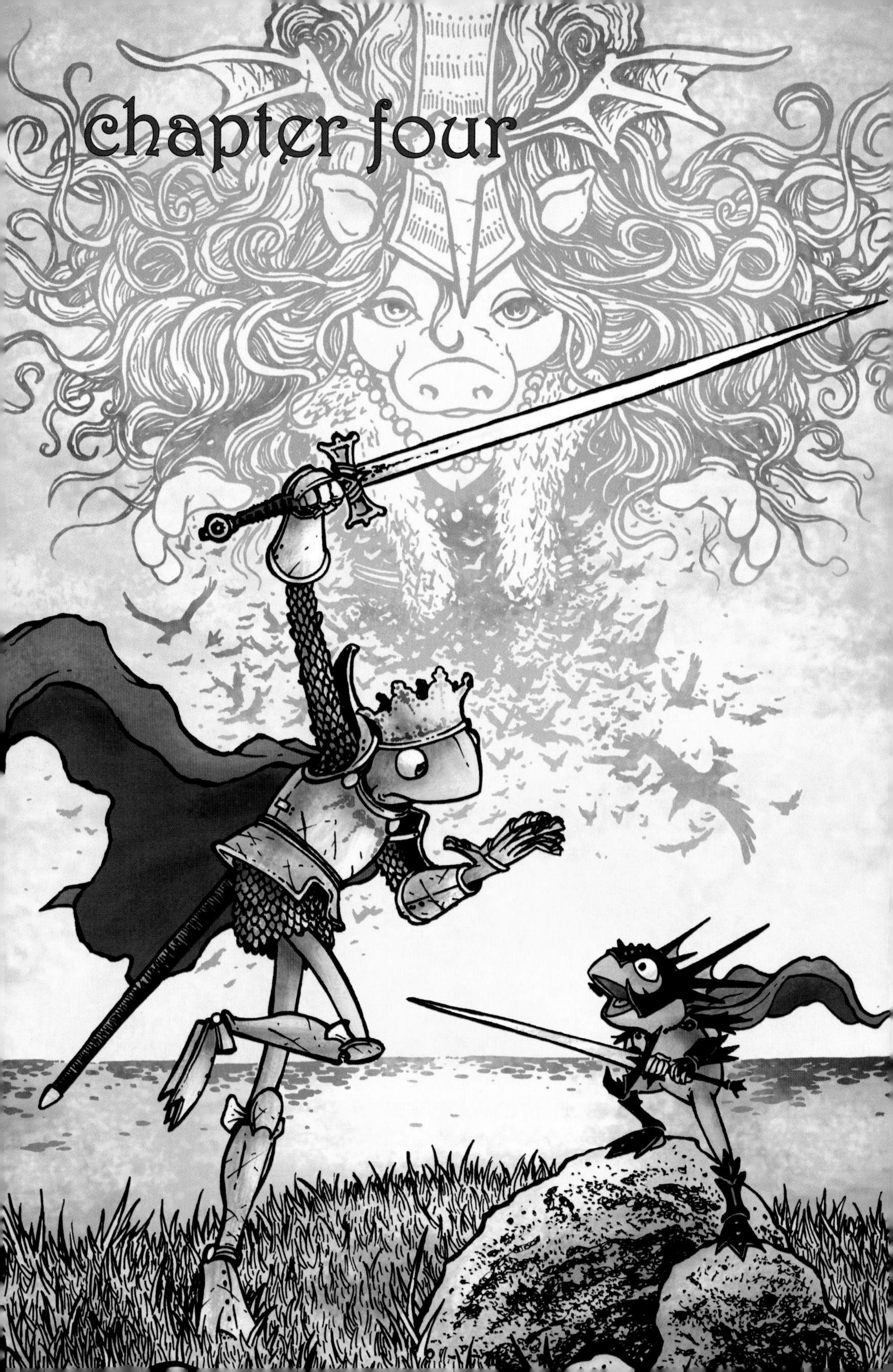

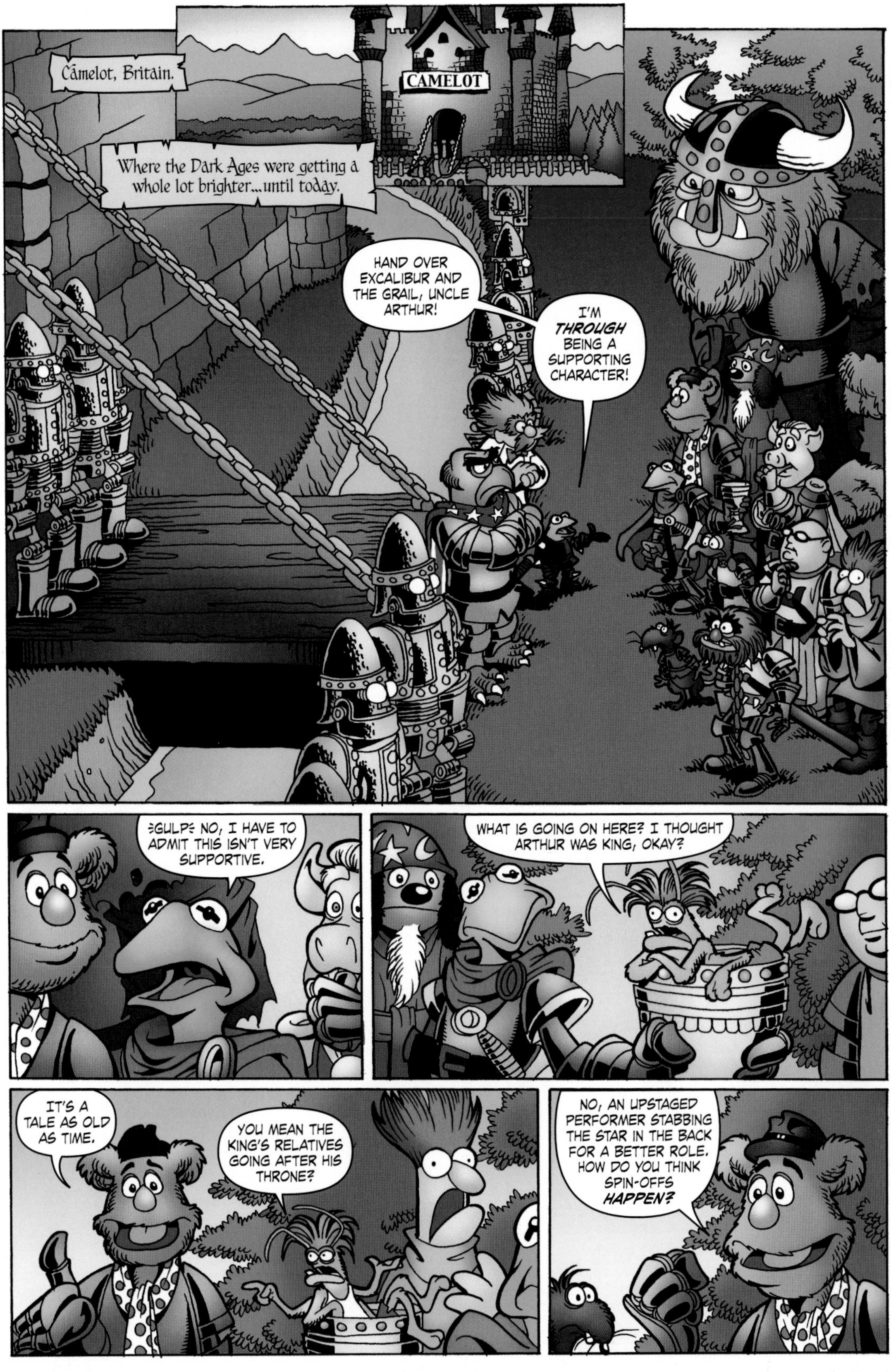
Câmelot, Britain.
CAMELOT
Where the Dark Ages were getting a whole lot brighter...until today.
HAND OVER EXCALIBUR AND THE GRAIL, UNCLE ARTHUR!
I'M *THROUGH* BEING A SUPPORTING CHARACTER!
=GULP= NO, I HAVE TO ADMIT THIS ISN'T VERY SUPPORTIVE.
WHAT IS GOING ON HERE? I THOUGHT ARTHUR WAS KING, OKAY?
IT'S A TALE AS OLD AS TIME.
YOU MEAN THE KING'S RELATIVES GOING AFTER HIS THRONE?
NO, AN UPSTAGED PERFORMER STABBING THE STAR IN THE BACK FOR A BETTER ROLE. HOW DO YOU THINK SPIN-OFFS *HAPPEN?*

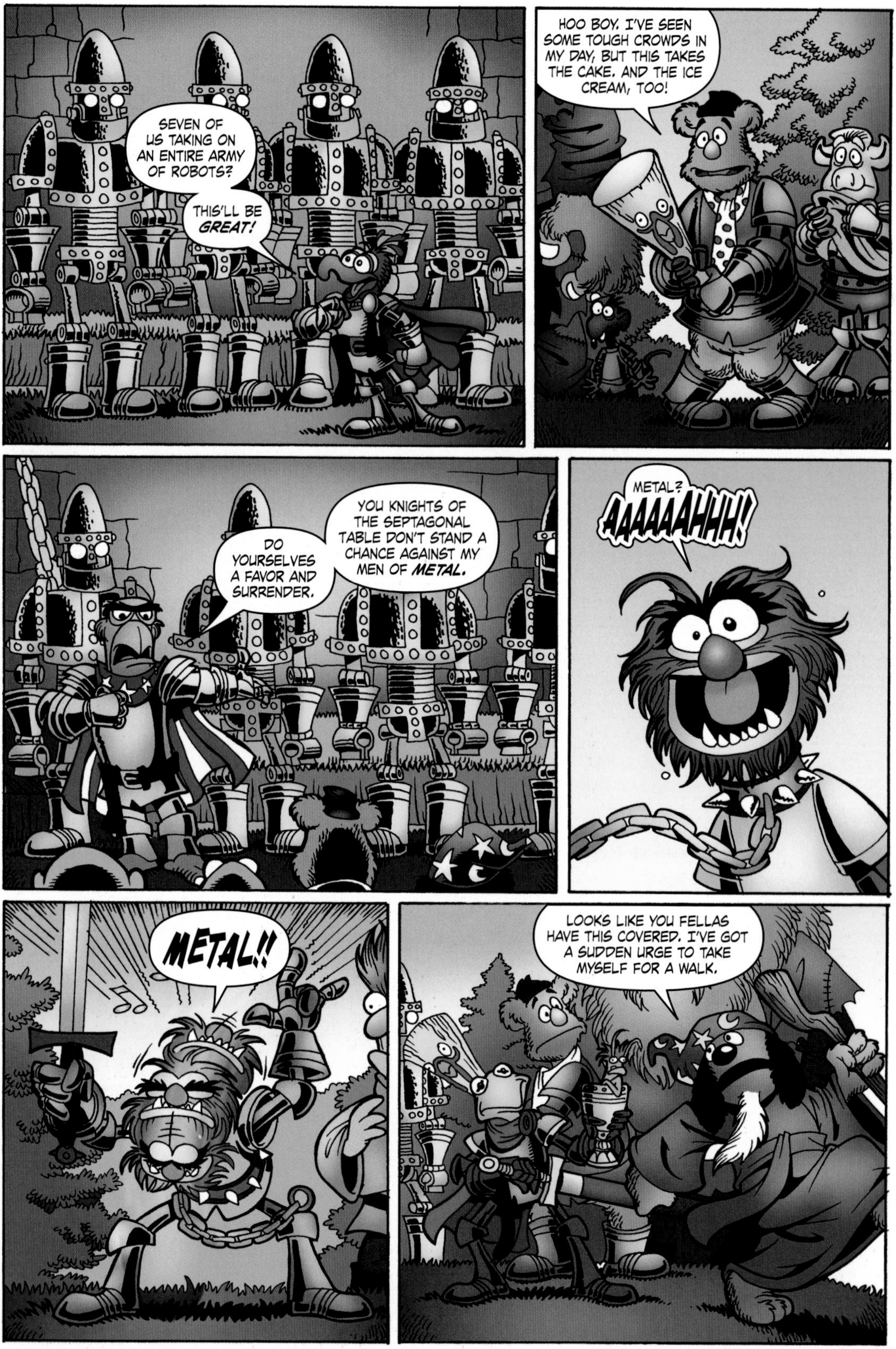

SEVEN OF US TAKING ON AN ENTIRE ARMY OF ROBOTS?
THIS'LL BE *GREAT!*
HOO BOY. I'VE SEEN SOME TOUGH CROWDS IN MY DAY, BUT THIS TAKES THE CAKE. AND THE ICE CREAM, TOO!
YOU KNIGHTS OF THE SEPTAGONAL TABLE DON'T STAND A CHANCE AGAINST MY MEN OF *METAL.*
DO YOURSELVES A FAVOR AND SURRENDER.
METAL?
AAAAAAHHH!
METAL!!
LOOKS LIKE YOU FELLAS HAVE THIS COVERED. I'VE GOT A SUDDEN URGE TO TAKE MYSELF FOR A WALK.

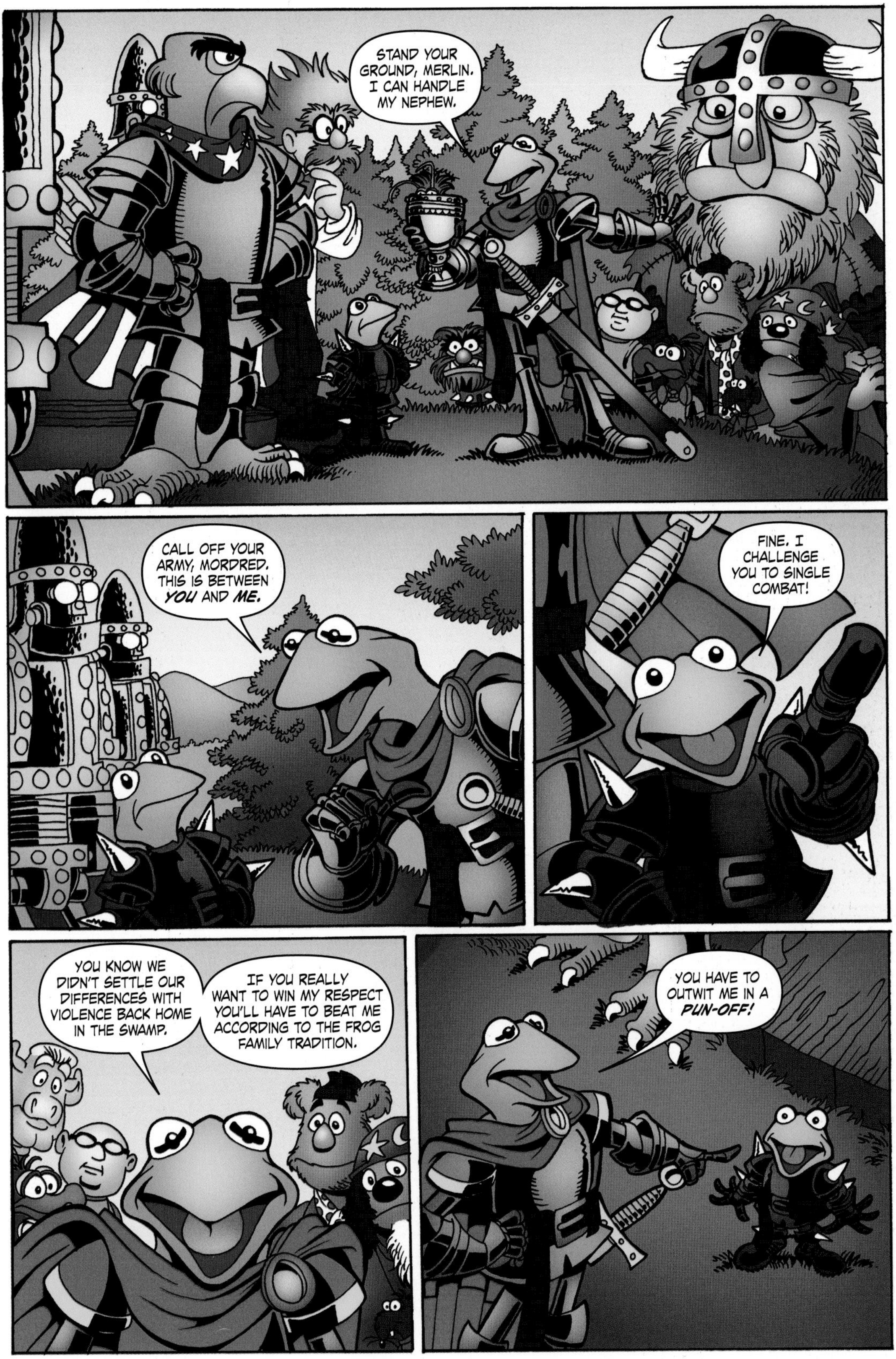
STAND YOUR GROUND, MERLIN. I CAN HANDLE MY NEPHEW.
CALL OFF YOUR ARMY, MORDRED. THIS IS BETWEEN *YOU* AND *ME*.
FINE. I CHALLENGE YOU TO SINGLE COMBAT!
YOU KNOW WE DIDN'T SETTLE OUR DIFFERENCES WITH VIOLENCE BACK HOME IN THE SWAMP.
IF YOU REALLY WANT TO WIN MY RESPECT YOU'LL HAVE TO BEAT ME ACCORDING TO THE FROG FAMILY TRADITION.
YOU HAVE TO OUTWIT ME IN A *PUN-OFF!*

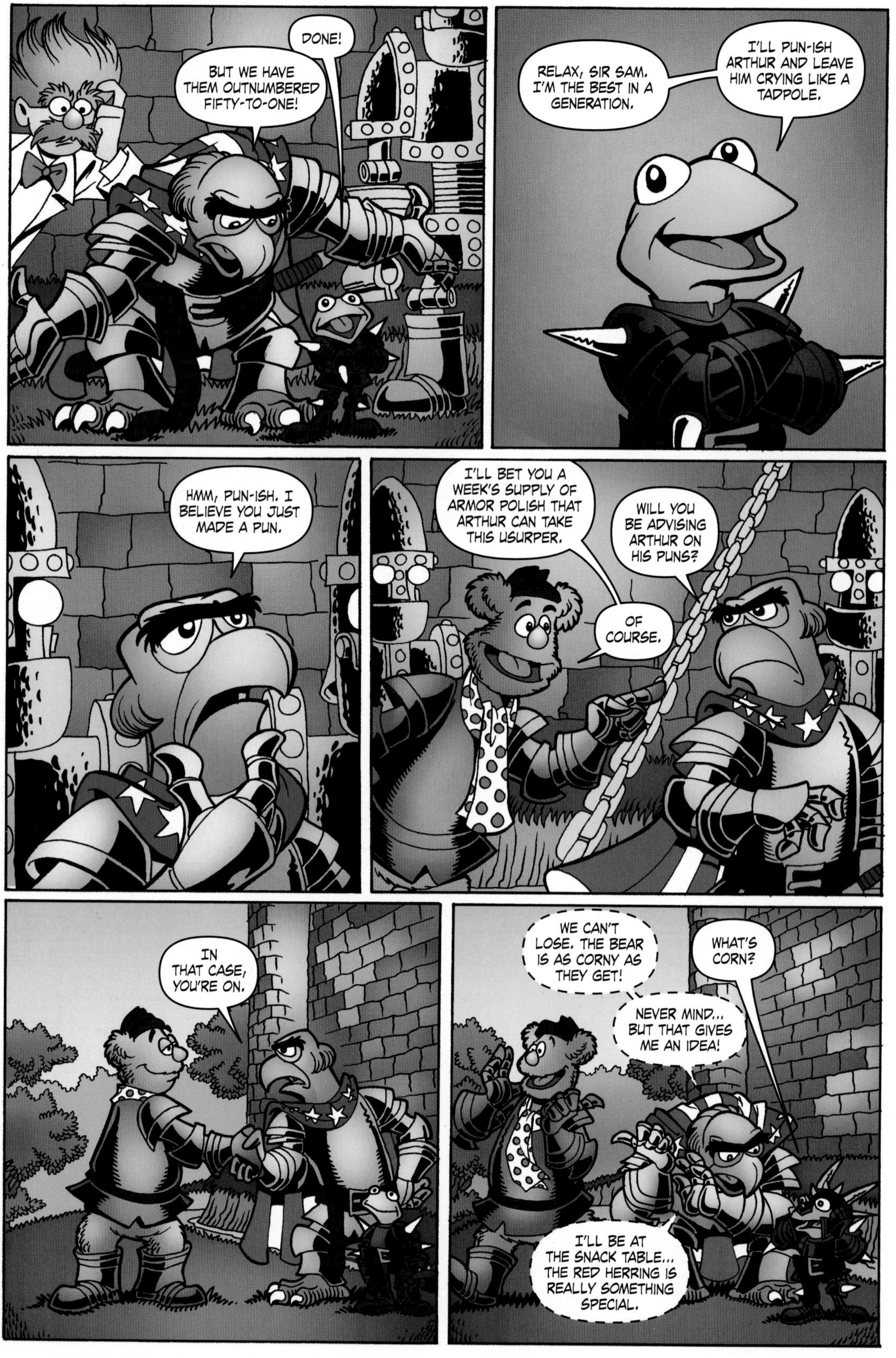
BUT WE HAVE THEM OUTNUMBERED FIFTY-TO-ONE!
DONE!
RELAX, SIR SAM. I'M THE BEST IN A GENERATION.
I'LL PUN-ISH ARTHUR AND LEAVE HIM CRYING LIKE A TADPOLE.
HMM, PUN-ISH. I BELIEVE YOU JUST MADE A PUN.
I'LL BET YOU A WEEK'S SUPPLY OF ARMOR POLISH THAT ARTHUR CAN TAKE THIS USURPER.
WILL YOU BE ADVISING ARTHUR ON HIS PUNS?
OF COURSE.
IN THAT CASE, YOU'RE ON.
WE CAN'T LOSE. THE BEAR IS AS CORNY AS THEY GET!
WHAT'S CORN?
NEVER MIND... BUT THAT GIVES ME AN IDEA!
I'LL BE AT THE SNACK TABLE... THE RED HERRING IS REALLY SOMETHING SPECIAL.

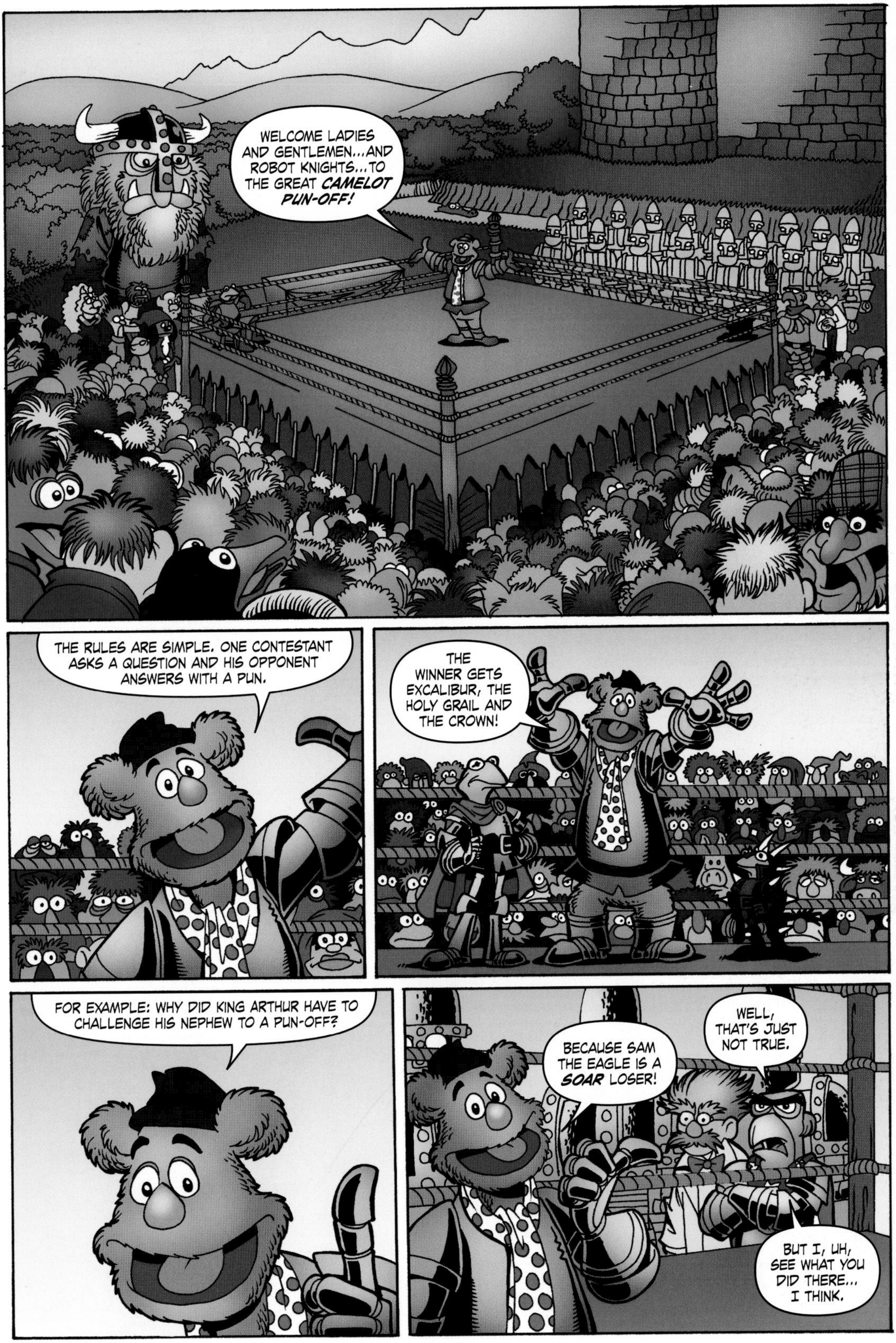
WELCOME LADIES AND GENTLEMEN...AND ROBOT KNIGHTS...TO THE GREAT *CAMELOT PUN-OFF!*
THE RULES ARE SIMPLE. ONE CONTESTANT ASKS A QUESTION AND HIS OPPONENT ANSWERS WITH A PUN.
THE WINNER GETS EXCALIBUR, THE HOLY GRAIL AND THE CROWN!
FOR EXAMPLE: WHY DID KING ARTHUR HAVE TO CHALLENGE HIS NEPHEW TO A PUN-OFF?
BECAUSE SAM THE EAGLE IS A ***SOAR*** LOSER!
WELL, THAT'S JUST NOT TRUE.
BUT I, UH, SEE WHAT YOU DID THERE... I THINK.

BWOCK BOCK. BWOCK BOCK BWOCK BOCK. BWOCK BOCK BWOCK BOCK BAWKA!

OH, HOW NICE OF GUINEVERE TO COME SUPPORT ME.

SHE *DID* SAY SOMETHING NICE, RIGHT?

≑SIGH≑ SHE SURE DID.

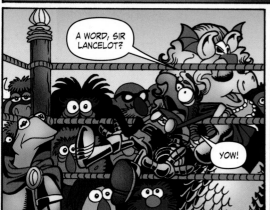

A WORD, SIR LANCELOT?

YOW!

LOOK, SHRIMP. YOU LIKE *HER* AND I LIKE *HIM*.

PRAWN!

OH. YOU MEANT HIM.

WHY DON'T WE WORK TOGETHER TO SPLIT THEM UP?

BUT WE'D NEED A REALLY DEVIOUS SCHEME TO DO THAT...

WHERE WILL WE EVER FIND SOMEONE DEVIOUS ENOUGH TO COME UP WITH SUCH A PLAN...AS IF I HAD TO ASK.

LEAVE IT TO ME.

I'LL SKIP THE DETAILS. I WATCHED NINETY MINUTES OF BROTHER CAVIL TELLING A BUNCH OF SPACE ROBOTS *HIS* PLAN AND IT JUST WASN'T WORTH IT.

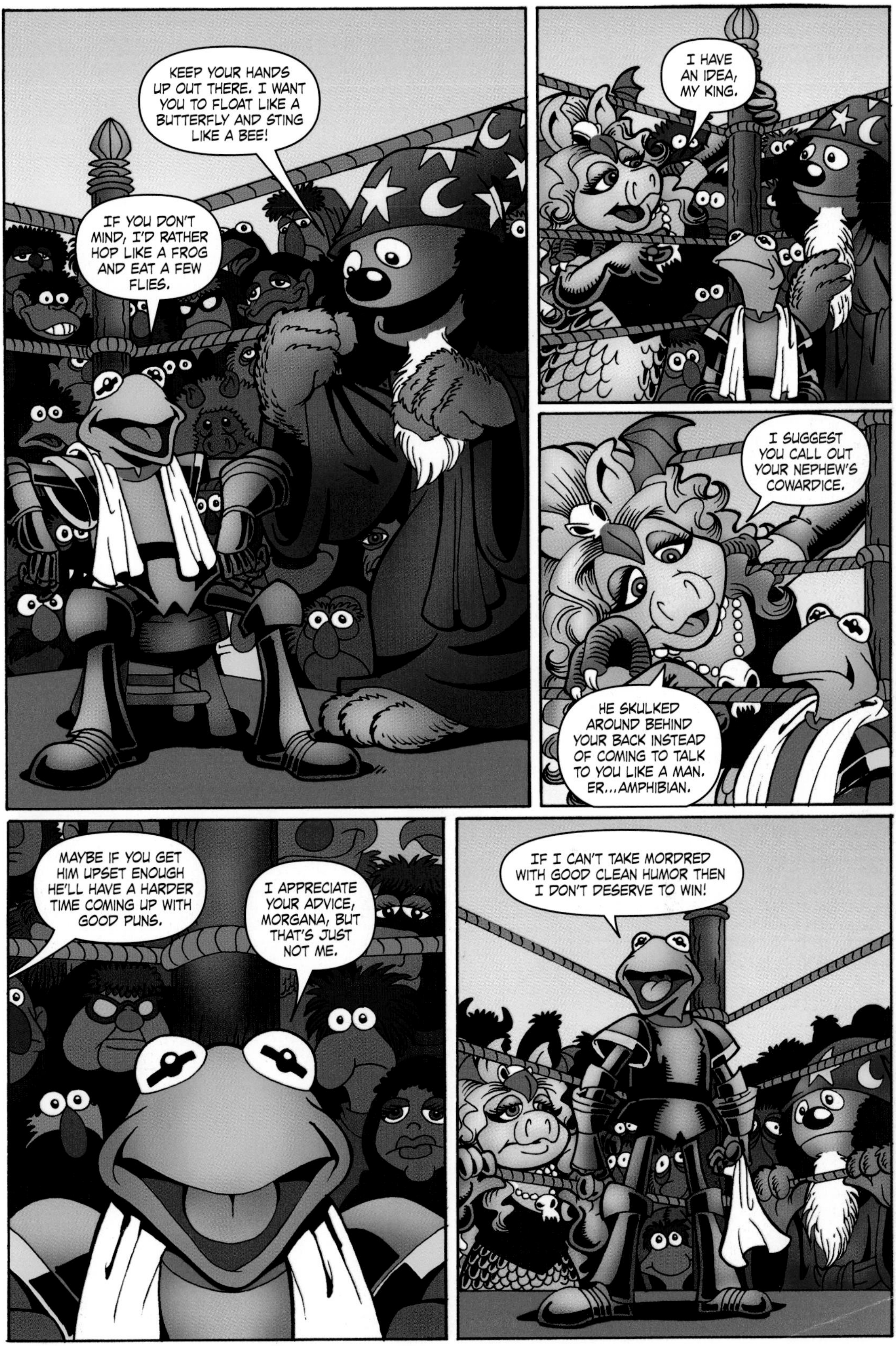
KEEP YOUR HANDS UP OUT THERE. I WANT YOU TO FLOAT LIKE A BUTTERFLY AND STING LIKE A BEE!
IF YOU DON'T MIND, I'D RATHER HOP LIKE A FROG AND EAT A FEW FLIES.
I HAVE AN IDEA, MY KING.
I SUGGEST YOU CALL OUT YOUR NEPHEW'S COWARDICE.
HE SKULKED AROUND BEHIND YOUR BACK INSTEAD OF COMING TO TALK TO YOU LIKE A MAN. ER...AMPHIBIAN.
MAYBE IF YOU GET HIM UPSET ENOUGH HE'LL HAVE A HARDER TIME COMING UP WITH GOOD PUNS.
I APPRECIATE YOUR ADVICE, MORGANA, BUT THAT'S JUST NOT ME.
IF I CAN'T TAKE MORDRED WITH GOOD CLEAN HUMOR THEN I DON'T DESERVE TO WIN!

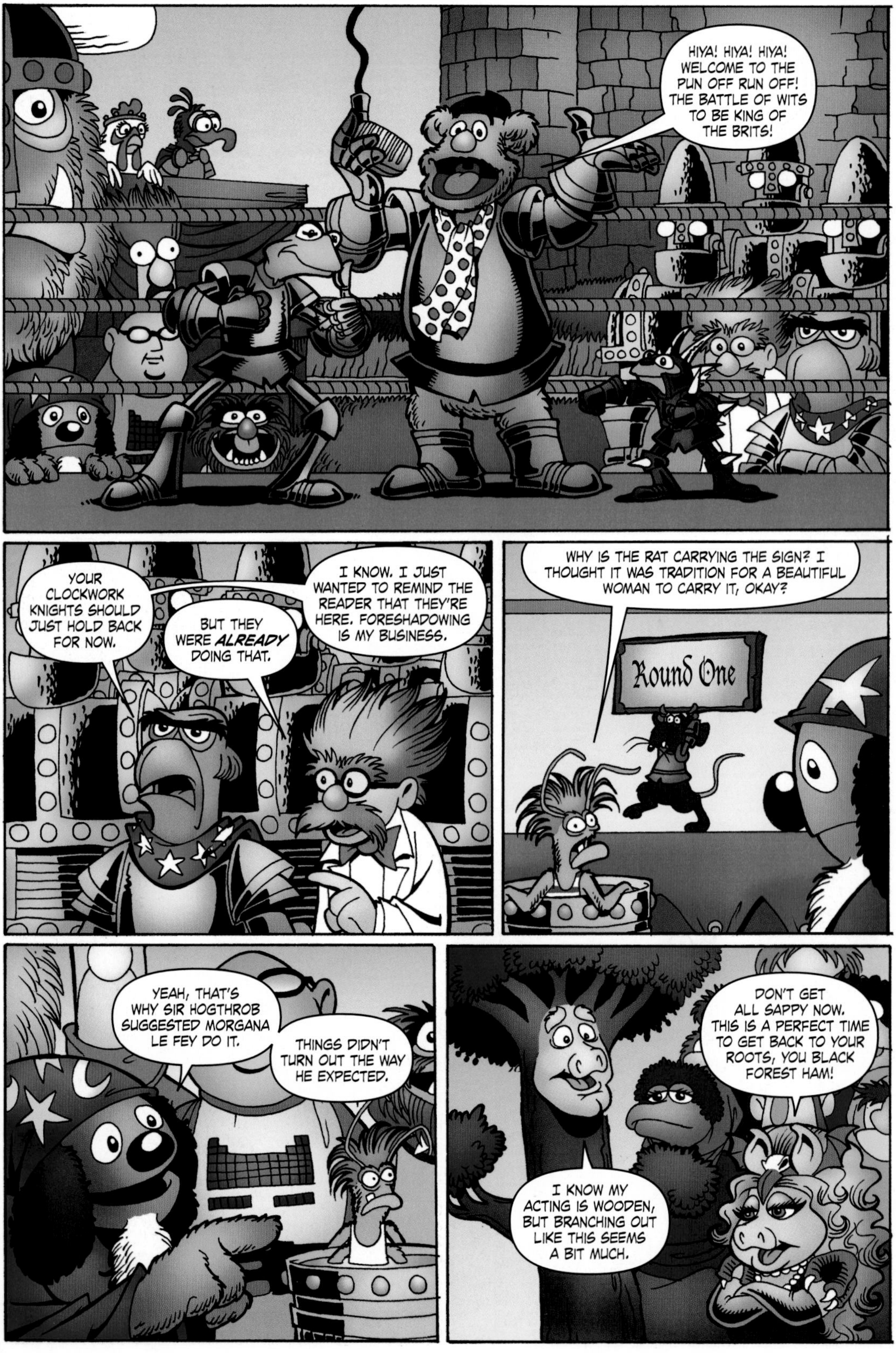
HIYA! HIYA! HIYA! WELCOME TO THE PUN OFF RUN OFF! THE BATTLE OF WITS TO BE KING OF THE BRITS!
YOUR CLOCKWORK KNIGHTS SHOULD JUST HOLD BACK FOR NOW.
BUT THEY WERE ***ALREADY*** DOING THAT.
I KNOW. I JUST WANTED TO REMIND THE READER THAT THEY'RE HERE. FORESHADOWING IS MY BUSINESS.
WHY IS THE RAT CARRYING THE SIGN? I THOUGHT IT WAS TRADITION FOR A BEAUTIFUL WOMAN TO CARRY IT, OKAY?
Round One
YEAH, THAT'S WHY SIR HOGTHROB SUGGESTED MORGANA LE FEY DO IT.
THINGS DIDN'T TURN OUT THE WAY HE EXPECTED.
I KNOW MY ACTING IS WOODEN, BUT BRANCHING OUT LIKE THIS SEEMS A BIT MUCH.
DON'T GET ALL SAPPY NOW. THIS IS A PERFECT TIME TO GET BACK TO YOUR ROOTS, YOU BLACK FOREST HAM!

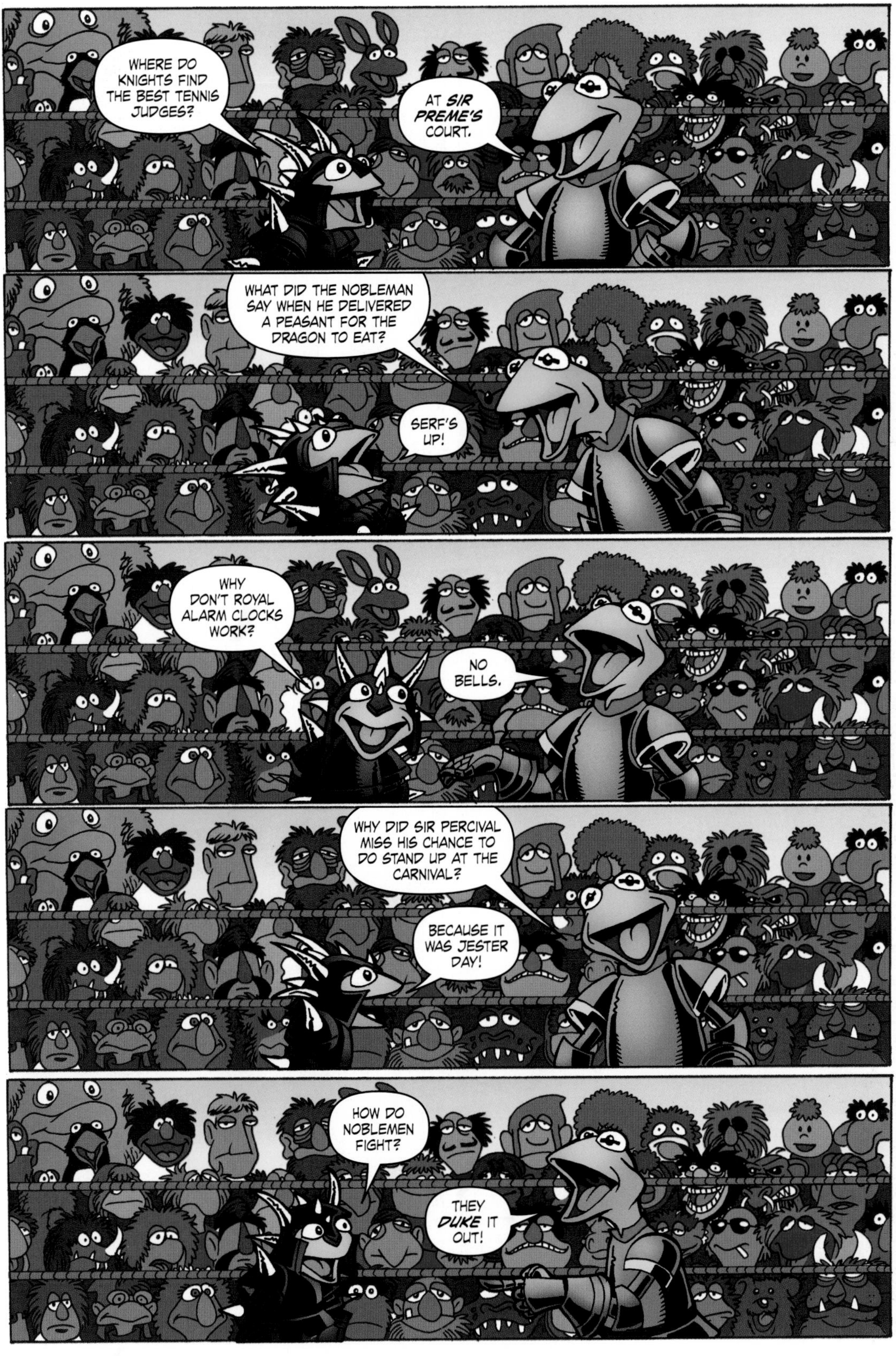
WHERE DO KNIGHTS FIND THE BEST TENNIS JUDGES?
AT *SIR PREME'S* COURT.
WHAT DID THE NOBLEMAN SAY WHEN HE DELIVERED A PEASANT FOR THE DRAGON TO EAT?
SERF'S UP!
WHY DON'T ROYAL ALARM CLOCKS WORK?
NO BELLS.
WHY DID SIR PERCIVAL MISS HIS CHANCE TO DO STAND UP AT THE CARNIVAL?
BECAUSE IT WAS JESTER DAY!
HOW DO NOBLEMEN FIGHT?
THEY *DUKE* IT OUT!

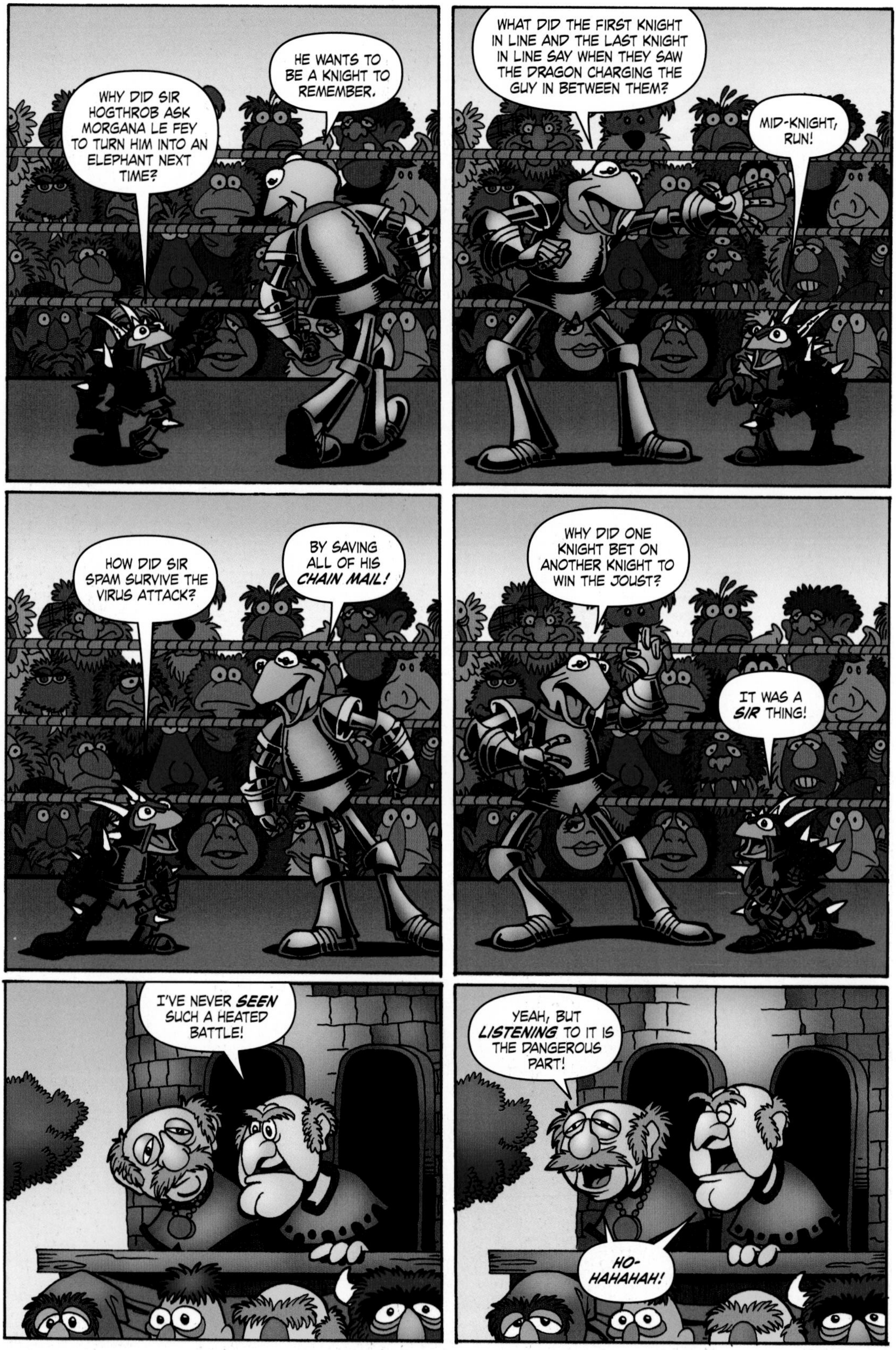
WHY DID SIR HOGTHROB ASK MORGANA LE FEY TO TURN HIM INTO AN ELEPHANT NEXT TIME?
HE WANTS TO BE A KNIGHT TO REMEMBER.
WHAT DID THE FIRST KNIGHT IN LINE AND THE LAST KNIGHT IN LINE SAY WHEN THEY SAW THE DRAGON CHARGING THE GUY IN BETWEEN THEM?
MID-KNIGHT, RUN!
HOW DID SIR SPAM SURVIVE THE VIRUS ATTACK?
BY SAVING ALL OF HIS CHAIN MAIL!
WHY DID ONE KNIGHT BET ON ANOTHER KNIGHT TO WIN THE JOUST?
IT WAS A SIR THING!
I'VE NEVER SEEN SUCH A HEATED BATTLE!
YEAH, BUT LISTENING TO IT IS THE DANGEROUS PART!
HO-HAHAHAH!

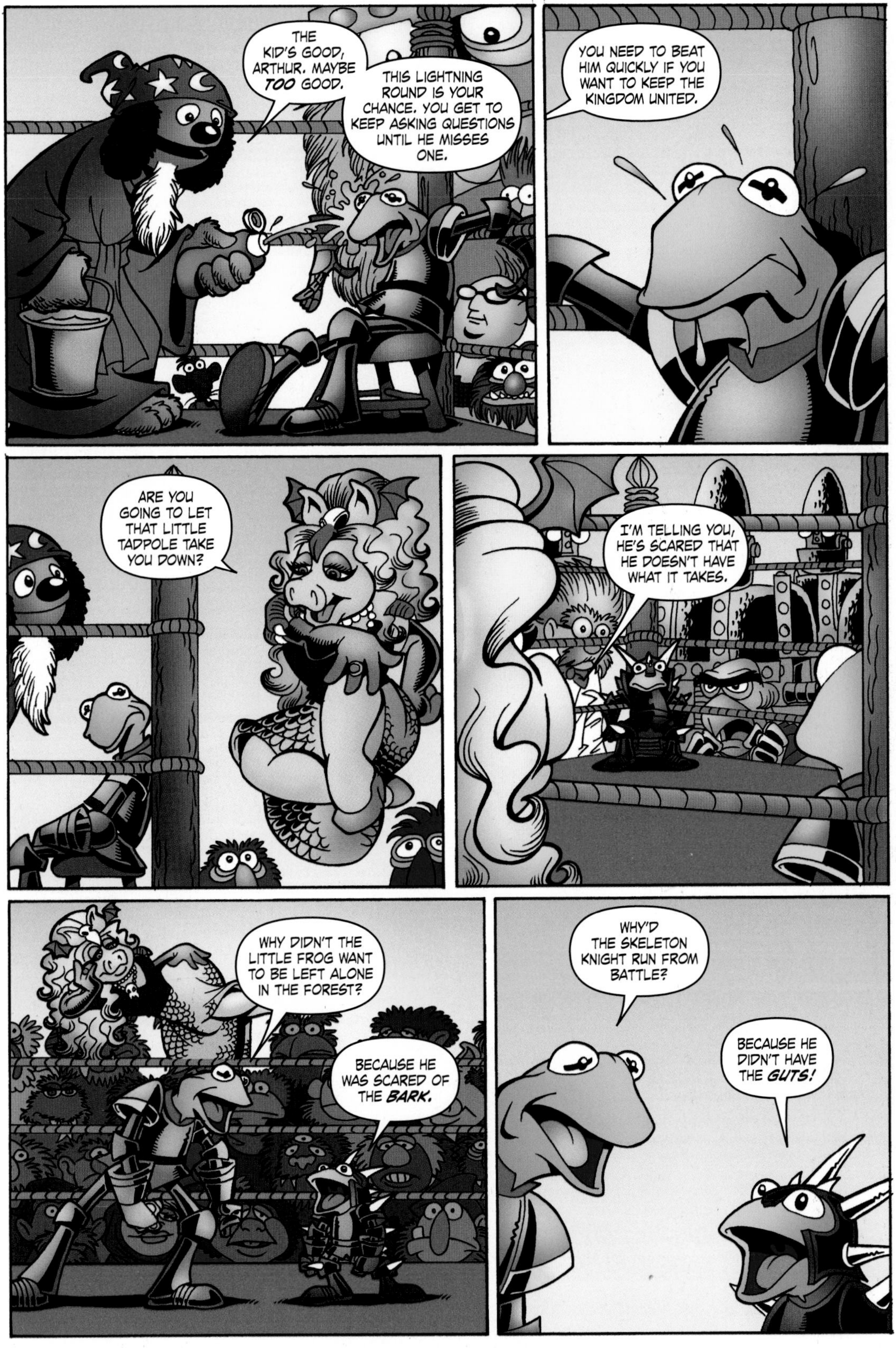
THE KID'S GOOD, ARTHUR. MAYBE TOO GOOD.
THIS LIGHTNING ROUND IS YOUR CHANCE. YOU GET TO KEEP ASKING QUESTIONS UNTIL HE MISSES ONE.
YOU NEED TO BEAT HIM QUICKLY IF YOU WANT TO KEEP THE KINGDOM UNITED.
ARE YOU GOING TO LET THAT LITTLE TADPOLE TAKE YOU DOWN?
I'M TELLING YOU, HE'S SCARED THAT HE DOESN'T HAVE WHAT IT TAKES.
WHY DIDN'T THE LITTLE FROG WANT TO BE LEFT ALONE IN THE FOREST?
BECAUSE HE WAS SCARED OF THE BARK.
WHY'D THE SKELETON KNIGHT RUN FROM BATTLE?
BECAUSE HE DIDN'T HAVE THE GUTS!

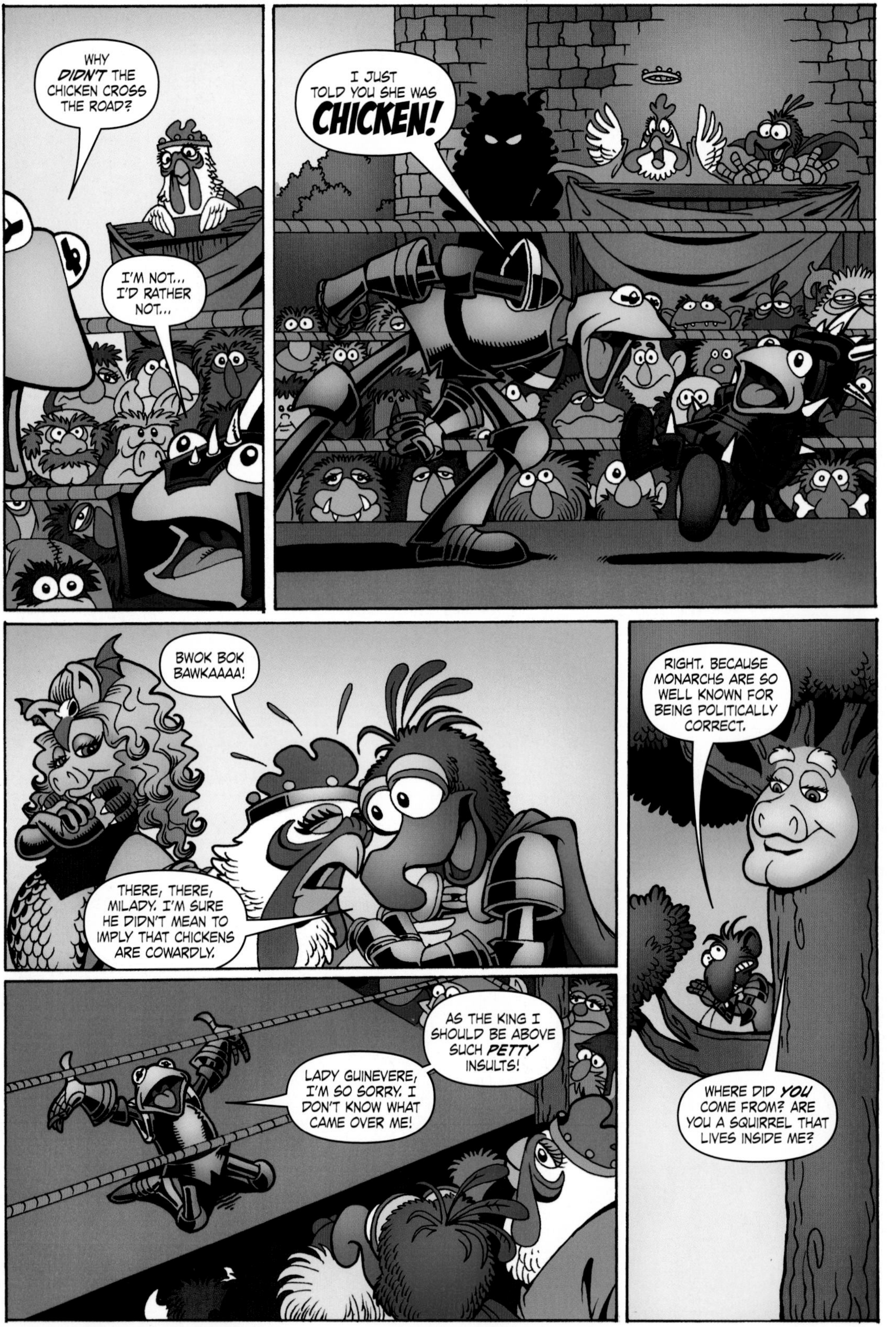
WHY *DIDN'T* THE CHICKEN CROSS THE ROAD?
I'M NOT... I'D RATHER NOT...
I JUST TOLD YOU SHE WAS **CHICKEN!**
BWOK BOK BAWKAAAA!
THERE, THERE, MILADY. I'M SURE HE DIDN'T MEAN TO IMPLY THAT CHICKENS ARE COWARDLY.
RIGHT. BECAUSE MONARCHS ARE SO WELL KNOWN FOR BEING POLITICALLY CORRECT.
AS THE KING I SHOULD BE ABOVE SUCH *PETTY* INSULTS!
LADY GUINEVERE, I'M SO SORRY. I DON'T KNOW WHAT CAME OVER ME!
WHERE DID *YOU* COME FROM? ARE YOU A SQUIRREL THAT LIVES INSIDE ME?

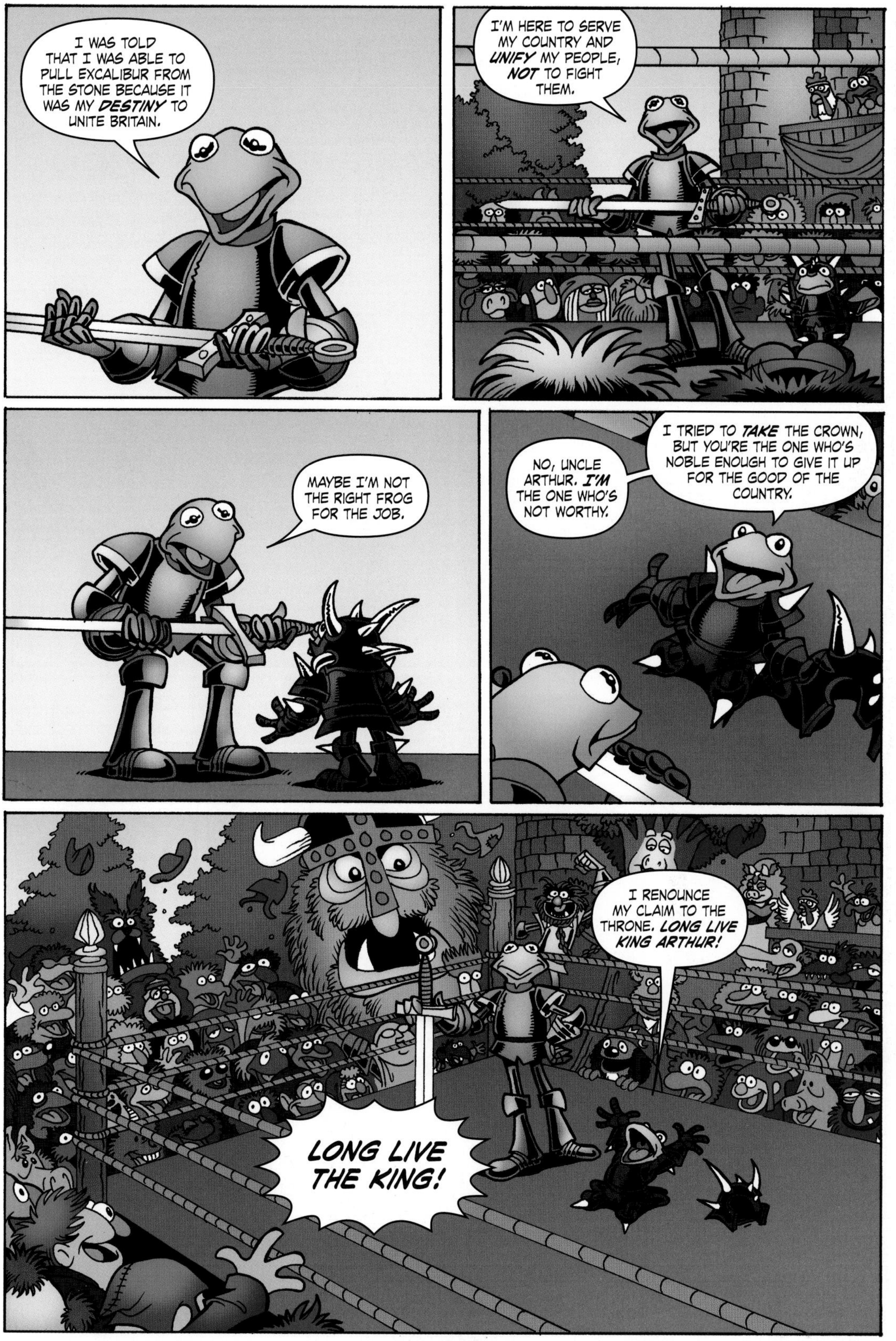
I WAS TOLD THAT I WAS ABLE TO PULL EXCALIBUR FROM THE STONE BECAUSE IT WAS MY *DESTINY* TO UNITE BRITAIN.
I'M HERE TO SERVE MY COUNTRY AND *UNIFY* MY PEOPLE, *NOT* TO FIGHT THEM.
MAYBE I'M NOT THE RIGHT FROG FOR THE JOB.
NO, UNCLE ARTHUR. *I'M* THE ONE WHO'S NOT WORTHY.
I TRIED TO *TAKE* THE CROWN, BUT YOU'RE THE ONE WHO'S NOBLE ENOUGH TO GIVE IT UP FOR THE GOOD OF THE COUNTRY.
I RENOUNCE MY CLAIM TO THE THRONE. *LONG LIVE KING ARTHUR!*
LONG LIVE THE KING!

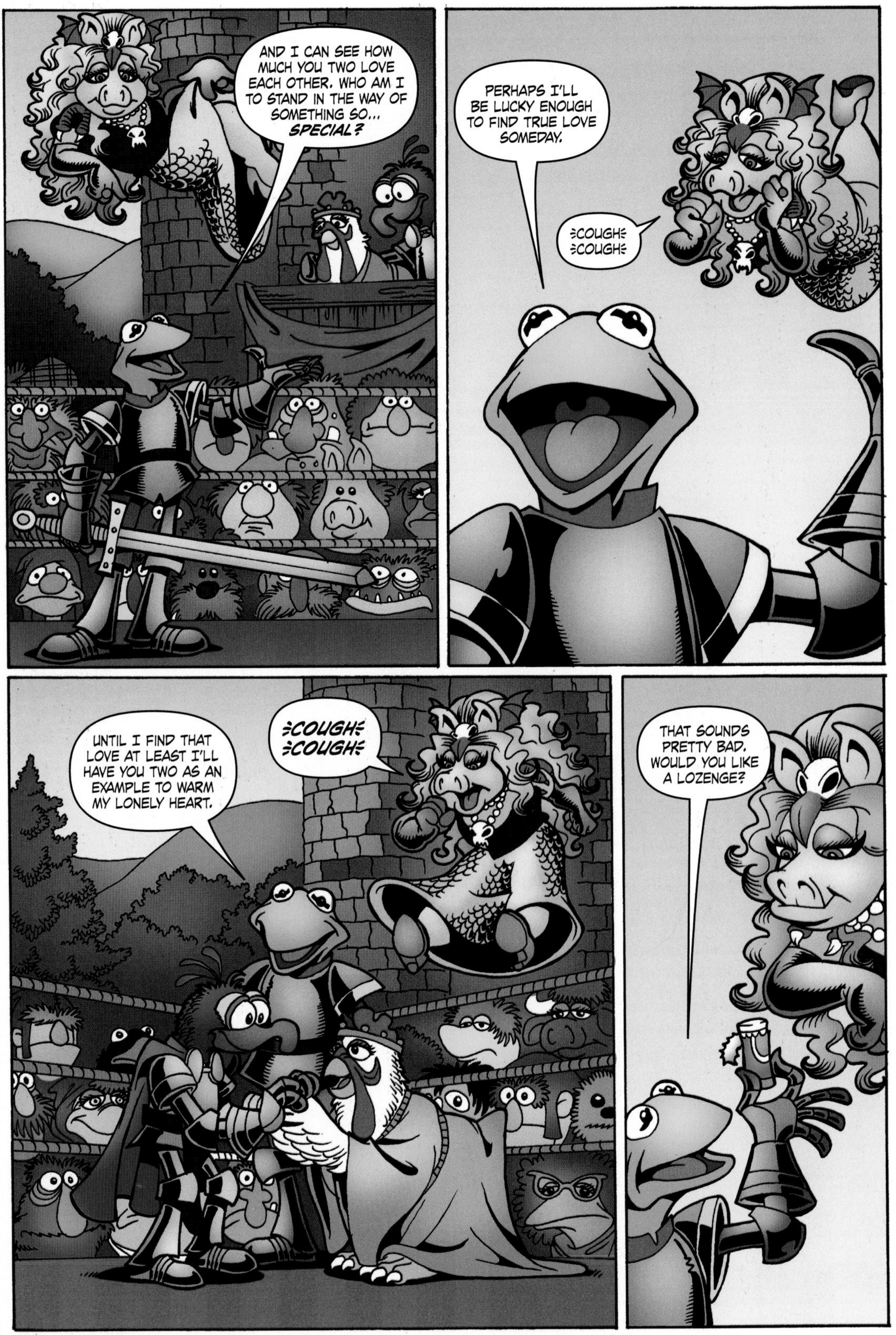
AND I CAN SEE HOW MUCH YOU TWO LOVE EACH OTHER. WHO AM I TO STAND IN THE WAY OF SOMETHING SO... SPECIAL?
PERHAPS I'LL BE LUCKY ENOUGH TO FIND TRUE LOVE SOMEDAY.
COUGH COUGH
UNTIL I FIND THAT LOVE AT LEAST I'LL HAVE YOU TWO AS AN EXAMPLE TO WARM MY LONELY HEART.
COUGH COUGH
THAT SOUNDS PRETTY BAD. WOULD YOU LIKE A LOZENGE?

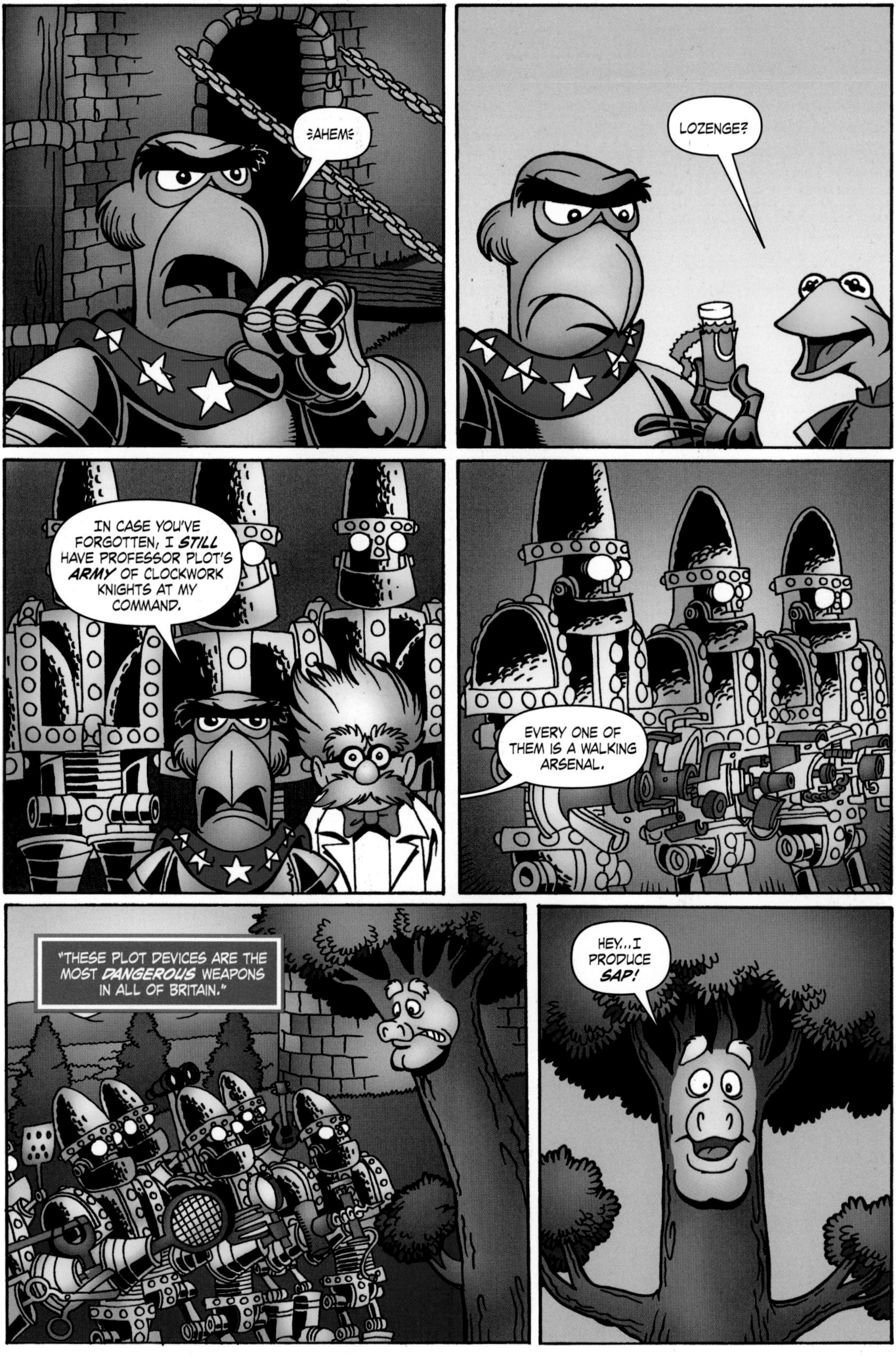

AHEM
LOZENGE?
IN CASE YOU'VE FORGOTTEN, I *STILL* HAVE PROFESSOR PLOT'S *ARMY* OF CLOCKWORK KNIGHTS AT MY COMMAND.
EVERY ONE OF THEM IS A WALKING ARSENAL.
"THESE PLOT DEVICES ARE THE MOST *DANGEROUS* WEAPONS IN ALL OF BRITAIN."
HEY...I PRODUCE *SAP!*

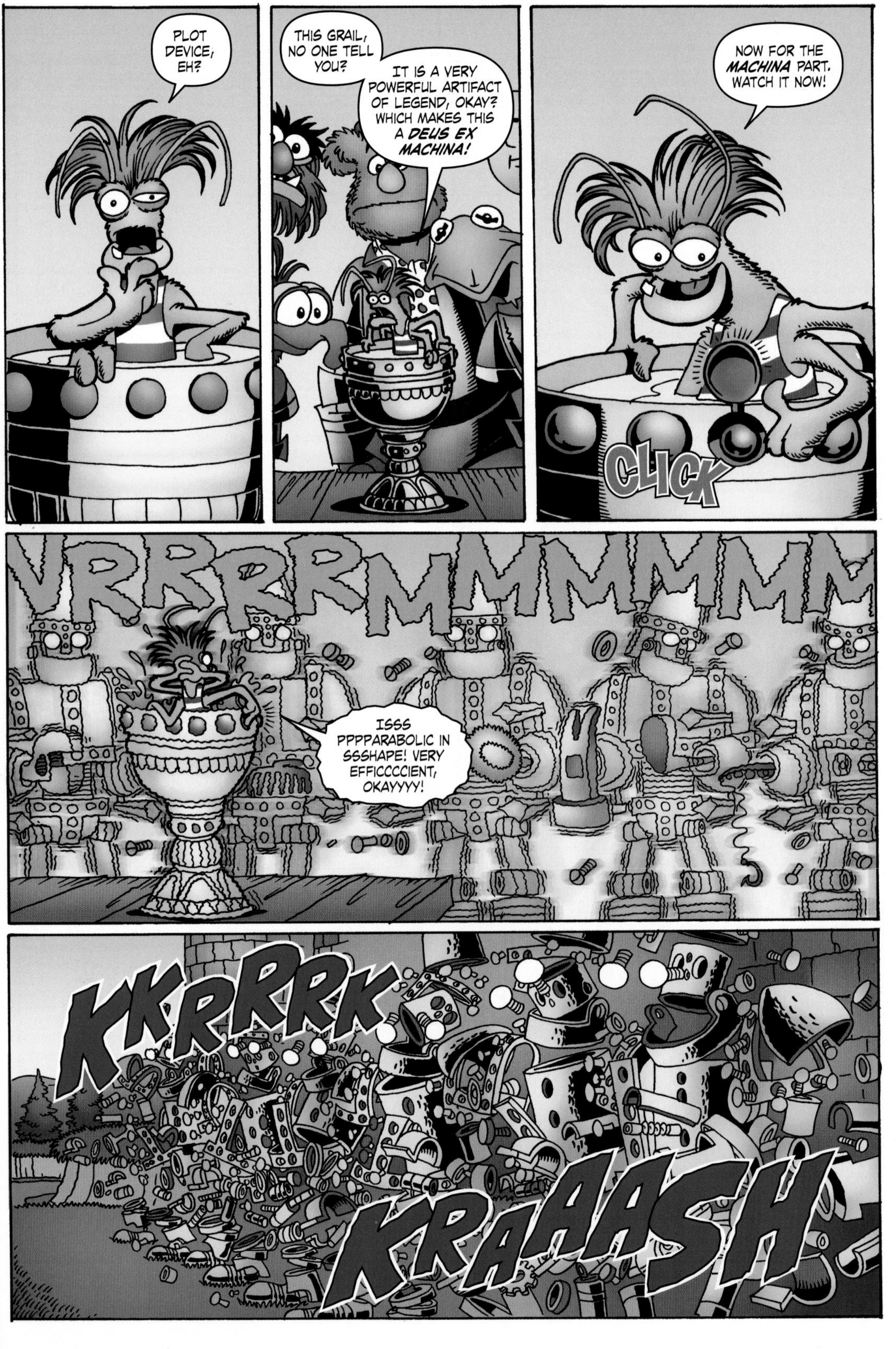
PLOT DEVICE, EH?
THIS GRAIL, NO ONE TELL YOU?
IT IS A VERY POWERFUL ARTIFACT OF LEGEND, OKAY? WHICH MAKES THIS A DEUS EX MACHINA!
NOW FOR THE MACHINA PART. WATCH IT NOW!
CLICK
VRRRRMMMMMMM
ISSS PPPPARABOLIC IN SSSHAPE! VERY EFFICCCCIENT, OKAYYYY!
KKRRRK
KRAAASH

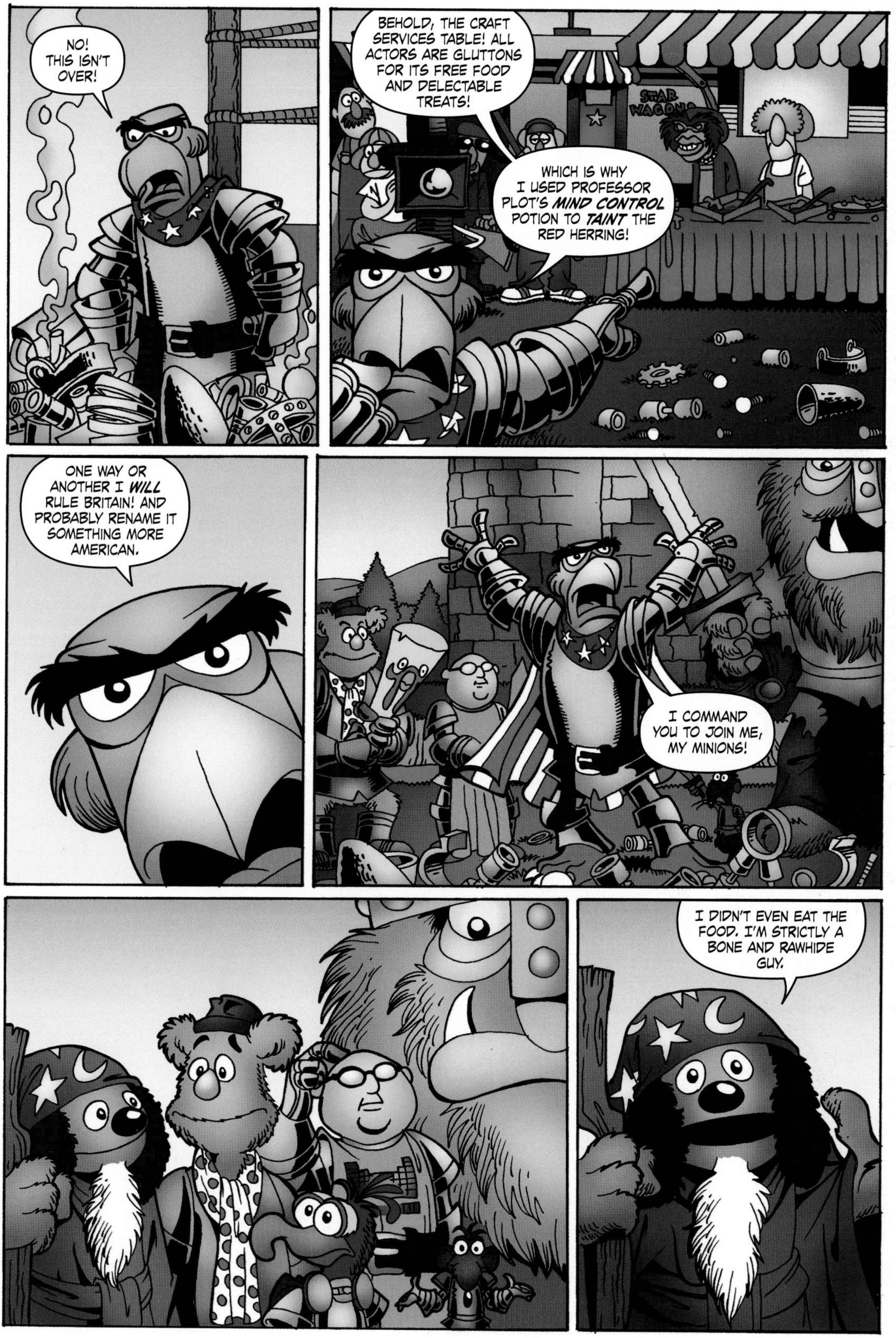
NO! THIS ISN'T OVER!
BEHOLD, THE CRAFT SERVICES TABLE! ALL ACTORS ARE GLUTTONS FOR ITS FREE FOOD AND DELECTABLE TREATS!
WHICH IS WHY I USED PROFESSOR PLOT'S MIND CONTROL POTION TO TAINT THE RED HERRING!
STAR WAGONS
ONE WAY OR ANOTHER I WILL RULE BRITAIN! AND PROBABLY RENAME IT SOMETHING MORE AMERICAN.
I COMMAND YOU TO JOIN ME, MY MINIONS!
I DIDN'T EVEN EAT THE FOOD. I'M STRICTLY A BONE AND RAWHIDE GUY.

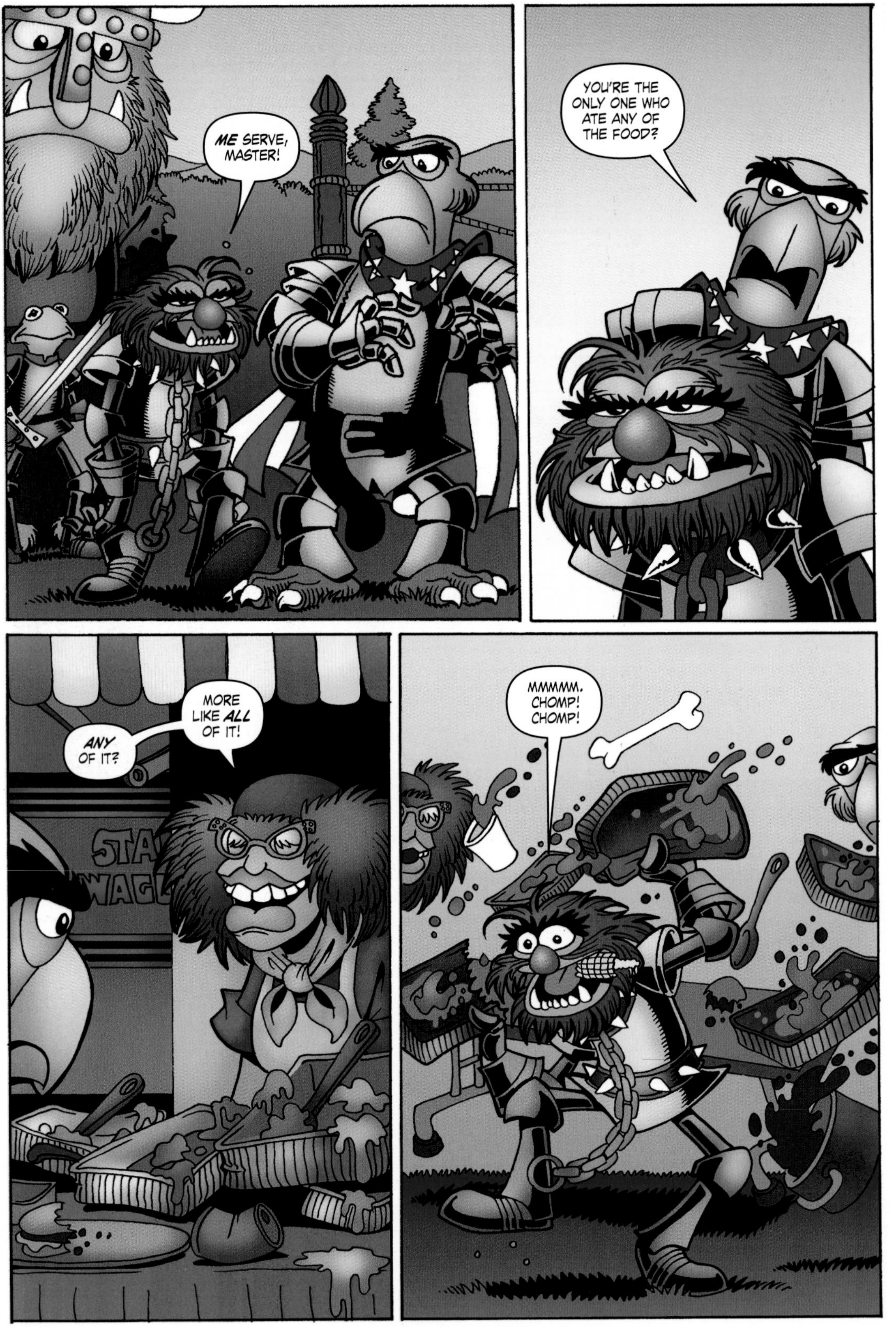
ME SERVE, MASTER!
YOU'RE THE ONLY ONE WHO ATE ANY OF THE FOOD?
ANY OF IT?
MORE LIKE ALL OF IT!
STA
WAG
MMMMM. CHOMP! CHOMP!

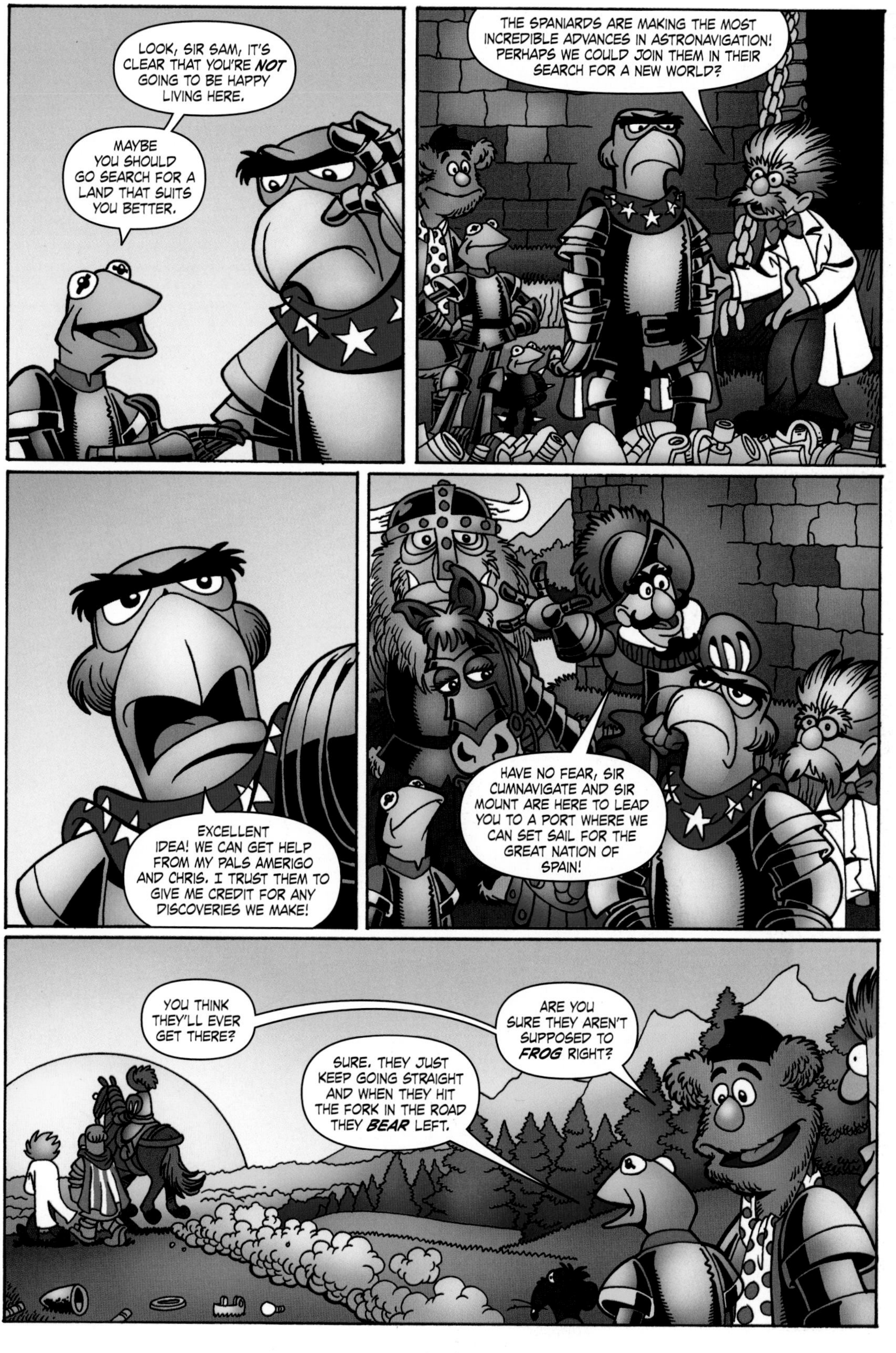
LOOK, SIR SAM, IT'S CLEAR THAT YOU'RE ***NOT*** GOING TO BE HAPPY LIVING HERE.
MAYBE YOU SHOULD GO SEARCH FOR A LAND THAT SUITS YOU BETTER.
THE SPANIARDS ARE MAKING THE MOST INCREDIBLE ADVANCES IN ASTRONAVIGATION! PERHAPS WE COULD JOIN THEM IN THEIR SEARCH FOR A NEW WORLD?
EXCELLENT IDEA! WE CAN GET HELP FROM MY PALS AMERIGO AND CHRIS. I TRUST THEM TO GIVE ME CREDIT FOR ANY DISCOVERIES WE MAKE!
HAVE NO FEAR, SIR CUMNAVIGATE AND SIR MOUNT ARE HERE TO LEAD YOU TO A PORT WHERE WE CAN SET SAIL FOR THE GREAT NATION OF SPAIN!
YOU THINK THEY'LL EVER GET THERE?
SURE. THEY JUST KEEP GOING STRAIGHT AND WHEN THEY HIT THE FORK IN THE ROAD THEY ***BEAR*** LEFT.
ARE YOU SURE THEY AREN'T SUPPOSED TO ***FROG*** RIGHT?

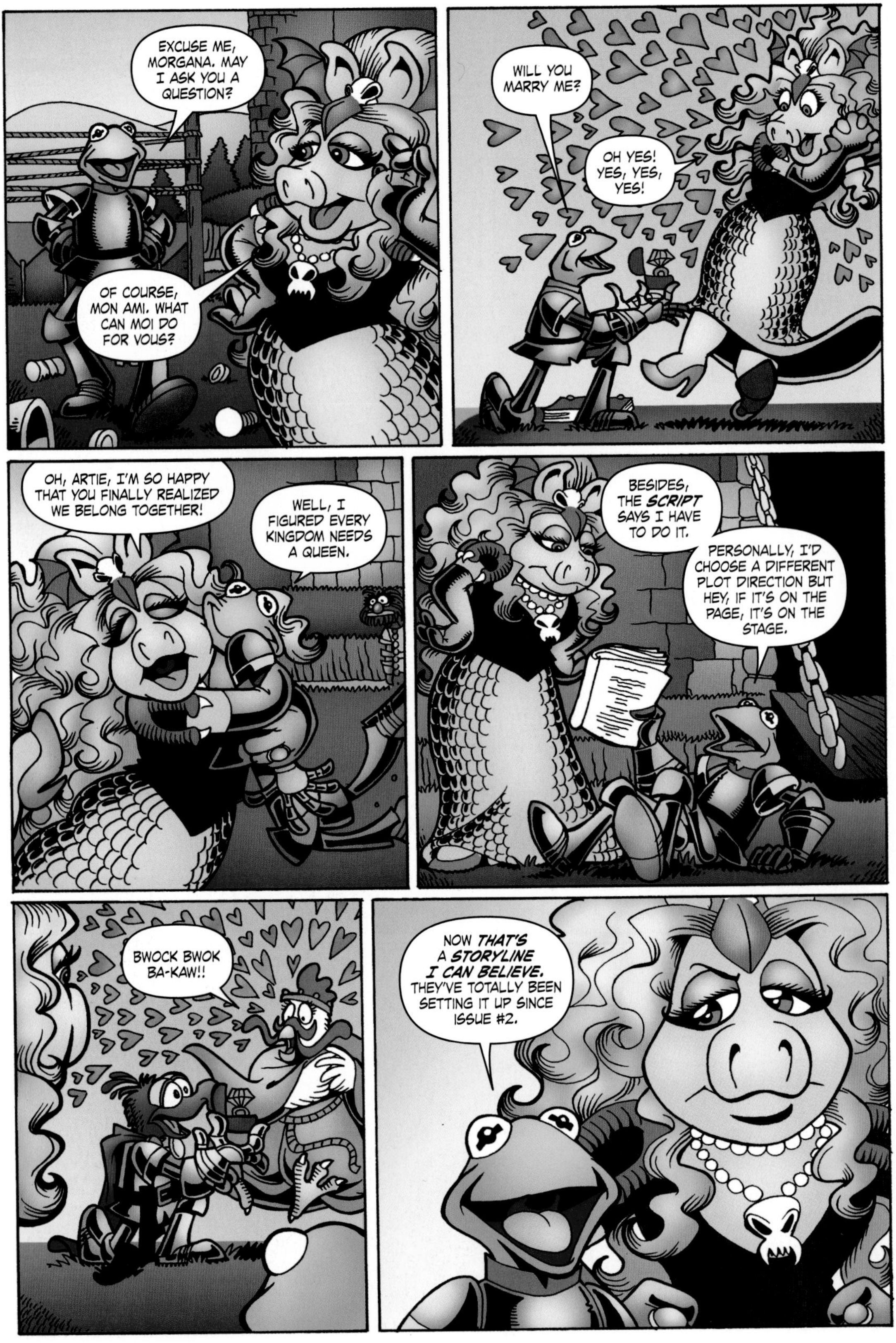
EXCUSE ME, MORGANA. MAY I ASK YOU A QUESTION?
OF COURSE, MON AMI. WHAT CAN MOI DO FOR VOUS?
WILL YOU MARRY ME?
OH YES! YES, YES, YES!
OH, ARTIE, I'M SO HAPPY THAT YOU FINALLY REALIZED WE BELONG TOGETHER!
WELL, I FIGURED EVERY KINGDOM NEEDS A QUEEN.
BESIDES, THE SCRIPT SAYS I HAVE TO DO IT.
PERSONALLY, I'D CHOOSE A DIFFERENT PLOT DIRECTION BUT HEY, IF IT'S ON THE PAGE, IT'S ON THE STAGE.
BWOCK BWOK BA-KAW!!
NOW THAT'S A STORYLINE I CAN BELIEVE. THEY'VE TOTALLY BEEN SETTING IT UP SINCE ISSUE #2.

FIGURES. I'M THE *REAL* STAR OF THIS BOOK BUT IT'S ALWAYS THE ONES WITH HANDS AND FEET THAT END UP GETTING THE GIRLS.

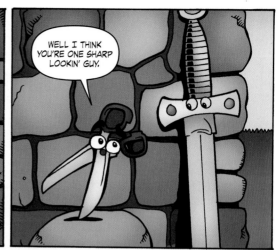

WELL I THINK YOU'RE ONE SHARP LOOKIN' GUY.

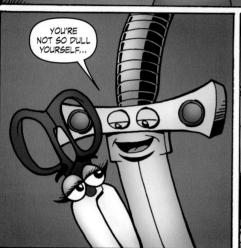

YOU'RE NOT SO DULL YOURSELF...

NOW THAT'S *REALLY* IMPRESSIVE. THEY STARTED SETTING THAT UP IN ISSUE #1.

BUT BACK TO WHAT'S IMPORTANT. A KING AND HIS QUEEN. WHAT SHOULD WE DO FOR A HONEYMOON?

I HEAR GREENLAND IS NICE THIS TIME OF YEAR.

*GREEN*LAND? THAT SOUNDS ROMANTIC! QUEEN MORGANA, PACK YOUR BATHING SUIT!

YOU KNOW WHAT MAKES THIS A HAPPY ENDING?

WHAT?

THEY STOP TELLING THE STORY!

HO-HAHAHAH!

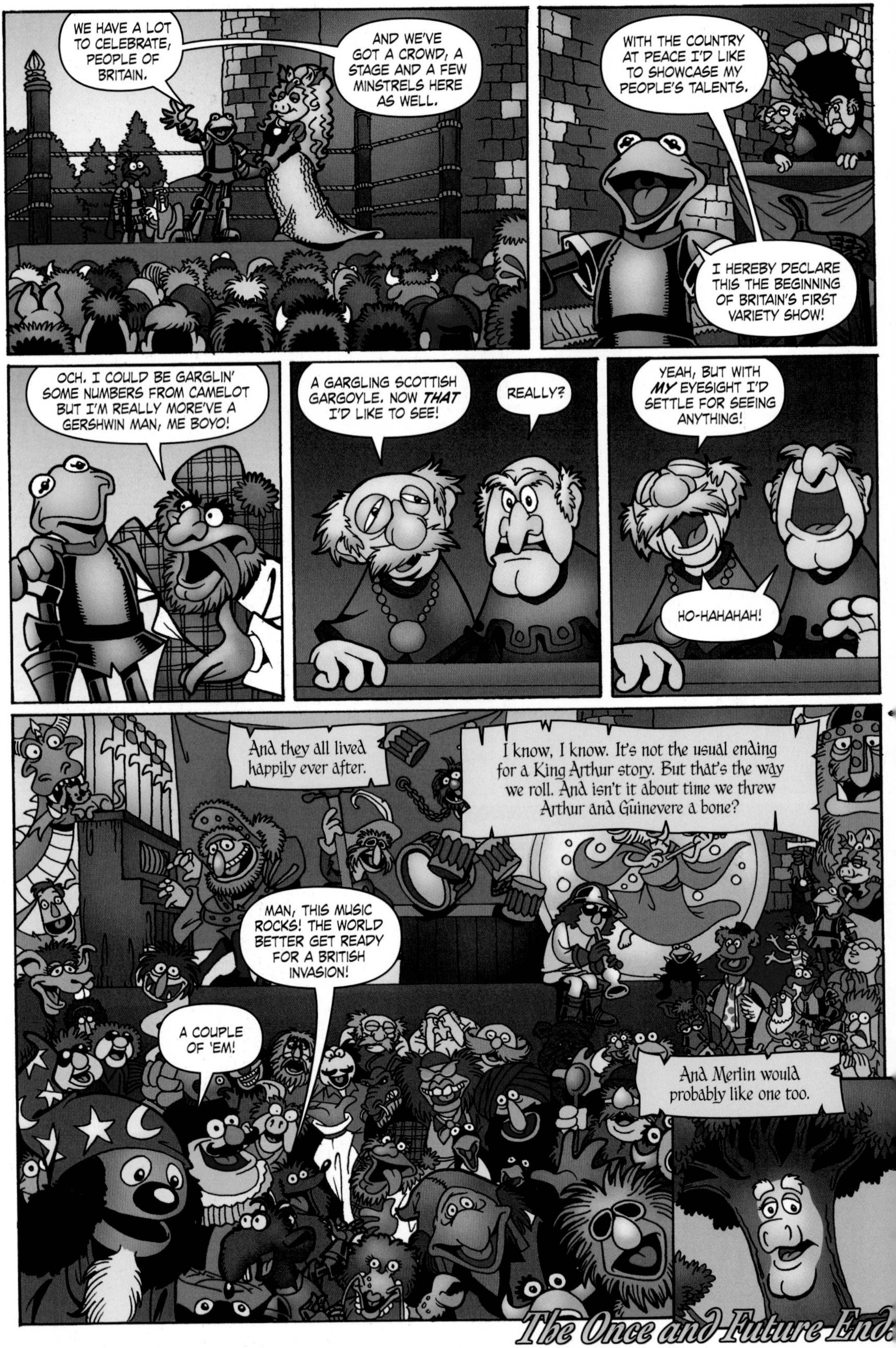
WE HAVE A LOT TO CELEBRATE, PEOPLE OF BRITAIN.
AND WE'VE GOT A CROWD, A STAGE AND A FEW MINSTRELS HERE AS WELL.
WITH THE COUNTRY AT PEACE I'D LIKE TO SHOWCASE MY PEOPLE'S TALENTS.
I HEREBY DECLARE THIS THE BEGINNING OF BRITAIN'S FIRST VARIETY SHOW!
OCH. I COULD BE GARGLIN' SOME NUMBERS FROM CAMELOT BUT I'M REALLY MORE'VE A GERSHWIN MAN, ME BOYO!
A GARGLING SCOTTISH GARGOYLE. NOW *THAT* I'D LIKE TO SEE!
REALLY?
YEAH, BUT WITH *MY* EYESIGHT I'D SETTLE FOR SEEING ANYTHING!
HO-HAHAHAH!
And they all lived happily ever after.
I know, I know. It's not the usual ending for a King Arthur story. But that's the way we roll. And isn't it about time we threw Arthur and Guinevere a bone?
MAN, THIS MUSIC ROCKS! THE WORLD BETTER GET READY FOR A BRITISH INVASION!
A COUPLE OF 'EM!
And Merlin would probably like one too.
The Once and Future End.

It's time to meet the Muppets once again! Join
Kermit, Fozzie, Gonzo, Miss Piggy and the rest of
the gang for a hilarious collection of madcap skits
and gags perfect for new and old fans alike!

THE MUPPET SHOW: MEET THE MUPPETS
DIAMOND CODE: MAY090750
SC $9.99 ISBN 9781934506851
HC $24.99 ISBN 9781608865277

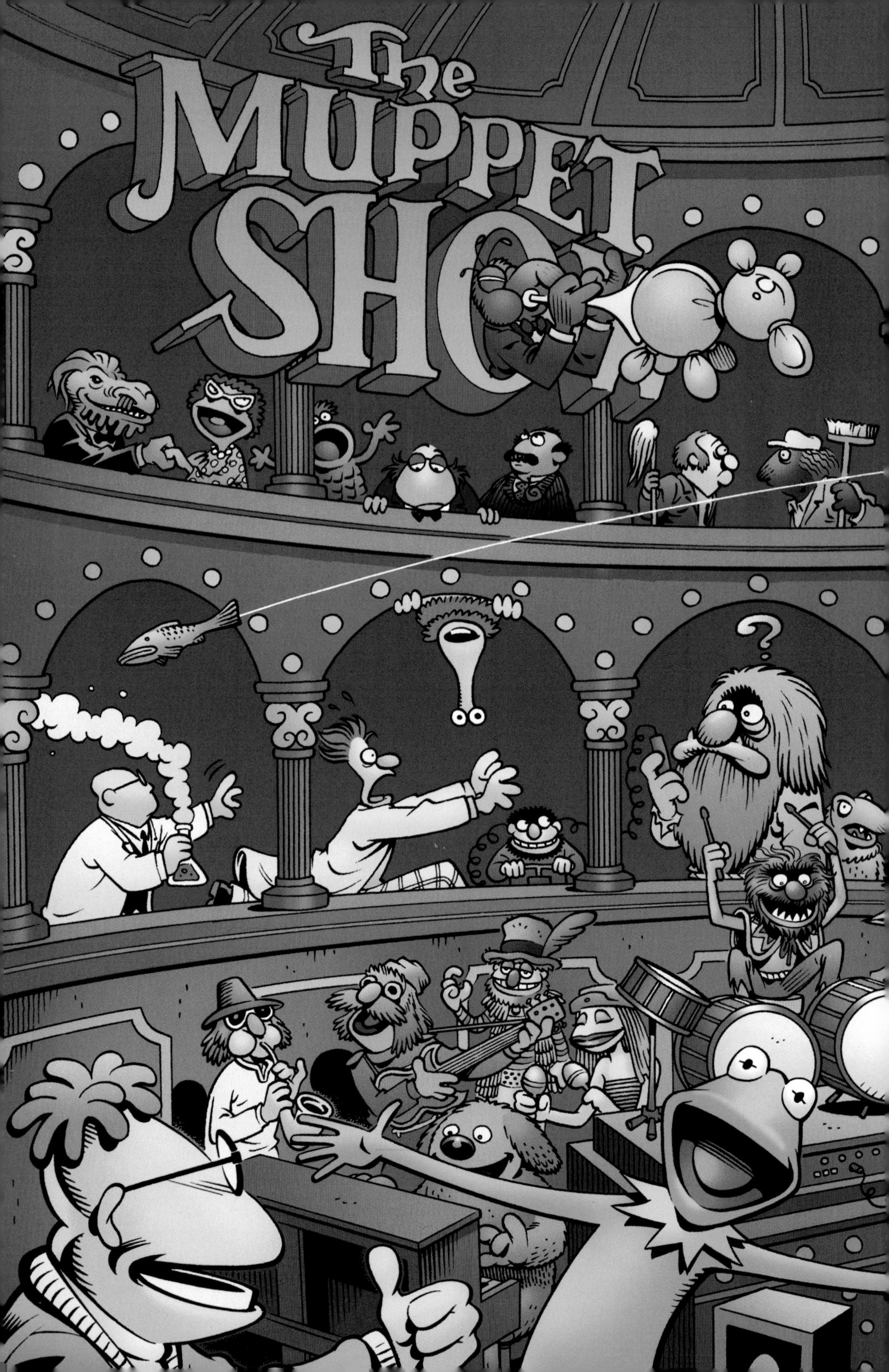
The
MUPPET
SHO

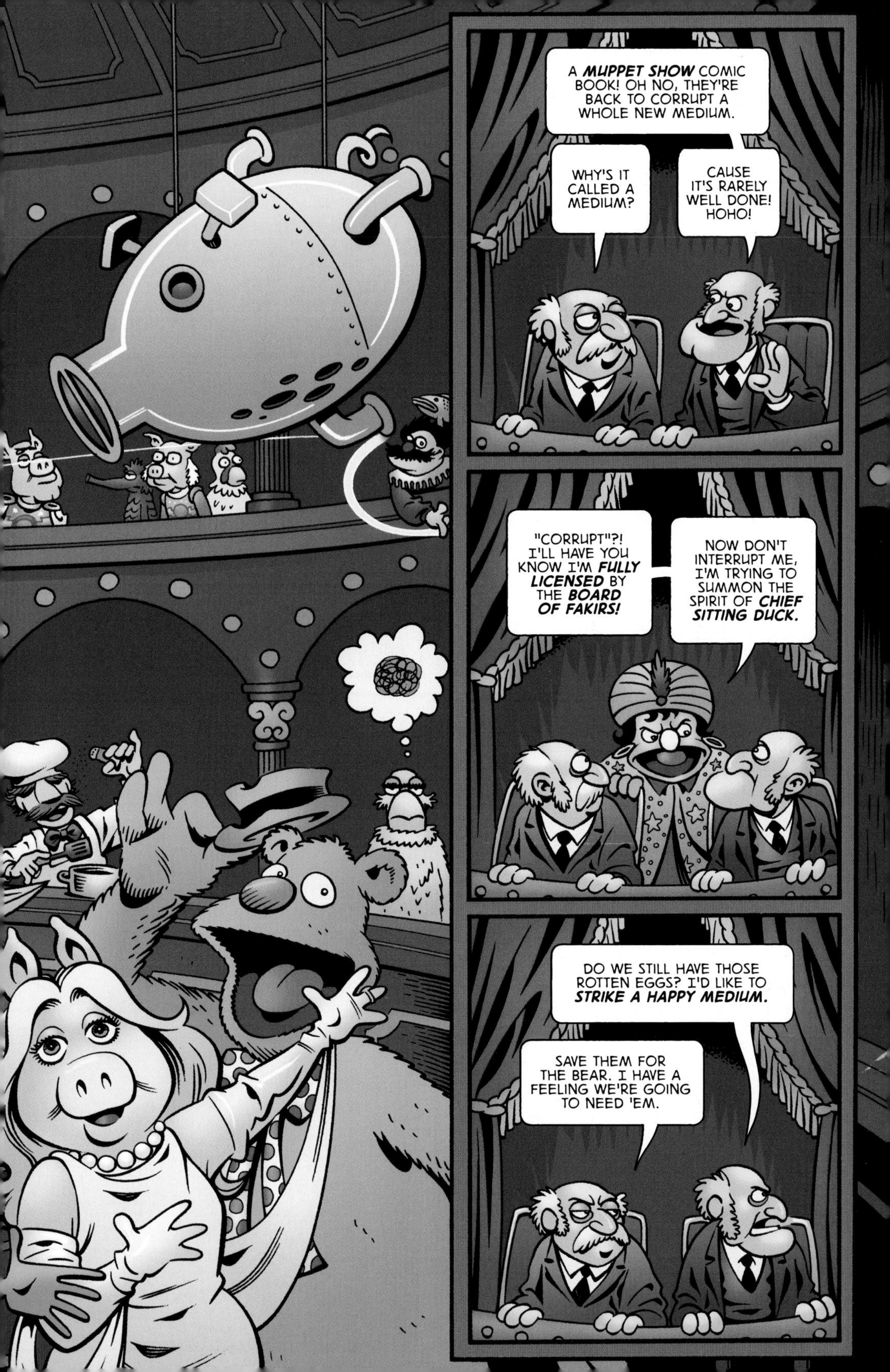
A MUPPET SHOW COMIC BOOK! OH NO, THEY'RE BACK TO CORRUPT A WHOLE NEW MEDIUM.
WHY'S IT CALLED A MEDIUM?
CAUSE IT'S RARELY WELL DONE! HOHO!
"CORRUPT"?! I'LL HAVE YOU KNOW I'M FULLY LICENSED BY THE BOARD OF FAKIRS!
NOW DON'T INTERRUPT ME, I'M TRYING TO SUMMON THE SPIRIT OF CHIEF SITTING DUCK.
DO WE STILL HAVE THOSE ROTTEN EGGS? I'D LIKE TO STRIKE A HAPPY MEDIUM.
SAVE THEM FOR THE BEAR. I HAVE A FEELING WE'RE GOING TO NEED 'EM.

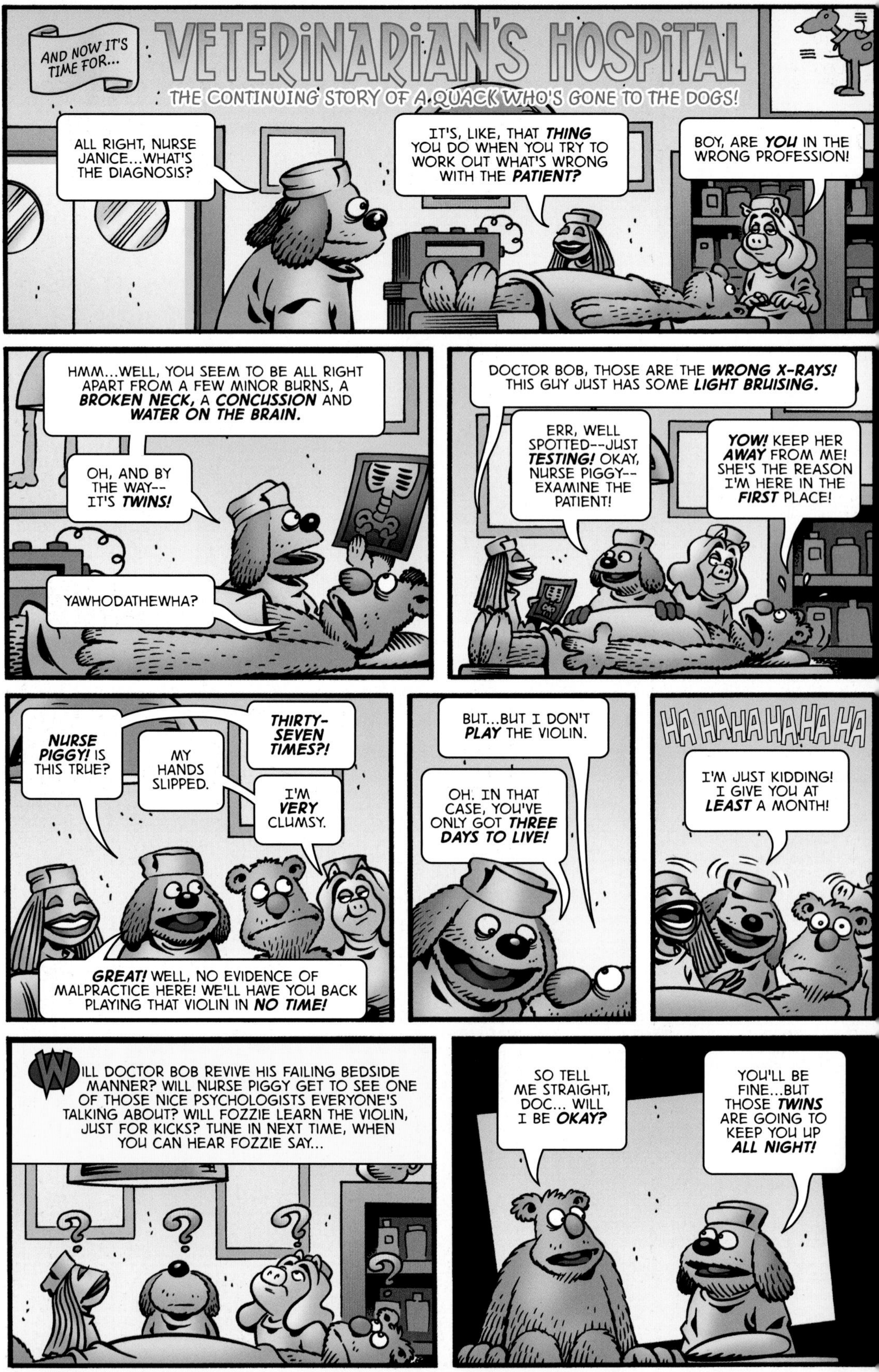
AND NOW IT'S TIME FOR...
VETERINARIAN'S HOSPITAL
THE CONTINUING STORY OF A QUACK WHO'S GONE TO THE DOGS!
ALL RIGHT, NURSE JANICE...WHAT'S THE DIAGNOSIS?
IT'S, LIKE, THAT THING YOU DO WHEN YOU TRY TO WORK OUT WHAT'S WRONG WITH THE PATIENT?
BOY, ARE YOU IN THE WRONG PROFESSION!
HMM...WELL, YOU SEEM TO BE ALL RIGHT APART FROM A FEW MINOR BURNS, A BROKEN NECK, A CONCUSSION AND WATER ON THE BRAIN.
OH, AND BY THE WAY--IT'S TWINS!
YAWHODATHEWHA?
DOCTOR BOB, THOSE ARE THE WRONG X-RAYS! THIS GUY JUST HAS SOME LIGHT BRUISING.
ERR, WELL SPOTTED--JUST TESTING! OKAY, NURSE PIGGY--EXAMINE THE PATIENT!
YOW! KEEP HER AWAY FROM ME! SHE'S THE REASON I'M HERE IN THE FIRST PLACE!
NURSE PIGGY! IS THIS TRUE?
MY HANDS SLIPPED.
THIRTY-SEVEN TIMES?!
I'M VERY CLUMSY.
GREAT! WELL, NO EVIDENCE OF MALPRACTICE HERE! WE'LL HAVE YOU BACK PLAYING THAT VIOLIN IN NO TIME!
BUT...BUT I DON'T PLAY THE VIOLIN.
OH. IN THAT CASE, YOU'VE ONLY GOT THREE DAYS TO LIVE!
HA HAHA HAHA HA
I'M JUST KIDDING! I GIVE YOU AT LEAST A MONTH!
WILL DOCTOR BOB REVIVE HIS FAILING BEDSIDE MANNER? WILL NURSE PIGGY GET TO SEE ONE OF THOSE NICE PSYCHOLOGISTS EVERYONE'S TALKING ABOUT? WILL FOZZIE LEARN THE VIOLIN, JUST FOR KICKS? TUNE IN NEXT TIME, WHEN YOU CAN HEAR FOZZIE SAY...
SO TELL ME STRAIGHT, DOC... WILL I BE OKAY?
YOU'LL BE FINE...BUT THOSE TWINS ARE GOING TO KEEP YOU UP ALL NIGHT!

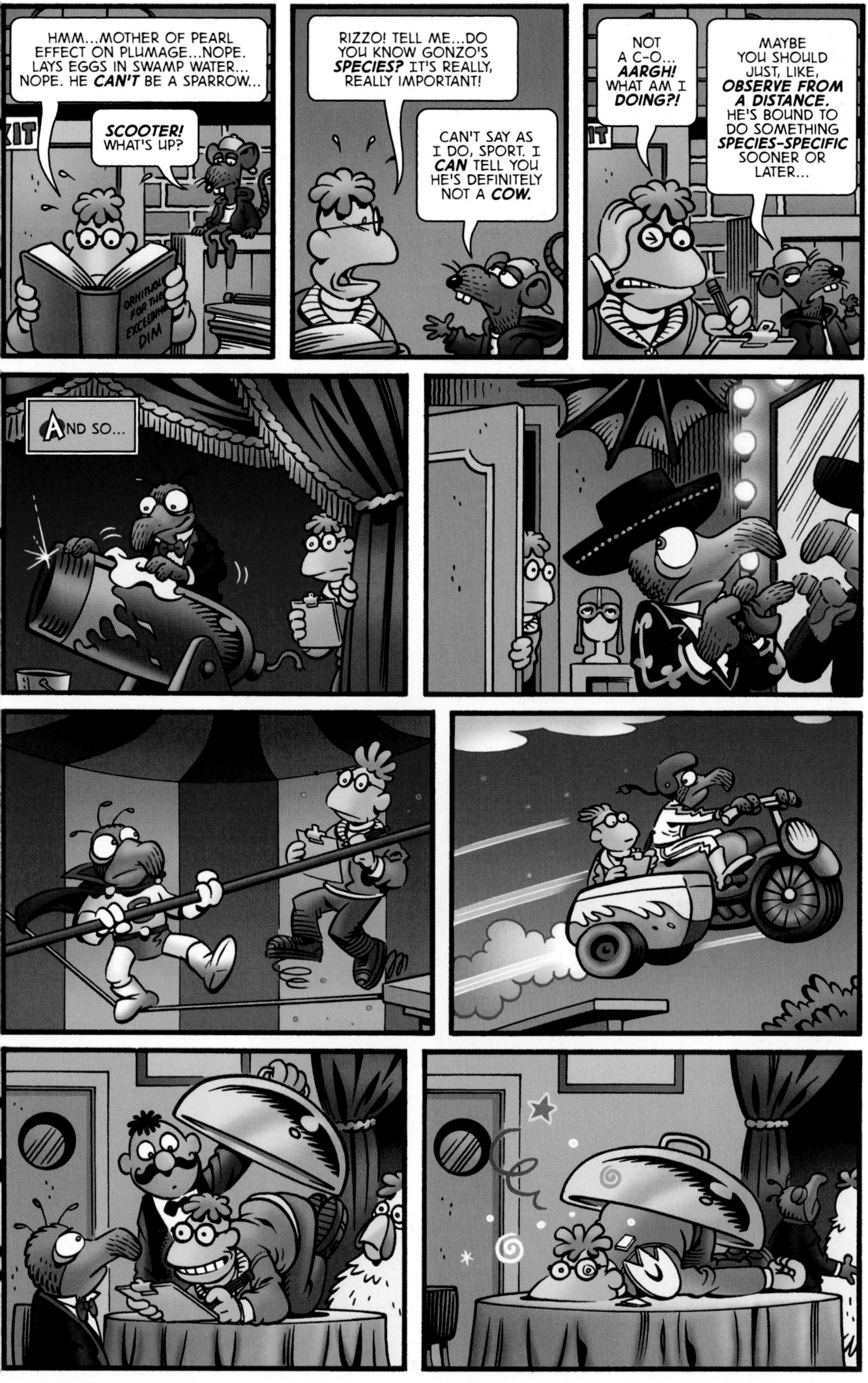
HMM...MOTHER OF PEARL EFFECT ON PLUMAGE...NOPE. LAYS EGGS IN SWAMP WATER... NOPE. HE CAN'T BE A SPARROW...
SCOOTER! WHAT'S UP?
RIZZO! TELL ME...DO YOU KNOW GONZO'S SPECIES? IT'S REALLY, REALLY IMPORTANT!
CAN'T SAY AS I DO, SPORT. I CAN TELL YOU HE'S DEFINITELY NOT A COW.
NOT A C-O... AARGH! WHAT AM I DOING?!
MAYBE YOU SHOULD JUST, LIKE, OBSERVE FROM A DISTANCE. HE'S BOUND TO DO SOMETHING SPECIES-SPECIFIC SOONER OR LATER...
AND SO...

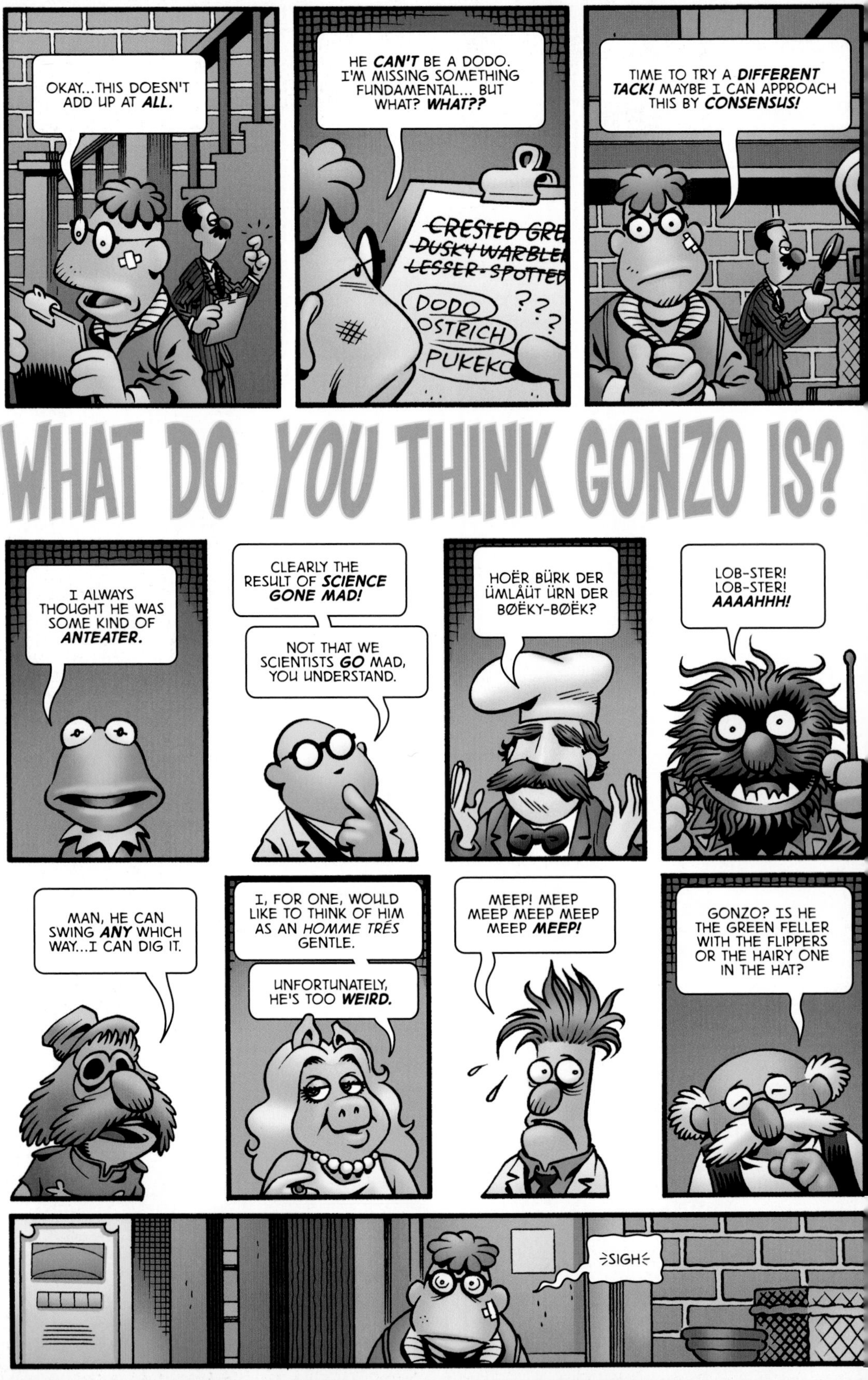
OKAY...THIS DOESN'T ADD UP AT ALL.
HE CAN'T BE A DODO. I'M MISSING SOMETHING FUNDAMENTAL... BUT WHAT? WHAT??
CRESTED GRE
DUSKY WARBLER
LESSER-SPOTTED
DODO
OSTRICH
PUKEKO
???
TIME TO TRY A DIFFERENT TACK! MAYBE I CAN APPROACH THIS BY CONSENSUS!
WHAT DO YOU THINK GONZO IS?
I ALWAYS THOUGHT HE WAS SOME KIND OF ANTEATER.
CLEARLY THE RESULT OF SCIENCE GONE MAD!
NOT THAT WE SCIENTISTS GO MAD, YOU UNDERSTAND.
HOËR BÜRK DER ÜMLÅÜT ÜRN DER BØËKY-BØËK?
LOB-STER! LOB-STER! AAAAHHH!
MAN, HE CAN SWING ANY WHICH WAY...I CAN DIG IT.
I, FOR ONE, WOULD LIKE TO THINK OF HIM AS AN HOMME TRÉS GENTLE.
UNFORTUNATELY, HE'S TOO WEIRD.
MEEP! MEEP MEEP MEEP MEEP MEEP MEEP!
GONZO? IS HE THE GREEN FELLER WITH THE FLIPPERS OR THE HAIRY ONE IN THE HAT?
SIGH

THE TREASURE OF PEG-LEG WILSON

When Scooter discovers that a cache of treasure is hidden
somewhere in the Muppet Theater, can Kermit keep the rest
of the gang from bringing the house down - permanently?
The laughs continue in this critically-acclaimed collection!

THE MUPPET SHOW:
THE TREASURE OF PEG-LEG WILSON
DIAMOND CODE: SEP090712
SC $9.99 ISBN 9781608865048
HC $24.99 ISBN 9781608865307

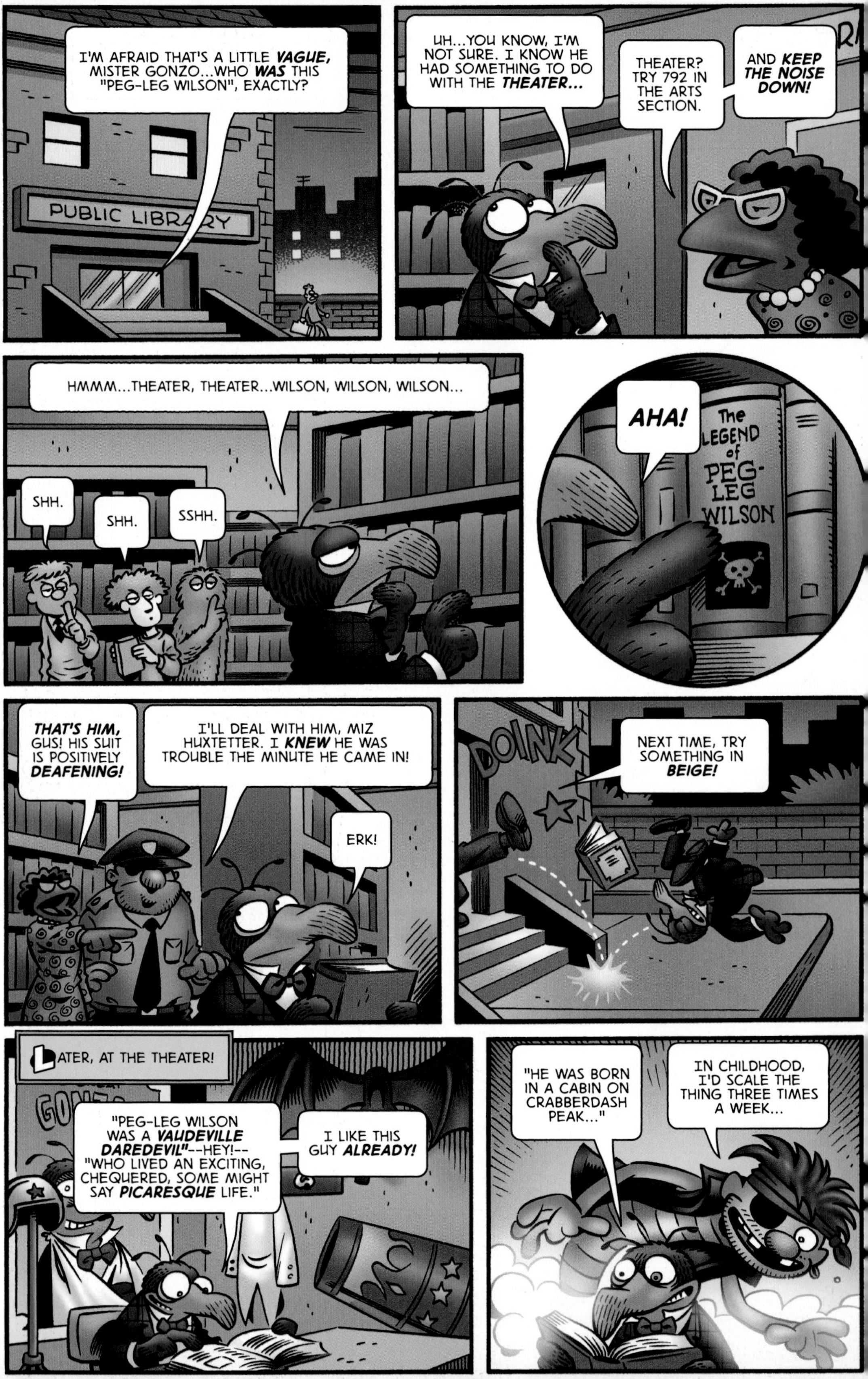
I'M AFRAID THAT'S A LITTLE VAGUE, MISTER GONZO...WHO WAS THIS "PEG-LEG WILSON", EXACTLY?
PUBLIC LIBRARY
UH...YOU KNOW, I'M NOT SURE. I KNOW HE HAD SOMETHING TO DO WITH THE THEATER...
THEATER? TRY 792 IN THE ARTS SECTION.
AND KEEP THE NOISE DOWN!
HMMM...THEATER, THEATER...WILSON, WILSON, WILSON...
SHH.
SHH.
SSHH.
AHA!
The LEGEND of PEG-LEG WILSON
THAT'S HIM, GUS! HIS SUIT IS POSITIVELY DEAFENING!
I'LL DEAL WITH HIM, MIZ HUXTETTER. I KNEW HE WAS TROUBLE THE MINUTE HE CAME IN!
ERK!
DOINK
NEXT TIME, TRY SOMETHING IN BEIGE!
LATER, AT THE THEATER!
"PEG-LEG WILSON WAS A VAUDEVILLE DAREDEVIL"--HEY!--"WHO LIVED AN EXCITING, CHEQUERED, SOME MIGHT SAY PICARESQUE LIFE."
I LIKE THIS GUY ALREADY!
"HE WAS BORN IN A CABIN ON CRABBERDASH PEAK..."
IN CHILDHOOD, I'D SCALE THE THING THREE TIMES A WEEK...

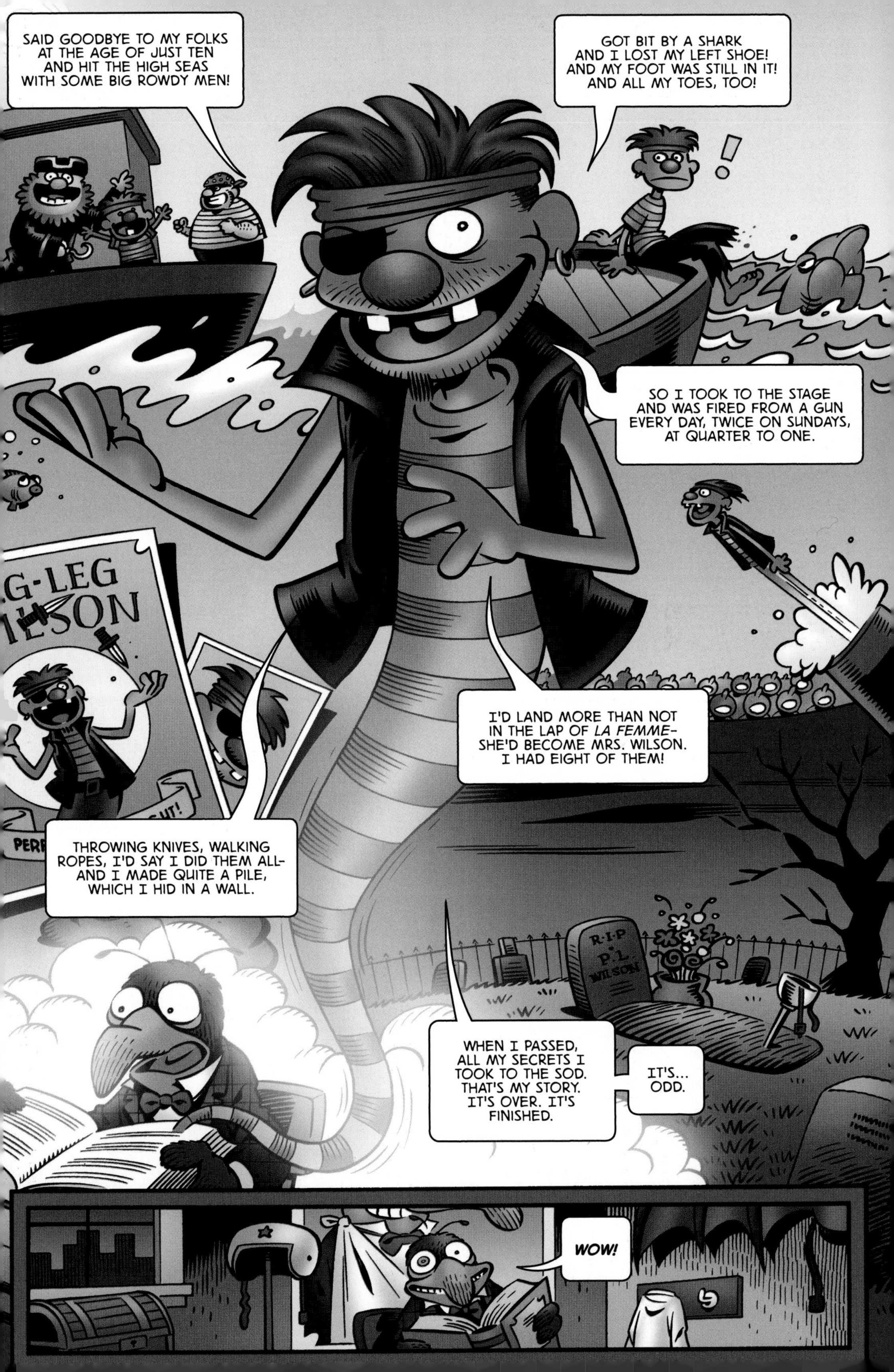
SAID GOODBYE TO MY FOLKS AT THE AGE OF JUST TEN AND HIT THE HIGH SEAS WITH SOME BIG ROWDY MEN!
GOT BIT BY A SHARK AND I LOST MY LEFT SHOE! AND MY FOOT WAS STILL IN IT! AND ALL MY TOES, TOO!
!
SO I TOOK TO THE STAGE AND WAS FIRED FROM A GUN EVERY DAY, TWICE ON SUNDAYS, AT QUARTER TO ONE.
THROWING KNIVES, WALKING ROPES, I'D SAY I DID THEM ALL- AND I MADE QUITE A PILE, WHICH I HID IN A WALL.
I'D LAND MORE THAN NOT IN THE LAP OF *LA FEMME*- SHE'D BECOME MRS. WILSON. I HAD EIGHT OF THEM!
R·I·P P.L. WILSON
WHEN I PASSED, ALL MY SECRETS I TOOK TO THE SOD. THAT'S MY STORY. IT'S OVER. IT'S FINISHED.
IT'S... ODD.
WOW!

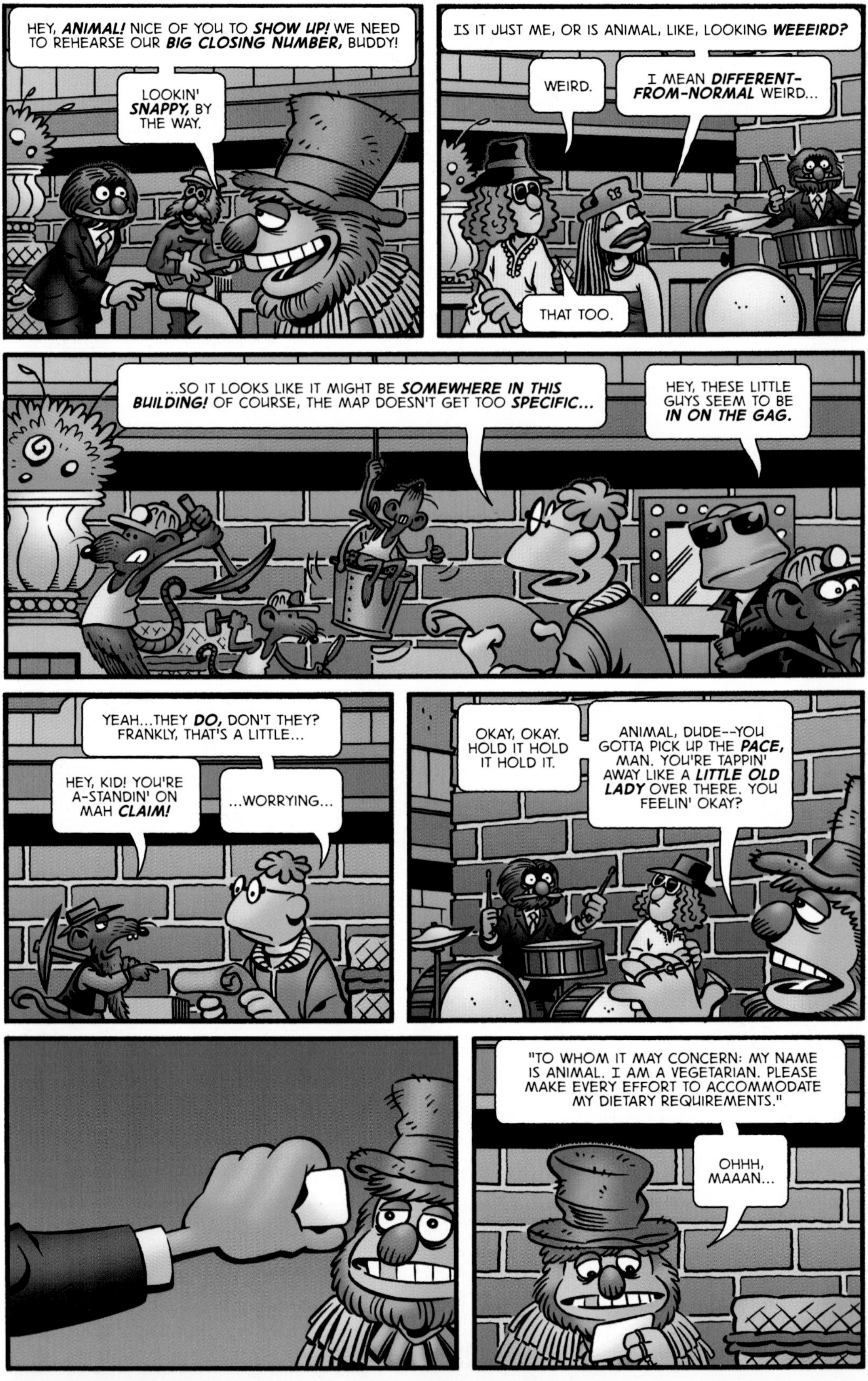
HEY, ANIMAL! NICE OF YOU TO SHOW UP! WE NEED TO REHEARSE OUR BIG CLOSING NUMBER, BUDDY!
LOOKIN' SNAPPY, BY THE WAY.
IS IT JUST ME, OR IS ANIMAL, LIKE, LOOKING WEEEIRD?
WEIRD.
I MEAN DIFFERENT-FROM-NORMAL WEIRD...
THAT TOO.
...SO IT LOOKS LIKE IT MIGHT BE SOMEWHERE IN THIS BUILDING! OF COURSE, THE MAP DOESN'T GET TOO SPECIFIC...
HEY, THESE LITTLE GUYS SEEM TO BE IN ON THE GAG.
YEAH...THEY DO, DON'T THEY? FRANKLY, THAT'S A LITTLE...
HEY, KID! YOU'RE A-STANDIN' ON MAH CLAIM!
...WORRYING...
OKAY, OKAY. HOLD IT HOLD IT HOLD IT.
ANIMAL, DUDE--YOU GOTTA PICK UP THE PACE, MAN. YOU'RE TAPPIN' AWAY LIKE A LITTLE OLD LADY OVER THERE. YOU FEELIN' OKAY?
"TO WHOM IT MAY CONCERN: MY NAME IS ANIMAL. I AM A VEGETARIAN. PLEASE MAKE EVERY EFFORT TO ACCOMMODATE MY DIETARY REQUIREMENTS."
OHHH, MAAAN...

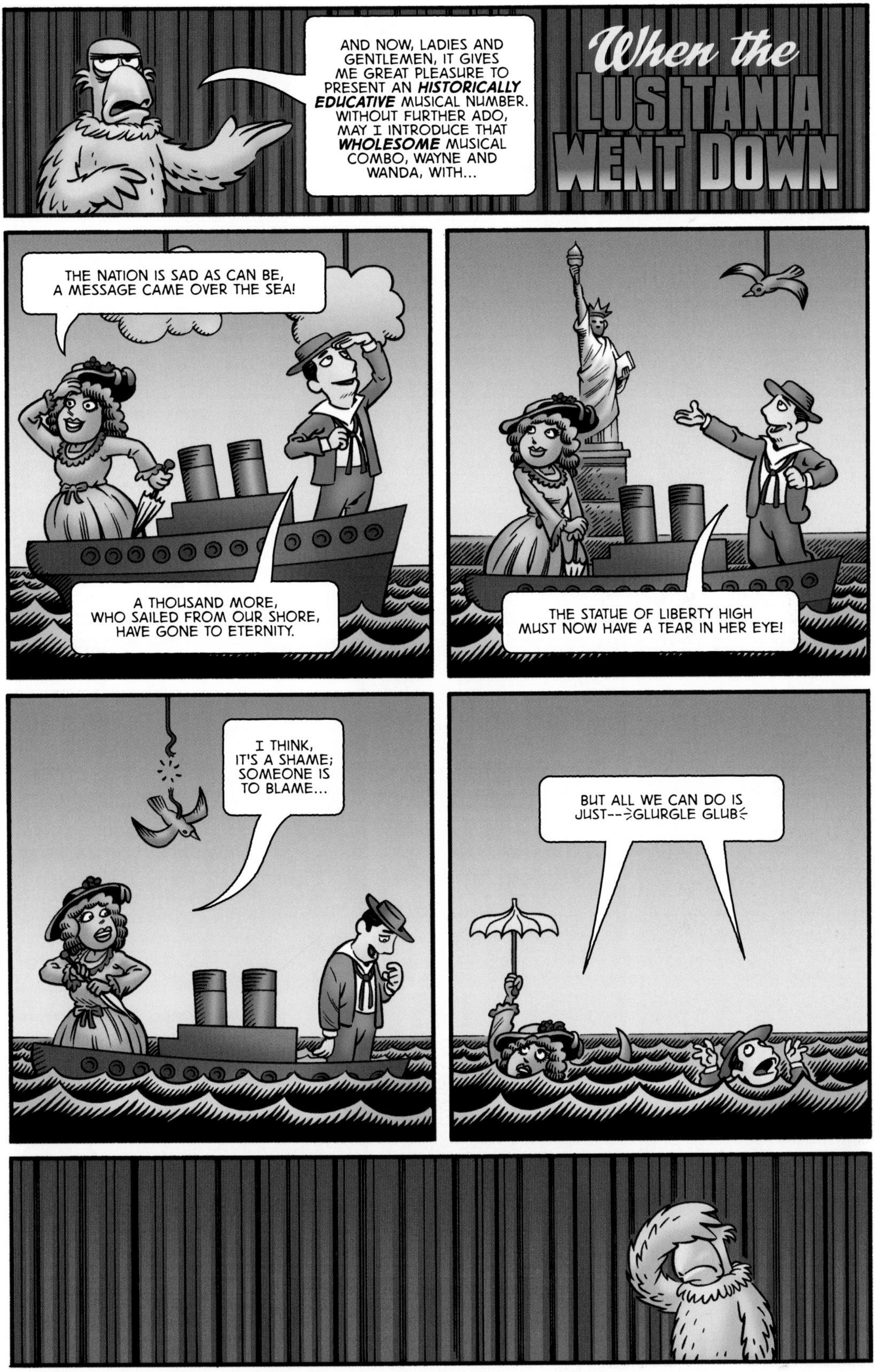
AND NOW, LADIES AND GENTLEMEN, IT GIVES ME GREAT PLEASURE TO PRESENT AN **HISTORICALLY EDUCATIVE** MUSICAL NUMBER. WITHOUT FURTHER ADO, MAY I INTRODUCE THAT **WHOLESOME** MUSICAL COMBO, WAYNE AND WANDA, WITH...
When the LUSITANIA WENT DOWN
THE NATION IS SAD AS CAN BE, A MESSAGE CAME OVER THE SEA!
A THOUSAND MORE, WHO SAILED FROM OUR SHORE, HAVE GONE TO ETERNITY.
THE STATUE OF LIBERTY HIGH MUST NOW HAVE A TEAR IN HER EYE!
I THINK, IT'S A SHAME; SOMEONE IS TO BLAME...
BUT ALL WE CAN DO IS JUST-- ⪢GLURGLE GLUB⪡

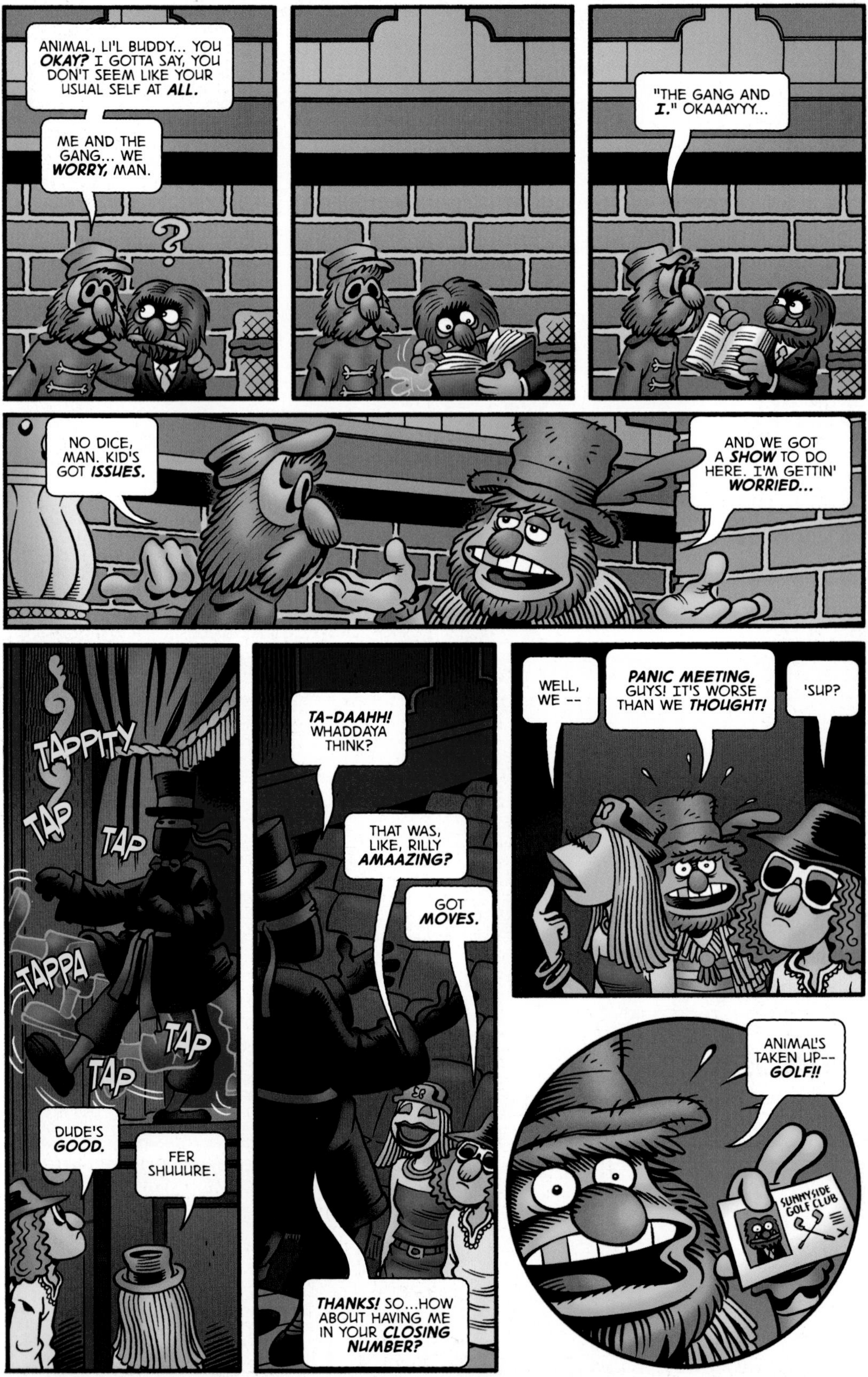
ANIMAL, LI'L BUDDY... YOU OKAY? I GOTTA SAY, YOU DON'T SEEM LIKE YOUR USUAL SELF AT ALL.
ME AND THE GANG... WE WORRY, MAN.
?
"THE GANG AND I." OKAAAYYY...
NO DICE, MAN. KID'S GOT ISSUES.
AND WE GOT A SHOW TO DO HERE. I'M GETTIN' WORRIED...
TAPPITY
TAP
TAP
TAPPA
TAP
TAP
DUDE'S GOOD.
FER SHUUURE.
TA-DAAHH! WHADDAYA THINK?
THAT WAS, LIKE, RILLY AMAAZING?
GOT MOVES.
THANKS! SO...HOW ABOUT HAVING ME IN YOUR CLOSING NUMBER?
WELL, WE --
PANIC MEETING, GUYS! IT'S WORSE THAN WE THOUGHT!
'SUP?
ANIMAL'S TAKEN UP-- GOLF!!
SUNNYSIDE GOLF CLUB

Peter Pan (Kermit) whisks Wendy (Janice) and her brothers to the magical realm of Neverswamp! Also starring Captain Hook (Gonzo) and Piggytink (Miss Piggy), this hilarious spin on the timeless tale is one

MUPPET PETER PAN
DIAMOND CODE: OCT090802
SC $9.99 ISBN 9781608865079

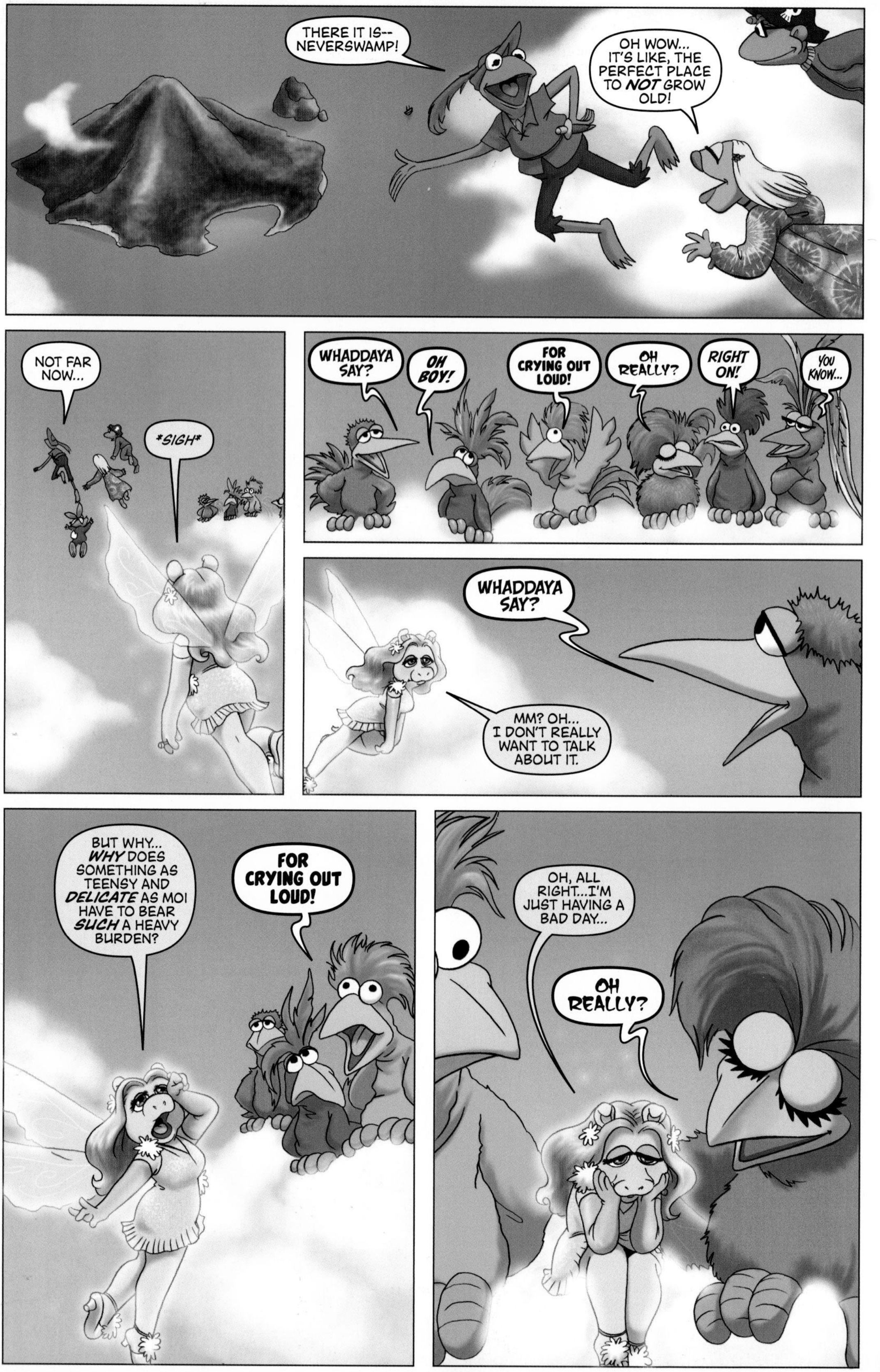
THERE IT IS-- NEVERSWAMP!
OH WOW... IT'S LIKE, THE PERFECT PLACE TO NOT GROW OLD!
NOT FAR NOW...
SIGH
WHADDAYA SAY?
OH BOY!
FOR CRYING OUT LOUD!
OH REALLY?
RIGHT ON!
YOU KNOW...
WHADDAYA SAY?
MM? OH... I DON'T REALLY WANT TO TALK ABOUT IT.
BUT WHY... WHY DOES SOMETHING AS TEENSY AND DELICATE AS MOI HAVE TO BEAR SUCH A HEAVY BURDEN?
FOR CRYING OUT LOUD!
OH, ALL RIGHT...I'M JUST HAVING A BAD DAY...
OH REALLY?

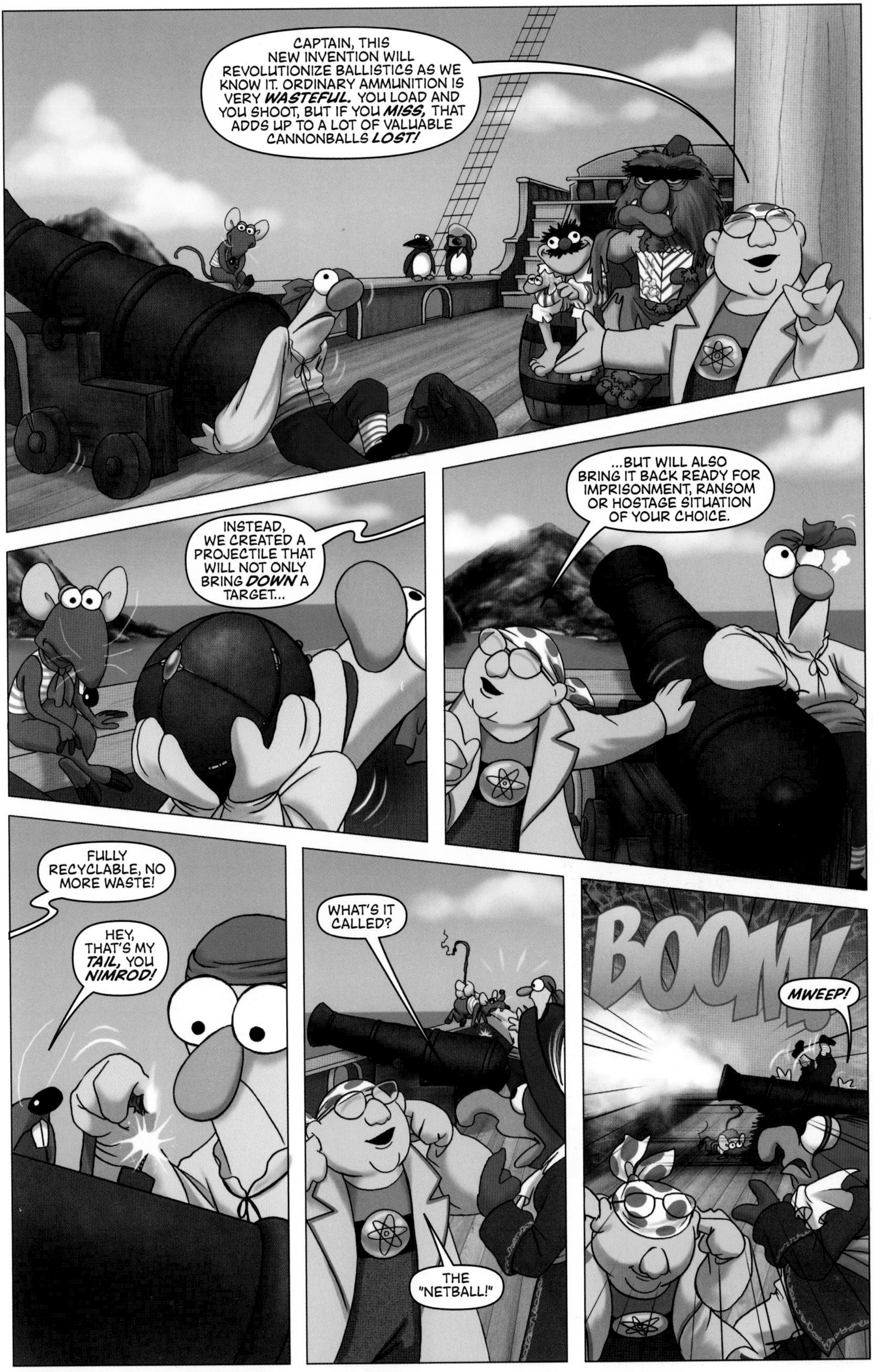
CAPTAIN, THIS NEW INVENTION WILL REVOLUTIONIZE BALLISTICS AS WE KNOW IT. ORDINARY AMMUNITION IS VERY WASTEFUL. YOU LOAD AND YOU SHOOT, BUT IF YOU MISS, THAT ADDS UP TO A LOT OF VALUABLE CANNONBALLS LOST!
INSTEAD, WE CREATED A PROJECTILE THAT WILL NOT ONLY BRING DOWN A TARGET...
...BUT WILL ALSO BRING IT BACK READY FOR IMPRISONMENT, RANSOM OR HOSTAGE SITUATION OF YOUR CHOICE.
FULLY RECYCLABLE, NO MORE WASTE!
HEY, THAT'S MY TAIL, YOU NIMROD!
WHAT'S IT CALLED?
THE "NETBALL!"
BOOM!
MWEEP!

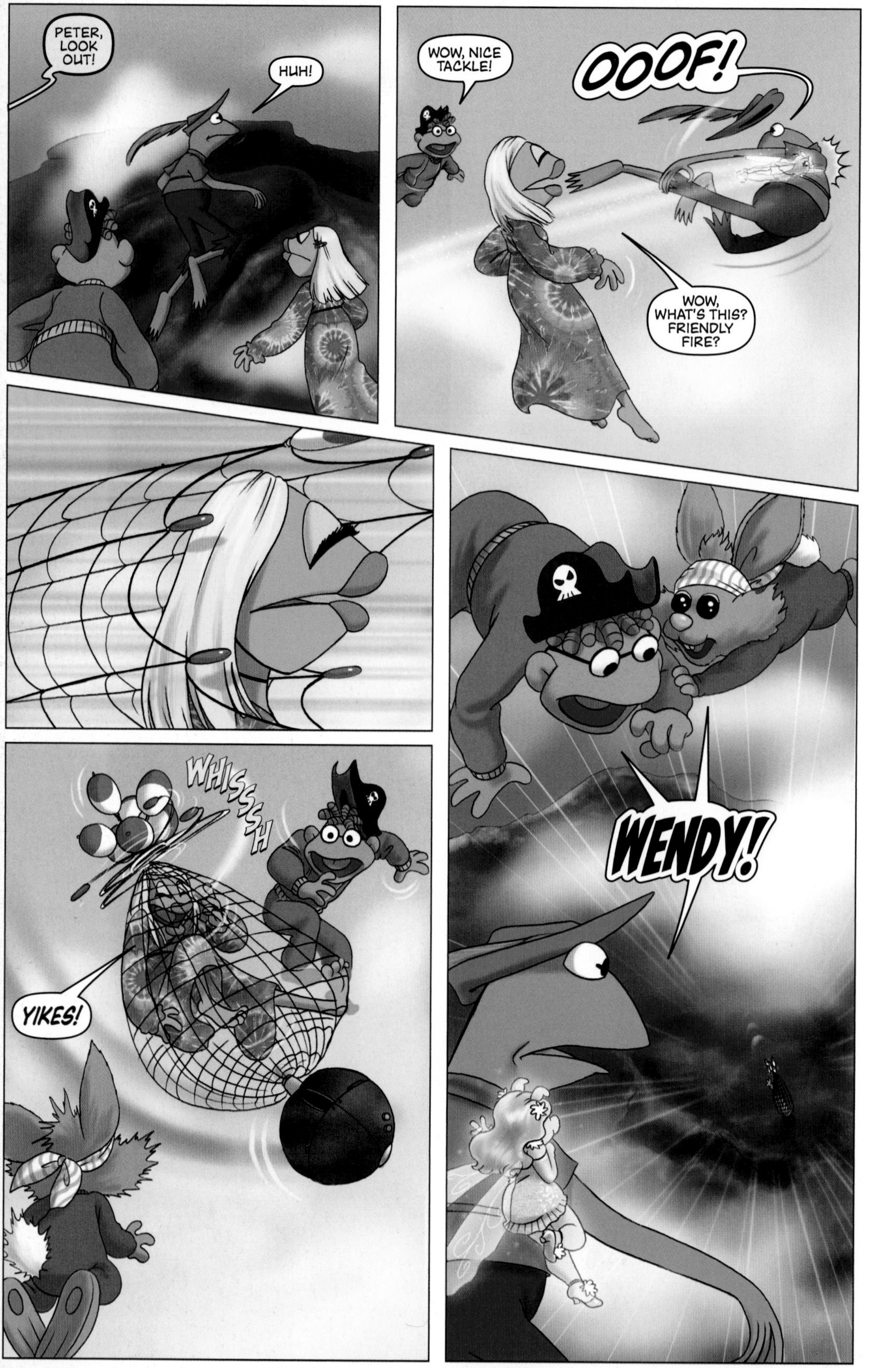
PETER, LOOK OUT!
HUH!
WOW, NICE TACKLE!
OOOF!
WOW, WHAT'S THIS? FRIENDLY FIRE?
WHISSSH
YIKES!
WENDY!

The Muppets tell the Robin Hood legend for laughs, and it's the reader who will be merry! Join Robin Hood (Kermit the Frog) and his band of Merry Men as they take on the stuffy Sheriff of Nottingham (Sam the Eagle)!

MUPPET ROBIN HOOD
DIAMOND CODE: JUN090792
SC $9.99 ISBN 9781934506790
HC $24.99 ISBN 9781608865260

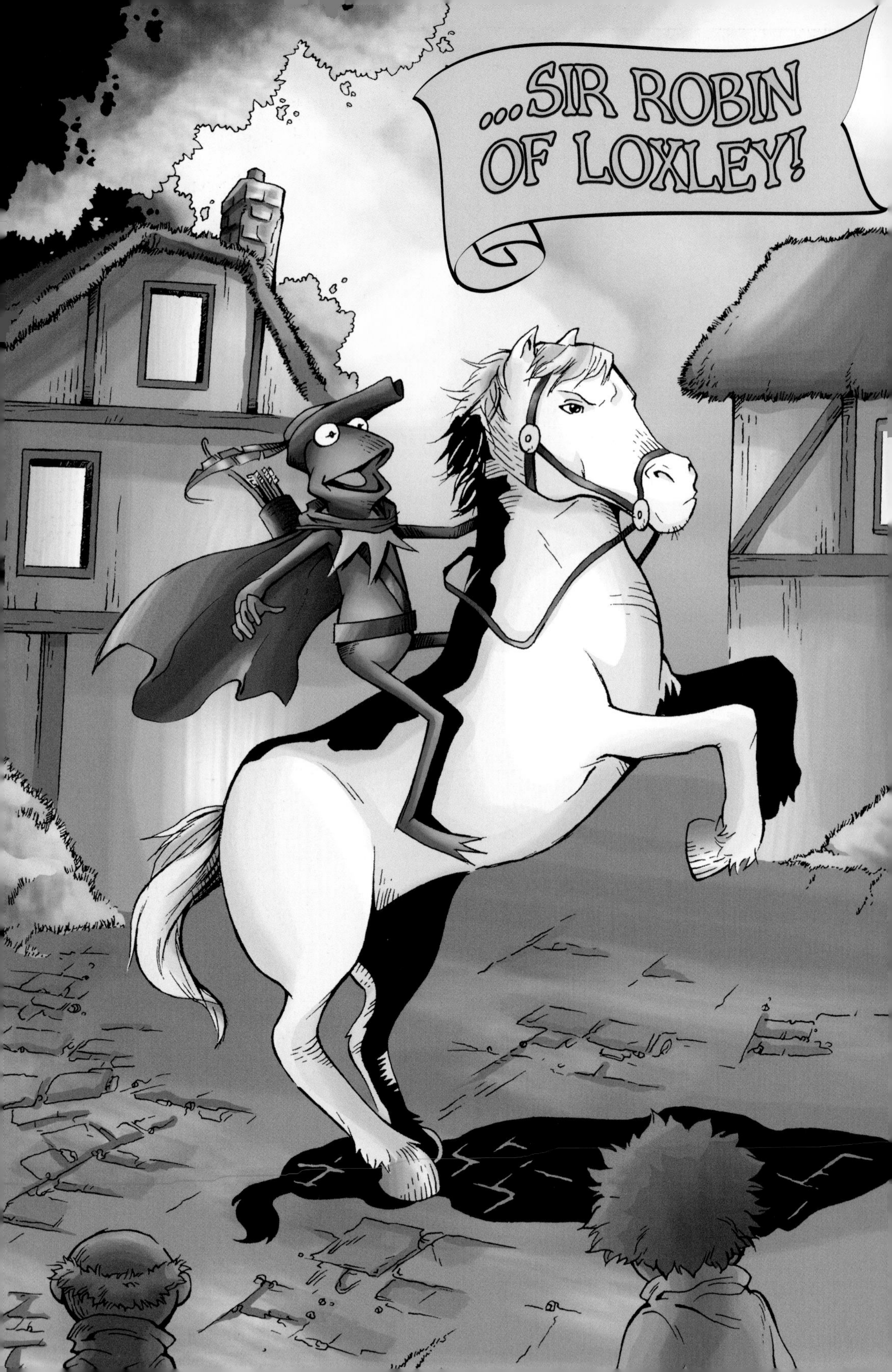
...SIR ROBIN OF LOXLEY!

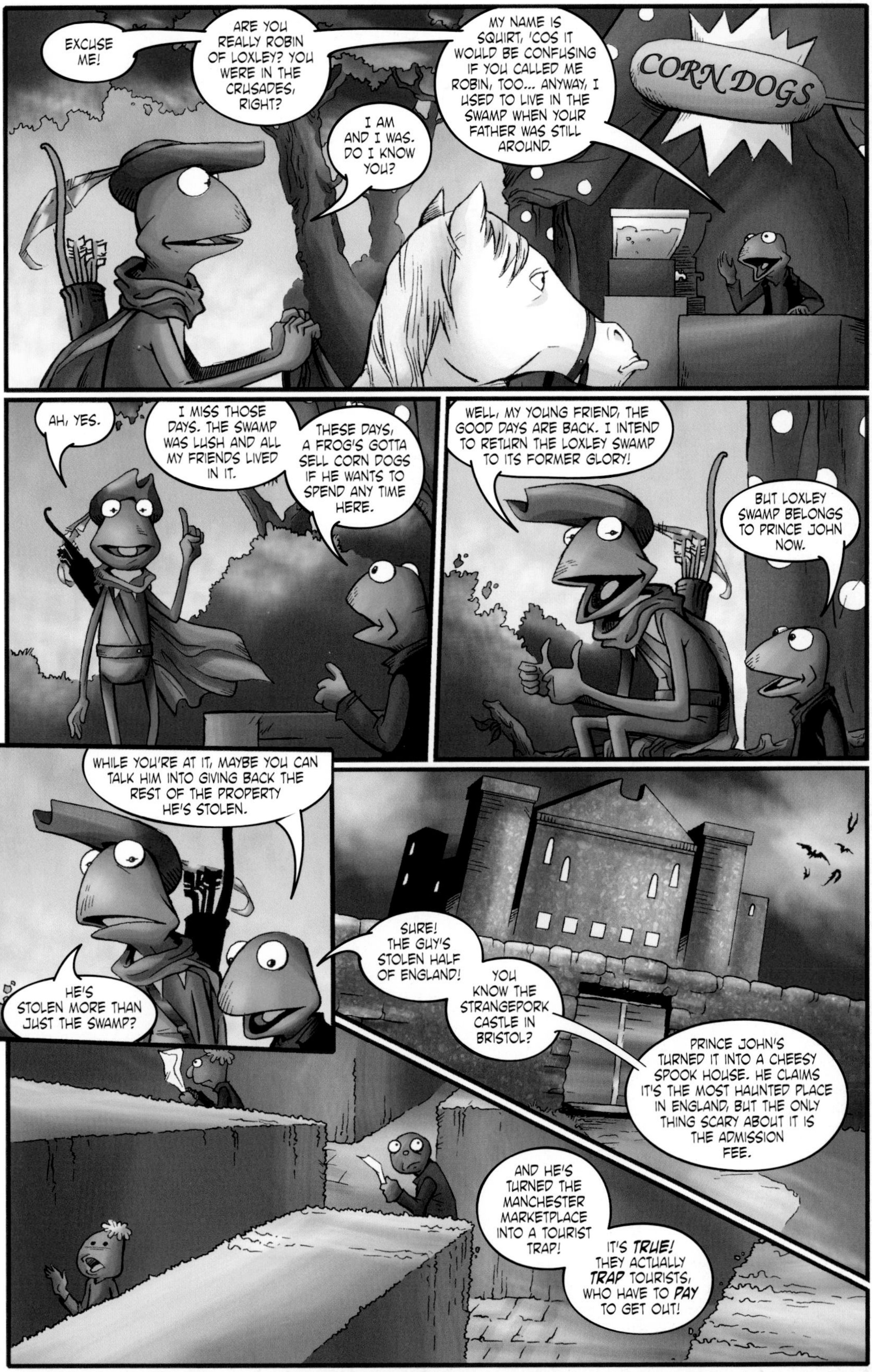
EXCUSE ME!
ARE YOU REALLY ROBIN OF LOXLEY? YOU WERE IN THE CRUSADES, RIGHT?
I AM AND I WAS. DO I KNOW YOU?
MY NAME IS SQUIRT, 'COS IT WOULD BE CONFUSING IF YOU CALLED ME ROBIN, TOO... ANYWAY, I USED TO LIVE IN THE SWAMP WHEN YOUR FATHER WAS STILL AROUND.
CORN DOGS
AH, YES.
I MISS THOSE DAYS. THE SWAMP WAS LUSH AND ALL MY FRIENDS LIVED IN IT.
THESE DAYS, A FROG'S GOTTA SELL CORN DOGS IF HE WANTS TO SPEND ANY TIME HERE.
WELL, MY YOUNG FRIEND, THE GOOD DAYS ARE BACK. I INTEND TO RETURN THE LOXLEY SWAMP TO ITS FORMER GLORY!
BUT LOXLEY SWAMP BELONGS TO PRINCE JOHN NOW.
WHILE YOU'RE AT IT, MAYBE YOU CAN TALK HIM INTO GIVING BACK THE REST OF THE PROPERTY HE'S STOLEN.
HE'S STOLEN MORE THAN JUST THE SWAMP?
SURE! THE GUY'S STOLEN HALF OF ENGLAND!
YOU KNOW THE STRANGEPORK CASTLE IN BRISTOL?
PRINCE JOHN'S TURNED IT INTO A CHEESY SPOOK HOUSE. HE CLAIMS IT'S THE MOST HAUNTED PLACE IN ENGLAND, BUT THE ONLY THING SCARY ABOUT IT IS THE ADMISSION FEE.
AND HE'S TURNED THE MANCHESTER MARKETPLACE INTO A TOURIST TRAP!
IT'S TRUE! THEY ACTUALLY TRAP TOURISTS, WHO HAVE TO PAY TO GET OUT!

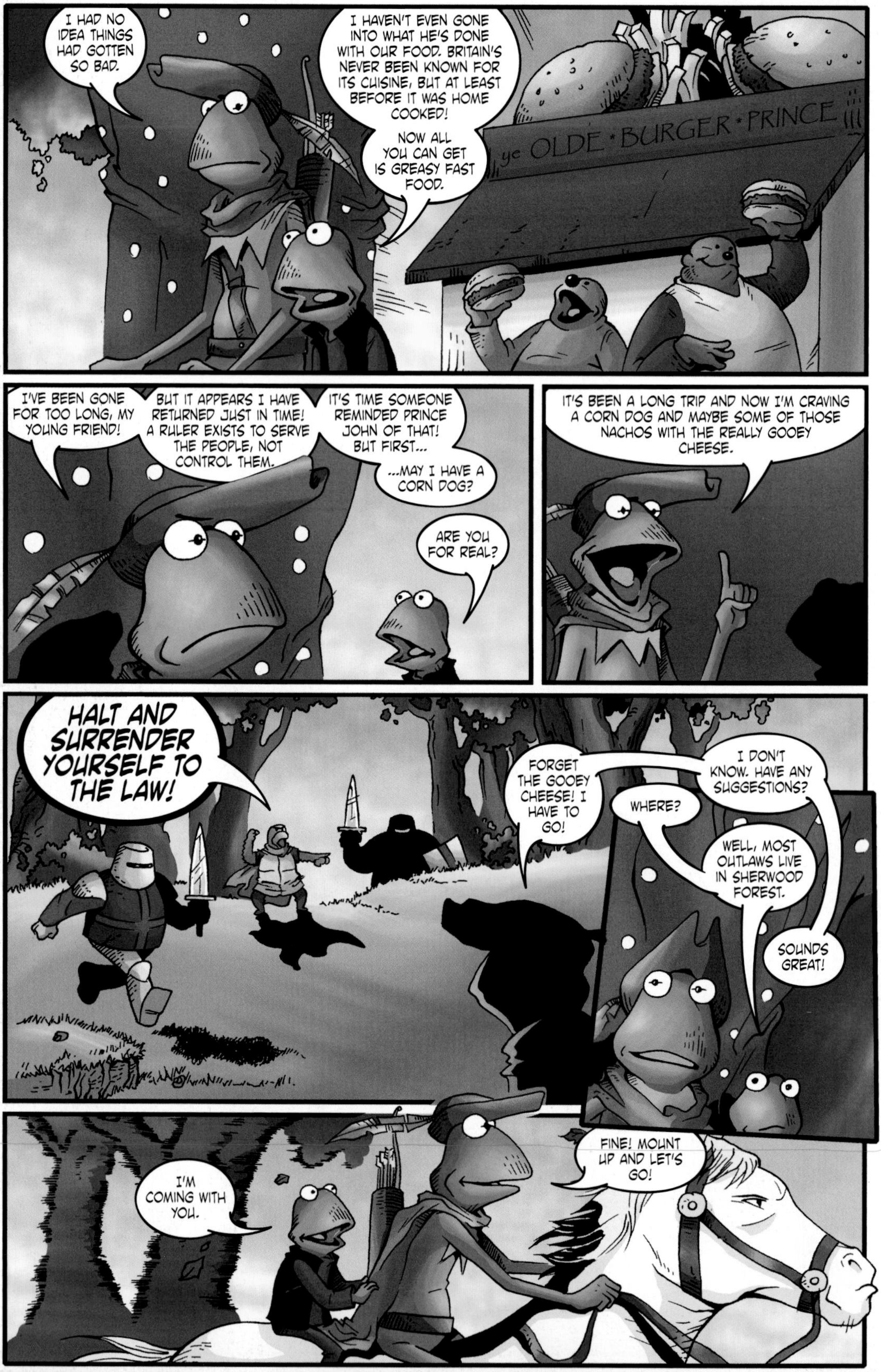
I HAD NO IDEA THINGS HAD GOTTEN SO BAD.
I HAVEN'T EVEN GONE INTO WHAT HE'S DONE WITH OUR FOOD. BRITAIN'S NEVER BEEN KNOWN FOR ITS CUISINE, BUT AT LEAST BEFORE IT WAS HOME COOKED!
NOW ALL YOU CAN GET IS GREASY FAST FOOD.
ye OLDE • BURGER • PRINCE
I'VE BEEN GONE FOR TOO LONG, MY YOUNG FRIEND!
BUT IT APPEARS I HAVE RETURNED JUST IN TIME! A RULER EXISTS TO SERVE THE PEOPLE, NOT CONTROL THEM.
IT'S TIME SOMEONE REMINDED PRINCE JOHN OF THAT! BUT FIRST...
...MAY I HAVE A CORN DOG?
ARE YOU FOR REAL?
IT'S BEEN A LONG TRIP AND NOW I'M CRAVING A CORN DOG AND MAYBE SOME OF THOSE NACHOS WITH THE REALLY GOOEY CHEESE.
HALT AND SURRENDER YOURSELF TO THE LAW!
FORGET THE GOOEY CHEESE! I HAVE TO GO!
WHERE?
I DON'T KNOW. HAVE ANY SUGGESTIONS?
WELL, MOST OUTLAWS LIVE IN SHERWOOD FOREST.
SOUNDS GREAT!
I'M COMING WITH YOU.
FINE! MOUNT UP AND LET'S GO!

A brand-new story that takes place before the hit film!
WALL•E finds himself isolated as more and more of
his companions shut down, until he finds a new friend
in the unlikeliest of places...and no, it's not Eve!

WALL•E: RECHARGE
DIAMOND CODE: JAN1100844
SC $9.99 ISBN 9781608865123
HC $24.99 ISBN 9781608865543

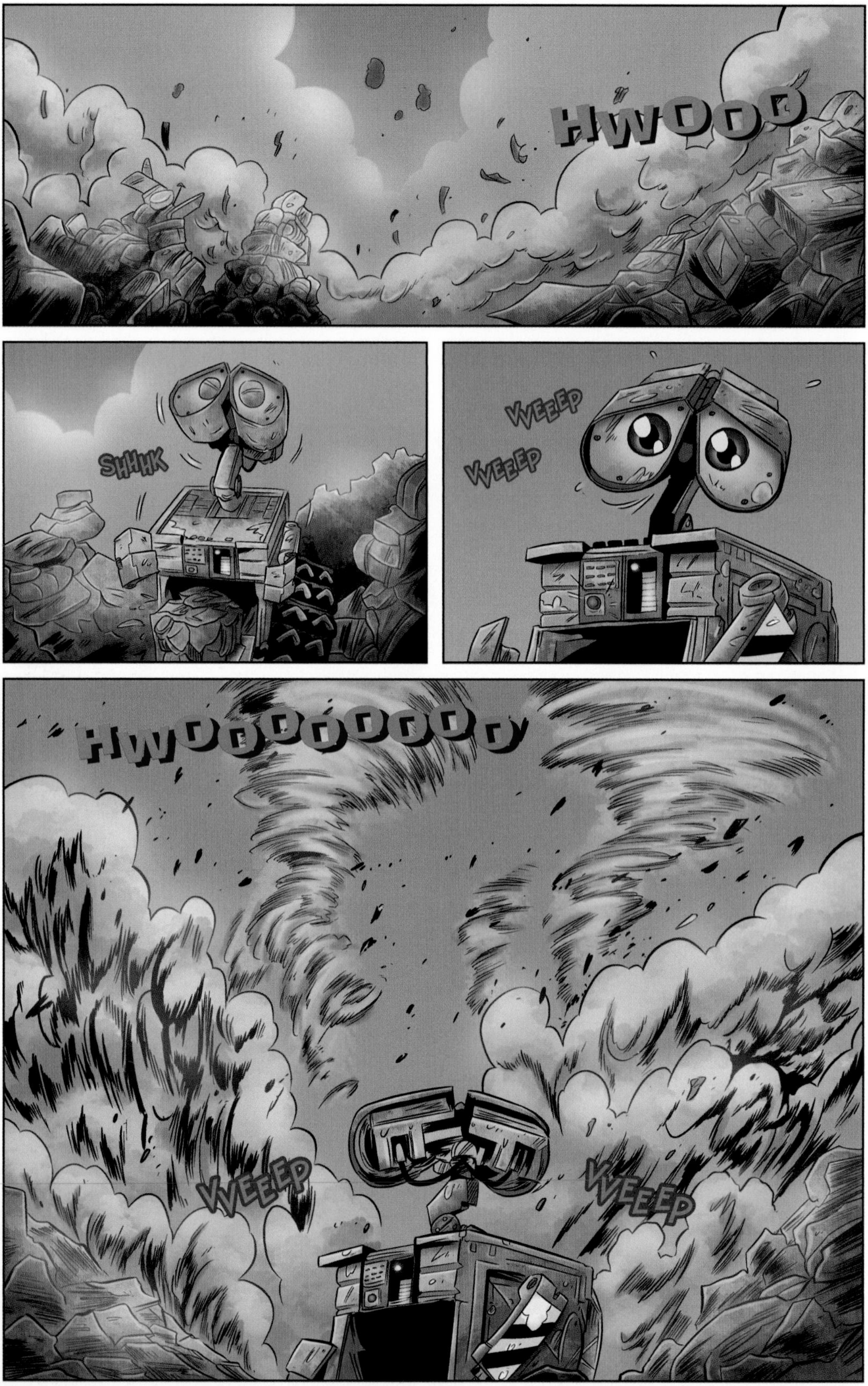
HWOOO
SHHHK
VVEEEP
VVEEEP
HWOOOOOOOOOO
VVEEEP
VVEEEP

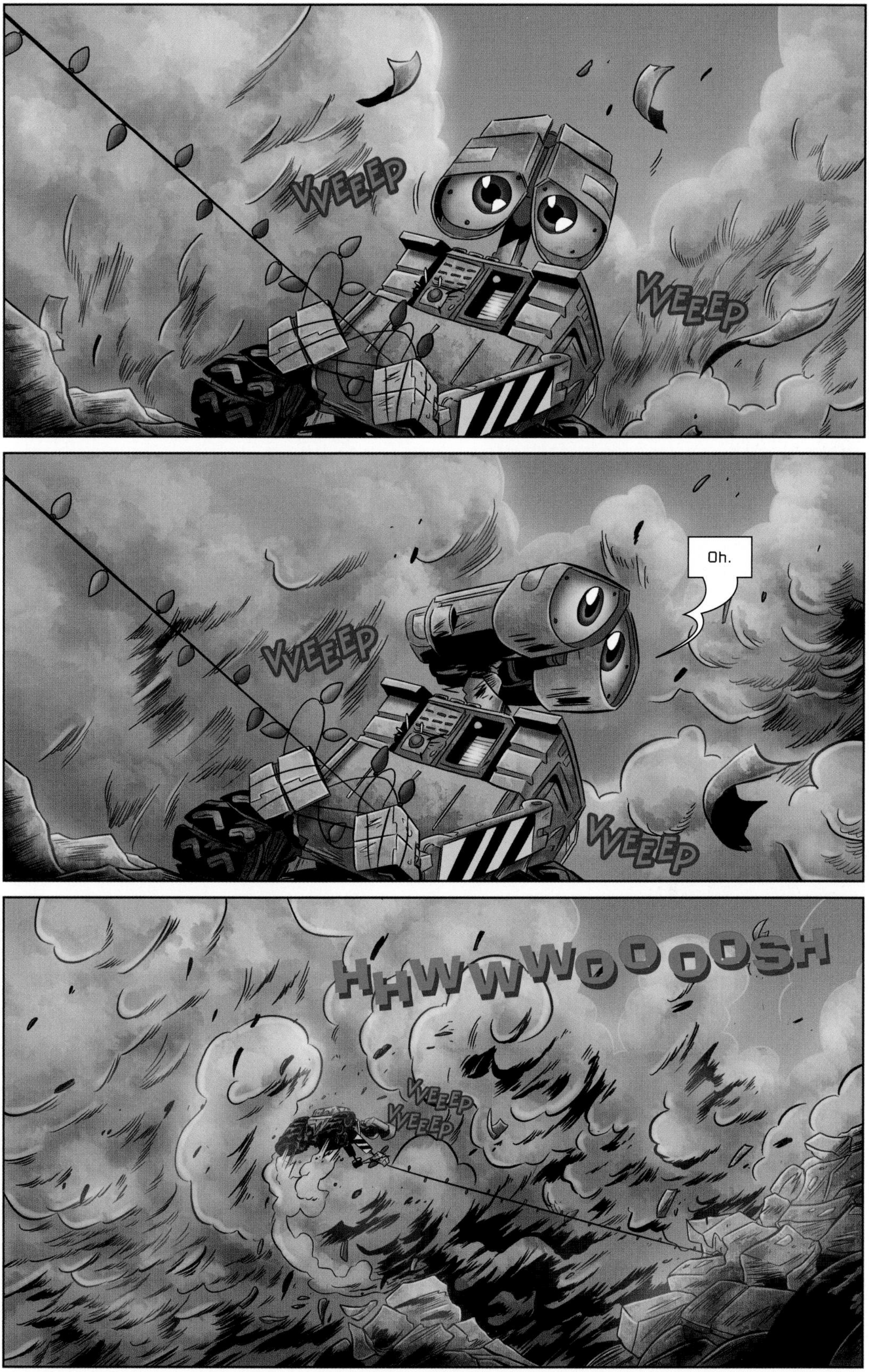
VVEEEP
VVEEEP
VVEEEP
Oh.
VVEEEP
HHWWWOOOOOSH
VVEEEP
VVEEEP

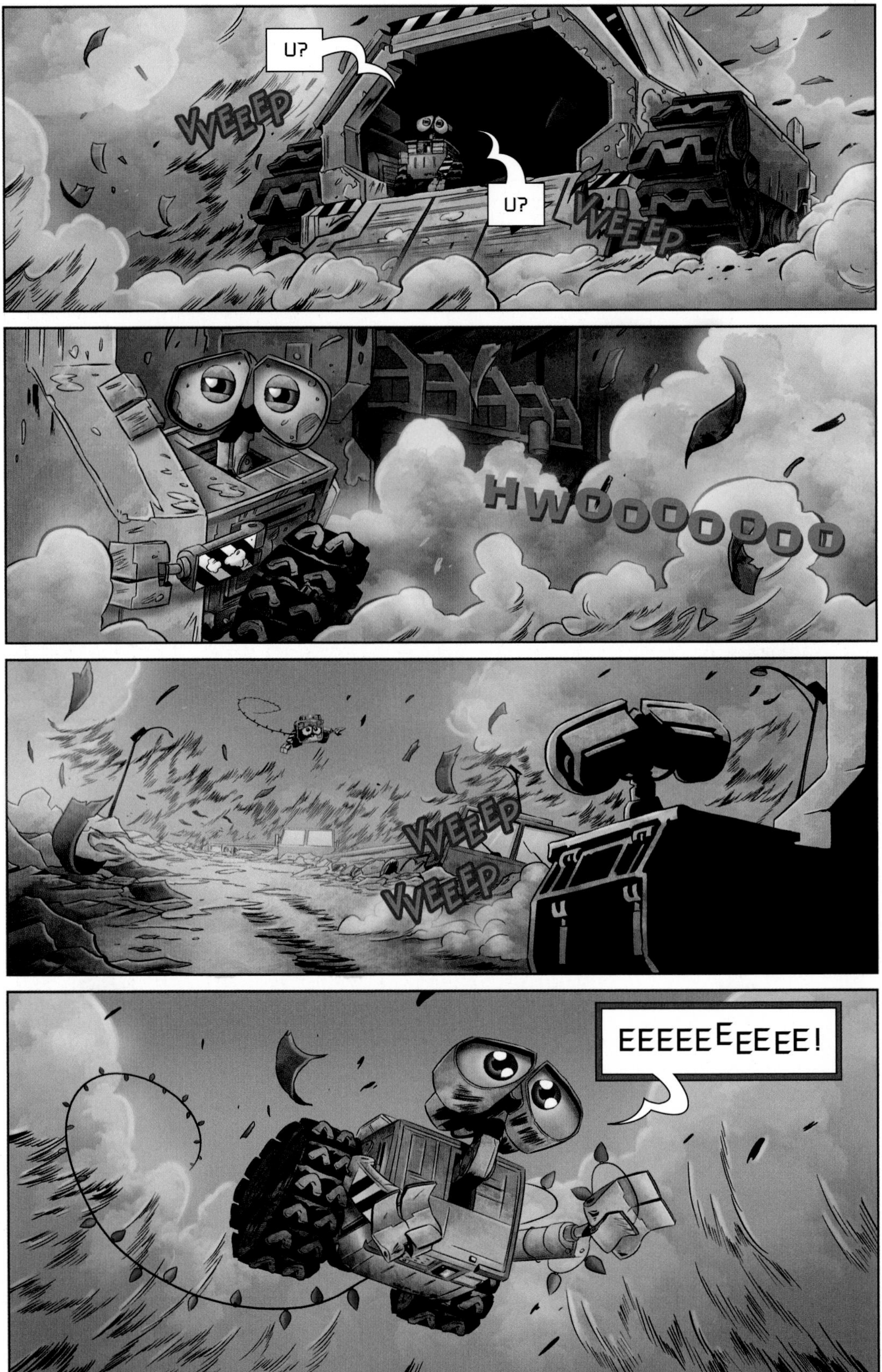
U?
VVEEEP
U?
VVEEEP
HWOOOOOOOO
VVEEEP
VVEEEP
EEEEEEEEEE!

GRAPHIC NOVELS AVAILABLE NOW!

TOY STORY: MYSTERIOUS STRANGER
Andy has a new addition to his room—a circuit-laden egg. Is this new gizmo a friend or foe?

TOY STORY: THE RETURN OF BUZZ LIGHTYEAR
When Andy is given a surprise gift, no one is more surprised than the toys in his room...it's a second Buzz Lightyear! The stage is set for a Star Command showdown!

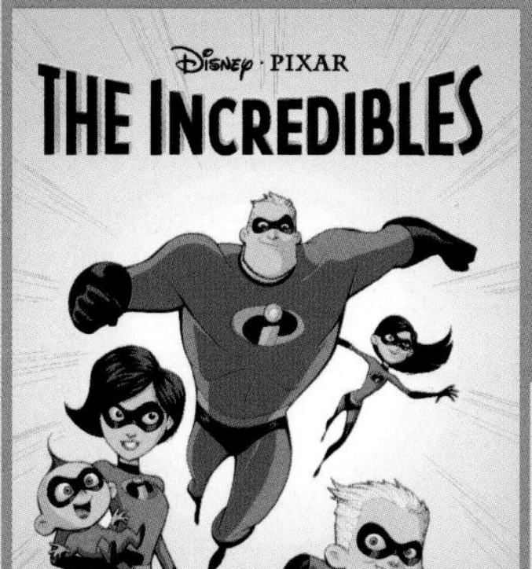

THE INCREDIBLES: FAMILY MATTERS
This action-packed trade collects all four issues of THE INCREDIBLES: FAMILY MATTERS. Acclaimed scribe Mark Waid has written the perfect INCREDIBLES story! What happens when Mr. Incredible's super-abilities start to wane...and how long can he keep his powerlessness a secret from his wife and kids?

THE INCREDIBLES: CITY OF INCREDIBLES
Baby Jack-Jack, everyone's favorite super-powered toddler, battles...a nasty cold! Hopefully the rest of the Parr family can stay healthy, because the henchmen of super villains are rapidly starting to exhibit superpowers!

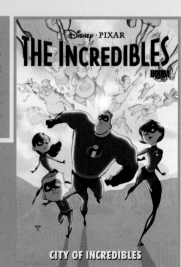

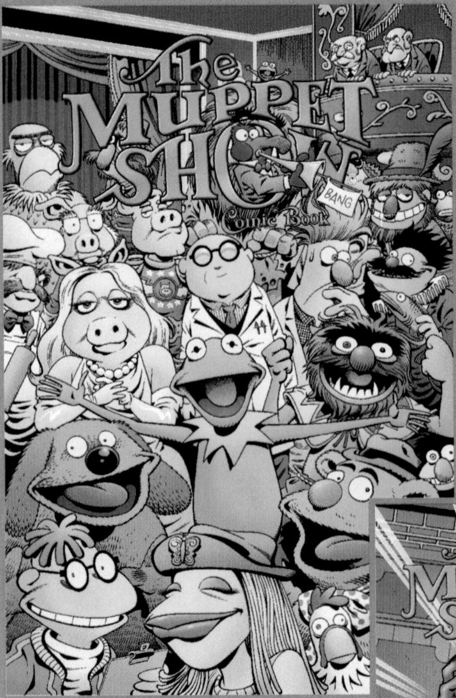
The Muppet Show
Comic Book
BANG

THE MUPPET SHOW COMIC BOOK: MEET THE MUPPETS
This hilarious trade collects the first four issues of THE MUPPET SHOW, written and drawn by the incomparable Roger Langridge! Packed full of madcap skits and gags, THE MUPPET SHOW trade is certain to please old and new fans alike!

THE MUPPET SHOW COMIC BOOK: THE TREASURE OF PEG-LEG WILSON
Scooter discovers old documents which reveal that a cache of treasure is hidden somewhere in the Muppet Theater...and when Rizzo the Rat overhears this, the news spreads like wildfire! Can Kermit keep everyone from tearing the theater apart?

THE MUPPET SHOW COMIC BOOK: ON THE ROAD
With the theater destroyed, the Muppets take their act on the road... but with two very familiar hecklers in every town, will the show be a hit, or will our Muppet minstrels be run out of town in tar and feathers? Also: Fozzie and Rizzo have plans for a big budget PIGS IN SPACE motion picture, but is Hollywood prepared?

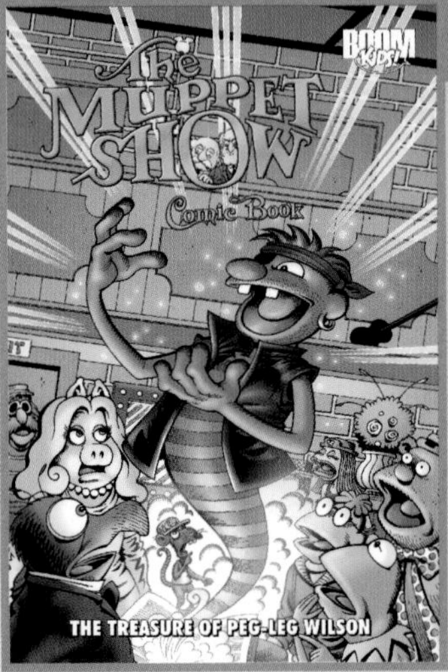
BOOM KIDS!
The Muppet Show
Comic Book
THE TREASURE OF PEG-LEG WILSON

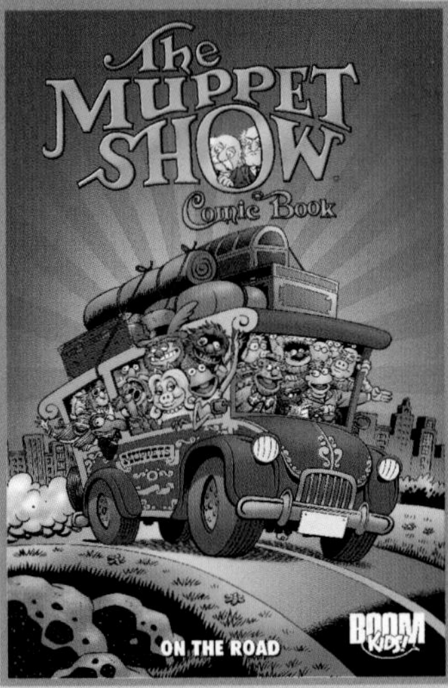
The Muppet Show
Comic Book
ON THE ROAD
BOOM KIDS!

THE MUPPET SHOW COMIC BOOK: MEET THE MUPPETS
SC $9.99 ISBN 9781934506851
HC $24.99 ISBN 9781608865277

THE MUPPET SHOW COMIC BOOK: THE TREASURE OF PEG-LEG WILSON
SC $9.99 ISBN 9781608865048
HC $24.99 ISBN 9781608865307

THE MUPPET SHOW COMIC BOOK: ON THE ROAD
SC $9.99 ISBN 9781608865161

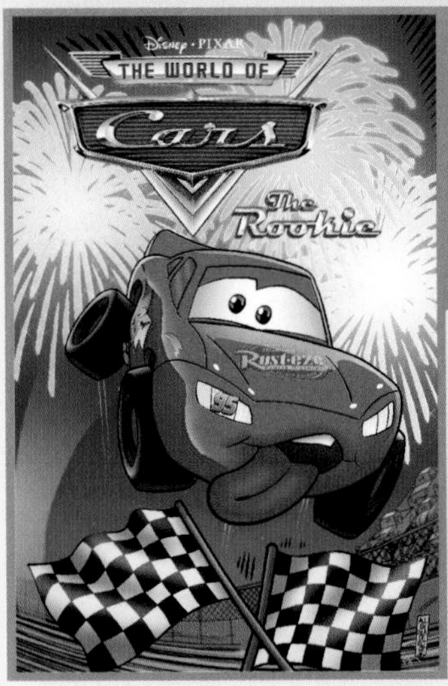
Disney · PIXAR
THE WORLD OF
Cars
The Rookie

CARS: THE ROOKIE
See how Lightning McQueen became a Piston Cup sensation in this pulse-pounding collection! CARS: THE ROOKIE reveals McQueen's scrappy origins as a local short track racer who dreams of the big time...and recklessly plows his way through the competition to get there! Along the way, he meets Mack, who helps McQueen catch his lucky break.

CARS: RADIATOR SPRINGS
From writer Alan J. Porter, this collection of CARS stories is perfect for the whole family! After his return to Radiator Springs, Lightning McQueen is hanging out with his friends at Flo's V8 Café when he realizes that everyone knows his story...but he doesn't know anyone else's! McQueen wants to know how his friends ended up in Radiator Springs...and more importantly why they decided to stay!

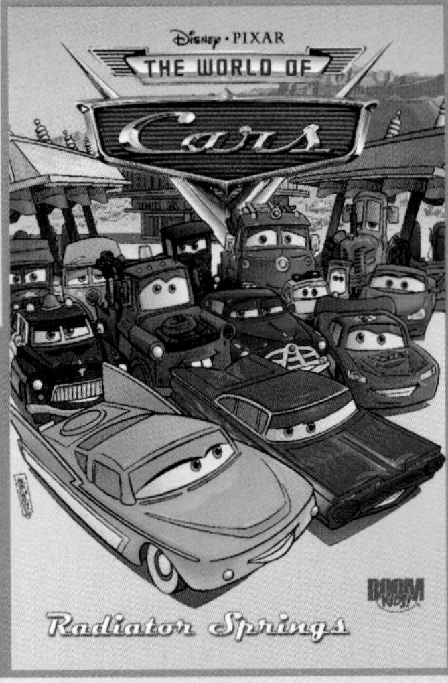
Disney · PIXAR
THE WORLD OF
Cars
BOOM KIDS!
Radiator Springs

CARS: THE ROOKIE
SC $9.99 ISBN 9781934506844
HC $24.99 ISBN 9781608865222

CARS: RADIATOR SPRINGS
SC $9.99 ISBN 9781608865024
HC $24.99 ISBN 9781608865284

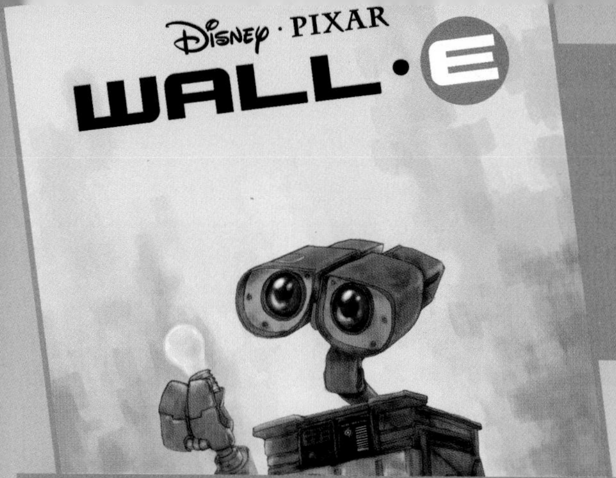

Disney · PIXAR
WALL·E

WALL•E: RECHARGE

WALL•E is not yet the hardworking robot we know and love. Instead, he lets the few remaining other robots take care of most of the trash compacting while he collects interesting junk. But when the other robots start breaking down, WALL•E must learn to adjust his priorities... or else Earth is doomed!

WALL•E: RECHARGE
SC $9.99 ISBN 9781608865123
HC $24.99 ISBN 9781608865543

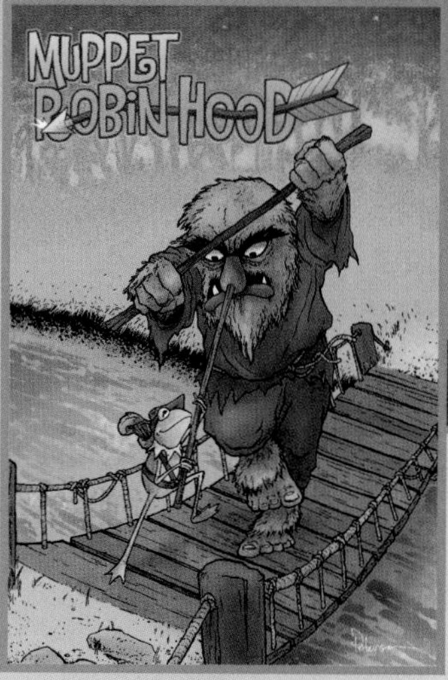

MUPPET ROBIN HOOD

MUPPET ROBIN HOOD

The Muppets tell the Robin Hood legend for laughs, and it's the reader who will be merry! Robin Hood (Kermit the Frog) joins with the Merry Men, Sherwood Forest's infamous gang of misfit outlaws, to take on the stuffy Sheriff of Nottingham (Sam the Eagle)!

MUPPET PETER PAN

When Peter Pan (Kermit) whisks Wendy (Janice) and her brothers to the magical realm of Neverswamp, the adventure begins! With Captain Hook (Gonzo) out for revenge for the loss of his hand, Wendy and her brothers may find themselves in a situation where even the magic of Piggytink (Miss Piggy) can't save them!

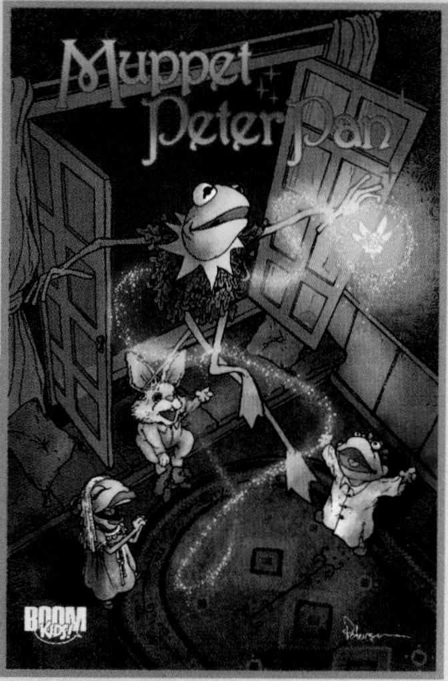

Muppet Peter Pan
BOOM KIDS!

MUPPET ROBIN HOOD
SC $9.99 ISBN 9781934506790
HC $24.99 ISBN 9781608865260

MUPPET PETER PAN
SC $9.99 ISBN 9781608865079
HC $24.99 ISBN 9781608865314

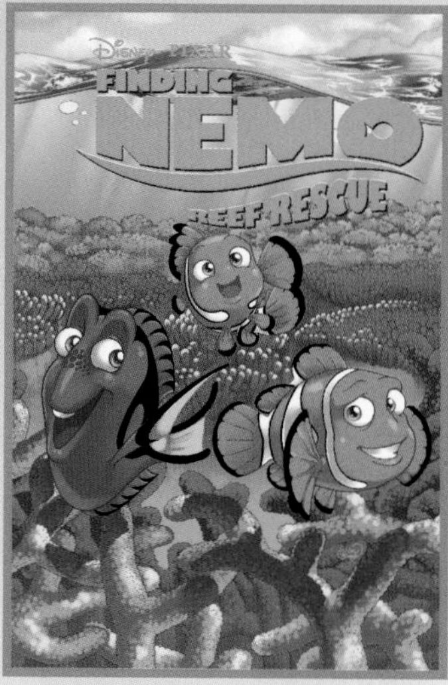

Disney · PIXAR
FINDING NEMO
REEF RESCUE

FINDING NEMO: REEF RESCUE

Nemo, Dory and Marlin have become local heroes, and are recruited to embark on an all-new adventure in this exciting collection! Their reef is mysteriously dying and no one knows why!

MONSTERS, INC.: LAUGH FACTORY

Someone is stealing comedy props from the other employees, making it difficult for them to harvest the laughter they need to power Monstropolis... and all evidence points to Sulley's best friend Mike Wazowski!

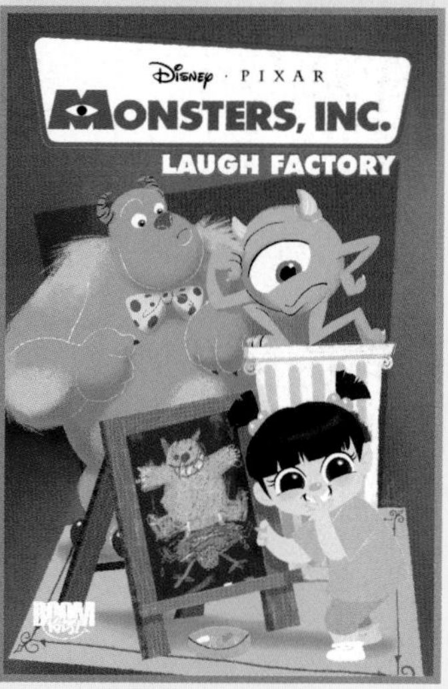

Disney · PIXAR
MONSTERS, INC.
LAUGH FACTORY
BOOM KIDS!

FINDING NEMO: REEF RESCUE
SC $9.99 ISBN 9781934506882
HC $24.99 ISBN 9781608865246

MONSTERS, INC.: LAUGH FACTORY
SC $9.99 ISBN 9781608865086
HC $24.99 ISBN 9781608865338

DISNEY'S HERO SQUAD: ULTRAHEROES

It's the year 2734 and the only one standing in the way of earth's utter destruction is...Mickey Mouse?! Join the four-colored fun as Mickey Mouse, Goofy, and Donald Duck take to the skies to save the world.

DISNEY'S HERO SQUAD: ULTRAHEROES
SC $9.99 ISBN 9781608865437
HC $24.99 ISBN 9781608865529

WIZARDS OF MICKEY: MOUSE MAGIC

Your favorite Disney characters star in this magical fantasy epic! Student of the great wizard Nereus, Mickey hails from the humble village of Miceland. Allying himself with Donald (who has a pet dragon named Fafnir) and team mate Goofy, Mickey quests to find a magical crown that will give him mastery over all spells!

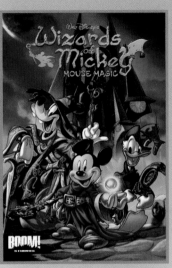

WIZARDS OF MICKEY: MOUSE MAGIC
SC $9.99 ISBN 9781608865413
HC $24.99 ISBN 9781608865505

DONALD DUCK AND FRIENDS: DOUBLE DUCK

Donald Duck as a secret agent? Villainous fiends beware as the world of super sleuthing and espionage will never be the same! This is Donald Duck like you've never seen him!

DONALD DUCK AND FRIENDS: DOUBLE DUCK
SC $9.99 ISBN 9781608865451
HC $24.99 ISBN 9781608865512

UNCLE SCROOGE: THE HUNT FOR THE OLD NUMBER ONE

Join Donald Duck's favorite penny pinching Uncle Scrooge as he, along with Donald himself and Huey, Dewey and Louie, embark on a globe spanning trek to recover treasure and save Scrooge's "number one dime" from the treacherous grasp of Magica De Spell.

UNCLE SCROOGE:
THE HUNT FOR THE OLD NUMBER ONE
SC $9.99 ISBN 9781608865475
HC $24.99 ISBN 9781608865536

WALT DISNEY'S
The Life and Times of
$CROOGE McDUCK
VOLUME ONE • BY DON ROSA
EISNER AWARD WINNER

THE LIFE AND TIMES OF SCROOGE MCDUCK VOL. 1

BOOM Kids! proudly collects the first half of THE LIFE AND TIMES OF SCROOGE MCDUCK in a gorgeous hardcover collection — featuring smyth sewn binding, a gold-on-gold foil-stamped case wrap, and a bookmark ribbon! These stories, written and drawn by legendary cartoonist Don Rosa, chronicle Scrooge McDuck's fascinating life. See how Scrooge earned his 'Number One Dime' and began to build his fortune!

THE LIFE & TIMES OF SCROOGE MCDUCK VOLUME 1 HC
HC $24.99 ISBN 9781608865383

THE LIFE AND TIMES OF SCROOGE MCDUCK VOL. 2

BOOM! Kids proudly presents volume two of THE LIFE AND TIMES OF SCROOGE MCDUCK in a gorgeous hardcover collection in a beautiful, deluxe package featuring smyth sewn binding and a foil-stamped case wrap! These stories, written and drawn by legendary cartoonist Don Rosa, chronicle Scrooge McDuck's fascinating life.

WALT DISNEY
The Life and Times of
$CROOGE McDUCK
VOLUME TWO • BY DON ROSA
EISNER AWARD WINNER

THE LIFE & TIMES OF SCROOGE MCDUCK VOLUME 2 HC
HC $24.99 ISBN 9781608865420

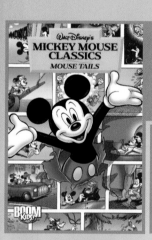

WALT DISNEY'S
MICKEY MOUSE
CLASSICS
MOUSE TAILS
BOOM KIDS!

MICKEY MOUSE CLASSICS: MOUSE TAILS

See Mickey Mouse as he was meant to be seen! Solving mysteries, fighting off pirates, and just generally saving the day! These classic stories comprise a "Greatest Hits" series for the mouse, including a story produced by seminal Disney creator Carl Barks!

MICKEY MOUSE CLASSICS: MOUSE TAILS
HC $24.99 ISBN 9781608865390

DONALD DUCK CLASSICS: QUACK UP

Whether it's finding gold, journeying in the Klondike, or fighting ghosts, Donald will always have help with Huey, Dewey, Louie, his much more prepared nephews, by his side! Carl Barks brought Donald to prominence, and it's only fair to start off the series with some of his most influential stories!

BOOM KIDS!
WALT DISNEY'S
DONALD DUCK
CLASSICS
QUACK UP

DONALD DUCK CLASSICS: QUACK UP HC
HC $24.99 ISBN 9781608865406

WALT DISNEY'S
Valentine's
Classics

WALT DISNEY'S VALENTINE'S CLASSICS

Love is in the air for Mickey Mouse, Donald Duck and the rest of the gang. But will Cupid's arrows cause happiness or heartache? Find out in this collection of classic stories featuring all your most beloved characters from the magical world of Walt Disney! Featuring work by Carl Barks , Floyd Gottfredson, Daan Jippes, Romano Scarpa and Al Taliaferro.

WALT DISNEY'S VALENTINES CLASSICS VOL 1 HC
HC $24.99 ISBN 9781608865499

WALT DISNEY'S CHRISTMAS CLASSICS

BOOM! Kids has raided the Disney publishing archives and searched every nook and cranny to find the best and the greatest stories from Disney's vast comic book publishing history for this "best of" compilation.

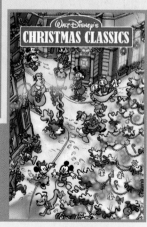

WALT DISNEY'S
CHRISTMAS CLASSICS

WALT DISNEY'S CHRISTMAS CLASSICS VOL 1 HC
HC $24.99 ISBN 9781608865482

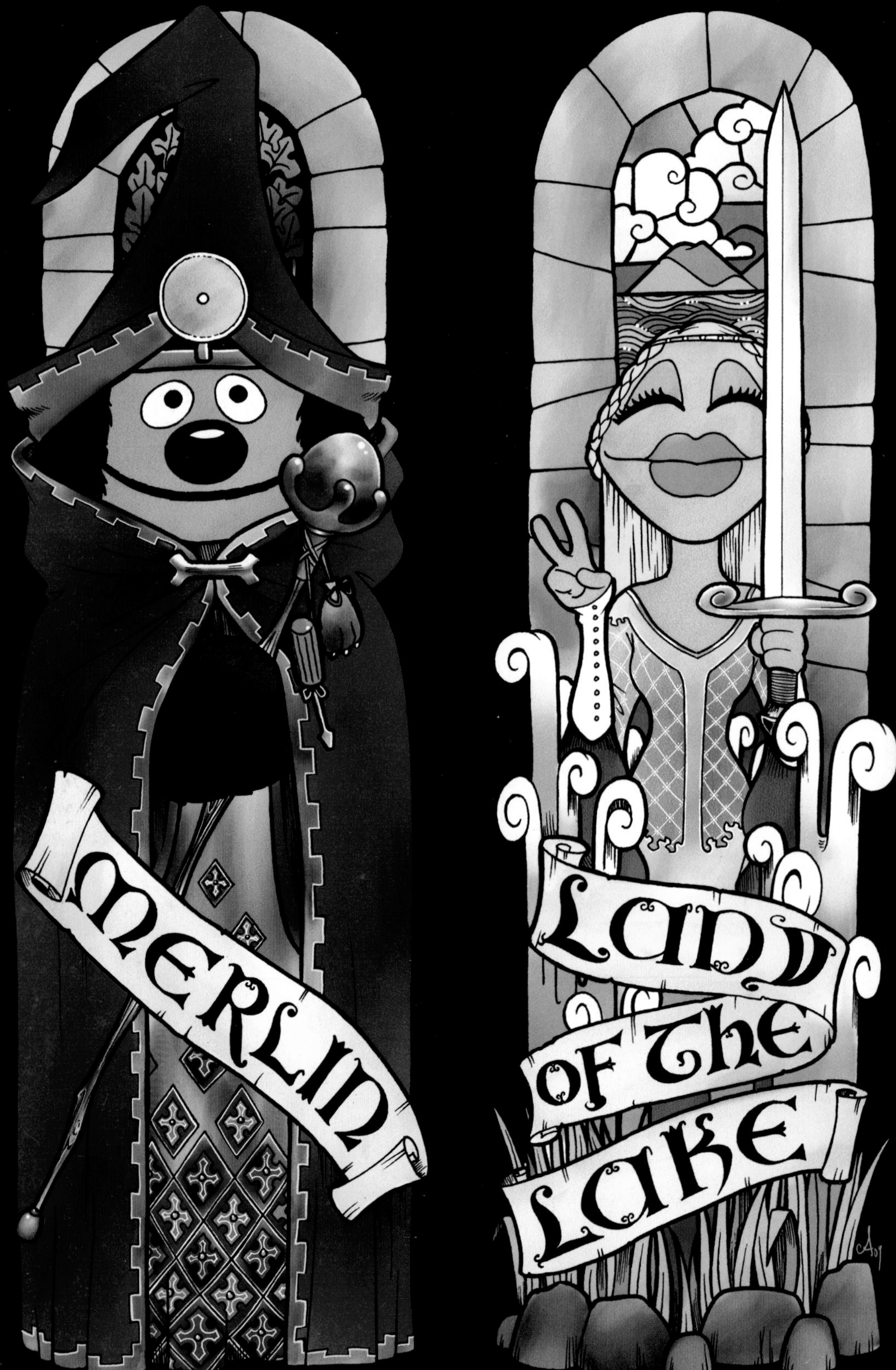
MERLIN
LADY OF THE LAKE